Seized ...
Body and Mind

Dear Victoria,
Never stop dreaming. Anything is
possible when you dream big enough.

Alex Mellou
x x x

Published by : ᴀ ᴍ Alex Mellow Books
Contact
Instagram : @alexmellowauthor
Facebook : @alexmellowauthor

Cover design by : Murphy Rae
Copy editing and proofreading services by : RJ Locksley

ISBN: 978-1-7392762-1-8 (paperback) 978-1-7392762-0-1 (e-book)
First Edition

the Hunter series
book one

Seized . . .
Body and Mind

ALEX MELLOW

ALEX MELLOW BOOKS

Sign up for the Newsletter

To receive up to date information on new releases, sales, sneak peeks, giveaways and other exclusive content.

Link: on author's Instagram account and Facebook page

What if home is not a place?
What if home is a person all along?

Billionaire CEO Sebastian Hunter doesn't bed his employees. He's vowed never to touch a nice girl. And he never brings a woman home. Yet on Alice Lake's first day as Sebastian's new secretary, Sebastian falls in instant lust—and breaks all his rules at once.

When Alice gets a concussion, Sebastian convinces Alice to stay at his soulless mansion while recovering, but his real plan is to win just enough of her heart to get her to sleep with him. But once they're living together, avid cook and virgin Alice turns out to be more than just a sweet treat. And Alice refuses to jeopardise her prized new job over a fling with a ruthless playboy...

Will Alice be able to resist Sebastian when the heart wants what the heart wants?

Also, a criminal mastermind has been stealing from the Hunter family business, and he'll do anything to stop Sebastian's investigation. A stalker lurks in the shadows, ready to crush any chance of happiness and a future together for Sebastian and Alice. And things are not what they seem.

They never are.

Seized ... Body and Mind, book one of the Hunter series can be read as a standalone.

This is a full-length, scorching-hot romance novel with Beauty and the Beast vibes, with no cliffhanger, no cheating, and a guaranteed happily ever after. It has lots and lots of emotion that will make you melt and root for this couple, as well as suspense and twisted little mysteries that will grip you from beginning to end.

Recommended for audiences 18+ due to mature themes and sexual content.

Trust.

The base of every relationship. The very foundation. The heart and soul of true love.

For my husband ... who taught me to trust.

Chapter 1

Alice

8.00 a.m. Hunter Corp
Canary Wharf, London

With my heart hammering inside my chest, I reach the building that houses all my hopes. The building that could give me the stability I so badly crave.

"Good morning," I greet the guards, swiping my pass over the scanner. My excitement is off the charts as I step inside the luxurious lift and, pressing a shaky finger to the button that indicates my floor, let my eyes wander back to the entrance one last time. Praying I can stay. Praying it's only a matter of time until the next stage of my life begins.

The elevator dings and I get off on the sixty-second floor, my eyes fixed on the six massive oak cafeteria doors as I walk down the hall. I inhale deeply and push my way in, relief filling me as I spot Linda at our table and hurry over to her, a smile spreading over my face.

"Good morning, sweetie!" She smiles back. As usual, she's beautiful in a black fitted skirt suit, much like my own, with a silky white blouse underneath. Her honey-brown hair is styled and tucked in a low bun, sitting loosely against her neck—again, much like my own dark tresses—and her makeup is minimal. "Come, sit. I've already picked up our breakfast," she instructs with a nod, bringing my attention to the spread of coffee and muffins on the table.

"You're the best, Linda. Thank you." I bend to kiss her cheek, my eyes suddenly burning with unshed tears. No one's ever been so kind to me, at least no one apart from my nana, so more often than not it still takes me by surprise.

Linda pulls me into a hug, rubbing circles on my back, as if she can sense how fragile I'm feeling. I can't help but tighten my arms around her, thankful for her friendship, her kindness, and her support, which have been invaluable since I started temping at Hunter Corp and met Linda on my first day exactly two months ago.

Back then I was lucky enough to land a position, even if a temporary one, as the junior secretary to the CEO and founder of the company, no less—Mr Charles Hunter, the charming billionaire and ruler of the Hunter empire himself. I've been working alongside Linda, his senior secretary, ever since.

Another blessing, really, since Linda and I clicked straight away. She turned out to be not just my supervisor but also my mentor, my advisor, as well as, I suspect, the main reason Mr Hunter is now considering keeping me on a permanent basis.

Linda denies this, of course, insisting he came to the decision all on his own. But I know she must've had a hand in it. It's a well-known fact Linda has a lot more sway in the office and over the Hunters than she lets on.

"I wasn't going to let you skip another meal," she says. "Now come, take off that coat and sit. Your coffee's getting cold."

"I mean it, Linda. Thank you for everything." After dropping my handbag on one of the extra chairs, I begin unbuttoning my coat.

She waves me off. "How are you this morning anyway?" she asks, looking at me over the rim of her mug. Her big, emerald-green eyes are trained on me the whole time as she takes a sip of her coffee, making me squirm. "And tell me the truth. We both know you can't lie worth a damn."

Yeah, she's not wrong about that. Lying is a skill I can't seem to master no matter how hard I try.

Sighing, I sit across from her. "I'm just nervous, I guess." I reach for one of the apple and carrot muffins—my favourite—and start picking at it. "I just wish my stomach wasn't so twisted up in knots from all this waiting. It's messing with my appetite."

Linda chuckles. "You have nothing to worry about. These things sometimes take time, that's all. And between all these new processes from HR and the employment laws that keep coming our way, we have to be careful. Play things by the book, you know? Although it does feel like a waste of time having to advertise the position. Not to mention interviewing countless candidates when we already have someone in mind."

"Yeah, doesn't mean you can't change said mind." I grimace. "What if Mr Hunter interviewed someone more qualified and decided I'm no longer a good fit?"

"Oh, Alice, but you *are* a good fit. You're young and smart, incredibly talented, and an exact match for what we have in mind. So stop worrying, you're just making yourself sick. Besides ..." Her eyes dart around the room, scanning for any unwanted attention before she continues in a hushed tone. "Do you *really* think I'd let the boss man change his mind?"

I finally smile, feeling somewhat mollified. I shake my head.

"Damn right I wouldn't. I'd bust his balls if he even tried, and trust me when I say he'll do anything, absolutely *anything* to avoid that." She widens her eyes at me, and we both burst into laughter.

Oh, I have no doubt she could make Mr Hunter feel sorry. Very sorry indeed, if she was so inclined.

"You're right," I agree as I use a napkin to dry my tears. "I am making myself sick, and it stops now."

"Good, then my work here is done." She lifts her mug to her lips.

I reach for my own mug and blow into it before taking a sip. "Oh, yeah! This is the stuff," I sigh, closing my eyes in pleasure as I let the richly flavoured coffee awaken my taste buds.

"I'll drink to that. Here's to getting toasty with a brew."

"Hear, hear!" I giggle, and we both take another sip.

"Now, young lady, let's talk about those cupcakes you brought in on Friday ... and how soon you can bring another batch."

With that we launch into a full-blown conversation about my favourite topic—food and all the joys of preparing it.

***

Located on the eightieth floor at the very top of the Hunter Corp, our office is almost entirely surrounded by glass. The floor-to-ceiling windows provide a view like no other of the city below and the Thames.

The decor is classy and modern, featuring dark, tasteful tones and soft lighting throughout the space. A few splashes of vibrant colour in the form of sculptures and paintings contrast with the glossy black furniture and the sophisticated grey wooden floors.

I love it. Love this space and how I feel when I'm here.

Today, however, not even this beautiful, zen environment can distract me from my nerves. And by the time Mr Hunter finally arrives, my insides are all twisted up as if my conversation with Linda never happened at all.

"How are my favourite secretaries this morning?" he asks as he comes into our office.

Standing at six foot four, in a navy three-piece suit and with not a strand of his salt-and-pepper hair out of place, Mr Hunter is the epitome of power. A strong, intelligent man, he'd look intimidating if it weren't for those playful blue eyes of his.

"We're your *only* secretaries, Charles," Linda retorts, her eyes narrowed. "So, what is it? What did you forget this time?"

He shoves his hands into his pockets. "Whatever do you mean, Linda? Are you implying I'm only nice when I need something from you?"

"Of course not. I don't imply things. What I say is exactly what I mean. So come on, out with it. What did you forget this time?"

"Nothing," Mr Hunter gasps with feigned outrage, and I snort.

To her credit, Linda does try to give me a reproving look. Her lips twitch until we all burst into laughter.

My heart warms. These two are worse than kids with the bantering, and the fighting, and the picking on each other every chance they get. It's like they're playing a tennis match, with me more often than not forced to play their referee.

In a way, it's endearing. Remarkable even. That despite everything they went through their friendship has not only survived, but remained just as strong after so many years. If not stronger, I'd say.

Especially since according to Linda, they were all the best of Friends back in the day—back when her husband and Mr Hunter's wife were still alive. Had been friends for most of their lives, since they all lived near each other and went to the same schools growing up. Which makes what happened to them even more devastating.

A shiver goes through me. *God, I can't even imagine a loss like that. I wouldn't survive.*

"Now, on a serious note," Mr Hunter says, pulling out his phone and checking it, "could one of you beautiful ladies please block the diary for the rest of the morning? The three of us will be having a meeting, and I don't want to feel rushed."

Oh. Ohhh!

I freeze—deer-caught-in-headlights kind of freeze—as I stare with my mouth agape at him.

Oh, my God. Oh, my God. Oh, my God! I scream internally. *This is it. No more waiting. No more agonising over an outcome that could possibly make or break my career—my life.*

Linda confirms she's blocking the diary, and Mr Hunter says we can start at ten, but I still can't move. Can't do anything but stare. It's like all my muscles went into complete lockdown.

"Thank you, Linda," Mr Hunter says. "Oh, and call the catering department so we can have something to eat."

"I'll do that now," I say in a rush, finally finding my voice. "So they know in advance."

"Yes. Good thinking, Alice. As always," he replies, and I feel as if I'm floating on air. My confidence builds with each kind word I receive from these two.

"Now, Linda, if you don't mind," Mr Hunter says as he slides his phone back into his pocket, "I need you to come into my office. I'd like to go over some of those tasks you mentioned last week."

"Tasks?" Linda asks. "Oh, the ... tasks. Yes, of course." With that she gets up, grabs her notepad, and, throwing me one last look over her shoulder, scurries down the corridor and into his office after him.

Frowning, I shake my head. *What was that all about? And was he flirting with her just now?*

Because with the look he was giving her, and the blush spreading all over her face, it definitely looked like it to me.

I laugh at the thought. Not that there's anything wrong with the two of them flirting, but I'm sure I'm just imagining things. All this excitement is messing with my head.

What I need is to calm down. Calm down and get on with my work.

Taking a deep breath, I place the call to the catering department. I check the clock again. *One hour. Just one more hour to go.*

***

"Thank you, ladies. I know how busy you both are, so I appreciate you taking the time to join me," Mr Hunter says as he sits across from Linda and me at his desk. "With that said"—he turns all his attention to me—"it gives me great pleasure to finally be able to tell you, Alice, that you got the permanent position. Congratulations, my dear. The job is yours if you want it."

Holy. Shit.

Slowly, very slowly, I release the shaky breath I was holding in.

My heart rate is going at a thousand miles an hour as I try to pull myself together enough to give Mr Hunter and Linda a little smile. Or at least what I hope is a little smile—at this point I've no clue what my face actually looks like.

"Thank you. Thank you both so much." I swallow hard, my voice thick with tears. "I won't let you down."

"Well, that's settled, then." Mr Hunter beams. "And welcome to the family, my dear, hopefully for many, many years to come." He and Linda exchange a look, and if I didn't know better, I'd say they also visibly relax.

Which is crazy, of course. They've nothing to be nervous about.

"Now, HR has already sent over your contract and some other documents. Take them home with you and read them tonight."

"Oh, God." I take a deep breath. "This is really happening, isn't it?"

Mr Hunter and Linda both begin to laugh.

"Here, Alice. This folder contains two copies of your contract, both already signed by me. One copy you keep, and the other we'll send back to HR once you've signed." He raises one eyebrow. "Unless you disagree with something, of course, in which case I urge you to come and speak to me so we can have it reviewed. I want you to be happy here, OK?"

"I ... I really appreciate the opportunity you're giving me, Mr Hunter. I'm going to give it my all. I promise."

"I already know that, Alice. You're a good girl. A good person. You'll be a great addition to the family. Won't she, Linda?"

"Yes, she most certainly will." A strange emotion flickers in Linda's eyes the entire time she holds my gaze. Pride? Hope? "She's also strong, our Alice, and can handle any kind of trouble thrown her way. That alone is fifty percent of the job, I'd say."

Mr Hunter nods. "We're very proud of you, Alice. And I'm confident you'll continue to impress us. Just remember you're everything we've been looking for, possibly more, so stop being so nervous. Relax. Just be yourself, and I promise you everything will be fine."

His words warm my heart, even if I don't quite know how to react. No one has ever said that to me. That they're proud. "Thank you. It means a lot coming from you. Both of you."

"Now," Mr Hunter says, "I have some really good news—or should I say *more* good news—I'd like to share with you ladies. As you both know, over the course of the last two years, Sebastian, my eldest, has been working personally with all of our managers in all of our sites. He's been working in our hotels in Paris for the past couple of months."

I nod. Linda made sure I was well acquainted with each of the Hunters' activities, contact details and whereabouts in the company.

"Sebastian," Mr Hunter continues, his eyes brightening, "was convinced it was the only way to improve not only our business, but also the way we *do* business in these new and challenging times. And he was right. So much so, and with such astonishing success, I've decided he needs to come home and do the same from here. He'll be with us in a week counting from today, this time as the CEO of the Hunter Corp ... and with you, my dear, as his senior secretary upon his return."

What? No! "I don't understand. I thought I was offered the position of junior secretary. To ... to assist Linda."

"Linda and I will be just next door if either you or Sebastian need us. We'll be covering for our CFO Arthur and his secretary so they can retire, at least until my middle son Luke comes back. Once he does, he'll take over as CFO, and hopefully we'll be able to step back a bit more." Mr Hunter steeples his hands together on the desk. "This company needs young blood, Alice, to continue leading it into success, and we, the old blood, deserve some free time to enjoy ourselves." He gives Linda a smile, and she blushes all over again.

Oh, that's cute. And understandable. I mean, the man might be in his fifties, but he's a total hunk. So yeah, something's definitely going on between these two. How did I not notice it before?

My grin takes over my face, and I have to hide it as they look at me again. I cover my mouth and cough into my hand as I look down to avoid their eyes.

In my defence, I did mention I was a terrible liar. It was only safe to assume my acting skills wouldn't be much better.

Mr Hunter clears his throat, obviously embarrassed I noticed their little exchange—and by my bad acting, no doubt. "We'll still be around. We want to support you and Sebastian, and Luke, of course, for as long as we can. That way everyone will be prepared long before it's our turn to retire."

"I understand, sir, and I'll do my best to help with the transition. You can count on me," I say, trying to sound confident, even if the thought of working for someone else feels like a punch in the gut.

"Thank you, my dear. And don't worry, we've already organised another secretary to join the team in order to assist *you*. She has experience, so that should be helpful, and she's available to start next week on Monday. The same day Sebastian returns. You can train her on the job, I'm sure."

"Of course. Thank you, Mr Hunter."

"No. Thank *you*, Alice. Linda and I have been looking for someone like you for a very long time. We're thrilled to finally have you here."

***

"You'll be fine, Alice," Linda says as we walk back to our office.

"Sebastian has been shadowing his dad ever since leaving university, and has been travelling back and forth between the office and every hotel and resort they own. He knows the business, and he'll tell you what he needs you to do. The rest are just daily tasks the new secretary can take over.

I nod, swallowing hard. "I'm just a bit anxious, that's all. I thought I'd be working with you. I felt more at ease because of that."

She smiles. "I know, sweetie, but I'll still be around. You can talk to me anytime you want. About work or otherwise."

"That's good to know." I say in a voice thick with emotion, stopping her in the middle of the corridor and hugging her tight. "'Cause I'm not ready for you to leave me just yet."

Linda hugs me back. "I'll always have your back. You know that, right?"

Drawing strength from her warm embrace, I take a shaky breath before letting go, psyching myself up for what I have to do next.

I have to ask, though. I need to know.

We start walking down the corridor again. "So, Linda ..." I gulp as we enter our office and reach our desks. "I've been hearing all kinds of rumours about Sebastian, and I was wondering if you could clear a few things up for me."

"Let me guess. You heard he's cold, intimidating, an asshole. Even abrupt with the staff at times, am I right?" She cocks a brow, and I nod.

"Um, yeah. Amongst other things. I didn't pay much attention to the rumours before, but now we're going to work together ..." I shrug. "I just need you to tell me how he really is. I already know he's not nice like Mr Hunter, but ... is he as bad as people describe?"

Her smile broadens. "Sebastian's nice in his own way. He's also intelligent, driven, confident ... and very, very determined for someone his age. So I guess he can come across as intimidating to some. He makes up for it with his good looks, though." She winks, and I laugh. "What? He's hot, as you youngsters say."

"Linda!" I admonish, laughing. "I don't want to know about that. I just want to know what it's like to work with him."

"OK, OK." Then she's leaning forward, her elbows on the desk and her chin on her hands as she regards me with a serious look in her eyes. "Sebastian can be quite demanding, as you can imagine, and often shows the patience of a five-year-old. But where he's strict he's also fair. That boy has a heart of gold, I can promise you that.

"Still, there'll be times when he's a pain in the ass. *Your* ass. Particularly when he's in one of his moods. Reel him in every once in a while. Trust me. It will do him good."

My eyes go wide as my chin drops. "Me? How am I supposed to 'reel in' the boss? He'll probably sack me on my very first day."

"Mr Hunter would never allow it. And I can't see you taking nuisance from anyone either. Not even your boss. That's how I knew you two would be a great match. Just be yourself, Alice, and don't let Sebastian get away with being an asshole. The rest will fall into place. You'll see." With that she unlocks her computer, ending our conversation, and leaving me alone with my thoughts.

Because now I get the whole 'match' thing ... and I'm not sure I like it. Not when I'm positive they were looking for someone who doesn't take shit from anyone, and also won't quit their job first thing after meeting Sebastian.

Damn it. I knew this was too good to be true.

And from what I can gather, it's bound to get worse. Especially when the guy has a huge fight in front of him.

With only half the staff behind him, Sebastian's left with the other half to convince, and they all seem too fearful and reluctant to accept the changes he's been wanting to implement. Changes he's now most certainly going to make.

I shudder just thinking about the hate and jealousy he's going to generate. The older, more conservative employees are resistant to change. They won't want to cooperate.

I inhale deeply and unlock my computer, a sense of dread stiffening my every move. I still don't know what to make of all this. Or Sebastian, for that matter. And I can't help but feel a little afraid. OK, very afraid. But who wouldn't in a situation like this? The guy is a first-class bastard from what I hear, and now I'm going to work with him.

Well, lucky me. He could be *my* first-class bastard for a very long time. Unless he sacks me on the spot, of course. I grimace.

No matter. I really need this job and I'm going to do it well. I just wish I could get rid of this uneasy feeling in my gut.

***

Back in my one-bedroom flat, I put away the shopping and go check on the herbs and vegetables I planted in the greenhouse out in the back garden—the main reason I chose this place and also why I can afford it. I made a deal with the landlady, who lowered the rent considerably in exchange for my promise to tend to the greenhouse and cook her a few home-made meals every once in a while.

The flat itself is old and run-down, but it's clean and it's got a fully equipped kitchen. Add in the white Ikea furniture (given to my landlady by her nephew when he redecorated), along with the cream two-seater that's been here since before I moved in, and this property is a total steal.

After a long, hot shower and a much-needed dinner, I sit on the couch with my favourite chamomile tea and read through the contract as well as all the other documents in the file.

It's a wonderful offer and I'd be a fool not to accept it. Not to mention the wage is higher than I thought. I huff out a laugh. *Guess I'll be earning every single penny dealing with the cold, stubborn womaniser my new boss apparently is.*

At least, that's what I was told a few weeks ago by the gossip suppliers. And by gossip suppliers, I mean the girls from main reception at Hunter Corp. Something I left out of my conversation with Linda, because I didn't want to get the girls in trouble. She'd know straight away it was them who told me.

I'm sure she already knows the little information I had, I heard from them. It's no secret they like to gossip and know every single thing that goes on in that place. Including every sordid little detail about the Hunter brothers' love lives. Particularly Sebastian's. They all seem to be crushing on him hard.

I shake my head. They even know about his rules on dating, which basically seem to be all about *not* dating, and never, ever having sex with people he works with or who work for him—much to the girls' heartbreak.

Still, considering he's the boss and also a 'love them and leave them' kind of guy—never having entered a relationship or gone back for seconds—it makes perfect sense to me that he wouldn't want to dip into the female population of the company. Literally.

God only knows how the girls find out about these things. Well, at least I'm safe with him. I've met some unsavoury characters in the past—as many young women still do in the workplace today—so that bit of information definitely gives me some peace of mind.

I lower my mug to the table and sign both copies of the contract. Mr Hunter has already signed his sections, so I keep my copy at home and put the other in my handbag to take back to the office tomorrow.

Well, it's done. I grab my mug and curl up on the sofa again. Now all I need to do is stop worrying myself sick.

I smile sadly into the cup. *Yeah, easier said than done, Alice. Easier said than done.*

I'm not that worried about the job itself. I know I can do it. But finding out I'm going to work for someone else? Especially when I already felt so safe, so happy? That's what's throwing me off. It takes a lot for me to trust people, and to my amazement, I already trust Mr Hunter and Linda with my life, so this whole thing is freaking me out.

What if Sebastian is horrible? What if I do my job well, but for some reason he hates me?

What if he makes my life a living hell?

***

The rest of the week goes by in a blur of meetings, phone calls and emails about the new CEO and CFO. Even my promotion deserves a post alongside Sebastian's and Luke's on the company's intranet. That surprised me, but Mr Hunter insisted.

Same with the meetings we held all day on Tuesday and Wednesday in the big conference room, since Mr Hunter wanted to inform the corporate staff of all the changes in person. A show of respect before they all received the emails and letters Linda and I were to send to every Hunter resort and hotel the following days.

Respect not many deserved, I dare say—more specifically the senior managers, with their constant interruptions during the meetings and empty threats of leaving the company. Mr Hunter told them any letters of resignation would be most welcome if it meant a better, stronger team for his sons to lead the Hunter Corp. into success.

I stifle a smile, remembering their dumbstruck expressions. Even I have to admit, if Sebastian is only half the man his father is, this company will still be in great hands.

Now, if only I could get a grip on my emotions …

"Alice, I'll see you on Monday, my dear. Have a lovely weekend." Linda does up the buttons on her coat, giving me a kiss on the cheek.

I smile. "You too, Linda. See you on Monday."

She turns and walks away, and I drag my tired body in the opposite direction towards the bus stop just a few feet down the road.

It's only the first week of March, so it's still freezing outside, meaning it's best I do my grocery shopping on the way home. After the crazy week I've just had, and with weather like this, I know myself too well to think I'll ever be arsed to go out during the weekend.

It wouldn't be the first time the cupboards were bare, anyway. At least this time it would be for a very different reason.

***

As planned, I spend my Saturday cleaning my tiny flat, doing the laundry, and even squeezing in some exercise after working on a new recipe for my book.

A passion of mine. Dream, really, since I love cooking and seem to have a knack for coming up with new recipes as well as taking apart existing ones to make them my own. I'm hoping one day I'll have enough material—and enough courage—to actually publish my work.

On Sunday I decide to have a proper break, a lazy day, and dedicate it entirely to myself. I read, have a nice, long bubble bath, and watch movies until I pass out on the couch. And finally, after spending the whole weekend in flannel pyjamas and fluffy bed socks, I'm a whole lot more relaxed and feeling much better.

I'm still anxious about meeting Sebastian tomorrow, but at least I'm not a bundle of nerves. I can only be myself, do my job well, and hope for the best. And if for whatever reason Sebastian doesn't like me or my work, then it's out of my control. Definitely not worth worrying about.

Besides ... he can't be *that* bad.

Can he?

Chapter 2

Sebastian

1.00 a.m. The Hunter Hotel
Trocadero, Paris

I open the door of the luxury suite we reserve for our most distinguished clients and wait for Cassandra to step out. I resist the urge to grimace. The suite is sophisticated and decorated mainly in reds and neutrals, with all the furnishings in light grey and the furniture in white, and Cassandra stands out like a sore thumb in her bubble-pink minidress. She's giving me a headache.

"Thank you for the lovely evening." My hand on the small of her back gives her a little push as I smile, making it quite clear it's time for her to go now.

What can I say? I'm a bastard.

She doesn't make any move to leave, though, and I sigh.

"Are you sure you don't want me to stay?" she asks, sliding her hand up my chest. "I can't help but feel we're not quite finished here." The look she's giving me is pleading.

I avert my eyes. Shit. This is always the hardest part. Getting rid of them.

Her hand moves to the back of my neck. I look down at her plastic face, taking in her huge, fake tits and bottle-blonde hair, and she smiles a knowing smile. She thinks I'm checking her out, that I'll cave in. What she doesn't know is that now the alcohol is losing its effect on me, she actually makes my stomach turn.

I never liked her type. Still don't. Guess that's why I can only fuck them from behind. She was a means to an end. A receptacle. And now that I'm done, I just want her out of my sight.

And yeah, I'm the worst kind of bastard, but in my defence, I did tell her I was one from the start. One thing I don't do is trick women into my bed. I never lie to them. And I'm not about to start now.

I grab her wrist, remove her hand from my neck, and let go of it as if it burned me. The soberer I get, the worse her presence is making me feel.

I take a step back, putting some distance between us. Both her smell and her touch are making me sick. "Believe me when I say we're quite finished, Cassandra. Now, be a good girl and leave."

Her eyes throw me daggers. Still my mask stays in place.

"Come on, you knew what this was. I didn't lie to you. I also remember telling you you'd have to leave once we were done. So don't act like this is anything more than a fuck. I don't date, and I don't do one-night stands. I fuck, and then it's over." My tone has its usual coldness to it, and her eyes become slits.

"You're an asshole," she hisses.

"Yes. Yes, I am. And now I'd like you to leave. I could always call security to escort you if you prefer?"

"That won't be necessary. I'll go." Her shoulders straighten and her frown turns into a bright smile as she fluffs out her hair. "I think you need some time to miss me, anyway. It's OK. You'll come to your senses soon enough. And then we can be together again."

I blanch at her words. She has to be mentally unstable. Or at the very least have a severe case of multiple personalities. I mean, just a second ago she was ready to cut my dick off, and now ...

She lets out a small laugh. "It's OK, babes. I forgive you. Relationships are hard in the beginning. But we'll be going home tomorrow. I'm sure we can do something about your fear of commitment then."

Bat. Shit. Crazy.

I rub at my eyes, feeling a migraine start to form as my anger increases. *Fucking hell, how did I end up fucking this slut? Oh, yeah, the bloody tequila.*

"Cassandra." I sigh. "*We* won't be going anywhere together. And we're certainly not seeing each other again. Is that clear?"

She lets out a laugh. "Well, we'll just have to see about that, won't we?"

My anger boils over. "OK, I think we're done here. You need to go ... now!" Annoyed, I point to the corridor outside. "I wish you all the best, Cassandra. Goodbye."

"Don't worry, babes, I won't let us lose this now that we've found each other. I know that when you push me away, it's really just a knee-jerk reaction. You don't know any better. I'm not going anywhere, though. There's no getting rid of me now. I can see how much you want me. I—"

"That's enough!" I whisper-shout. I'm this close to calling security.

I could throw her out myself, but she's clearly unstable and might say I attacked her or some shit like that.

Not that I'm too worried about the authorities. A man in my position can never be too careful, so I always record the audio of these encounters. Still, I'd like to avoid a scandal if at all possible.

"Leave. Now!" I growl.

"See you soon, Sebastian. I promise you that," she says, her tone sickly sweet.

Is she threatening me? Because that definitely sounded like a threat to me.

I grit my teeth, but hold my tongue, giving her only silence in return.

She finally crosses the threshold, and I don't miss a beat. I shut the door just as she's about to turn back towards me.

I blow out a breath. *What the fuck is wrong with that girl?*

I shake my head, threading my fingers through my hair as I walk back to the living room and fall into one of the red couches. *What a nutcase.* Definitely the craziest one I've picked up so far. And I've picked up my fair share of crazies.

Crazy and greedy, all of them.

I shake my head again in disgust, seeing visions of myself and the sick, twisted women I fucked, reminding me of their endless thirst for power. Their games. Their confidence in my stupidity for sleeping with them, making them twice as stupid for believing once they'd put out, they'd have me by the balls—and on my knees, proclaiming my undying love for them. Preferably with a sizeable rock in my hands.

Hilarious, really. Like I couldn't see their money-hunger and malicious plans from miles away. That's why they're easy pussy. All of them. No exceptions.

No. No. If I was looking for a wife—which I'm not, of course—it wouldn't be any of them.

They're too rotten, too ugly. Inside and out. Their plastic faces and fake boobs. Their greed and shallowness, making them good for one thing and one thing alone.

Definitely not wife material.

No, I'd have to look for a real woman. One with the natural beauty and smarts I crave so much. Kind, and funny, and ...

"Jesus," I mutter, dragging a hand over my face. "What the fuck is the matter with me?" I've been travelling a lot, that's all. Been feeling a bit lonely these past few months. More so than usual, anyway. And all these bimbos are losing their usefulness.

Hell, lately I have to be drunk off my ass just to get laid. I'm not even sure how I get it up most of the time.

I can't fuck a good girl, though. I *won't* fuck a good girl. That's dangerous territory, and I don't want to hurt anyone's feelings.

Feelings have no place in my sex life. Hence the bimbos.

We use each other. I get what I want, and they get some nice gifts in return. They might not get the rich husband they were hoping for, but I usually make it up to them.

Money, jewellery, and cars, I find, have a way of softening women. And I have no qualms in being generous if it means they won't run their mouths about me.

It won't work with Cassandra, though. No, not with Cassandra. In fact, I think it's best if I cut all ties with her after today.

***

I hear my phone ring and go back into the bedroom to retrieve it.

'Dad' appears on the screen and my face contorts into a grimace. *Shit. I really don't feel like talking to anyone right now. Especially Dad.*

Not to mention he's been doing this a lot—calling just to check up on me, even if he pretends it's about work most of the time.

I sit on the plush red armchair facing the bed and accept the call. "Hey, Dad."

"Hey! How are you, son?" I can hear him smiling on the other end.

"OK," I say, feeling my own lips stretch into a smile. "Just going to bed."

I eye the bed and it feels wrong. I don't think I can sleep on it tonight. The smell of sex and the expensive perfume the crazy bitch was wearing lingers in the air. It makes me feel sick to my stomach.

I get up, pick up my work phone and go sit in the lounge.

"Are you all packed and ready to come home?"

"Yeah, Dad, all good." I text François, my hotel manager, telling him I need to be moved to the Hunter family suite right away and to send someone to help. "I'm actually excited this time," I continue. "All this travelling is finally getting to me, I guess." Then I shoot a text to Ryan, my head of security and best friend, to let him know of the changes.

I frown. Should've stayed in the family suite from the beginning, but in my defence, I didn't want to take any of the women up there. Next time I'll just stay in the suite ... and use one of the guest rooms for the deed.

"Been there myself, son. And it can get pretty lonely, pretty fast. Not to mention everything feels like work and no fun."

"Yeah, but I'm glad I did it. Now, not only do our hotels follow the same processes, but our staff is also in sync—doing the same things, *saying* the same things, even communicating with each other, which we both know hasn't been the case for years."

"I know. I know, and I'm the first to take my hat off to you. It's commendable the job you've been doing with all of our sites. It's done us a world of good, and I can already see the impact on our business."

"Thank you, Dad. I didn't do it alone, though. François and Philippe, and all our good staff across the sites, have been unstoppable in their mission to help me. And I suspect that's the reason why we made such good progress so fast. I mean, we even managed to cut down on expenses. If that's not saying something, I don't know what is."

"Oh," he says, and I can hear the surprise in his voice. "I didn't know you were looking at the expenses. I thought we were going to wait for your brother before tackling those."

"Actually, it's because of Luke I checked. He found some irregularities with the invoices in the Dominican resorts and brought them to my attention when we spoke on the phone."

"What kind of irregularities?"

"Mainly that we were being overcharged for goods and services we don't actually need. And the ones we do need, we could get elsewhere for a much better deal." I run my fingers through my hair, shaking my head. "It's weird, Dad, but some of these suppliers seem dodgy as hell. Even when we contacted both our legal team and theirs, in hopes of renegotiating or cancelling the contracts, they did everything to avoid us and our paperwork."

"Hmm, and are you boys still having trouble with them?" He sounds worried now, preoccupied, and I blow out a breath.

I didn't want to worry the old man. It's just that unfortunately ... I'm a bit worried myself. My gut keeps telling me there's more to this than meets the eye. That's why Luke and I will investigate the matter further once we're both back in the office and can go through the archives.

Something is wrong with this picture, and I'm intent on finding out exactly what.

"A little, but thanks to our legal team, we were able to pull out of most contracts. They added a clause that allows us to end any agreement if we're offered or find a better deal. Now it's just a few of the older companies we seem to be stuck with, since those contracts didn't include the same clause."

Which is royally pissing me off. How could our staff let something like this slide? What were they doing back then?

"How long until we can sever our connection to them?"

"Another year." I sigh again, my frustration at an all-time high. I'm used to getting what I want, when I want it, no matter what. Always. And because of our own, I'm having to submit. To hold back. When I don't hold back for anyone.

Fuck. I run my fingers through my hair. "But we'll talk about all this in detail when I get back, Dad."

Yeah, I still want to find a way. The fucking leeches have already sucked too much, robbing us for years. Not to mention that most of the luxury goods we've been paying serious coin for can't be found anywhere. Even when I did the inventory check myself at Luke's request.

"OK, son. You must be tired, so I'll let you go."

"Fucking knackered," I reply with a yawn, and then smile when my dad laughs at my more-than-honest response.

I'm about to say goodnight to him when I remember my secretary situation. "Oh, Dad, I almost forgot. Did you manage to find someone?"

There's a knock on the door, and Ryan steps in with a housekeeper and a porter trailing behind him. I acknowledge their presence with a nod and point to the bedroom.

"Yep. That's all been taken care of, son," my dad says smugly, bringing my attention to our conversation again.

"Experienced?" I specifically asked for someone with experience.

"Two months' training with us, but don't worry, we found you the most delightful little lady for the job. You'll like her. She's very competent, professional, and a perfectionist too."

An older lady then. Good. The last thing I need is another young thing swooning over me at the office. The gawking I get from our receptionists is already annoying enough. "If you're sure."

"As I said, she's very competent. A professional. You'll get along just fine."

"And what does Linda say?"

"Funny you should ask, because the two of them get along like a house on fire. They're already the best of friends."

"Good to hear. Definitely one less thing for me to worry about."

Whoever this lady is, if she's already managed to get Linda's approval, I'm impressed. Linda may look sweet as pie, but she can smell bullshit, including my own, from miles away. There's no pulling the wool over that woman's eyes.

That's why I trust her more than anyone. With her you know exactly what you get.

"No, no worrying necessary," Dad says. "You can just come home and enjoy the benefits of our hard work. And believe me, this time you will, son. This time I guarantee you will." He laughs wholeheartedly, and I can't help but feel amused by his tone.

My dad must really like this new lady. And here I was thinking he had a thing for Linda.

"Well, it took you long enough to find this unicorn secretary, so ..."

"First, don't let Linda hear you talk about her like that. She'll get jealous. And secondly, I'll have you know we also found you a junior secretary to help with the smaller tasks around the office, young man."

"Oh?" I say, impressed.

"Yeah, Sharon from the accounts department. She's retired now, but didn't want to give up work altogether, so we thought it would be a good fit."

"Sounds good. And it makes sense with the workload we have in the office."

"Good, I'm glad you agree. Now go get some sleep. We'll see each other tomorrow and catch up properly over dinner."

I smile. I've missed the old man. "See you tomorrow, Dad."

"Have a good journey, son. Come back safe to us."

My face falls as emotion grips me by the heart. "I will, Dad. I will."

***

Ringing off, I let out a big sigh.

Come back safe to us. That's what my mum used to say to my brothers and I.

She didn't come back safe, though. She didn't come back at all.

I close my eyes, swallowing hard at the sudden pain in my throat and chest.

I was only fifteen when a car crash took her away from us ten years ago. My younger twin brothers, Nathan and Mason, were twelve and my middle brother, Luke, was fourteen. And my dad, a middle-aged, self-made billionaire, was left alone and broken with four kids.

His soul, his heart withered. And I suspect he wanted nothing more than to follow his wife to the grave.

He stayed, though. A great dad, despite the tragedy surrounding our family. A great dad, despite his pain. And the reason why, I suppose, I avoid falling in love like the plague.

I won't let what happened to him happen to me. I won't depend on someone else for my happiness.

I saw what that did to him—how *love* ripped him apart piece by piece, until we could barely recognize what was left of him—and I don't want it. Don't want any part of it.

To be honest, I don't think I'm even capable of the feeling. I've never grown attached to any female. Never wanted one in a romantic kind of way. So perhaps I'm no longer capable of such emotions.

Even if one day, who knows, I may live to regret it.

Ryan walks out of the bedroom. A wide grin stretches over his face as he shakes his blond head at me.

"Don't, man. Just don't say anything," I groan, running my hands through my sweaty hair.

I need to shower. Need to wash that skank off my skin.

He laughs at my pained expression. "I told you that girl was crazy, man. Now look at you, changing suites in the middle of the night. What did she do? Try to bite your dick off or something?" He falls into the couch in front of me.

"Shit. Crazy doesn't cut it." I huff out a laugh. "She actually threatened me. *Really* threatened me when I wouldn't let her stay the night."

"She did what now?" His brows bunch together as I tell him everything, down to the tone she used and the expression she wore when she said I would see her again soon.

Ryan's eyes narrow, his lips pressed into a tight line, but he doesn't interrupt, listening intently until I'm done.

"Do you know who she is?" he finally asks, and I can tell he's worried about this. We're used to a bit of whining, a few tears every now and then, but never the crazy shit I witnessed today.

"Her name's Cassandra Oakes. I met her briefly during a charity ball."

"Yeah, I figured as much when you told me to stand down on the background check."

I nod regretfully. "She comes from old family money. Prestige. And we both know her dad. Stephen Oakes, the politician?"

Ryan's features soften at this. "Hmm ... Oakes seems to be a good man. He's a supporter of a lot of good causes, including many of the Hunter charities. Still, I think I'd feel better if you let me run a background check. You know, do a little digging about her and dearest old Dad." He's already pulling his phone out of his jeans pocket and typing furiously on it. Probably emailing Jamie, our most trusted hacker-slash-IT guy. "Someone like her has to have history. A previous meltdown, a complaining ex-boyfriend, some kind of mental illness. Her behaviour isn't normal. That has to leave a trail somewhere."

I pinch the bridge of my nose. He's right. We need to know more about her and the kind of reach her family has. "Do it." I give the order even though he's already on it. "And Ryan, I'm sorry I stopped you before." Our gazes meet and I hold his sky-blue eyes. "It won't happen again. I promise." And I mean it.

I made a mistake this time. A stupid mistake. One I'll never repeat.

***

We make our way to the Hunter family suite in silence.

I'm tired. Dead tired. So exhausted, in fact, I just want to go to sleep. Something I should be doing already, since our jet will be leaving at eight a.m. and it's now two forty-five.

Fuck. I rub my eyes, knowing it's my own fault I'm here instead, swapping rooms.

Ryan and Michael, my other trusted bodyguard, go in as soon as I open the door and start doing their security sweep of the suite. It smells nice in here. Clean and fresh, like someone just polished. I perch on the couch, looking around the ample living room with renewed interest.

The decor is still the same from the remodel two years ago. The furnishings are all in silver and dark blues, with the sofas and chairs in cream, and the furniture is in a shiny white that simply screams expensive.

Modern and elegant, the theme carries into the bedrooms with slightly different colour variations and patterns, but still very much the same, leaving no doubt it was done by a professional.

It's good. Better than good. Like everything the Hunters do in this business. And a sense of pride invades my chest.

Now, if only I felt the same whenever I think about my personal life, everything would be just dandy.

Ryan and Michael finish checking the rooms and come back to the lounge. "Have a good night, man," Ryan says, and I look up from my place on the couch.

"Yeah, you too, mate." I nod towards Michael as he leaves, and he nods back. "And Ryan ... thank you." I feel bad for standing in his way when he was only looking out for me. We're best friends. I'm not just a job to him.

He pats my shoulder on his way to the exit. "Just get some sleep, Sebastian. I'll see you tomorrow."

"See you tomorrow," I say, and he leaves, closing the door behind him with a soft click.

After a much-needed shower and two ibuprofen, I brush my teeth and finally collapse on the bed. I'm more than ready for this night to become a distant memory.

My eye catches the bright-red wrappers on the nightstand, even when I turn away, trying my best to resist. But it's no use. And before I know it, I'm taking one of the dark truffles from its wrapper and shoving it into my mouth. It melts on my tongue, and I sigh, the rich notes of dark cocoa and strong coffee beans taking over my senses as I finally relax.

I close my eyes. After this night from hell, I should just eat the whole bowl. Give in to my sweet tooth and swear off having sex ever again.

I laugh, and shut down the rest of the lights. Hopefully tomorrow I'll be going home and all this fucking travelling will stop messing with my head.

"Home." I say the word out loud, folding my arms under my head. Yeah, more like a huge-ass box of brick and glass that's just as empty and as hollow as my life.

My mansion is as elegant and as modern as can be. A cleverly crafted work of art with every gadget, luxury and comfort known to man. And not once have I ever felt at home when I'm in it. Don't think I ever will, to be honest.

The opulent property just feels way too big and too impersonal to me. Not one bit like the welcoming home it was designed to be. If anything, I think it makes me feel worse.

Because it *is* a family home. Complete with the enclosed, heated pool, the huge gardens, and more than enough space for kids to play. My dad's idea of a perfect gift. A gift he built and designed along with three other houses, which he gave to my brothers.

The old man is sneaky that way. And hopeful we'll start forming our own families soon. So it came as no surprise when he made sure we stayed close to each other—and him.

Guess hope is truly the last emotion to die. Otherwise, he would've given up on the idea years ago.

Never mind. He'll get the picture soon enough.

I close my eyes and turn on my side again.

All I know is that I need to get back to London, to familiar territory, and surround myself with faces and memories from my childhood. The places and smells that make me feel right, centred. That's what 'home' should really mean, in the end.

I'll feel better once I go back. Feel like myself again.

I just have to hold on a little longer.

Chapter 3

Alice

The bus stops, and I fly through its halfway-open doors as if the Devil himself is chasing me

Oh, God. Oh, God. Oh, God!

My soles squeak on the pavement, my face is a sweaty, flustered mess, and I feel like I'm about to faint by the time I reach the Hunter Corp. "Good morning!" I shout at the guards, who all smirk, but thankfully hold one of the lifts open for me.

Grr, no time for breakfast either.

I shake my head and, getting inside the elevator, press the button for my floor. I hate it when my days begin like this. Stupid, stupid bus was twenty minutes late! And now I can't even get coffee before I start work.

"Coffee!" I groan out loud, dropping my head back until it rests on the wall. Oh, what I wouldn't give for a hazelnut latte right now.

The lift dings and I run through the open doors and down the corridor like a maniac. I drop my handbag under the desk and throw my coat over my chair. I turn on the lights, the computer, and the printer and am just about to sit to replace my trainers with the sensible heels I wear in the office when I notice the silence.

No beeping, no humming, no flashing lights, nothing.

"What's wrong, sweetie?" I coo, petting the dark monitor. I find our electronic equipment temperamental, and a little TLC usually goes a long way. I press the 'on' button again, and still nothing happens.

OK. The main lights are on—even with the big windows surrounding us, the overhead lights are always on during the day. And the printer is also working. So the computer must be unplugged somehow. That, or the IT guy who was here on Friday screwed up and I'll have to call him again.

The socket is somewhere on the floor under the desk. "Well, no time like the present," I mutter, getting on my hands and knees and crawling under the damn thing.

Hmm, the plug is in, so maybe it's the socket that's off. I feel around until I find the switch ... and then there's that familiar sound of electronic equipment coming back to life.

"OK, baby, you're all better now." I smile, crawling out backwards when a deep, baritone voice says from behind me—

"Who are you? And what the fuck are you doing under the desk?"

Startled, I let out a yelp and jerk upwards. The back of my head hits the very edge of the desk hard. "Aaah!" I hear my anguished scream and screw my eyes shut. Pain stabs through my brain, making me crouch even lower to cradle my head.

"Mmm," I moan, dazed. Little white dots appear behind my eyelids, and I swoon from side to side. God, it really is like seeing stars, isn't it?

"Shit! Are you OK?" Big hands close around my waist and I'm suddenly lifted into an upright position.

Oh, bad idea. Bad idea.

Dizzy and with a throbbing headache, I feel my knees wobble and I'm sure I'm going to pass out. I fall against the hard wall behind me.

"I got you, sweetheart. I got you." An arm slips under my knees and I'm lifted into the air.

I take a chance opening my eyes, and through the dizziness see the most beautiful face I've ever seen on a man. The electric-blue eyes looking down at me are so intense, I feel they can see right into my soul. I shiver and look away, my eyes closing again, turning everything black.

* * *

"Come on, sweetheart, wake up. You're worrying me now," a voice says, its sound so soothing, I don't want it to ever go away.

I just need a few more minutes, though. Just a few more minutes and I'll be up.

"Come on, beautiful."

I feel a caress on my cheek. "Mmm." It feels good, so good, and that voice ...

Something cold presses against my forehead, helping clear the fog away. "Can you try opening your eyes for me?" the voice asks.

"Blue eyes," I mumble.

"Yeah, that's me. Now open yours, sweetheart."

Slowly, very slowly, I open my eyelids, trying to focus only on what's in front of me. I don't want to get too dizzy, or, worse, throw up.

The first thing I see is those electric-blues staring intently at me. I stare back, my gaze fixed on the most sensual, full, kissable lips I've ever seen and a smooth, clean-shaven face that's so freaking beautiful it hurts to look at it. This guy could easily be an actor or a male model.

"How do you feel? Are you still dizzy?"

"I ... yes." I avert my eyes, embarrassed. "I feel sick."

Oh, God, don't let me throw up on this guy. Please.

"Yeah, you banged your head pretty hard. I checked and you don't seem to have any cuts, but there's quite a big bump forming."

I touch the back of my head tentatively and feel the bump. The light touch of my fingers makes me wince, it's so tender.

"You gave me a fright," I accuse. "It was you, wasn't it?" I note I'm in my boss' office, lying on his couch. I can't believe this guy. The cheek.

"Sorry, didn't mean to scare you," he says, but then frowns. "Who are you, anyway? And what were you doing in that office in the first place?"

Oh, he must be security. Probably one of the guys in my new boss' personal team. "I'm Alice, Mr Hunter's secretary," I reply.

"Charles Hunter?" he asks, his eyebrows raised.

"No, Sebastian Hunter."

Blue Eyes blinks, and then blinks again. "What? Are you fucking kidding me right now?"

I cover my ears. "Stop shouting. Seriously, what is wrong with you?"

"I ... sorry. I guess I'm just a bit ... surprised. You look too young to hold such a position." He gives me an assessing look from head to toe and back to my face again. "You look barely eighteen. Are you even legal yet?"

"Legal?"

"To fuck, to drink. You know, are you an adult?"

I gasp. Oh, this idiot needs to go. I don't even care if I never get to see his handsome face again. "You come in here, make me hit my head and pass out, shout and swear at me, and now you offend me? I think it's best you leave. I want you to leave ... now!" I try to sound as assertive as I can, but my voice comes out shaky and weak.

His laughter fills the room. "You want me to leave, sweetheart? Then you better be ready to throw me out yourself. Think you're up for it?"

I'm fuming. Who does this guy think he is? "Listen here, asshole. My boss should be arriving any moment, and he won't like that you're in his private office being rude to his personal secretary, capisce? So you need to leave. Now!"

"Oh, and why's that, Alice? Are you sleeping with the boss? Is that why he'll care?"

"What? Of course not. He's well-mannered, a gentleman like his father, that's why. I'm warning you, if you don't leave, I'll call security."

"Easy, tiger." Blue Eyes smiles broadly, like this is the most fun he's had in years. "As far as I'm concerned, I'm only here because I'm helping your boss' dainty, clumsy secretary anyway. So quiet down, smart mouth. Don't get your panties in a twist."

Annoyed, I go to tell him whose panties I'll twist when there's a light knock on the door and a blond young man steps in. "Everything's ready, they're just waiting for us to arrive. Oh, and the new secretary is here. She's asking for Alice. They're supposed to work together."

"That's Sharon. She's the junior secretary starting today. I'm supposed to train her," I say, already trying to get up.

Blue Eyes gently pushes me back down with his hands on my shoulders. "You're in no shape to do that. Besides, the only place you'll be going is the private hospital I'm taking you to."

"No, there's no need. I'm fine now and I have work to do. Also, I'm not going anywhere with you. I don't know you."

He looks irritated. "Alice, you've hit your head pretty hard and I'm worried you might have a concussion. You were unconscious, remember? And you're still feeling dizzy and sick. I'm not taking any chances." I puff out my cheeks in frustration, and he raises one thick eyebrow at me. "I'm taking you to the hospital, and that's final."

He turns to the other guy, and this time I follow his gaze to the door.

Seriously! Where are all these hot guys coming from?

Tall, with sky-blue eyes, muscled and gorgeous, Blondie has an unreadable face and is most definitely security. I can sense that eerie vibe emanating from him from miles away. The same vibe I'm getting from Blue Eyes, if I'm being honest. And it's confusingly attractive. It makes me wonder just how hard I hit my head.

I turn to Blue Eyes again, taking advantage of the fact he's not looking at me, and let my eyes roam freely. Jet-black hair, super-long lashes, and tanned skin. I take in every detail of his straight nose, strong, masculine jaw, and that mouth ... God, that beautiful, kissable mouth of his ...

He looks back at me, and I quickly avert my eyes, making the room spin.

Damn it.

"OK, just tell Sharon to mind the phones and do what she can until Linda gets here," Blue Eyes says. "Oh, and call Linda again. Tell her that if Alice has a concussion, she has to carry on with the training herself."

I bite my lip, trying to stifle my smile. Even through my dizziness and nausea, I can't help the surge of excitement running through my veins when he says my name for the second time.

"Come on, little thing. Let's get you checked." His arms go under my back and knees and then he's lifting me from the couch.

I gasp, and instinctively my arms wrap around his neck. Jesus! Someone sure had their breakfast this morning.

He's strong. Not to mention tall. So very tall. And OK, most people are tall compared to my five foot two, but this guy ... this guy must be at least six foot five.

"I can walk," I try to protest, but end up sounding like a nagging child.

"Not today, sweetheart."

"But ..."

"I'm carrying you. End of story." Commandingly, that's how the asshole talks to me.

I narrow my eyes. "Seriously?"

Ignoring my death glare, he carries me out of the office.

Sharon gets up as soon as she sees us and gives me a smile. Her plump, short figure and grey hair remind me that she's not only a mature lady but also a work colleague.

My cheeks heat up. I'm so embarrassed right now I could die. It's not enough that this brute manhandled me and shushed me like a child, now I'm being carried around like an invalid. And OK, my balance is not great at the moment. And I'm a tad overwhelmed when it comes to decision-making. But still, how dare he? How—

"Good morning, Sharon. I'll be taking Alice to the hospital now, if anyone asks. Oh, and thank you for your help this morning. It most definitely has been an interesting one." Blue Eyes gives her a lopsided, panty-melting smile, and I almost laugh when the poor woman blushes. If I wasn't so preoccupied checking my own panties are still in place, I'd be doubling over, no doubt.

Sharon recovers quickly, I'll give her that. With a polite nod towards the cheeky bugger, she turns to me with another smile on her bright-pink lips. "I hope you feel better soon, my dear." She reaches for my hand, comforting me. "And don't worry about a thing. Linda and I, we've got this."

"Thank you, Sharon," I say.

Blue Eyes' gaze is hot and boring into my cheek. "Right, we're off." He clears his throat, turns and with a quick goodbye to Sharon is rushing us down the corridor towards the lifts.

***

I frown, not recognizing my surroundings as Blue Eyes enters a different lift and we arrive in an underground garage. The Hunter building is ginormous, and to be honest the whole journey is a bit of a blur. So much so, by the time we're inside a car and moving, I don't remember most of it. Also, the dizziness is still bad, there's a hammer banging inside my head, and I'm unable to focus on much apart from the gorgeous man who has me sitting on his lap, my head on his chest, his hands rubbing my back, my shoulders, my ...

Wait! Why is he holding me like this, and, more importantly, why am I allowing it?

I squirm, trying to move and sit by his side, but his arms tighten around me. "We'll be there soon, sweetheart."

"I can sit by myself. It's not right I'm sitting on your lap."

"You're right where you need to be, beautiful. Now quiet down and rest. Try to relax, 'cause I'm not letting you go."

He caresses my cheek then, and I give up, too tired to argue with him. I'll just close my eyes for one second. Just one second ...

I'm moving, and it's fast and bumpy. In fear of falling, I grasp what's closest to my hands, only to realise it's the thick fabric of a coat and that I'm being carried again. My face is so close to the crook of his neck, his scent envelops me like a warm blanket. Blue Eyes smells spicy, musky and clean—wonderfully masculine. It's comforting and disturbing at the same time. Comforting because it makes me happy. And disturbing because of the sexual need it awakens in me.

"Almost there, sweetheart," he whispers in my ear, and I shiver, goosebumps spreading everywhere as his warm breath fans over my skin.

Seriously, what is this man doing to me? And why is my body behaving like this? It's like I have no control over it.

"You cold?" he asks, and I tentatively open my eyes to look at him.

"I'm OK. Don't worry." I notice then that I'm wearing my coat and scarf—he must've put them on me in the car, and I have to fight the urge to kiss him on the cheek. Or worse, his mouth.

I'm thinking about it. Imagining it, really. I'm shocking the hell out of myself. It's never happened before, me thinking about a man like this, wanting to kiss him, touch him.

I know it's only because he was nice to me. Not to mention sweet and thoughtful with the coat thing. It's confusing, that's all.

I couldn't possibly want to kiss a man I just met. A man I know nothing about.

I look at him again and the same vision assaults me. I bite my lip, and his arms tighten around me. Comforting, protective.

Shoot, this man is dangerous. He's dangerous to me, I can feel it.

"Good morning, sir. How can I help?" A smiling blonde greets us from behind a tall, white marble desk.

"Morning," Blue Eyes rasps, and I have to fight the smile his voice brings to my lips. But then he speaks again, and I can't believe my ears. "Sebastian Hunter … and this is my fiancée, Alice Lake, to see Dr Smith."

I gasp.

What? What's he saying? Sebastian? As in my boss, Sebastian? Oh, God, he's my boss. Wait … fiancée?

With great difficulty, I lift my head from his shoulder and stare at him, transfixed. My headache is getting worse by the second, as is the ringing in my ears.

He smiles a knowing smile and gives me a little squeeze. "It's OK, baby. Everything will be fine." He kisses my temple.

"Yes, Mr Hunter. We've been expecting you. Please follow me and I'll take you to Dr Smith right away."

With that Sebastian turns and follows the receptionist to the consulting room with me still in his arms. I'm so shocked, I don't say anything. There's nothing remotely appropriate I can say.

Dr Smith is a short, bald-headed man, ultra-skinny, and surprisingly nice. He asks me a lot of questions and checks my eyes with a light. He's convinced I have a concussion and wants to do an MRI. He talks mainly to Mr Blue Eyes, though, seeing as I keep falling asleep and can't concentrate.

To add to my embarrassment, I also throw up three times. Once on the radiology nurse, then on the expensive wooden floor of the outpatient waiting area, and another time just inside the consulting room, luckily in the sink.

Sebastian even cracks a joke, thanking me for throwing up on the nice nurse instead of him.

I don't laugh. In fact, I could kill him in that moment for the jokes and for hiding his identity from me. Which he apologises for countless times and explains he didn't do it on purpose. Still, I'm angry.

After all the tests are done, Dr Smith confirms that I have a concussion. The force of lifting my head in fright and hitting the desk was strong enough to jolt my brain. He prescribes painkillers, some tablets for the nausea, and lots and lots of sleep so my brain can heal. Dr Smith also tells Sebastian to wake his lovely 'fiancée' every two hours, for a minimum of twelve, and ask her questions to assess if she's OK.

Ha. I almost snort. As if that's going to happen.

Before long, we're saying our goodbyes, with the doctor handing Sebastian his card and telling him to call in case he has any concerns.

"I can walk on my own, thank you." I try my best to sound assertive, sure of myself. My head's throbbing in time with my heartbeat, but I don't care. All I know is I have to put some distance between us.

Already bending to pick me up, Sebastian reluctantly straightens to his full height and lets go of my waist. "Are you sure? You still look unsteady on your feet."

"I'm fine," I lie, just as a new bout of nausea comes over me and I have to ask myself why the hell I'm doing this.

Oh, yeah, I remember. I'm adding 'hot and bothered' to my endless list of symptoms. I can't help but wonder if I should've told the doctor. Maybe he'd have a prescription for that too.

Sebastian frowns, both hands on his hips as he shakes his head at me. "I don't like this. The last thing you need is a fall right now. Let me at least hold on to your arm. Please."

Sighing, I acquiesce. Who am I fooling anyway? "OK, but just my arm."

I take a tentative step, swallowing hard as bile rises up my throat. My hands fly towards Sebastian when I feel as if I'm about to fall.

He lets out a frustrated groan, bends and picks me up in his arms. Then, without another word, he sets off to the car. And just like that, the discussion is over.

Resigned, I loop my arms around his neck, my fingers brushing against his dark, soft hair and sending a jolt of arousal straight to my core. My toes curl and I feel myself getting wet. He has lovely hair. Silky and strong beneath my fingertips, and so fragrant it's as if I'm not even awake. It's as if I'm dreaming. Dreaming and fantasising about him.

I sigh and run my fingers through the dark tresses again. "You need a haircut," I blurt out before I can stop myself, my face burning.

God, I can't believe I just said that.

"Do I, now?" He smiles a slow, boyish smile. "And who's going to give me one? You?"

I look away. "It's your funeral. I wouldn't trust myself with a pair of scissors right now." He chuckles and holds me closer to his chest.

Feeling self-conscious, I rest my hands on his right shoulder, only to get more flustered when the thick, hard bulges of his muscles ripple underneath my fingertips. The strength and size of his arms is evident even beneath his suit and winter coat.

Seriously, what's with all the muscle on this guy? Surely he doesn't need to be this big, does he?

My mouth slackens, watering when my hands close of their own accord, giving him a little squeeze.

Then again, big feels really good right now. Hard and strong and a little dangerous at the same time.

"Having fun?" Sebastian rasps, making me snap out of my newfound perverted ways, and I fist my hands. The heat on my face spreads to my ears and chest as I lean my head on my own shoulder and close my eyes, unable to meet his.

One knock to the head and I'm already behaving like a slut. I stifle a groan. This is so unlike me. Feeling up a man, a stranger no less—my boss, for Christ's sake.

Jesus, my boss! What am I doing? Please just kill me now.

"It's OK. I liked it," he whispers, his lips touching my ear ever so slightly, giving me goosebumps all over again.

"What?"

"I liked that you touched me," he breathes with his lips still on me, causing me to shiver, and him to groan as he buries his nose in my hair.

When we get to the car, he sits with me on his lap again, and this time I don't argue with him. No, I just lay my head on his chest and let myself enjoy it before falling asleep.

I figure, if I have a concussion, I might as well take advantage of it. I'm confused, and right now Blue Eyes just smells too good and looks too handsome to pass up on the opportunity. Later, I can just claim I wasn't feeling like myself—which is the truth, anyway—or that I don't remember. Which I hope to hell is not the case.

I don't want to forget a single detail about this man.

***

"Time to wake up, Sleeping Beauty."

Mmm, I don't want to. I turn away from the voice.

"Alice, sweetheart, I need you to answer some questions."

My head hurts, everything spins, and I haven't even opened my eyes. So, no, I don't think so.

"Alice, come on, tell me how old you are."

Wait. Am I in a hospital? Did I have an accident or something?

Slowly, I open my eyes, my vision hazy as it takes in the shape of a man. I blink rapidly until his face is no longer a blur. Then everything that happened comes back in a rush. I remember him. All the other bits are foggy, but him I remember.

"Twenty-two. I'm twenty-two years old," I whisper, also remembering this is the reason I'm here, in his house, in his guest bedroom, since he's responsible for babysitting me for the next twelve hours and insisted it'd be easier to do it in his home.

"Good, sweetheart. Good. And how are you feeling?"

My brows furrow. There's a part of me that's still mad at him for hiding his identity from me, even if he's right about what he said at the hospital—that he didn't lie to me and I never did ask him his name. Still, it stings. "I need the bathroom. Can you help me up, please?"

"Of course. I'll take you there and leave you near the sink so you have something to hold on to."

He lifts the covers off of me, and I notice he removed my jumper and shirt, leaving me only in my tank top and trousers. "I took them off so you'd be more comfortable," he tells me, picking me up in his arms.

Automatically, my own arms wrap around his neck and I hold on tight. It's weird, but there's this sense of familiarity between us. This closeness already. Which, of course, shouldn't be there to begin with. We aren't friends, and the only reason why he's helping me is because he's feeling guilty. The rest I probably imagined.

Surely a man like him wasn't flirting with someone like me. And even if he was, that's all it will ever be—innocent flirting, as there can never be anything else between us.

I clear my throat as he walks us to the bathroom. "That's OK. I'm sure I'd be too warm with them on, anyway."

He smiles a beautiful smile, but doesn't say anything, not even one of his smartass replies. Then his eyes drop to my lips, and it's there again, that charge, that crackling current between us, making my heart beat like mad against my ribs. The attraction I feel towards my boss is so thick it's almost palpable, and the way I'm drawn to him is so strong, so overwhelming, I know I'm in way more trouble than I believed.

"Here you are." He puts me down, and I grab hold of the sink. Only then does he let go of me. "Are you sure you can manage? I don't mind helping you out. I could at least help you sit, then step outside to give you some privacy."

"No," I almost shout. Haven't I suffered enough humiliation for one day? "I mean, thank you, but that won't be necessary."

"I'll be right outside, then. Just call me once you're done." He closes the door behind him, and I breathe out a sigh of relief.

God, give me the strength. Seriously. I take a deep breath and turn towards the toilet, only to go still.

Bloody hell!

I take a look around, my eyes wide as saucers as they take in the gorgeous walk-in rain shower at the back, the huge flat screen TV mounted to its right, and what looks like a built-in glass sauna to its left.

Simple, light-grey tiles cover the entirety of the walls with darker-grey slabs of the marble covering the floors, and all the porcelain features are white with the accessories in silver and glass. The bathtub—a jacuzzi, really—is big enough for six and sits right in the centre of the floor, and I'm ... well, I'm speechless. Lost for words as I stare at the beauty of it all.

Never have I ever seen anything like this, at least not outside of magazines or TV shows, and I can't wrap my brain around the fact that this is someone's home.

After a minute to compose myself, I finally use the toilet and wobble back to the huge counter near the entrance. My chin hits my chest again when I see the his-and-hers sinks and the magnificent silver mirror on the wall.

I rub my eyes. Holy water! How on earth did I miss that when I came in? And, more importantly, did I miss it because of Sebastian or because of how hard I hit my head?

God only knows.

Groaning, I push my hair away from my face, but avoid the mirror altogether. Don't need to add my reflection to my list of problems as well.

A knock sounds at the door as I wash my hands, and I smile, telling Sebastian to come in. He promptly whisks me into his arms and takes me back to bed, where I fall asleep.

***

"Alice."

Nooo, I'm too tired. Go away.

"Come on, sweetheart, it's question time again." Sebastian brushes the hair off my face, tucking it behind my ear, and I open my eyes a little. "Hey, can you help me out here?"

I nod, regretting the action as soon as I do it, and then he's asking me a bunch of questions from his list. Yeah, because he's anal like that.

"Good, you're doing really well," he says, putting away the notepad where he's been writing all my answers too. "Now, how's the nausea? Think you can try to eat?"

My stomach turns. "I'm not sure. It's not too bad at the moment, but I'm afraid food might make me sick."

"I'll just get you some tea and toast." He shrugs. "If you can't hold it in, we'll just try again later."

"OK," I say, unsure.

"Here, take the anti-sickness tablets now, and I'll be back in a few minutes." Sebastian hands me a box and a glass of water and leaves.

After taking the tablets, I put the glass on the nightstand, and all I can think is that I really, really don't want to throw up on this bed. I run my fingers over the covers.

The bedding is lovely, with the duvet in silver and the sheets and pillows in a pristine white and ultra-soft. The bed itself is huge and upholstered in the same silver as the duvet with a matching panelled headboard that is also the biggest and most luxurious I've ever seen, which makes my nerves skyrocket at the prospect of messing it up. Especially by throwing up on it.

I glance around, noticing for the first time the black-brown furniture and white walls. A silver ottoman sits at the end of the bed and two matching large couches are tucked away in the corner of the room by the floor-to-ceiling windows.

Deep-red throw pillows and blankets lie carelessly on the seats, where Sebastian has been working since morning on his laptop, and silver and white heavy curtains are pulled shut to keep the afternoon light at bay. An array of decorative pieces and sculptures tie the theme together, as well as black and white paintings of the most exquisite nudes.

And once again my jaw hits my chest. All I know is that this is serious money, the kind you don't get to see, let alone experience, and I've never felt more vulnerable or out of place in my life. Not to mention that it's just too personal, me being here in Sebastian's guest room. In his house.

There are lines between employer and employee that shouldn't be crossed. And this is one of them.

I wrap my arms around myself, sighing.

The room does feel a little too intimate, though. Too much like Sebastian and his vibe. Which is strange, of course. Why would a guest room feel so much like him? Yet I can feel his presence everywhere, his soul.

And that's when it hits me. Oh, God, I'm not in a guest bedroom, am I? I'm in his bedroom, his bed. I press a hand to my mouth.

This has to be the craziest shit that's ever happened to me. Along with all the attention Sebastian is giving me.

And that's exactly why I need to leave. I'm getting too comfortable. Too familiar with him. So much so, I didn't even think about where I was when I first woke up. All I know is once I saw Sebastian's face, I felt safe, protected. Like nothing could ever harm me or touch me as long as he's around.

I laugh humourlessly. Yeah, it just goes to show how hard I hit my head.

***

When Sebastian returns, he places a bed tray over my legs and helps me get more comfortable by adjusting the pillows behind me. Then he sits on the side of the bed and watches me as I eat.

"Thank you. For looking after me, I mean." I cautiously take a bite of my toast and a sip of my tea. I need to tell him I have to go home now. That he doesn't need to feel responsible for me.

He smirks. "It's been a pleasure."

"Sure it has," I say sarcastically, massaging my temples to ease the pain that's still slicing through my brain. "What's not to like about carrying a dizzy, confused, covered-in-vomit woman around and having to take care of her? That's everyone's idea of fun."

He laughs. "At least you're funny. I'll give you that."

And you're handsome, says a voice in the back of my head.

Stop it. Stop it right this second.

"I do have to correct you, though. The poor nurse you threw up on was the one covered in vomit, not you."

"Don't remind me." I groan, covering my face with my hands. "God, I feel terrible. That poor lady. And she was so nice to me. Even afterwards."

He grins. "Also, you're only tiny. I could carry you around all day and not break into a sweat."

"I'm sorry for disrupting your day nonetheless," I say, choosing to ignore his last comment as I pick at my dry toast again. "You were supposed to be back at the office, not dealing with all this."

"I caused all this, remember?" He frowns. "I shouldn't have startled you like that. I should've waited until you were clear of the desk to talk to you. It's just that I ..." He presses his lips together, and my curiosity is piqued.

"What? You what?" I want him to tell me. I want him to tell me everything.

"It's probably best if you don't know."

"Tell me. Please."

Sebastian sighs. "I wasn't expecting to find someone I felt so immediately attracted to right outside my office door, OK? It caught me off guard, and I ... well, I didn't know how to react."

Embarrassed, I avert my eyes. "I don't know what to say to that."

"You don't need to say anything." His eyes bore into mine, and I feel the air get stuck in my throat. Blushing furiously, I remain quiet this time, and his lips pull into a sinful smile.

Oh, he's enjoying this.

He motions to the tray. "If you're done, I'll take that back."

"Thanks," I reply, and then hesitate, choosing my words. "Sebastian, I ... I just wanted to say that I really appreciate everything you've done so far, and that as soon as I can be on my own, I'll go home. You don't have to feel responsible. Not for me."

He moves the tray to the coffee table in the lounge and sits again by my side. "Alice ... I'm afraid you won't be able to be on your own for a while. Dr Smith explained that even when these first twelve hours pass, you'll still be experiencing a lot of symptoms. And because everyone recovers differently and these types of injuries are so complicated, he can't be sure for how long."

"It's OK, I'll be careful. And if I feel unwell, I'll just call 999. There's no reason why I can't be by myself."

"It's not that simple. You might be incapacitated, too confused to call for help. You might even fall and hit your head again. I'm sorry, but I'm not prepared to take that risk. I'm not letting you stay by yourself and that's final."

"Look, you're being very nice and all, but it's my decision." I push my hair back, trying to remain calm, but I'm getting so mad, I just want to punch him in the face. "Also, I need to go back to work soon. Sharon needs training, and Linda has her own job to do. I'll take a couple of days off, of course—I know I need the rest.

But I'm pretty positive that with work and my normal routine my brain will heal much faster and go back to what it was in no time."

"Alice, you won't be able to go back to work either, sweetheart. At least not for another couple of months, remember? Dr Smith was adamant about that. He gave us a sick note to hand over to HR." Sebastian raises his eyebrows like I'm supposed to know this, and I blanch.

"What? Is he crazy? I can't be off work for that long." My head is pounding, the hammer is back in full force, and my skull might just explode after all.

"Of course you can. This is your health we're talking about. Besides, I agreed with him, and so did my dad. You need to rest. Work can wait."

"You don't understand. I'm on my probation period. I won't get paid. I won't be able to afford my rent, my bills. I won't be able to survive." Tears spring to my eyes. "What am I going to do?" I whisper.

"Stay here with me." Sebastian shrugs. "It's really no big deal. That way you can focus on getting better, regaining your health, and I'll have my chance to make amends. Problem solved."

"No, you still don't understand. I'll lose my flat, my deposit, not to mention people will think I'm taking advantage of you."

Sebastian huffs out a laugh, and I give him a reproving look. "I'm going to get an ice pack for your head and some painkillers," he says. "You look tired. I'm sure you'll fall asleep again soon."

With that he gets to his feet and leaves the room, and I'm left gaping after him.

Two months. Two whole months without a job or an income. And I can't stay here.

You also cannot afford not to stay here.

My eyes water again. It's true, I can't. Staying with Sebastian might be the only way to keep my flat. It's just that I'm afraid. Afraid of him. Afraid of myself. Afraid of my feelings. Afraid I came this far just to lose everything.

Sebastian comes back with the ice pack and the painkillers, and in no time I'm back asleep in his bed, just like he said I would be.

In fact, over the course of the next twenty-four hours, I do nothing but sleep. Sebastian, of course, diligently looks after me and wakes me up every couple of hours, claiming he's not confident the standard twelve hours is actually enough and that he needs to do this for his own peace of mind.

I don't question it. To be honest, I'm too out of it to argue with him again.

What I need is to get better and regain control over myself, my emotions. Then I'll find a way, and he won't be able to stop me.

I turn on my side and pull the covers up to my face, inhaling them deeply. Smelling him on them. Wishing with all my heart we were different people, living different lives. That we'd never met, and I'd never found out I could feel this way towards a man.

"God," I groan. "Who would've thought hitting one's head on a desk could land a girl in so much trouble?"

Chapter 4

Sebastian

Twenty-four hours earlier...

"Abuse," I repeat after Dr Smith in disbelief.

Alice sleeps peacefully on the examination table inside the consulting room. I take in her sun-kissed skin, heart-shaped face, plump cheeks and pink full lips, her long mahogany hair and delicate frame, and my stomach somersaults at the thought of anyone harming her.

How? How could someone hurt something so beautiful? So sweet?

"I shouldn't be telling you any of this, Mr Hunter."

My eyes fly back to the good doctor. "A bit late for that now, isn't?" I ask impatiently, seeing we've already made a deal where he gives me full disclosure of Alice's health status and medical history, and I pay him sixty thousand pounds for the trouble. I press my lips together. "How about I throw in an all-inclusive holiday for you and the family? Wherever you want. Hawaii, Maldives?"

Smithy sighs, resigned, I think. After all, he's already sold his soul to the Devil. "We found signs of previous head injuries. Nothing that affected her brain, but serious enough that we can still see the fractures—all old and healed now—on the X-rays that we took.

"That, together with a broken arm and a fractured wrist—also from when she was only a kid—led me to believe she was mistreated as a child. Which makes me even more concerned about the concussion she has now, as well as the emotional impact it may have on her, if being hurt like this reawakens unhealthy feelings or bad memories from her past."

I shake my head, dumbfounded. My eyes close and I cover my face with both hands, imagining her as a small child—tiny, fragile, defenceless—and fuck, I still have trouble believing.

Logically, I know it's true, of course. Even if everything in me is repulsed by the idea, there's too much evidence to ignore.

"I'm sorry, Mr Hunter," Dr Smith says regretfully. "I'm sure she'll tell you herself when she's ready. Just be patient and give her time. She'll come to you eventually."

"Time. Yes, I'll give her time. All the time she needs," I agree, a plan for how to take her for myself already forming in my head. I deepen my expression to one of worry. I'll put the hurt little bird back together. Mend it for my own pleasure before releasing it into the wild. "Problem is, time isn't something she's great at."

Dr Smith frowns. "What do you suggest we do?"

I give the good doctor a purposeful look, lean my elbows on the desk, and in less than five minutes not only have I convinced him to write Alice off work for two whole months to recover from her concussion, I also have him agreeing she should be monitored for most of that time.

"Maybe tell her she should be admitted or at least have someone living with her," I suggest, knowing full well by then, thanks to Ryan, that she lives by herself with no one to help. No one except her very new, very loving fake fiancé, who is more than willing in this case, even offering to have her move in with him so she won't have to stay in hospital.

"I will recommend all of your suggestions to Miss Lake, verbally and in writing. My secretary will send over a clinical letter together with her sick note. But beware, Mr Hunter, that on the hospital's medical report it will show that my recommendations were requested by you and therefore a direct result of your worry and concern for your fiancée. I cannot risk anyone in the hospital looking into it and questioning my judgement."

"That shouldn't be a problem, Doctor. I don't see Alice requesting her medical records any time soon. And if she does, I'll make sure no repercussions fall on you."

***

"What the hell am I doing?" I groan, scrubbing at my face as I pace the floor in my living room. I practically kidnapped the poor girl, and I can't bring myself to regret it.

I just couldn't help myself. It's like I lost all sense of what's right and wrong since my eyes fell on her, and I just had to have her. I still have to have her.

Christ, what is the matter with me?

I run my fingers through my hair, savagely pulling as if to punish myself.

Alice doesn't deserve this. She doesn't deserve what I'm about to do to her, to her life. Not when she has been through so much already.

I clench my hands, my nails digging into my palms as I fight the urge to slam my fists through the fucking wall. It's been hours since Dr Smith told me his findings and still I can't wrap my brain around it.

I relax my hands and rest my elbows on the black grand piano specifically bought in to decorate the front of the room. How shallow. How privileged I've always been compared to Alice.

And now here we are—me already taking over her life, and Alice ... well, exactly where I want her. In my bed, in my house. Under my protection and dominion, where hopefully soon I'll be able to do whatever I like to her.

My dick twitches and I press a hand to my trousers, squeezing it hard.

My beautiful prisoner. My beautiful, broken angel whom I can't wait to teach about the pleasures in life. My dick twitches again and I hiss through my teeth at the pleasure-pain sensation shooting up my spine.

God, I need to fuck her. Need to kiss her.

That's all I think about. Kissing her all over and taking that smart little mouth. I groan at the vision, my mind already conjuring up images of my lips on hers and my hands exploring all the curves and planes of her hot body.

Fuck. I close my eyes, inhaling deeply. Never have I desired a woman so much or reacted so intensely. And it's driving me wild, compelling me to do things I can't even explain. To crave things

I never wanted before. Against my better judgement, I can't let her go. At least not until I've had a taste. Until I know what she looks like and how she sounds with me buried deep inside her.

I know it's wrong, I know I'll probably hurt her in the end. That's the main reason why I vowed never to fuck a nice girl, but I can't stop myself. I'm a bastard. Have been one for most of my life, and old habits die hard.

I'll make it up to her. Buy her whatever she wants once I'm done. A flat, a house, a car. All of it, if she so desires. And money—I'll give her plenty of money. Enough to set her up for life. Enough she won't have to work another day if she so decides. And then she'll be free. Free to find someone good for her. Someone who isn't a monster. Someone who will love her and worship her like the exceptional creature she is.

Someone who isn't me.

The pang of pain and jealousy in my chest is as sharp as it is unexpected, leaving a foul taste in my mouth as bile rises up my throat.

I run my shaky fingers through my hair. I was never 'the good guy', but even I know this is what will inevitably land me in hell.

Yet I can't bring myself to care. Can't bring myself to stop.

For now, heaven is right here on Earth, and I will do anything—absolutely anything—to keep it that way.

Eventually, hopefully, I will grow bored. Grow indifferent as I go back to being my normal self. Then I'll stop thinking about her. Stop wanting her so fucking much and let this go. Move on with my life and allow her to move on with hers.

I push myself off the piano and go pour myself a glass of the whisky I don't even like. I sit my sorry ass on the couch.

My plan is simple, but brilliant. Just as long as I continue to play my part right and act like the unexpected hero, the white knight in Alice's life. I smirk. At least until she cares deeply about me. Then I will pounce. All I have to do is pretend to be the good guy and sweep her off her feet.

She will fight me at first, of course. In fact, I expect nothing less from her. I have a bad-boy reputation, and she's ... well, she's a good girl to the core. Then there's the fact that I'm her boss, and she won't easily cross that line. Not unless I sway her. Make her see just how good we can be together. How happy we can make each other if she only gives us a chance.

I neck my drink and place the glass roughly on the coffee table as shame comes over me. This is the other reason I never go for good girls. They're not easy. And all this lying and deceiving is not me. I never lie. Never cheat.

Never ... until today.

Jesus! What is she doing to me? What the fuck is this tiny, beautiful girl doing to me?

I've been numb and in control for so many years, I don't know how to deal with all this. Don't even know what 'this' means, to be honest.

All I know is she makes me feel, and now that I found her, now that I've seen her warmth, her light ... I can't let her go. I'm addicted.

I want her. Need her. And so I shall have her.

I pull my phone out of my pocket, unlock it and proceed to find the contact HR sent only half an hour ago. My teeth sink into my lower lip as I press the call button and wait.

"Hello?" A soft, elderly voice comes down the line.

"Mrs Hayes." I sit up. "My name is Sebastian Hunter. I'm calling with regards to your tenant, Alice Lake—I'm afraid there's been an accident."

***

Four days later ...

Hearing a small sound from behind me, I turn, still clutching a loaf of bread, a pint of milk, a bag of croissants and a newspaper, only to see Alice enter the dining room and make her way towards the kitchen.

My lips twitch at her disobedience as I lower my morning shopping to the island. Well, Michael's morning shopping, really, seeing I don't go to the shops myself. I tell my security team what I need and one of them goes out and gets it for me.

See, obedience. Obedience I get from everyone around me except from the little thing. Obedience I was expecting after reminding her only yesterday she needs to stay in bed and rest, and that I'd bring her breakfast just as I've been doing since the beginning of the week.

I shake my head, stifling a grin. It seems as if my rebel of a guest has other plans, though, since she's already down here and has beaten me to it.

It's annoying. And oddly refreshing, if I'm being honest.

Even if it messes with my carefully laid out plans for the rest of the day. My grin comes out and I shake my head.

I admire her, I realise. Not that I'll ever admit it. Not out loud, at least. No one can ever know how much power she already holds over me, least of all her. Which means I'll have to tread carefully here if I want to continue being the one who pulls the strings.

I scowl and, with a long exhale, turn towards the entrance again, my face a mask of feigned disappointment as I lean against the island and cross my arms, ready to give her the speech. The 'my way or the highway' speech. The one I give anyone who chooses not to listen to me.

But I should know. She isn't just anyone. She's her. My little thing. And when she waves in that dorky, adorable way that's entirely Alice, smiling at me, I can't help but smile back like an idiot.

Like me, she's still wearing her pyjamas—some deep-red cotton trousers with small white polka dots and a white tank top sans bra—and my dick couldn't be happier to see her. I swallow hard, trying to keep my drool from hitting my chin. The movement of Alice's hips, slow and hypnotic, renders me speechless. Her plump cheeks are flushed pink and her eyes are extra-wide as she takes in her surroundings, and I can feel my grin growing bigger.

She's gorgeous, and I knew she'd like the house. The whole place has this open-plan feel to it, with minimal walls and lots of furniture divisions.

The living room and kitchen occupy opposite sides of the ground floor, with a spacious dining room as well as another sitting area between them—the homework room, as Linda likes to call it, much to her delight and my annoyance, with its big, round table, bookshelves, and a cosy reading nook built into the wall.

The perfect space for kids to play and do their schoolwork while you rustle up some dinner. Malevolent little witch, Linda. Always knowing which buttons to push to fuck with me.

I vanish all the thoughts of kids and their homework out of my mind. Thoughts like that have no business in my head. Thoughts like that have no business in my life, period.

Alice's mouth falls open when she enters the kitchen, her eyes turning wider and rounder somehow as they land on the conservatory and its incredible, high ceiling. Bright sunlight spills in, a show in itself with the back of the house covered in floor-to-ceiling windows. The conservatory serves as the eating area as well as the lounge to the kitchen.

"God, Sebastian, this house is insane. And this kitchen ..." Her sparkling eyes scan the place again as she spins, and I remember her saying something about how much she loves to cook in our countless conversations this week.

This is good. And something I can use to distract her.

She smiles and runs her fingers over the kitchen island, and I can't help but look around too, trying to see what she sees.

Shiny white cupboards with stainless-steel handles and black marble countertops line the entire wall on the right, giving it a clean, contemporary look. A huge island with a cooker, sink, and breakfast area sits right in the middle of the room. And a table for twenty is on the left by the conservatory's window overlooking the gardens. At the very far end of the room there's the pantry, the laundry room, an American fridge-freezer, and a top-of-the-range triple-deck oven that, to be honest, has never been used.

And I get it. I do. It's a chef's kitchen. Her dream kitchen, staring her right in the face.

"You're very welcome to use it if you want. In fact, consider it yours for as long as you stay." I slide my hands into my pockets and let my eyes flicker back to hers.

She makes a face, clearly still not happy about her living arrangements, and I almost laugh. Ever since Linda brought her some clothes and personal items from her flat, she's been like this. Difficult. Moody. Constantly testing my patience and resilience.

Well, too bad for her I'm not the backing-down kind. Too bad for her I'm just as stubborn as she is, if not more, and the last thing I'd do now is give up.

Besides, she's too shiny. Too new of a toy for me to get over that easily. No, it would drive me insane to give her up when I know I'm getting close to the prize. And no way am I denying myself my fun. No way am I leaving her alone before she gives me what I want.

"Should you be up anyway?" I ask, trying to defuse the situation.

She rolls her eyes. "It's been four days, Sebastian. I had to get out of that bedroom. Not to mention I'm feeling much better now, so there's no reason for your concern."

I nod and take a sip of my coffee, trying to hold in my tongue. After the first day and a lot of arguments from her, I had to move her from my bedroom to the guest room across the corridor just to shut her up and keep the peace.

I'm still sour about it, though. I'm not used to being told what to do. Much less in my own house. And even if Alice is the hottest female I've ever seen and it makes my cock that much hungrier for her when she tries to resist me, my control over her is still important to me. My dominion over her is still important to me.

My dick stirs at the idea of me dominating Alice in bed, giving me a hard-on I'm not entirely sure my thin pyjama bottoms will be able to conceal.

"So ..." I clear my throat. "How about some breakfast?" I move towards the cupboard to get her a plate and a mug and grab an apron along the way. "Think you can have some coffee and toast? Or can you manage a croissant this morning?" I tie the apron around my waist.

She smiles. "I think I can manage a croissant. Maybe two. I'm absolutely starving today."

"Good, let's get you fed then. And afterwards, maybe I could give you a tour of the house."

"Yes," she squeaks, clapping her hands together as she jumps on the spot, and my heart skips a beat. My black, empty heart, which is now feeling fuller than ever as I stare at the laughing, beautiful girl, my prisoner, in my kitchen.

***

Day six

"What if I worked from home instead?" Alice asks at dinner, looking hopefully at me from the other side of the dining room table as I pause with my fork mid-air.

Well, fuck. Now why didn't I think she'd think of something like that?

I frown and, lowering my fork to the plate, pick up my glass of wine. I gulp some of it down. She's been pestering me all day about going back to work, and quite frankly I'm becoming increasingly frustrated with the topic. "Sweetheart, you know that's not a good idea. You're still healing and right now work would just be a setback. That's why Dr Smith wanted you home. Remember?"

Her face falls, and my heart squeezes tight inside my chest. I try to stay strong. I need her to be under my protection, under my control, if I want any hope of having her under me.

She nods and picks up her fork, still in absolute silence, and I follow suit, shoving the most wonderful steak I've ever had in my life into my lying, filthy mouth.

My eyes close in pleasure. Like everything she does, it's fucking magnificent.

And yeah, it's safe to say I'm enjoying myself tremendously since little Alice moved in. I mean, what's not to like? She cooks all these amazing meals, is insanely gorgeous, and on top of that she makes me laugh. Not to mention she's intelligent, smart, and incredibly talented in everything she does.

Noticing she's been quiet for a while, I flick my eyes over to her and release a heavy sigh. She's also a woman, and a very sensitive one at that.

I soften my voice. "Alice, you don't need to worry about work, OK? I've told you before, the job will be there when you're ready. In the meantime, cook, write, exercise, make sure you enjoy yourself. Think of this as a holiday, if it helps. But please, let's wait until you're actually better."

She nods, averting her eyes. I can't stand to see her like this. "Hey, look at me," I cajole. "Stop worrying, OK?"

She pushes her hair back with a frown, shaking her head. "I've worked most of my teenage years and all of my adult life, Sebastian. Working is all I know."

"And you're still working now. I mean, look at all the amazing meals you've prepared for us. Look at how beautiful and welcoming my house is. I don't think I've ever seen it looking this good."

And that's the honest-to-God truth. Not even the cleaning crew, whom I've got coming to the house three times a week, has managed to do whatever it is she does.

It's like she enchanted the place. I almost laugh. Well, she most certainly enchanted the owner.

She finally smiles, and I let myself relax further into my seat. "So you don't think the candles and flowers are too much?" she asks shyly.

"I think they're great." Just like you are, I want to say, but somehow manage to hold it in. Now's not the time for that.

Now's the time to be sensitive. As sensitive as I possibly can.

Her smile grows wide and she finally begins to eat.

I join her, keeping the rest of our conversation light and easy, steering it to safer topics—like the latest recipe she came up with and my training session at the gym.

"Oh, is it OK if I use the gym with you tomorrow?" Alice asks, placing our plates by the sink when we finish our meal.

Before I have time to reply, she turns and walks straight into me. Her little hands fall onto my hips as she gasps. Our eyes clash, and the same electricity I've been feeling all week buzzes between us. The energy around us is so heavy and thick I can barely breathe.

Fuck, I want to kiss her. I want to kiss her so bad my whole body begins to shake with need.

As if sensing it, she takes a step back, her breathing ragged and just as laboured as mine. She runs her hands down her jeans as if drying her palms, and I lower our glasses to the sink.

"You ... you want some tea?" she stammers, and I nod before turning on the tap, breaking the spell between us.

Alice turns on her heels and goes in the direction of the kettle and the mugs to start prepping our teas, and I bite into my lower lip, every instinct in me telling me to grab her and kiss her. I inhale deeply and close my eyes on the exhale.

She's not ready yet, and it's my turn to do the dishes. I'll get my kiss some other time. I know I will. Besides, I'm enjoying myself. Why ruin that by rushing into things?

***

Day seven

"How dare you speak to my landlady before I did?" Alice sneers as soon as I walk through the front door.

I frown and place the box I'm carrying on the floor. Jesus, she's been waiting for me. Straightening, I pull the sleeves of my sweater up to my elbows as she narrows her eyes.

My hands drop to my hips and I let out a long sigh. That's all I seem to do nowadays: sigh. What an exasperating woman.

"Alice," I say, a hint of frustration in my tone. "She was going to make you give her a month's notice, remember? Pay her additional charges? This way, she felt pressured into letting you go. You know, with me being your boss and all. And my family's name."

Alice shakes her head. "I was hoping she'd let me keep the flat. That she'd give me a payment plan once I went back to work. I thought she'd be open to it." Alice screws up her face as if she's about to cry, and I can't help but take a step forward and grab her hand.

"Sweetheart ..."

"I don't understand." Alice's other hand shoots up to cover her mouth. "She always liked me, and I could've paid her at least another month's rent. I'd owe her, what, two months at the most? But she wouldn't listen. She wouldn't even hear me out."

"Alice ..." I start, and that's when Ryan comes in, pushing two large suitcases into the hall. He cringes when he notices Alice, but by then it's too late.

"Are those my things?" she gasps before throwing me the dirtiest look of all time through her tears. And if up until then I wasn't sure if I'd made it onto her shit list, there's no doubt in my mind I'm at the very top of it now.

"You went through my stuff?" she shrieks, pulling her hand away from mine and taking a few steps back. "You went through my flat?"

Shit! "Sweetheart, calm down. Your head ..."

"Don't tell me to calm down, you ... you big, overbearing, controlling asshole!" she screams, and my eyebrows shoot up. That's the first time she's ever sworn in front of me, yelled at me, since knowing who I am, and I must confess I'm surprised. Maybe even a little impressed.

I glance over at Ryan and he presses his lips together. The look in his eyes is pity and amusement at the same time as he tries to stop his grin. Fucker.

"I can't believe you did this. I can't ... I can't ..." Alice sways a little as she presses her hands to her temples, a moan of pain escaping her lips. And I don't even think. In two strides I'm holding her up by her waist.

"Alice. Alice!" I pick her up, and she wraps her arms around my neck, her head leaning on my shoulder as she screws her eyes shut.

"Sebastian," she murmurs, and I press my lips to her hair.

"I've got you, baby. I've got you. It's OK. Let's just get you into bed and medicated. You'll be all right in no time. I promise."

***

Day eight

The bag swings heavily as I do a series of punches. My breathing is all over the place as I grab it with both arms, hitting it over and over again with my knee before releasing it. Then I twist and kick it as high as I can.

I'm angry. Fucking pissed. Sweat drips down my forehead and back, but I don't stop. I can't.

I don't even know who I'm angrier at. Me or her. I fucking hurt her. I fucking hurt her again.

I kick the bag particularly hard and hear a gasp from behind me. Turning, I find Alice wearing tight, black yoga trousers and a baby-blue sports bra with her hair tied back in a high ponytail, and my mood takes a dive for the worse as my cock hardens against my shorts. Yeah, I'm gonna need a real fight soon, the bag is no longer enough.

"Mind if I join you?" Alice asks tentatively.

"You sure you want to be near the overbearing, controlling asshole who's ruining your life?" I retort, reminding her of her own words.

"I'm sorry," she says, her eyes cast down, and I no longer have the heart to stay mad at her when she's behaving like this.

Sweet. Remorseful. Guilty.

I sigh, and, after removing my gloves, thread my fingers through my damp hair. Damn it, she even robs me of the capacity to stay mad.

"I shouldn't have said those things to you. I …" She shakes her head and her eyes rise up to meet mine.

"Forget it," I say. "And you were right anyway. I should've spoken to you. I should've told you what I was planning on doing before contacting your landlady." I dry my face and chest with a towel I pick up from the floor, enjoying the way her eyes follow my every move as I walk closer to her. "I was only trying to help, though. I'd never do anything to hurt you. You know that, right?"

"I know," she says, still looking at me through her long, black lashes. "That's why I feel so bad. I was unfair to you last night when you've been nothing but kind to me."

At her words, I feign even more hurt. I know this is my chance to get closer to her, to gain her trust. I just wish I wasn't feeling so fucking bad for deceiving her.

"I guess we both did and said some stuff we regret," I whisper.

She gives me a sheepish smile. "Yeah … I guess we did."

"So, what do we do now?" I ask, staring at her. I can't help it.

"We make up," she says, and extends a hand to me. "Friends again?"

I take her hand in mine before kissing the back of it. Her breath hitches and her gaze softens under my touch.

"Friends again," I agree.

With that she smiles and, letting go of my hand, saunters to the far side of the gym. Where she unrolls a bright pink yoga mat and begins her warm-up exercises in front of me.

I clear my throat and, after drinking some water, resume my training at the punching bag … or at least I try, seeing as it's impossible to concentrate on what I'm doing. I can't ignore that fine, fine body of hers doing all kinds of twists and turns and stretching positions on that fucking neon yoga mat.

"Maybe sometime soon you can give me some pointers. Or lessons, perhaps, if you wouldn't mind," she says from her place on the floor where she's touching both her feet with her hands, startling me.

"Lessons?" I ask, distracted, still watching her like a hawk in the mirrors, looking down the cleavage of her bra.

"Yeah, on how to fight. Self-defence moves and all that."

"Sure," I say, before I really have time to think of a proper answer.

All I know is that all this sexual tension and anticipation is messing with my head, making me less rational, less tactful, and a lot less careful than I usually am.

"I mean, we can do that once you're fully recovered. Yes." I try to retract, but at the look of disappointment on her beautiful face I find myself changing my mind yet again. I blow out a breath. "Well, maybe we can start you on a gentle course for now. Nothing physical. Just some theoretical dirty moves and explanations to go with them."

She laughs, and I can't help but laugh with her. "OK, and thank you. You didn't have to agree to that. Why the dirty moves, though? I don't understand."

"Because, little missy, there's no way someone your size can fight straight with someone like me. You'll need some help. Some tricks up your sleeve. That is, if you actually want to stand a chance."

"Tricks? Like kicking someone in the groin and stuff?" she asks, blushing.

"To start, yeah. But also understanding how to use your strength and your surroundings to your advantage. Like if you hit a guy who's attacking you, hit him with the heel of your hand right under his nose. You'll break his nose for sure, might even kill him if you hit him hard enough. Or if you're in a work environment—an office, for example—use a pen to stab him in a leg or in the neck so you can get away."

Her eyes grow wider. "Wow. I never thought of a pen as a weapon."

"Most things can become weapons, Alice," I say as she mounts the exercise bike. "You just have to know how to use them."

She starts pedalling, and I decide to lift some weights, sitting my lucky ass on the bench that's fixed right behind hers so I can fully appreciate the view. I beam out a smile.

Yeah, life's good again. Life's really good ... when we're back to being friends and she's back to speaking to me.

***

Day ten

Laughter rings across the dining room as I serve my dad, Luke and Linda more wine. We've just finished dinner, a roasted rack of pork with various vegetables and rice, and my dad is sitting at the head of the table, telling stories about my brothers and I growing up.

"Once we even had a nanny come all the way from France. We were assured she was the best of the best and wouldn't run away after any number of childish pranks." My dad sighs dramatically, and Linda and Alice begin to laugh.

Luke, my younger brother, and I glance at each other and grin, knowing what's coming.

"Well, let's just say Sebastian took that as a challenge, and every night after her first, he'd place live frogs and snails under the covers of her bed." The women erupt into a fit of laughter, and my dad shakes his head. "Safe to say the poor woman didn't last a week, let alone a year."

"Oh, my God, that's disgusting," Alice says, sitting across the table from me, her smile bright and contagious.

"God, I'd forgotten all about that." Linda giggles at her side, covering her mouth with both hands.

"Yeah, but you know what he said when I questioned him?" My dad chuckles, and I press my thumb to my lips, trying to contain my smile. It's good to see him like this. Happy. Laughing. "He said he read somewhere the French liked to eat frogs and snails and that he was only looking out for her, making sure she wouldn't go hungry just because she was away from home. He was five years old back then."

Everyone roars with laughter, but my eyes stay glued to Alice, taking in her perfect smile, her white teeth and sexy little mouth as she bites her bottom lip.

"He was a good kid, though. They all were," Dad adds.

What's he on about now?

My brows furrow and he smiles before looking back at the women. "But Sebastian was always the most protective one, you know. Always looking out for his brothers. I remember he even broke his arm once trying to save Mason from a fall."

Alice looks straight at me then. Really looks at me. No shy glimpses or stolen glances. Amazement is clear in her eyes, as if for the first time she's actually seeing me.

Umm ... My face warms and I shrug, getting genuinely embarrassed. I don't know why, but I am. This part of me is only known to my family, and I wasn't yet sure if I wanted to share it with Alice. Seems like Dad took away my choice. "He thought he could fly and threw himself out of a window," I rush to say like it's no big deal. I don't want her to think I'm a saint. I'm no saint. Even if I'm not the Devil either. "It was only the ground floor, though. And he was only three."

"I broke my arm too, you know?" Luke chimes in, grinning at me before he turns his attention to Alice. "In two different places." He gives her one of his playboy smirks, and I frown.

What's he playing at? I already warned him I'd cut his balls off and feed them to him if he stepped out of line with her. In fact, I remember warning him again just as soon as he got here—and so rudely crashed our dinner, trailing after Dad and Linda, who were actually invited.

Seems I'll have to remind him yet again. Just as soon as the others are out of earshot and I can be clearer on what the score actually is.

"You were riding your bike, Luke," Linda deadpans, and everyone bursts into laughter again.

"Does everyone want coffee with their dessert? It's chocolate cake," Alice says, getting up and gathering our dishes.

Linda signals for me to sit when I rise to help Alice and starts helping her herself.

"I'll have some, thank you," I say, falling back into my seat.

"Me too, please," Luke replies, sending me a wink.

Fucker.

"I'll make the coffee, ladies. You can do the dishes and deal with the dessert," Dad offers, following the women to the kitchen, and I finally turn to Luke with what I assume is murder in my eyes.

"Stop flirting with her or else," I order, my voice hard with rage.

Luke laughs, and it grates on my nerves. In fact he's been grating on my nerves ever since he arrived, earlier than expected, last week and suddenly can't get enough of my house—of Alice. "You have it bad, bro. You have it really bad if you're threatening me again."

"You're delusional," I say.

He raises one thick brow, his eyes and face so much like my own it's like looking in a fucking mirror. He's a better person than me, though. Younger, funnier, not as damaged. Which is why I don't like him hanging around Alice so much. Because any day now, she might see it too. That she'd be better off with someone like him. "Yeah, maybe so. But why threaten me then?"

I sigh. "Because she's too good. Too good for the likes of us."

"Bullshit. You wanna fuck her and don't want anybody else to have a fighting chance."

"Seriously, Luke, stay away from her. Or else."

"Or else what, Sebastian?"

I fix him with my eyes. I want him to know I'm serious. "You don't want to know."

He smiles at my answer as if it was exactly what he was expecting. "You have feelings for this girl. Anyone can see it. Anyone except you, that is."

"Fuck you, Luke," I growl, and he opens his mouth to speak.

Just then, though, the wheels of the serving trolley squeak and my dad's voice reaches our ears.

Luke grins. "Guess we'll have to end this conversation another time, bro."

I glare at him, and force myself to unclench my fists. "Yes, bro … I guess we will."

***

Four days later …

5.45 a.m. Hunter Corp

After a full hour on the treadmill and some serious weightlifting in the gym downstairs, I'm finally feeling a lot more focused and relaxed than when I arrived at the office almost four hours ago.

I lift the steaming cup to my lips and smile like an idiot into my coffee before taking a sip. I swipe my thumb over my phone again and a different picture of Alice comes up. She's smiling in this one, looking directly at the camera—at me—and my heart squeezes tight. So tight, in fact, I have to close my eyes for a full minute just to regulate my breathing.

You're a fucking wimp, Sebastian, the voice at the back of my head says, and I huff out a humourless laugh, opening my eyes again.

I pay it no mind, though, and move on to the next picture, recognizing it at once as one of the most recent photographs I took of Alice—and the reason why, if I'm being honest, I've been working out in the office since two this morning, have already showered, and have been slaving over our new contracts for the last couple of hours or so.

But when one finds themselves in a sleeping girl's bedroom, ogling and taking photos of her, one needs to take a step back and really think about what one is doing.

I exhale heavily and sit back on my comfortable, black leather chair. I couldn't sleep much anyway. No surprise there. Except today, I needed to concentrate. Needed to work with a clear head on my shoulders. Something that's becoming increasingly hard to do with Alice around.

Not to mention all this sexual tension and pent-up desire building between us over the course of these past few days. It's a wonder how I've been able to last so long. How I've been able to keep my distance and not cross any boundaries with her, despite my wanting to.

And I want to. I want to so badly, it's all I think about.

Fuck. I rub my face.

Two weeks. Two whole wonderful weeks have gone by since I brought her into my house, and everything feels so damn different already. I feel different already.

Which doesn't even make sense when there's nothing physical going on.

So why should that be the case? Why should I be so hung up on the girl when I'm not even getting my dick wet?

I frown and drop my phone back on the desk. It lands with a thud in the otherwise silent room. She's different. I don't know why, but she is. And the thought alone has been enough to give me pause. She intrigues me, confounds me.

The distance, the careful conversations and shy behaviour—her defences are the ultimate aphrodisiac. The energy that keeps drawing me in on top of her intelligence, kindness and beauty.

Even if it's her trust I crave the most, her faith in me. It makes me want to break down her walls and peel away the layers until she's as exposed as I feel. Until there's nothing new left to explore between us.

Resting my elbows on the desk, I hide my face between my hands. God, I'm so obsessed with the girl it's borderline psychotic. My behaviour is crazy and sick. And I'm fucked ... I'm thoroughly fucked if I have to wait another day without at least getting a kiss. Just a little kiss.

I spin my chair around and watch as the first rays of sun pierce through the heavy, grey clouds in the sky.

I'll still take it slow, I'll still give her time, but tonight ... Tonight I begin taking what's mine.

Chapter 5

Sebastian

A knock on the door startles me, bringing me out of my reverie.

"Hey, can we talk?" Luke asks, pushing the door open and popping his head inside.

What's he doing here so early? I glance at the computer, and it's only six a.m. "Sure, come on in," I reply, resisting the urge to bait him.

He looks sombre, grim, making all kinds of alarm bells go off inside my head.

"What's wrong?" I ask, straightening in my chair as he enters and closes the door behind him.

He hesitates for a moment, pausing with his back still turned to me as if to gather his thoughts, and I brace myself for the worst, knowing this is not his typical behaviour. Then he turns and crosses the room towards my desk, and it's my turn to frown, wanting to wipe the worry off his face.

"You know my team and I have been looking into all of our business deals, past and present alike," he says, grabbing hold of a chair and sliding a hand into the trouser pocket of his navy, three-piece suit.

I nod, my anxiety levels spiking when I realise what this is about. Ever since we found out we were throwing money down the drain with some of our suppliers, Luke and I launched a full investigation into the matter. He and his team have spent many a night in the office lately going through boxes and boxes of contracts, invoices, receipts, and pretty much any other document they could get their hands on in order to help us figure this out.

"Go on," I encourage, and, leaning forward, lock my hands together on the desk, giving him my undivided attention.

"Well, there's a pattern." He sinks into one of the chairs opposite mine, his eyes troubled when they rise to meet my gaze.

"What do you mean?"

"I mean this shit has happened before. In fact, it's been going on for years. Many years." He shakes his head in frustration. "Sebastian, whoever these people are, they targeted us. They knew exactly what they were doing from the beginning. They used different names, different companies, most only existing for the duration of our contracts with them. Making us one of very few customers, and, more often than not, the only customer they had."

He frowns. "And I know this whole thing almost sounds too fantastic to be true, but it's too much of a coincidence that the majority of these businesses no longer exist. That apart from the few companies we're still trying to get rid of, all the others declared bankruptcy and shut down once our contracts came to an end. The money ... gone. Simply vanished into thin air."

"Fuck," I mutter. "This is serious, Luke. A lot more serious than I originally thought."

He nods, his eyes narrowed as they rise to meet my own. "They produced documents, of course. Bullshit stories to justify their losses, using other businesses and even some bad investments abroad to leak the profits. Essentially ..."

"Essentially making the money disappear," I interrupt. "Probably into offshore accounts, if I have to guess."

Luke grimaces, but nods again, confirming my suspicion.

I press my fingers to my temples, feeling a headache already starting to form. "So whoever's behind this has been robbing us blind for years."

"Basically ... yes," Luke says, sliding his fingers through his hair and pulling at the ends.

His mannerisms are so much like my own, so much like my dad's, it's disconcerting at times. Especially when we're like this, pissed as hell and trying to collect ourselves. Trying to calm down before we do something we'll most definitely regret.

"Dad never noticed it because the money was small, and going out as payments for what seemed to be legitimate bills," he continues. "The dodgy expenditures blended in with the real ones and were never high enough to bring attention to themselves. Until now, of course. And only because I decided to go over our expenditure with a fine-tooth comb. Still, over the years, someone made close to a hundred million pounds on the back of our family's business."

"Fuck," I murmur, rubbing my face with both hands as I come to another conclusion. And if I'm right, this is surely a whole other level of fucked-up even for us. Pinching the bridge of my nose, I take a deep breath. "It's one of our own, isn't it? It has to be one of our own for it to go on for so long."

We exchange a look, and I know I'm right straight away. Shit.

"Unfortunately, there's no other explanation. Which is why I followed my gut and continued to dig."

"Did you find out who it is?" I ask, my voice rough and menacing.

The way his nostrils flare tells me I'm not gonna like this. "From what I was able to gather, these deals began shortly after Arthur became CFO."

"Motherfucking son of a bitch," I growl, my fists closed so tight I can feel my nails cutting into my palms.

"I know, man. I know." Luke's jaw is clenched so tight I'm surprised he's still able to talk.

God, how could Arthur do this to our dad? Our dad, who was always there for him. Our dad, who never turned him down ... even when Arthur's own wife left him. Even when Arthur began stalking said wife and exchanged his job for the bottom of a bottle.

It was my dad who stopped him. Who got him cleaned up and gave him a job. Who saved him from himself and got him through the divorce. They were supposed to be friends. And Arthur ... Arthur was supposed to be loyal.

"Are you sure he was involved?" I ask, hoping for even a sliver of doubt in my brother's face.

"Positive." Luke sighs. "That's why my team and I have been going through the archives. I didn't want to say anything before because all I had were suspicions. I just couldn't get my head around the fact something like this had been going on for so long and the CFO never noticed. Never raised a query about it. I expected him to ask questions, to want to know about the constant change of companies, or about the bankruptcies at least. But I didn't find anything. I didn't find any evidence whatsoever he was looking into this ... and that was when I knew. The fucker had to have been involved. There's no way he wouldn't have noticed there was an issue with these companies, even if our expenditure wasn't raising any alarms on its own. So I kept digging, and as it turns out ... Arthur dealt with all those contracts himself. He's a liar, Sebastian. A cheat. A thief who took advantage of our dad and has been stealing from our family ever since.

"He would've gotten away with it too if it wasn't for you. I have a feeling that if we hadn't gone to the hotels and resorts in person when we did, those contracts would've come to term and that would've been the end of it. Most likely we'd never have found out about this."

I sigh heavily. "Where is he now? Do we know?"

"No, he's gone. Left the country two days after his retirement date," Luke says, biting on his thumbnail. "Sebastian, we have to sit down with Dad at some point and tell him about this. I want to contact the police and also recruit our own team of investigators. I don't know if I'm going to be able to uncover much more on my own, and we need to start following the money ... that is, if we want to have any real chance of finding out where he is."

Hmm, he's right. The money trail is our best option if we ever hope to catch the son of a bitch.

I nod. "We should get a few more hackers too. They can join our security team and work together on this. Let me get Ryan up here, and we can start setting that up right away."

"What about Dad?" Luke asks, concern evident in his eyes.

Yeah, that's one conversation neither of us will be looking forward to. It's going to break the old man's heart. "Let's talk to Ryan first, then we'll talk to Dad. Together, OK?"

* * *

I find her in the living room asleep, her small form sprawled on the couch and her long mahogany hair spread all over the pillow like a dark halo. Her tablet rests on her stomach and I smile, reaching for it, knowing she was reading one of those steamy romance novels she pretends not to like. She never falls asleep when she writes recipes for her cookbook, that much I already know about her. I lower the tablet to the coffee table, careful not to wake her up.

Then I turn and stay just like that, unable to move or even blink as I stare at her. I just need a minute. Just a minute longer before I have to break the spell. Before I have to see her soft features hardening because she still feels the need to be careful around me.

Sliding my hands into my anthracite suit trouser pockets, I scan down her body. In a light pink tank top and the world's tiniest grey shorts, lying barefoot on my couch, she's a vision. Easily the sexiest woman I've ever seen, and my mouth begins to water at the sight.

My cock throbs and swells to an unbearable size, pushing painfully against my zipper until I barely restrain myself from touching her, kissing her. Fuck me, but this girl is playing with fire.

And if I didn't know any better, I'd think she was trying to lure me. Tempt me. Seduce the shit out of me until I lose it, grab her, and bury myself inside of her, giving us both what we need. What we want. What we would've been doing from the moment we met if it was up to me.

Fuck. I drag a hand slowly down my face before threading my fingers through my hair, pulling at the ends. I do know better, though. And I do know Alice. Enough to know whatever I'm imagining right now is nothing more than wishful thinking.

My beautiful girl moans a deep, throaty moan, her delicate features relaxed, her expression serene. And that mouth—that sensual mouth of hers that makes her look just like a doll—parts as if she's waiting for a kiss. Oh, my sweet, sweet girl, the things I'd do to you if you'd let me.

I inhale deeply, my hungry eyes dropping down her throat, the swell of her breasts, her tiny waist ... God. I stifle a groan, my dick so fucking hard I'm afraid it might break through my zipper. Precum leaks onto my stomach and boxers, coating me in my arousal. And still my eyes continue their descent, memorising every single one of her curves.

It's pathetic. Embarrassing. How my need for her has grown so great I want to be near her all the time, talk to her, laugh with her, spend my days getting to know her.

Because now it's not just about the sex, no. Or the thrill of getting her to sleep with me. Now I want more. Need more. Something I can't even explain.

We just have this ... connection. This crazy thing between us. This warmth. Like she fills a void deep inside my chest, a void I didn't even know was there, and now I'm addicted. I'm addicted to my little thing.

She stirs again, and I crouch. "Alice," I say, smoothing a hand over her hair. "Sweetheart, wake up."

"Sebastian," she murmurs, half-asleep, making me smile. The warm feeling in my heart tells me how much I like the fact she knows it's me. How much I enjoy it's my voice she recognises. "You're home."

"Yeah, just got here," I murmur, standing again next to the sofa as I look down at her. I clear my throat and slide my hands into my pockets, catching myself. "Something smells really good, by the way. It's making me hungry." And it's not just her, I swear.

She yawns, looking cute as fuck, and I stare at her lips. "Yeah, dinner should be almost ready. I'm making us chicken pot roast with carrots and baby potatoes today," she says lazily right before she stretches and groans. My jaw clenches.

God, she wants me to lose it, the little vixen. She wants me to go mad.

"Why don't you go and have your shower, Sebastian? I'll prepare the salad in the meantime."

"Sounds good," I rasp as my cock jerks inside my trousers. "I'm in desperate need of a shower." Yeah, a cold shower and a wank, and not necessarily in that order.

Alice smiles, and I smile down at her. "Want to join me?" I ask. A guy can ask, right?

"And you were being so nice," she says incredulously.

"You know me, sweetheart. Besides"—my eyes drop down the length of her body suggestively before rising back to meet her gaze—"a girl like you? Can't blame a guy like me for trying."

She blushes, making me chuckle as I turn and walk away. Doesn't matter how many times I flirt with her, there's always that surprised look on her face. That glint of shyness in her eyes, right before she brushes it off and goes back to ignoring me.

It's a defence mechanism. She thinks I'm kidding, and she's trying her damnedest to protect herself.

She doesn't know that it doesn't matter. That she's already lost.

And that soon, very soon, I'll be showing her just how hot and serious we are destined to be.

* * *

"More wine?" I offer, already holding the bottle over her glass. We've been sitting at the dining room table for the last half an hour or so, talking, eating and drinking, and already this is the best half an hour or so of my day.

"Just a little. Thank you." She smiles. And I smile with her as I pour her yet another drink.

I'm not trying to get her drunk, though. I just want her to relax. Maybe some of her defences will fall that way. Maybe she'll finally open up and let me in.

And I know, I know it sounds like I'm going all soft and shit, but I don't care. Nothing matters when it's just the two of us like this. Laughing, talking, enjoying the wonderful meal she made.

"How was your day?" she asks.

I love that she asks about my day. That she actually listens and cares. That she makes me feel valued, important. Like I'm the only person who matters to her.

Before I know it, I'm telling her everything about my meeting with Luke today, about Arthur's betrayal, and the subsequent conversation with my dad.

Alice shakes her head. "I can't believe someone could do this to your father. He's such a good person, a good man. So kind and caring ... fair ..."

I blow out my breath. "It's greed. Envy. Unfortunately, it always comes down to money when you have it." I start picking at my place mat as I look down at my plate. "The worst thing about all this is that the old man was really crushed. He trusted Arthur. They were close friends. The son of a bitch did more than just rob my dad, he betrayed their friendship, and that's what Dad can't forgive."

Alice's small hand covers mine, and I inhale deeply, probably for the first time since Luke came into my office. I feel lighter already, better now I've told Alice what happened. As if the burden has lessened somehow because she's here to listen. To help me make sense of things.

I frown. I left nothing out—something new and unprecedented for me.

And when her hand covers mine, I turn it around, holding it in mine as I intertwine our fingers together. Realising I want this. Need it. Can't go on without it any more.

"What about you, Sebastian? How are you feeling about all this?" she asks.

No one ever asks how I'm feeling. If I'm hurting. My eyes search hers, and before I can stop myself, the words are tumbling out of my mouth again.

My eagerness surprises even myself when I tell her just how horrible and sad the whole situation is making me feel, as well as the plans Luke and I are making for the company and the investigation we're about to launch to find that piece of shit Arthur and his cronies.

And once again, she listens, giving me her undivided attention, her kindness, her heart.

This woman amazes me. Confounds me, even. Making me do things I never thought I'd do in a million years. Making me speak with no reservations, no filters.

Never in my whole life have I confided in someone like I do in her, and maybe it's dangerous, maybe I'm setting myself up for regret, but I can't bring myself to stop. I'm too lost in her beautiful eyes. In the way she bites her lower lip just so every time I lick mine. In the way she takes my breath away by simply existing. By simply being here with me.

So when she gets up from her seat, wraps her small arms around my neck, and pulls me into her embrace—I almost fucking sigh in relief. Loving the way she's holding me, the way she smells, and particularly the way her soft breasts feel under my cheek.

What? I'm feeling down. I didn't turn into a saint all of a sudden.

"I'm so sorry, Sebastian. Your family doesn't deserve this," she murmurs, running her fingers through my damp hair in a comforting motion.

"The hardest part was telling my dad about it. Luke and I really struggled with it." Fucking Arthur. The hurt in my dad's eyes was like a punch in the gut, twisting at my insides even now.

"You're both good men, good sons. Your father is very lucky to have you."

My heart squeezes at her words, beginning to pound all over again. The anger, the hurt feeling like salt on an open wound. The betrayal like an actual dagger stabbing me through the back.

So I throw my arms around her, clinging to her small frame as she offers me her strength.

She hugs me back, and to my surprise, there's nothing sexual about the embrace. I actually needed this, needed her.

I tighten my hold on her, and she kisses my head. "All you can do now is move forward, Sebastian. Sooner or later Arthur and his accomplices will get caught. You'll see. Just focus on all the positive changes you're already making in the business and the rest will fall into place. I believe in you. You'll do great things. I believe in you more than anyone." She whispers the last part, and my chest swells with pride, joy and something else I can't quite understand.

It makes me feel good, though. Better. She makes me feel better. Like anything is possible. I can't help but be grateful that she's here by my side when I know in my heart I don't deserve such a blessing.

* * *

Alice stiffens in my arms as if just realising what she's doing. Her hands drop to my shoulders and she tries to take a step back from me.

I take a deep breath and let go of her, also getting to my feet. I clear my throat and start gathering our dishes.

She moves to help, and I stop her, deciding to give her some space. "Why don't you go and choose a movie for us to watch, sweetheart," I offer. "Something funny. God knows I can use the distraction, and that way we can both relax a bit before bed."

"I ... I can do that," she stutters, a deer-in-headlights expression written all over her face. With that she turns and saunters in the direction of the living room, and I carry our dishes to the sink.

Turning on the tap, I can't help but snicker at how domesticated I've become when less than three weeks ago no one would catch me throwing out the rubbish, let alone doing the washing up. Now look at me. Rushing home for dinner after work. Looking forward to spending time with Alice. Even doing chores if that means having her around for a bit longer at night.

I smirk. Shit, it sounds as if we're married or something, which is fucking hilarious, really. Ridiculous, of course. Even if the thought doesn't freak me out nearly as much as it did in the past. Quite the opposite, in fact. I feel this weird rush of excitement, this energy, spreading through my veins at the prospect of having Alice as my wife.

I could have all this. All this and so much more if I let her stick around. As my wife, there'd be no doubt as to whom she belongs to, and as her husband, I'd be entitled to have her in my bed every night. Fuck her whenever and wherever I felt like.

Shaking my head, I put away the last of the dishes and turn off the tap. I exhale, my eyes closed as I hold onto the sink.

Fuck. What the hell am I thinking?

I could never do that to her. Or anyone else for that matter. I'm too damaged. Too fucked up in the head to screw with someone else's life like that.

Especially Alice's.

No, I made my mind up a long time ago, and she deserves better than this. Better than me, a miserable fuck who's too scared to feel. Too scared to lose her if she ever became that important to him.

Besides, a pretty girl like her will find someone in no time. A good man who'll deserve her. A good man who'll love her and cherish her the way that I can't. A man who's the exact opposite of me.

"Fuck," I growl, fighting the urge to punch the sink, the usual feelings of rage and hate taking over every time a similar thought enters my head. My jaw tightens and I grind my teeth together.

Truth is, I don't want her to leave. Don't want her with anybody else but me. But how can I do that to her—to myself—and not live to regret it?

What if I put us through all that—a relationship, marriage and all that it entails—just to lose her anyway? Could I do it? Could I try?

She'd be mine. Completely mine, yes, but what if we're already living on borrowed time?

I groan, shaking my head in defeat. No ... no, it's not right. And I can't. I just can't put myself through that. I know I wouldn't survive.

I bring my glass of wine to my lips and take a gulp, wishing it was something stronger.

Just get your head on straight, you idiot.

All we have is the now, the present, and I have too much work in front of me to waste my time on a doomed relationship.

We can have some fun, enjoy each other for a while. That was the plan, anyway, and I should be sticking to it. She's already too much work as it is, too much effort.

She's probably out there torturing herself right now just for hugging me. Blaming herself for allowing such an intimate moment with her boss to happen despite us clearly being attracted to each other.

I take another long drag of my wine.

Well, unfortunately for her I'm done.

Done with giving her time, done with waiting for her.

Done with this crazy, unhealthy obsession of mine ... when all the while she's holding the cure. She is the cure.

She is my cure.

Chapter 6

Alice

At the risk of being caught, my eyes drift from the television to Sebastian again.

Half-naked and sprawled out on the sofa, he's a sight to behold. Easily the sexiest man I've ever seen, and I can't take my eyes off of him. There's just this energy about him, this pull, this 'je ne sais quoi' only a few men possess and even fewer know what to do with.

I bite my lip and press my thighs together as I try to resist, my panties getting wetter and wetter the longer I stare at him. I take in his broad, strong shoulders, his powerful, muscular chest, and those abs—God, those abs that keep calling to me—and I shiver, goosebumps spreading everywhere.

It's like this man was made for me. Every part of him, every muscle, every dimple, every look from him makes me come alight, aflame. Makes me want to do everything and anything with him.

My face heats up and I almost laugh at how ridiculous I sound.

Logically, I know it's all that kickboxing and weightlifting he does before the crack of dawn that makes him look like this. Not some sort of divine intervention designed to make us fit.

But wow—my stomach flutters—these are some damn fine results, if you ask me.

My core tightens and I force myself to look away, to focus my attention on the grand living area and the formal dining room across from it, hoping it will distract me from him. I know it's an impossible task, but focus my eyes anyway.

Both rooms are huge and beautifully decorated, with light-coloured oak flooring and modern, dark wooden furniture with grey, blue and cream furnishings throughout. Fresh flowers adorn the long dining table, as well as twenty velvety grey chairs that match the big corner sofa and plush wingback armchairs in the lounge. Bold, abstract art covers the walls, with exotic-looking plants standing in every corner, and there's even a real stone fireplace, making the whole space look warm and cosy despite its size.

My smile grows bigger and I bite into my thumbnail, looking at Sebastian again.

This place is gorgeous. Insane, but gorgeous, and so him.

I stare at the god sitting across from me, my eyes dropping to his washboard stomach, the prominent V-line that disappears into his black pyjama bottoms, and I can't help but squirm a little in my seat. This man is simply too good to be real, and the way his strong, powerful body calls to mine frankly scares the shit out of me.

He's dangerous. This is dangerous, and I shouldn't be checking him out, but I swear it's like having a supermodel in the house. What's a girl supposed to do?

I scrunch up my face in disgust at myself. I can't get caught, though. Sebastian wouldn't behave like a gentleman. No, he'd take it as an opening to make even more of his dirty remarks. And although he's not as bad as he was when I first moved in, he still says things he shouldn't ... things he shouldn't even be thinking about me.

My teeth sink into my lower lip. Yeah, the man certainly has a filthy mind, and has no problem being verbal about it. The only problem is, he doesn't sound like a creep at all. He has this way of making everything sound sexy, tempting, leaving me—the voice of reason— to constantly remind us both that he's my boss.

Even when I'm undeniably shaken and want nothing more than to give in to him. To lust.

Still, one of us has to be responsible, right? One of us has to be mature.

"Do you want to take a closer look, sweetheart?" His voice jerks me out of my thoughts, and I flush, realising this whole time I've been staring at him. "Come sit next to me," he drawls as he pats the empty space next to his thigh.

Damn it! He'll be insufferable now. Embarrassed, I avoid his eyes and tuck my feet under my legs. A pillow sits over my lap and I hug it for support, hiding behind it really, as I wrack my brain for a reply.

I wish the ground would swallow me whole. I feel mortified. Absolutely mortified.

"I ... I don't know what you mean." Face burning and heart racing, I keep my eyes glued to the television, hoping he'll just let it go.

"I don't mind, you know?" he says, getting up and crossing the room to sit next to me. "Besides, I stare at you all the time, so it's only fair."

God, he smells good. All spicy, and manly, and so utterly delicious my brain almost short-circuits on the spot.

Then he's sliding one arm behind me and pulling my quivering body to his. His free hand holds my jaw up, giving me no choice but to meet his gaze.

Electric-blue eyes, now almost black with desire, stare back at me. The blue I love so much is nothing but a small rim around his pupils as he slowly licks his lips, and just like that he draws me in.

I can't move, can't look away. The intense look in his eyes excites me, thrills me, and most of all frightens me, because I can no longer resist this beautiful man.

He's fascinating to me. His mind, his darkness, the danger exuding from his much larger and taller body.

So even as my hands come up to push against his chest, desperately trying to put some distance between us, I already know it's a lost cause. Still, I push harder, fighting and squirming in his hold, but I might as well be pushing against a brick wall.

He's strong, too strong, and I'm glad. I'm glad because now I can finally give in, succumb ... knowing I did everything I could to stop this madness.

"Alice, we both want this. It's time we let it happen." His voice is thick with desire, cajoling, raising goosebumps all over my skin as I tremble under his touch.

Liquid heat pools in my panties, and I try to look away. He doesn't let me, though, his hand on my jaw still holding me firmly in place. "Don't deny me this, baby girl," he whispers, lowering his head and grazing my lips with his. Just a feathery touch at first, making me tingle all over right before he captures my mouth in a slow, sensual kiss.

The pillow—my protection, my shield—falls to the floor as his large hand slides down my side and reaches my waist, squeezing me a little before it settles on my hip. And when his tongue tenderly licks between my lips, seeking entrance, I open for him, melting and moaning in his arms as the last of my resistance disappears.

"Alice," he groans and begins to stroke my tongue with his, his grip on me turning almost violent as he deepens the kiss, stealing my breath away, shutting down my brain until I can no longer remember why on earth I was pushing him away.

All I can focus on is him. The feel of his hard body pressed up against mine. The rapid rise and fall of his chest and rippling muscles under my palms. All too good to keep denying myself. Too good to keep running away—especially now I know how perfect he is.

He pulls away, both of us breathing hard as our eyes lock on each other's. "So sweet," he growls, dusting his thumb over my lower lip before he sucks it into his mouth. "So fucking sweet."

Then he's kissing me again, the kiss so hot and passionate that when he grabs me, places me astride his lap, and puts his hands on my ass, all I can do is submit, moaning helplessly into his mouth as he takes what he wants from me.

God, no one's ever touched me like this, made me feel like this, and I think I'm about to lose my sanity. Sliding my fingers through his hair, I hold on tight as he begins to trail open-mouthed kisses down my jaw, my neck, along my collarbone.

"Sebastian," I moan as he sucks and nibbles his way back up to this spot just behind my ear. I gasp, my body shivering as his tongue flicks over the sensitive skin again and again, and before I know what I'm doing, I'm grinding myself shamelessly on him.

He groans, gripping my hips, pushing me down onto something hard, and ... oh, God, that's his ...

"I'm so hard for you, baby girl. I want you so fucking bad." His hold on me tightens, guiding me, forcing me to rub myself on the huge erection between his legs, and soon enough my hips have a mind of their own.

It feels good, though. He feels good, and as his big hands cup my ass again, squeezing it hard, I almost orgasm on the spot.

"Fuck, this ass has been driving me mad," he snarls, kneading my flesh as I whimper and grind my clit harder on his cock.

And I'm lost. Lost in the waves of pleasure travelling up my belly. Lost in the way he touches me and makes me surrender. Lost on how he takes charge of my body, like it belongs to him ... like it has always belonged to him.

Leaving a trail of open-mouthed kisses down my neck, Sebastian fists my hair and sinks his teeth into my shoulder. The sharp pleasure-pain sensation pushes me higher and higher until I feel as if I'm free-falling from the sky.

Startled, I gasp. And he shoves the strap of my tank top down, following its descent with his mouth.

His skilful tongue licks down my chest, drawing patterns on my skin and making me see stars.

"Sebastian," I try, but my voice is weak and breaks down. "Sebastian," I try again, my tone a tad stronger this time, and his hooded eyes finally rise to meet mine.

A dark smile spreads over his lips for just a second, right before he slides the strap of my top the rest of the way down and in one swift move covers my breast with his mouth.

"Oh, God," I cry out, arching my back and curling my fingers in his hair. The feel of his lips and wet tongue suckling on my stiff nipple proves to be too much, too good, and I can't hold back any more. I need the connection, need to be close to him.

And call me stupid, but I'll take whatever I can get.

Sebastian groans into my breast, the sound travelling straight to my clit, and I can't think, can't rationalise what he's doing to me any more.

The pull of his mouth, the vibrations of his groans, his touch are all I can focus on, and as my core begins to spasm and more wetness rushes out of me, soaking my panties, I think I'm about to climax just like this. With my boob in his mouth.

Next thing I know, though, he's releasing me. His heavy-lidded eyes bore into mine, and I don't understand. Confused, aroused, it takes me a moment to realise what he's doing, but by then it's too late. And when he grips the front of my top with both hands, ripping it apart, I'm too stunned to react. Too shocked to do anything but stare into his beautiful face.

Then he's on me again, his mouth wet, and warm, and heaven on my skin. His hands are rough, and hard, and yet so gentle on my breasts, and I don't care. I can't stop, not when there's so much need, so much pressure building inside me, and I feel like I'll combust if I don't experience this with him.

"Fuck," he growls, grabbing my ass and rubbing me all over his length, his expert mouth still doing wicked, wicked things to my flesh. "You're so beautiful, baby. So fucking beautiful you take my breath away."

Our eyes meet, unmoving and lingering on each other, and in this moment I'm his, completely and utterly his.

Then his mouth's covering mine, swallowing my moans in a savage kiss, and our grinding increases, our movements urgent and frenzied as we push our bodies towards release.

"Come for me, baby girl," he rasps, gripping my hair and kissing his way down my neck, barely in control any more. "Show me ... show me how you come. I need to see you."

And just like that, as if trained to comply with his every command, my whole body convulses, exploding into a thousand fragments as I come with a scream. "Sebastian. Oh, God, Sebastian."

"Perfect. So ... fucking ... perfect," he grunts out, his grip on my hip tightening as he grinds himself harder on me. "Oh, fuck. Fuck, baby. Alice," he groans, pulling me by the hair for a kiss as his whole body shudders and stiffens under mine.

Exhausted, I collapse on his chest, my nose pressed up to his neck as I breathe in his spicy scent.

Heaven, pure heaven.

He closes his arms around me and presses a tender kiss to my temple.

Both of us are breathing hard and soaked with perspiration, a hot, wet mess as we hold each other close. And yet he's still looking at me as if I'm special. As if I'm everything he desires.

Then he's searching for my lips again, capturing them in a sweet, slow, tender kiss that brings tears to my eyes, and the last of my control dissipates.

Oh, why does he have to be so perfect? So dreamy? Because that's what this is. A perfect kiss with the perfect man in the most perfect moment in time, making me wish we could stay just like this, just the two of us, forever.

Smiling into my lips, he tucks my hair behind my ear. His knuckles brush my cheek as he looks down at me adoringly.

And it finally hits me. God, what must he think of me?

Probably that I'm a slut. A cheap, dirty slut who's going to bed him from now on. A whore who's going to tend to his every need and dirty desire in the office and at home. No wonder he looks so happy.

My stomach lurches and I bury my face in his chest, unable to keep looking at him. What was I thinking? He's my boss, for Christ's sake. I'll lose my job, my dignity, myself, not to mention Mr Hunter and Linda will never forgive me. They'll probably think I was some kind of gold-digger, after Sebastian's money all along.

No, no, no. I can't do this. It doesn't matter if I have feelings for him. It wouldn't even matter if I loved him. This is madness, and I've no excuse.

I knew he was a player. I just stupidly thought I was safe because he never goes for the staff, and at the end of the day—even if we're not working together yet—that's all I am to him, a member of staff.

Damn it. I stiffen as he kisses my head. We shouldn't have crossed the line. Our relationship was already complicated enough with Sebastian having to take me in and look after me since the accident, but now ... now it may be ruined forever.

Cursing myself, I shut my eyes tight in regret.

It's OK for him, he can always sack me if this backfires. But what about me? I'll end up heartbroken and jobless, with no prospects for a better job, and I've worked too damned hard to lose it all like this.

No, I have to stop him, and I have to stop him now. I need to protect myself. Nobody else will.

Barely holding my tears, I push against Sebastian's chest and climb out of his lap. He looks puzzled, but helps me up. "Are you OK, sweetheart?"

I shake my head, clutching the two halves of my ripped top whilst avoiding his eyes. Never in my life have I felt as humiliated or as small as I do right now, standing like this in front of him.

That is, until my eyes fall to the wet spot between his legs where we both released our fluids, and to my utter horror Sebastian follows my gaze. A devilish grin spreads on his lips as he sees the reason why my cheeks are burning up.

Great, now he's amused by my embarrassment.

"What's wrong, Alice?" His eyes come back to mine, and he grips his still-hard cock, stroking himself through his trousers.

"This," I say, waving a hand between us. "This is wrong and it can't happen again. You're my boss, and ..."

"There's absolutely nothing wrong with what we just did," he growls, sitting up. "In fact, this is just the beginning. There's much, much more on the cards for us, Alice. Believe me."

"No, there isn't," I yell, going into full defensive mode. "And don't you ever touch me again."

"Stop!" he orders. The severity in his tone makes me jump back as my poor heart almost leaps out of my chest.

Christ, now I went and pissed him off, and I don't like it when he's pissed. He looks scary when he's angry, downright dangerous in fact, and I'm not strong enough right now to deal with him.

Taking deep breaths, I try to calm my racing heart. He won't harm me. He'd never hurt me. Sebastian's a good man.

"I can't promise not to touch you," he rasps, eyes burning into mine. "All I can promise is that I'll keep my distance tonight." Running his fingers through his hair, he takes a deep breath and blows it out, obviously still trying to rein in his temper. "Now go to bed, Alice. We'll talk tomorrow once we've both calmed down."

I don't want to talk at all, but I don't argue. It wouldn't be wise right now.

So I turn and run as fast as my feet can carry me all the way up to my bedroom, where I lock the door, change into my nightgown, and hide under the covers of my bed, hoping tomorrow everything will be OK ... that we'll be OK ... and, most importantly, that it's not too late for us to go back to how things were right before our kiss.

* * *

Sleep evades me all night as thoughts of Sebastian and how it felt to kiss him play like a movie in my head.

I sigh and turn on my side, wishing for sweet oblivion for what feels like the millionth time.

I should leave, it's for the best.

But where would I go with no money?

I could ask Linda.

No, she'd know something was wrong. And my former landlady is out of the question too. Which is pretty pathetic, really. I should have friends, family, people who care about me.

There's no one, though. Not a living soul who actually gives a damn.

Crap, why did he have to go and do this? And, more importantly, how can I make him see sense?

He doesn't need me. He can have any woman he wants. Any woman but me.

Pain lances through my body and I curl myself into a ball. Just the thought of Sebastian with another woman hurts more than I can bear.

Which, once again, is pretty pathetic of me. He's not mine to keep. He's not mine at all.

Yet I can't help the way I feel. I think I love him. In fact, I'm sure I do. And I don't want him to be with anybody else. Just me.

Of course, I'm not as naive as to think he'll ever feel the same about me. He's a Hunter, a CEO and billionaire, and I'm ... me.

Touching my lips with trembling fingers, I feel the first of many tears spill from my eyes.

I'll never forget him, though ... and I'll never forget our kiss.

* * *

Breakfast is painfully awkward as Sebastian ignores me as if I'm not even there.

It's upsetting. We usually talk and have coffee in the kitchen together before he leaves for work. And now he's treating me like this.

Another sign that I'm doing the right thing, that I have to keep my distance.

The silence is deafening, though, gritting at my nerve endings until all I want to do is shout at him, lash out and push him to say something, anything ... but I don't. I'm not making the first move.

He's the one who started all this, he should be man enough to finish it. And he knows we have to talk, he even said so himself last night. So what's the deal with the silent treatment now?

Ten more minutes tick by, and I'm going out of my mind as he sips his coffee and reads the news on his phone.

Grrr, asshole.

I can't stand it. We've never gone so long without exchanging a single word, and it feels wrong. Mainly because it hurts, but also because now I know for sure that if I become a problem, he won't think twice about getting rid of me. Sacking me and scratching me out of his life as if I never even existed.

Well, I've got news for you, Mr Hunter. I'm not letting that happen. I've worked too hard and too damned long to let my job go just like that. So we're sorting this out today. Once and for all.

Sebastian gets up to wash his mug and plate, and I begin to panic. Shit, what do I say? What do I say?

I look down at myself, still wearing my white satin nightgown and robe, and cringe. I should've gotten dressed for this.

He's already in his trademark bespoke suit, looking all sleek and put together in grey slacks and a white shirt, and I haven't even brushed my hair.

Suddenly I don't feel so brave. Maybe I should wait until this evening. Yes, we can talk over dinner, I decide.

But then he's turning and leaving—not bothering to even glance my way—and before I know what I'm doing I'm rushing to his study after him.

* * *

"Sebastian, can we talk?" I ask nervously as I stand by the open door.

I'm furious, though. Furious at him for treating me like this. Furious at myself for allowing it.

"Sure, I still have some time. Come on in." His eyes stay cold and glued to the laptop in front of him.

I frown. Jeez, he can't even look at me any more. Can't even look me in the eyes.

Wounded pride at my rejection, that's all. He doesn't care. Not really.

"About last night," I say, taking a few steps inside and stopping not too far from the door. Just in case. "I think it'd be best if we forget what happened and stop all this"—I pause, choosing my words carefully—"overfamiliarity between us."

His lips press together, and I take a deep breath, straightening my back. "So, I'll address you as Mr Hunter from now on, and start doing some tasks for the office again. Here at the house, of course," I rush to say at the small rise of his brows. "I could get remote access, do some of the smaller tasks from here." I sigh, frustrated. I'm not getting through to him. I can feel it. "Sebastian, please. This will help. If we keep our relationship professional, maybe we can still ..."

The first chuckle that comes out of his mouth stuns me into silence, and his eyes finally rise to meet mine. "We can still what, Alice? Work together? Pretend I didn't kiss you, didn't make you come?"

Embarrassment clogs my throat, and for a moment I have to look away. How dare he? This isn't funny. He continues to laugh, though, and it takes everything in me not to walk up to him and slap the funny right off his face.

"Oh, Alice." He tuts, shaking his head. What's he trying to do? Humiliate me? Hurt me? Seriously, the cheek of this man! "I must say I'm impressed. Not many people have the balls to tell me what to do. Still"—he gives me a twisted smile—"I'm afraid this can't be helped. I want you, and you want me, so I'm not forgetting, nor am I stopping anything. You know as well as I do this attraction between us has been there from the start. We have chemistry, Alice. Insane, off-the-fucking-charts chemistry, and I'm not passing up on that. So don't ask me to back off, because I won't. We'd be fools not to act on this."

"I don't know what you're talking about. I don't want you, and, to be quite honest, I've had better than last night. That was ... mediocre, at best." Avoiding Sebastian's eyes, I do my best to sound convincing, I really do, but my voice comes out high-pitched.

"Mmm, you and your smart mouth," he drawls. "Perhaps I should fuck it. Coat your throat and your tongue in my cum. Bet that would rid you of your smart-mouth syndrome altogether." He smirks devilishly at me. "And if that doesn't do the trick ... well, maybe when I make you come on my cock the first time, I will shut you up once and for all."

Heat rushes into my cheeks and then my throat, leaving me burning and feverish as it spreads towards my chest. And yet again, much to my surprise, my core spasms, my panties are drenched, and the need to climb up his body and rub myself all over him makes me shake like a leaf.

God, how embarrassing is this? Nothing even remotely similar ever happened to me before him. Sure, I've experienced a certain level of excitement when watching a heated scene in a movie or reading a romance. What girl doesn't?

But this? This is on a whole other level, and it's all because of him. Because of that gorgeous face and delicious body of his ... all huge, and muscular, and tall, and ... No, no, no. Don't think about his body. Don't even think about his face. Just don't think about him at all.

I shake my head, annoyed he has such an effect on me. "Just stop. Stop saying those things to me. They're not happening. There's not even an if for us, let alone a when."

"Oh, they're happening, Alice. And the sooner you get over the nonsense going through your pretty head, the sooner we can get on to the good parts."

"Not in this lifetime, I can tell you that much," I snap, not sure who I'm trying to convince any more, me or him.

"You keep saying that to yourself, baby. But after last night, forgive me if I don't believe you."

"I'm not your baby," I hiss. "And if you continue to behave in such an inappropriate manner with me, you leave me no choice but to talk to your father."

His eyes narrow, and before I know it, he's on me, forcing me to stumble back. He stalks after me, following and matching my every step until my back hits the wall. Predator and prey. Hunter and deer facing off.

"Mr Hunter, what are you doing?" Silence. "Sir, please."

Caging me with his arms, he leans into me as my hands come up to push against his chest. He smiles, our faces mere inches apart, and once again I get lost in his eyes, in the power exuding from his body, in the clean, spicy scent of his cologne, and I can't think straight. Can't look away from him.

My heart starts beating maniacally inside my chest, the butterflies in my stomach making it impossible for me to even act calm.

With my luck, I'll probably throw up on him. Which he totally deserves, by the way.

I just don't think I can handle any more embarrassment today.

"Inappropriate, huh?" he asks, his voice raspy and laced with desire as he pins me with his eyes. "Mmm, what about when I make you come again, Alice? Will that be inappropriate too? Or when I make you cry out in ecstasy as I fuck you with my mouth, my tongue, my fingers? What about when I sink balls deep into that tight little cunt of yours and fuck you hard? Tell me, sweetheart, 'cause either way, it's going to happen."

I gasp, his crude words unsettling, but also intoxicating, and to my utter shame, I become even more aroused. "Mr Hunter, please let me go."

He smirks, looking every bit like the handsome devil he is, and moves closer to whisper in my ear. "You think that by calling me 'Mr Hunter' or 'sir', you're going to stop me, Alice?" He chuckles, the sound rich and deep in his throat, raising goosebumps all over my skin. "Because I can tell you right now that you won't." Pulling back, he licks his bottom lip as he ravishes me with his eyes. "Fuck, if anything, you're making things worse, baby girl ... because now all I can picture is you calling me 'sir' while I spank that hot little ass of yours into submission."

My breath hitches, and he licks his lips again, his eyes burning with the same fire I saw last night right before he kissed me.

Holy mother of all things sexy. How am I supposed to resist him when he's like this?

Then he's leaning in further, his face so close to mine, I can feel his minty breath brushing my lips. "I could make you feel so good, Alice. Make us both so happy. Just let me in. Let me take care of you and show you how perfect we can be."

His tone is cajoling, tempting, and I have to look away because there's a dangerous possibility I might give in.

"Fuck, that blush is driving me wild," he growls, burying his face in my neck, licking and sucking on my sensitive skin like a man possessed. "It's as if you fucking enjoy taunting me with your innocence." Pretty soon my hands are clenched tight around his shirt instead of pushing him away. My knees almost fold as wave upon wave of pleasure travels through my body.

"No," I whisper, somehow coming to my senses. "Sebastian, please stop." My voice is all breathy and needy, annoying the crap out of me as I push hard into his chest.

Because you're a stupid girl, Alice. Nothing but a stupid girl who has fallen for the wrong man.

Giving me the most delicious smile, he reluctantly steps back, lowers his arms to his sides and slides his hands into his pockets. His movements are so smooth, I can't help but swoon a little on the spot.

Well, screw him and his hotness. I'm nobody's toy. Yesterday I was caught off guard, letting myself melt in his arms like that, but not today. With all my might and not a second to waste, I raise my hand above my head and let it fall across his face.

See, I can be fast too, Mr Hunter. Now put that in your pipe and smoke it, you ... you stupid, arrogant, entitled idiot!

The red mark on his cheek forms almost immediately. It should be all the proof I need that I hit him hard enough. Except he didn't even flinch, nor is he showing any signs of regret like I was expecting.

No, he's grinning like a fool, and all I seem to have accomplished is a throbbing hand and wounded pride, not to mention a heavy conscience for having slapped the bastard.

His stupid grin broadens, the glint in his eyes making him look dangerous and dark, winding me so tightly, I fear I might snap at any time.

God help me, looking this good should be illegal, especially when he's not right in the head.

"I deserved that. So I'll give it to you." Sex drips from his voice as he stares down at me. "But only that one, Alice. There'll be hell to pay if you do it again, understand?"

I huff, unimpressed, and a small snort escapes his mouth. "On second thought, maybe I should punish you now. Make you repent on your knees with my cock in your mouth. Would you like that, baby? Is that what you want from me?"

I'm seeing red when I go to slap him again, but this time he's ready for me and catches my hand mid-air, pinning it easily over my head. My other hand shoots out, and he repeats the process just as effortlessly, pausing to press his lips to the inside of my wrist.

"Careful, baby. As much fun as this is, I don't want you hurting yourself." The gentleness in his voice takes me by surprise. "I'm sure your little hand is already throbbing, yes?"

I raise my chin defiantly. "You're an asshole, you know that?"

"And you're beautiful, you know that?" He bites his lip as if daring me to kiss him. To surrender to this madness and let him take what he wants.

"Stop making fun of me, Sebastian. This is not a game," I whisper, dejected. This might be amusing to him, but it's definitely not amusing to me.

"Hey," he says, and releases my wrists to hold my face in his hands. "I'm not making fun of you. Why would you say such a thing? Can't you see what you do to me? Can't you see how much I want you?" His lips brush my cheek, kissing a path towards my ear, and my hands fall to his sides. God, he's so big and broad, I can feel every muscle tensing and contracting under my palms.

He sucks my earlobe into his mouth, pressing his erection to my hip, and I gasp. "Can you feel how hard my cock is for you, baby?" he murmurs. "Does this feel like a game to you?"

I pull back, watching in a trance as his eyes darken with arousal, boring into mine with such need, such fire, I can barely think. "I ... I don't understand. They said you don't get involved with women you work with, and you ... you keep laughing at me."

"It's a well-known fact I don't mix business with pleasure, Alice.

A rule that has always served me well, until you showed up"—a slow smirk forms on his lips—"and all sense and logic jumped out of the window along with my pride. But then again, I've never wanted someone as bad as I want you," he drawls, running his thumb over my bottom lip. "Never needed to possess one like I need to possess you."

I go to speak, but he shushes me, pressing his thumb to my mouth.

"I'm not finished," he rasps, making me glare at him. The nerve on this man. "So fiery!" He laughs, and I glare harder. If looks could kill, he'd be laughing for the last time. "I like it. I like it a lot. And for the record, I wasn't laughing at you. Just think it's funny that someone as tiny as you is so ready to pick a fight with someone like me, a physical one, no less."

"Just leave me be, Sebastian. I need my job, and you're my boss, for Christ's sake. Stop this madness now." I push into his chest, trying to reason with him. He must see this. There's no way he could be so selfish. "And for the record," I angrily mimic his words, "I could seriously hurt you if I wanted to."

"Oh, I've no doubt you could hurt me, baby. You're a very capable woman. Which is why I promise to keep that in mind in all my future interactions with you." He winks, and I shove him harder, releasing an exasperated grunt when he doesn't budge an inch.

"Come here, kitten," he says, lifting me by the waist and parking my behind on the side table next to the wall.

"Let me down!" I yelp. "Let me down right this second."

"Or what?" he asks, tucking a loose strand of hair behind my ear, the gesture so intimate and tender, my poor heart skips a beat before resuming its crazy rhythm inside my chest.

This is something I'd expect from a boyfriend. Something I'd expect from Sebastian if he was mine and I was his.

Gripped by sadness, I look down to avoid his gaze, and that's when my eyes almost fall out of their sockets. Holy shit. I thought he was big when I felt him on my hip, but nothing prepared me for the huge bulge that is now tenting his slacks.

"I know it's big, sweetheart. But don't worry, I promise to go slow on you the first time we fuck." He laughs, the sound low and throaty, sending chills up and down my spine, and I can feel myself melting further into him.

He kisses my blazing cheek. "Did you really think I wouldn't notice the way you look at me, Alice? You can't hide, you know? You can't hide how much you want me. I wouldn't be pursuing you so relentlessly if I didn't see lust in your eyes."

He's right, I do want him. I want him more than anything, but it doesn't give him the right to treat me like this.

His face falls, erasing all traces of his cocky grin, when the tears I've been fighting all morning finally fill my eyes. "Hey, what's wrong, baby?" he asks as he lifts me off the table and places me back on the floor. "Fuck, did I hurt you? Please tell me if I hurt you, Alice."

Chapter 7

Alice

Despite how hard I try to control my emotions, my vision blurs and more tears spill with a will of their own.

"No," I manage to push past the lump in my throat. "You didn't hurt me. Not the way you think, anyway."

His brows furrow as he searches my eyes. "What do you mean? Tell me." The gentleness in his voice makes me feel worse.

I inhale deeply. "Sebastian, I'm not one of your 'girls'. I don't do one-night stands. Nor do I have cheap, dirty affairs, flings or whatever the hell they're called these days. That's not me. I'm not wired that way. So I'll ask you again. Please stop. Don't do this. You'll only hurt me in the end," I sob, and with a sigh he pulls me into his arms, burying his face in my hair as he cradles me to his chest. "You're so selfish. You sleep with me and then what?" OK, I'm ugly-crying now.

He tries to soothe me, rubbing my back in circles and swaying me in his arms, but now I've started talking, I've no idea how to stop. "You'll cast me aside like yesterday's news, and once I'm ready to go back to work, you'll probably sack me just so you don't have to see me again. You won't even want to look at me."

Wracking sobs shake my whole body as my fingers clench around his shirt, now soaked with my tears. "Sebastian, please." I hiccup. "I'm not the kind of girl who can separate sex from emotion. I'd get attached. I'd end up jobless and with my heart broken."

"I'd never sack you," he murmurs, and I laugh humourlessly in response. "OK, I admit when I brought you home with me, I didn't exactly do it out of the goodness of my heart." He blows out a heavy breath. "But I'm a guy, Alice, and an asshole at best. Back then I thought I wanted to fuck you much more than I wanted to help you. I convinced myself that's all I wanted from you ..." He pauses, seemingly reluctant to continue. "The thought of transferring you to a different department once we were done did cross my mind."

I tense in his arms, and he rushes to explain. "But I dismissed it just as fast, Alice. I promise. I think even then you were changing me. I just didn't realise it." He sighs into my hair. "I could never hurt you that way, baby. And you must know my dad wouldn't allow it either, or Linda. They adore you."

I scrunch my eyes tight. He's right, he's an asshole, and I'm an idiot for falling for him. "So you'd just transfer me? That was your brilliant plan? Don't you know these things have a way of coming out? That I'd be ridiculed at the office? I can already hear the whispers, the snickers behind my back. The 'joke', the 'slut'. An easy target for all the perverts working for you, thinking that once the boss is done, they're entitled to the scraps." I massage my temples, trying to keep the mother of all headaches at bay. "And that's not even the worst. No, the worst would be the disappointment in your father's and Linda's eyes." My voice breaks and I press a hand to my mouth. "God, your father would probably sack me himself and save you the trouble. Getting rid of the gold-digger who tried to seduce his very rich and very handsome son."

Sebastian's chuckles interrupt me. "You think I'm handsome then?"

I sniffle as I meet his gaze with my swollen eyes. Now I've opened the floodgates, I can't seem to stop. "From everything I've just said, that's the only thing you heard?" I hiccup.

"I heard everything you said, angel," he says, kissing my nose. "I just think we should discuss the part about me being handsome in greater detail, that's all."

Upset, I begin to struggle in his arms, and he pins me to the wall, both of his arms caging me as he leans in and presses his forehead to mine.

"Fuck, baby. I won't sack you," he whispers, breathing hard, obviously aroused as he tries to hold himself back. "And I won't transfer you, either. I already told you that. It was rotten of me to even think it, I know, but I'm glad I told you the truth. From now on, I want us to be completely honest with each other."

"I've always told you the truth, Sebastian. You're the one who had secrets all along." I sigh, letting my hands slide down his rock-hard chest as he pulls back to look at me. "I think deep down I knew. I knew you couldn't be so kind. That men like you always expect something in return."

He exhales heavily. "Look, you were right to be suspicious before. It's even understandable if you feel that way now."

No shit, Sherlock!

"But woman, you've got one hell of an active imagination, and, quite frankly, a very cynical view on life, on people." He pauses, his eyes searching mine. "And I think ... I think I can understand you better for it. I myself have trouble seeing past the bad, the ugly. Even when the good is staring me right in the face." He shrugs. "I guess it's just easier to always expect the worst. That way you don't get disappointed, don't get hurt, and ... fuck, I guess what I'm trying to say is we're very much alike, you and I, more than you could ever imagine."

Surprised he finally told me something real about himself, I don't quite know how to react. He's ripping me wide open before his eyes, and my first instinct is to run, hide, push him away. Yet he's also giving me a little glimpse into his mind, the first in all this time, and I can't help but feel intrigued.

Searching his face, I hope to find more answers to the enigma that is Sebastian Hunter, but in the end, it's the vulnerability and sadness I see in his beautiful blue eyes that finally gets to me.

He's being honest this time. I can tell. And, in his own way, trying his damnedest to open up to me.

But is it enough? I wonder. Enough to let him in? To take the risk?

Because I get the feeling a man like him will never let me in as much as he's forcing his way into my heart, and I don't think that will ever be enough for me.

"Alice, I know I behaved very badly. In fact, I can't remember a time when I haven't, but the truth is you've had me from the start. Something in me changed since the very first moment I saw you, and even if I was being stubborn and kept telling myself all I wanted was to have you in my bed, I think deep down I always knew it wasn't true. I need more. I need you ... all of you."

He holds my face between his hands, his expression intense, sincere as he wipes the remaining tears from my cheeks. "Alice, the day I met you my heart became yours."

I'm still stunned by his words when he draws me into his arms, his lips lingering as they gently kiss my forehead, my cheeks, and then move towards my mouth, capturing my lips in the most beautiful, deep, sensual kiss of my life.

Damn, Sebastian Hunter can kiss. Was born to kiss, and no fantasy of mine could ever measure up.

Moaning, I slide my hands into his hair, tugging him, holding him close to me as his tongue tangles and twists deliciously with mine. He groans and the kiss turns hard, his lips taking possession of mine, breaking down my resistance, my fears, my doubts, until there's only his sweet taste in my mouth.

He sucks on my lips before releasing them, and then goes on peppering kisses all over my face. "Delicious. So fucking delicious. You're fucking everything to me now," he whispers, his eyes smouldering hot, and for once I'm thankful for the strong grip he has on my ass. I'm sure that with the way my lungs are burning and my knees are shaking, I'd be having a close encounter with the floor otherwise.

"Mine. This sweet little mouth is mine, Alice. Do you understand? You're mine!" And before I can even think of a reply, he's kissing me again, possessing my mouth like he owns it, like it's his. Showing me with every lash and stroke of his tongue that he means it. That my body now belongs to him.

My caveman's staking his claim. Marking his prize like any dignified barbarian would.

And I think I like it ...

I think I like it a lot.

Straightening to his full height, he uses the grip he has on my behind to lift me into his arms, making my legs automatically wrap around his waist.

God, he's turning me into a slut. A few kisses with this man and I don't even recognise myself. But then he's sucking on my tongue, pulling it into his mouth, and all rational thought leaves my brain.

Next thing I know, he has me on his desk, his lips still glued to mine and his hips between my thighs as he grinds the huge erection in his trousers against my centre.

He grunts, and papers scatter all over the floor. A muffled thump in the background seems serious, and I think I may be sitting on his phone, but I can't bring myself to care.

No, at this moment, all I can think about is the mouth devouring mine, the delicious movement of his hips between my thighs, and this warm, tingling feeling spreading in my chest, telling me that I finally belong to someone. That I finally may have found the person who also belongs to me.

So screw it. You only live once. And slutty or not, this feels way too good to be bad.

Or maybe it is bad, and that's why it feels so good. I don't know.

Whatever this is, though, I've only ever felt it with Sebastian. Only he can make my body come alive like this.

When he's nibbling and sucking on my lower lip. When he's groaning into my mouth. When his hands are all over my body as if he'll die if he doesn't touch me.

"From now on these luscious lips will only be swollen from my kisses," he murmurs into my lips right before he sucks them into his mouth. "We're together now, exclusively, do you hear me? So no more crying, and definitely no more kissing—unless it is with me." Holding my jaw, he forces me to meet his gaze, his eyes intense.

"Does that go for you too?" I ask, my tone incredulous. "Do you really expect me to believe that?" I don't mean to sound so harsh, but jealousy is sinking its teeth into my heart. Throw some trust issues and an active imagination into the mix—as Sebastian so kindly pointed out—and voilà, bitchy Alice is in the house.

He blows out a breath, and I close my eyes to block him out. "Alice, look at me," he says, and I reluctantly meet his gaze. It's open, honest, and dark with desire.

Can I trust myself to read him, though? Or better yet, can I trust him not to hurt me?

"I don't want anybody else. Just you. Only you."

For now, but what will happen to me when he changes his mind? How will I survive?

Frowning, he scans my face with fiery eyes. "Is there someone else? Is that why you're coming up with excuses?"

Christ, jealous much? I almost laugh at the thought. He gave me my first kiss, for heaven's sake. He must know I'm not experienced, so why is he asking about other guys?

"Answer me. Now," he demands, his voice quiet, too quiet. Shit, he's scary when he talks like this.

Still, my body doesn't seem to care as my core clenches and my nipples tighten to the point of pain. Scary Sebastian, with all his intimidating energy, is sexy as hell, and I can't help but get excited. Yearning for this beast of a man to do whatever he wants with me.

Heat rushes to my cheeks and I swallow hard. Seriously, what is the matter with me?

"There's no one else," I rasp. "Just you." His jaw unclenches, and a slow smile takes over his features again. "I was just thinking you'll get bored with me soon, and ..."

"Hey, I told you that's not going to happen," he says, hugging me tight. "You need to trust me on this, all right? I'm not lying to you. I promise."

Mollified, for now at least, I bury my face in his neck and breathe out a sigh of relief.

"I know you must've heard stories," he begins, his voice husky and deep. "That I'm a playboy. That I sleep around. That I use women and leave ... but that's all over now." My heart begins to beat frantically inside my chest and I close my eyes. Dare I believe?

"Besides, all the women I got involved with knew the score and agreed. So my past will only matter if you let it. I was always upfront with them. There was never the option for more, only sex. I never had a girlfriend, you know? Not even as a boy." He caresses my cheek.

"Why?" I ask as I lean into his touch.

His smile broadens. "Because I never met anyone I wanted. Never met anyone I needed to be with that way ... until you, that is. I only want you, Alice. Fuck, I need you so bad, it's driving me crazy. Especially when I know you want me."

He holds my jaw up, brushing my lower lip with his thumb. "I can feel your need for me every time we kiss, in the way you slide your little hands into my hair and tug, in the way you look at me ..."

His lips touch mine ever so lightly, his tongue licking across my open mouth as I melt, readying myself for his kiss.

He pulls away, though, a knowing smile on his lips as he pins me with his gaze. "There's no reason for us not to be together if we choose this. And I choose this. I choose you, Alice."

"You're my boss, Sebastian," I whisper, naming the main reason why we shouldn't get involved.

"I think we both know by now the only place I want to be your boss is in the bedroom," he drawls, a devilish smirk spreading over his lips.

"I'm being serious," I huff, frustrated he keeps making light of everything I say.

"So am I. Tell me this, then. Apart from your sick leave, when have I ever acted like your boss? Come on, give one example."

"I ... erm ..." I've got nothing. Nothing. Sure, he's strong-willed, frustrating, even insufferable at times, but he's never given me a direct order so far. Quite the opposite, in fact. He fusses over me. He's sweet, kind and offers to help me all the time. Not exactly what you'd expect from a boss at all.

Which makes me realise that this whole time he has actually been treating me like his equal, his friend ... perhaps even his lover.

I look back at him.

"Exactly," he says. "Because I can't act like your boss when all I want is to kiss you. When all I want is to have you in my bed, my bedroom, my house ... Even when you're mad at me and being totally unreasonable."

I press my lips together to stifle a smile. "Even when I'm telling you off?"

"Especially then." He winks, and I can feel myself blush. "You look cute as a button when you're all riled up."

I snort. "I only get riled up because you're messy and easily distracted." He rolls his lips as if to stop his smile from growing bigger, and I press my forefinger to his chest. "Don't you dare laugh. You'll be lucky if Sharon doesn't kill you before I do, you know? Just carry on losing stuff all the time and not listening to anyone. You'll see."

"Trust me, I only lose things at home," he says, and I frown.

What's he on about? He wouldn't do those things on purpose, would he? No. Even Linda and Sharon agree he can be exasperating at times. "Please elaborate," I say, narrowing my eyes at him.

"Well, Miss Lake, to begin with, I blame you for my distracted state of mind." He kisses the tip of my nose. "You can be very … distracting. A man would have to be dead not to take notice of you. And as you know, I'm always very much alive when you're around."

Right on cue his hips roll into mine, emphasising his point, and I gasp. The sensation makes me temporarily forget what we were discussing.

Annoyed that I keep giving in to him, I push into his chest. "Behave." He leans back to look at me, his eyes dancing with mirth. "What about you being messy and losing all your stuff? Is that my fault too? Are you seriously going to blame me for that? And be careful, Mr Hunter. Depending on your answer, I may or may not be in a helping mood for a very long time."

"But you are to blame. You and your tight little ass, of course. I particularly enjoyed that time I got you on your hands and knees, fishing papers from under the couch. Of course, I did shove them there for that purpose alone, but the result … hmm, the result was even better than I could've imagined. Hell of a sight, and again, very distracting. Couldn't hear a word you said, though. Remember how you got mad I wasn't listening?"

I nod, still in shock, and a snort escapes his mouth. "Well, now you know why. And you were right. Men really do suck at multitasking."

I remember that. As well as him saying that a folder fell to the floor and that's why the documents slid under the couch. Unbelievable! "Are you saying you've been behaving like a dick on purpose?"

"You truly are a breath of fresh air, you know that?" he drawls before nuzzling my neck. "Mmm … I wish I didn't have to go to work today," he groans, and I grin, letting my head fall to the side, giving him better access.

His lips continue to caress my sensitive skin. "We'll be having words about this later," I moan, closing my fists around his shirt and pulling him to me. "Don't think I'll forget."

He chuckles into my neck. "The thought didn't even cross my mind. I told you, you look too damn cute when you're all riled up with me." I smile, fixing his tie and the collar of his shirt. "But maybe we can leave that conversation for tomorrow. Tonight, I want to talk about us. No more fear, no more doubts, and most importantly, no more hiding what we feel. I want to put your mind at ease. I want you to believe in me, in us." His eyes hold mine. "Sooo ... I'm taking you out to dinner."

"You're taking me on a date?" I ask, surprised, excitement bubbling up in my chest, my stomach.

"Yes, I'm taking my girl on a date." He chuckles, and I smile so big I think my face might split in two. Then he's sliding his tongue across my mouth as I melt against him, his lips sucking and teasing mine until my breath rushes out, and he takes them in the most wonderful slow, lingering kiss.

God, he's amazing. This is amazing ... and I don't want it to ever end.

Too soon he's pulling away and placing me back on my feet, eliciting a small wail of complaint to leave my still-tingling lips. Breathing hard, he presses his forehead to mine. "I have to go before I end up fucking you on my desk," he growls, sending shivers down my spine. His words are strangely exhilarating.

"Yes ... you should ... go," I breathe. I really should tell him I've no experience, and that being 'fucked on a desk' is not how I pictured my first time. But for some reason the words won't leave my mouth.

"Come on then," he says, turning me away from him and slapping my behind.

He laughs out loud when I yelp in surprise. Then he puts on his jacket, grabs his phone from the desk, and, holding my hand in his, leads the way to the front door.

When we reach the main hall, he turns to face me. "Stop worrying until you hear me out, OK?" He clasps my chin, forcing me to look into his eyes.

I nod, feeling suddenly shy. This guy is way too sexy for me. "OK," I reply.

"Trust me. You have nothing to fear, I promise. I'll see you this evening, sweetheart." Sebastian drops a chaste peck on my lips and opens the door.

I step outside with him and stand by the open door. "Have a good day," I rasp, shaking slightly from the morning chill as I wrap my arms around myself.

I watch him until he reaches the car, swooning like a schoolgirl with a crush when he throws me one last look over his shoulder and winks at me before getting inside.

Oh, my, I'm in trouble here.

Especially now my heart is in his hands—and my happiness depends entirely on what he does with it.

* * *

Back inside, I close my eyes and lean with my back against the door, unable to move. Unable to speak. Unable to do much of anything, really.

He said he wants me. That he wants to talk about us, and that his heart is mine. He called me his girl.

Covering my face with both hands, I muffle my excited scream as I begin to jump like a crazy person on the spot.

Oh, God! Oh, God! Oh, God! I can't believe this is happening. I can't believe Sebastian really wants us to be together. Like together together, as in a proper relationship.

Then again, what if I'm reading too much into this? I gasp. He said he wants us to be together, he didn't say anything about it being official.

My hands drop to my chest and I freeze. This could just be a ploy to get into my pants. A ploy where he asks me to be his girlfriend, yes, but with the stipulation that we keep it quiet for a while. For work, his family, to protect his public image ...

Shoot! Dejected, I slump against the door again as a lump forms in my throat.

Well ... I guess I'll find out tonight, won't I?

Of one thing I'm sure, though, I have to at least hear him out. I owe it to myself.

And if he does indeed disappoint ... Maybe it will make it easier to forget him. Maybe it will make it easier not to think about him.

Smiling sadly, I shake my head, already knowing that's not true.

No, I won't forget him any time soon. But I won't stay with him either. I'd much rather spend an eternity alone than feel lonely and hollow for even a second in the arms of the one I love. It'd kill me knowing he didn't love me back. That being with me or any other woman means exactly the same to him.

Thank you, but no, thank you. I have more dignity than that, and if that means that by tonight I'm unemployed and sleeping on the streets, then so be it. Because with him, either I get the whole package or nothing at all. I won't compromise on this.

The sound of my phone snaps me out of my thoughts, and I rush to the kitchen. A ridiculous smile spreads over my face as I recognize the ringtone and almost trip over my own two feet in my haste to answer the call.

"Hello," I say, a little breathless.

God, I really need to get a hold of myself. This guy is turning me inside out already.

"Hey." He's smiling too, I can hear it in his voice. And it makes me so giddy, I have to roll my eyes at myself.

"Did you forget something?" I ask, my smile growing wider. I can't help it.

He chuckles. "No, sweetheart. I have everything I need, exactly where I need it."

"OK," I say, confused. "Then why are you calling? We just talked."

"Ouch, baby. Didn't you miss me? I thought you'd like to hear my voice," he says in a fake-wounded tone, sounding so out of character, I can't help but giggle down the phone. "And now you're laughing at me. Oh, God, the pain. I don't think my heart can take much more." His chuckles reach my ears, and I love it. Love this light, happy version of Sebastian. Love the mood he's in.

"Sebastian, stop," I say between giggles. "You know what I mean."

"I have a surprise for you. Go to your room. I left it on your bed."

"What surprise?" I ask, already making my way to the bedroom. "When did you have time to leave something up there?"

"Impatient little thing, aren't you?" He laughs just as I reach the top of the stairs and turn to walk down the corridor. "You'll find out soon enough. Where are you now?"

"Almost there. I'm just opening the ..."

Oh, my word! I gasp, pressing a hand to my chest.

Hundreds of deep red roses are spread in clear crystal vases all over the space. A large, silver box with a black ribbon and a big, thick bow on top sits proudly in the centre of the bed. And a solitary rose and white card are lying diagonally on it.

God. I'm speechless. I cannot say a word.

"Alice, are you there? Alice?"

"Yes ... I'm ... I'm in my bedroom now," I whisper through a sob.

"Shit. Sweetheart, why are you crying?" he asks, concerned. "You don't have to keep it if you don't like it."

"They're happy tears, I promise. Besides, I haven't looked inside the box yet. I've only seen the flowers."

"So you're happy with just the box and some flowers? Well, that simplifies gift-shopping for you. A lot." He laughs, and I laugh with him despite the tears.

Excited, I climb onto the bed and kneel in front of the box. I put the phone on speaker, placing it on a pillow beside me, and lift the rose to my nose, inhaling deeply. I smile at the scent before laying it next to my phone.

Taking a deep breath, I pull the card from under the ribbon and read it.

To the most beautiful girl in the world.
My girl. My Alice.
Sebastian

Another sob leaves my throat, and Sebastian becomes audibly distressed. "Sweetheart ..."

"Sorry. I'm so sorry," I cut him off, shaking my head the whole time at how surreal this situation actually is. "I'm just not used to receiving gifts, that's all. Pay no mind to me." The words leave my mouth before I can stop them, and I wince as I wait for what I said to sink in.

For him to ask me about my family and friends. To ask me what I mean.

To my relief, he doesn't, though. He just teases me until I'm laughing and smiling again and with another deep breath finally begin to unwrap my gift.

"Now I feel like I'm missing out," he grumbles. "I would've loved to have seen your face, the surprise in your eyes. Fucking meetings."

I smile, thankful he understands my little slip is a touchy subject for me and decided to let it go. Most people would've asked me to elaborate. They would've asked me to talk, and I'm not ready for that. Not yet, anyway. "Don't say that. It means a lot to your dad you're presiding over the staff meetings today. Besides, we're seeing each other tonight. We have a date, remember?"

"How could I forget? That's all I can think about. Now what's taking so long? Tear that fucker up. Come on!"

"Nooo," I cry. "Now who's being impatient?"

His chuckles are music to my ears. "Don't tell me you're one of those people who's careful with unwrapping. Damn it, just my luck."

"It's so lovely I don't want to ruin it. OK, I'm lifting the cover now." God, I'm so giddy my heart might explode.

There's a ton of black, silky tissue paper inside, and I begin to pull it out. And then ...

Then I see it.

A dress. A stunning midnight-blue, chiffon dress. The colour is so rich and sophisticated, I can't help but run my fingers over the fabric, pulling them away almost immediately, afraid I'll ruin it somehow.

Tears fill my eyes. No one's ever given me anything so beautiful in my whole life.

Carefully, I take it out, gasping as a pair of silver stilettos and matching clutch catch the light, sparkling. There's even lingerie—blue, just like the dress, silky and lacy, and a lot racier than anything I usually wear.

Oh, Mr Hunter is a bad boy all right. A bad boy with extraordinarily good taste.

I shake my head, my cheeks ablaze as I pull the last of the tissue out, only to find an entire line of beauty products covering the bottom of the box.

"Sebastian ..." I whisper.

Creams, makeup, perfumes ... I cover my mouth with a shaky hand. Everything a girl would need to prepare for a date and more.

Such a sweet thing for him to do.

And even if part of me—the poor part, I guess—hates to admit it and kinda wants to feel offended, the truth is, I don't own anything this nice. I've never owned anything this nice, which I think is the exact reason why Sebastian is doing this.

He probably didn't want me to feel less or embarrassed when we went out tonight. Especially if he's planning on taking me to one of those swanky places I only ever read about in magazines.

At least that's why I hope he's doing this. He'll be sadly mistaken if he thinks he can buy me.

"So, what do you think?" Sebastian asks, sounding unsure.

Smiling, I pick up the dress and walk over to the mirror. I hold it in front of me. Sexy, fun and sophisticated, it features a teasing Greek neckline, delicate straps and a fitted waist. The skirt is flared and falls just below my knees, and the fabric is so soft and flowy, I can't wait to try it on and spin around like a little girl.

"Do you like it? As I said, you don't have to keep it if you ..."

"I love it! I absolutely love it. All of it," I reassure him. "But this is too much, Sebastian. These things look very expensive, and I can't accept such a gift."

"Do you like it or not?"

"Yes. I told you I do, but that's not the point."

"Then you're keeping it. And Alice, don't deny me this. It's quite rude not to accept a gift, especially when so much thought was put into it."

I frown and walk back to the bed, sitting with the dress on top of my lap. It really is gorgeous. I'd be lying if I said I didn't want it. "I'm sorry. I didn't mean to sound ungrateful. I do love it. It's just that I worry ..."

"I told you not to worry. This is included in the 'not worrying' deal."

"But ..."

"No buts." His voice is tender and raspy, raising goosebumps all over my skin. "I want you to be happy, Alice. It makes me happy."

My heart skips a few beats, and I have to make a conscious effort not to blurt out that all I need to be happy is him.

Shit, I really am in trouble.

"Thank you. You can be very sweet when you want to."

He chuckles. "I guess there's a first for everything. Which reminds me. Margaret, who is my personal shopper, and actually very sweet, is coming to the house this afternoon."

I frown. What?

"She's bringing a whole new wardrobe and some other essentials for you to choose from, as well as a hairstylist and a beautician from her team to help you get ready for tonight."

My frown deepens. No!

"I want you to feel like a princess, Alice. My princess, starting today."

OK, I'm putting my foot down. This is way too much, and he has clearly lost his mind. "Sebastian, no. I can't let you do that. It's too much, and ..."

"Alice, don't argue with me. Margaret has the key, and if you don't work with her, she'll just leave the whole lot there and quite possibly bring more. It's your choice."

Stubborn man! Can't he see I don't care about his money? Can't he see all I care about is him?

"I don't want to take things from you, Sebastian. It's not right, and it makes me feel uncomfortable." I sigh. "So please don't buy me anything else."

"It makes me happy, Alice, and it's non-negotiable. Besides, I've already paid for everything, so you can wear my gifts or leave them to gather dust in the wardrobe. Either way, they're being delivered today."

He already paid? Is he crazy? Unless ... he's doing all this because he really wants something serious and got carried away.

I'm sure he wouldn't invest so much time and effort in a fling, right? Not to mention his money. Christ, how much money did he spend?

Doesn't sit right with me, that's for sure. He's all I want. "You're impossible, you know that?"

"And you're gorgeous, you know that?"

"Stop, I'm being serious," I chastise, or at least I try, seeing he's making me smile again.

I shake my head. Why does he have to be so freaking sweet all the time? Makes it quite difficult to stay mad at him.

Maybe tonight he'll finally give you a reason to succeed, says a small voice in the back of my head.

He laughs. "Just stop overthinking this, Alice, and enjoy being pampered for once. Come on, let the girls help you. You deserve it, sweetheart."

I rub my forehead. Maybe he's right. Maybe I am overthinking this. "Well, you're definitely making me feel like a princess getting ready for the ball."

"That's how you should always feel, baby. I'll make sure of it," he says, his voice low and husky, making me ache, making me tremble for him.

Ryan says something in the background, and a deep groan from Sebastian reaches my ears. "We're here, sweetheart. I have to go." I giggle at how upset he sounds, and he laughs. "I'll pick you up at six."

"OK. I'll see you this evening, Mr Hunter."

"Looking forward to it. Miss Lake. And Alice, please stop worrying. There's nothing to worry about."

Chapter 8

Sebastian

The elevator pings and the doors slide open on my floor.

I slip my hands into my suit trouser pockets and step out, my face nearly splitting in two as I cross the foyer towards my office at the back. "Good morning," I say to the girls at the front desk.

"Good—good morning, sir," they both stammer at the same time.

I don't believe I've ever spoken to either of them. Guess there's always a first time.

My smile grows wider. It's crazy, but I feel like I could take on the fucking world today.

She's mine. Alice is finally mine and isn't going anywhere.

I remember how fucking awesome she felt against me last night, imagine how much better she'll feel tonight, and I almost groan at the vision. Christ, I can barely wait.

My head is still spinning from our earlier conversation this morning, though, and that wasn't something I expected. At least not when the plan was to make things harder for her. Avoid her until she couldn't take it any more, and then pounce.

Fuck, I almost couldn't keep a straight face when she followed me into the study. What I didn't plan was for her to be so honest, so pure. And those tears ... those fucking tears cut right through my cold, numb heart.

Next thing I knew, I was spilling my guts to her. Telling her things I shouldn't. Things I've never told anyone.

And even if in the end it all worked out to my advantage, I still cringe at how much I actually told her about me.

We're already attuned to each other, picking up easily on one another's moods, emotions, needs and feelings. Even when I do my best to hide mine from her. So I can't help but worry that maybe I told her too much, showed her too much, and she'll use this information to weaken me. To burrow her way under my skin and make me need her even more. And not in a sexual way either, but in a way I haven't needed anyone in a long time.

It scares me. That and her thirst for knowledge. Her need for honesty at all times. She's got dignity, guts, more than any other woman I've ever met and ever will. I already know that.

Which makes me even more nervous, since she's also the only woman I've ever lied to in my whole life. Not to mention the only one who didn't deserve it.

Fuck, I knew this was going to come back and bite me in the ass. I drag a hand over my face.

In my defence, I was desperate. Still am. I've never felt this way before, and the need to keep her and get close to her was overwhelming, taking away all sense of logic and reason until I just couldn't help myself. Couldn't stop myself no matter how much I tried.

Now she matters. More than I'll ever admit to her or even myself.

More than I should ever have allowed her to.

* * *

Luke is already waiting for me and talking to Sharon when I walk past her desk.

"Good morning," I say to both of them, perhaps a little too cheerfully, making me regret the words as soon as I register the looks of shock written all over their faces.

Great, now I've probably freaked them out. I'm not exactly known for spreading cheer and joy around the office.

I keep walking, not stopping to chat. Which is probably for the best. God only knows what else I'll let slip when I'm feeling like this.

"Good morning, Sebastian. Your coffee's already inside," Sharon calls.

"Thank you, Sharon. And hold my calls, will you? I'll let you know when I'm ready."

"Hey, wait up," Luke says, running after me.

I speed up, already knowing what he wants. Nosey bugger.

"What happened?" he asks with no preamble as soon as he's by my side.

I draw my brows together. "Nothing. Nothing happened. Why?"

"Come on, man. You're never this happy. Especially in the morning. So spill. Why is Mr Grinch smiling like a kid on Christmas morning?"

That makes me chuckle. "Well, good morning to you too, bro. And seriously, the Grinch? You couldn't come up with a nicer analogy for me?"

His hand on my shoulder brings us to a halt and he moves to stand in front of me. "You fucked her."

The way he says it, it's not even a question, it's a statement. "Careful," I grit out, my jaw clenched tight. Luke's my brother, but right now, I could break his neck.

He stares me down, assessing, then grins. "Yeah, you fucked her."

"That's none of your business." I go to move, but his hand on my shoulder tightens.

"Of course it's my fucking business. You've been way too distracted with her. Maybe now she's opened her legs, you can focus on work again."

"What the fuck did you just say to me?" I growl, getting in his face, my happiness replaced by the need to tear into something with my bare hands. And fuck, I'm almost as high on it as I was elated.

He continues to grin, but a flash of worry crosses his eyes. Good. He knows I'm serious then. "Calm down, man. I just meant that now she can help you relax instead of giving you added stress. You know, keep you satisfied, so you can stop obsessing over her."

"I'm warning you, Luke. Don't you dare talk about her," I push out between my teeth. My hands close into fists, my whole body readying for a fight.

Luke's smile broadens, and I narrow my eyes at him. I've never hit my brother before, at least nothing outside sparring matches and training, but I know he won't back down. We're too alike. All four of us are. "She must be a very hot fuck if you keep threatening me like this." I clench my jaw. "Hmm, intriguing. Who knows, maybe if I ask nicely, she'll give me a taste."

I lose it then. I just fucking lose it, and before I know what I'm doing, I'm punching my brother in the face. Blinding rage guides me as I throw myself at him. And then we're falling, rolling on the floor and grunting as each of us tries to overpower the other.

In a pussy move, he manages to land a punch to my side. I feel the force of it travelling down my ribs, barely registering any pain. Instead, I welcome the new surge of adrenaline coursing through my veins, his little stunt only serving to fuel my anger.

He's a big guy, but I'm bigger. I'm also older and stronger, so I find myself on top. I pull back my arm and throw another punch, and another, and another, making sure his jaw will have a nice, big bruise to go with his split lip.

"Sebastian!" Strong arms pull me off him, and I struggle against their hold, teeth bared and growling like an animal as I reach for Luke again. Now that I've started, I just want to finish the fucking job.

"What the hell is going on here?" my dad booms, getting between us just as Luke gets up—ready to make another move for me, no doubt—forcing Dad to place a hand on each of our chests to keep us apart. "Stop this! Now!"

Ryan has me in a tight chokehold, but is struggling to keep me subdued. Not many men are capable of pulling me off someone in the first place, let alone holding me back when I'm like this.

"Calm down, Sebastian. Calm the fuck down!" Ryan grinds out, and I give Luke a threatening grin.

"My brother has a fucking lesson to learn, and I plan on doing the teaching," I snarl as I almost break free.

Tightening his hold on me, Ryan pulls me back, and my dad gets in my face. "Sebastian, stop! Stop this, son!"

Minutes pass, but eventually I focus on him, his face, his voice, and the fury inside me starts to subside. Adrenaline is still coursing through my veins. I'm high on it, but at least I'm not trying to beat Luke's face into a pulp any more.

Ryan feels the difference and releases me, giving me a few hard slaps on the back. "OK, man. OK, that's good. Just take a deep breath."

"What did you do?" Dad growls, turning on Luke like the Devil.

"Why do you always assume I did something? That it's somehow my fault?"

"Because your brother doesn't usually behave like this," Dad shouts. "I'll ask you one last time. What did you do to turn him into a raging lunatic?"

"OK, OK. I might've said some inappropriate stuff about Alice—"

"You're such a fucking asshole," I growl, launching myself at Luke just as my dad gets in the way, holding me back. "Inappropriate, my ass! You'll never speak her name again! You hear me? I'll fucking end you if you speak her name again!"

"Why, Luke? You know Alice is special to your brother," Dad says.

"Yeah, she's special all right. I get that," Luke says. "What I don't get is why the fuck he's not telling us the truth about how he really feels about her."

"It's none of your fucking business," I hiss through my teeth. "I told you not to talk about her."

"You never had any qualms discussing your whores before. What's so different about this one?"

Seeing red, I shove my dad out of the way and throw Luke against the wall. I knee him in the gut a few times, then, gripping the front of his suit jacket, I lift him clean off the floor and roar in his face. "She's my woman, you bastard. The woman I fucking love and—" I gasp, unable to finish the sentence. I feel like I'm the one who got hit in the gut.

Love. I love Alice. I fucking love her.

I swallow hard. I think deep down I've known for a while. I just didn't let myself admit it.

It was easier to believe the lie. To focus on the lust I was feeling. But love? Fuck, it couldn't be. I just couldn't accept it. Couldn't open myself up to it. Even when I realised that what I felt for Alice was stronger than anything I'd ever felt before.

Still, I resisted. Alice is intelligent, gorgeous. Sex on legs. She's also kind and witty—downright funny, come to think of it, always making me laugh and feel good about myself—and caring. She's so fucking caring, that girl.

My chest constricts. I'd already accepted that I liked her, that I like myself better when I'm with her. And with my obsession growing stronger by the second, I'd even decided to ignore my fears and make her mine.

"Sorry. I shouldn't have ... I ... I went too far." Luke shakes his head. "I'm sorry, Sebastian. I just wanted you to admit your true feelings, that's all."

I don't react. I can't. Can't let go of him yet. Even seeing him struggle to catch his breath doesn't faze me.

Then my trembling body is once again pulled off Luke, and moments later I find myself inside my office, sitting on the couch with no recollection of how I got here.

"Calm down, Sebastian. Calm down." My dad pats my shoulder as he stands next to me. "You're OK. It's OK, son. This is a good thing. Alice is perfect for you. You couldn't have chosen a better woman."

"No. No, it's not OK." My voice comes out harsh, the muscles in my jaw working overtime as I shake my head. "What if I lose her? What if she leaves?" Resting my elbows on my knees, I hide my face between my hands. "I can't do this. I can't. It will destroy me." Suddenly I can't get enough air. My head spins out of control and my heart begins to beat against my ribs.

Fuck, what's happening to me?

"Boys, please leave," my dad says, and then his hands are holding my face. "Breathe, Sebastian. It's OK, it's just us now. Come on, breathe, son," he pleads, but I can't focus on anything. "Look at me," he shouts, shaking me once, and finally precious oxygen fills my lungs. "That's it. Nice and slow now. In and out. In and out."

Breathing hard, I focus on his voice, his face, on the worry still obvious in his eyes, and I begin to calm down. I'm nowhere near normal, no, but at least I'm not about to pass out.

"Talk to me, son." He's crouching in front of me, holding my shoulders. "I'm your dad, Sebastian. No one in this world could possibly want you to be as happy as I do. Talk to me."

I shake my head, the words stuck in my throat, my eyes burning as if I'm about to cry. No, not possible. I haven't shed a tear since ...

"Is this because of your mum?"

I don't react, don't move a muscle as I stare into his eyes.

He sighs and sits next to me, our shoulders touching as he also rests his elbows on his knees. "Losing your mum is the hardest thing that's ever happened to me." He pauses, as if steeling himself to talk about her.

"I loved her so much ..." His voice breaks and he swallows hard. "More than life itself. I thought we would have our whole lives together." He looks at me with so much pain and love in his eyes, I drop my head down into my hands again.

"That said, if I were given the choice to go back in time and not meet her, not be with her ... I wouldn't change a thing. Because being with your mum is also the very best thing that's ever happened to me. So how could I deny myself the most wonderful years of my life, years I got to spend in her company?"

Slowly, I raise my head and meet his eyes. They're glassy with tears. Same as mine, I'm sure.

"Dad ..." I whisper after swallowing the lump in my throat. "How can you say that? I saw you crumble into pieces with my own eyes. You became half the man you were before."

"I know, son. I know," he says, his eyes fixed on mine. "And for that I'll always be sorry. Your mum took a piece of my soul when she left us, and I didn't know how to make myself whole again." He sighs. "It took me a long time to realise that she also left a piece of her soul with me."

I frown. "What do you mean?"

"I mean you." He throws his arm over my shoulders. "You and your brothers. My memories with her. Our undying love for each other. Because make no mistake, I will always love your mother. I'll love her until the day I die, and I was lucky that she loved me the same way. That's what life is all about. Nothing else matters."

"I don't think I could go through something like that and survive," I admit.

"You don't. No one does. No one's ever the same. But what are you going to do? Let the love of your life get away? Not live your life to the fullest because you're afraid? The truth is we're all dying from the moment we're born, son. That's what gives meaning to life. You know this is what you have. The here, the now. So you have to seize it. Make it count. The plans you both make will always be important and special, even if you don't get to live them. Because those moments you lie in bed talking about them, sharing secrets and desires and loving each other, those moments will forever be yours, and no one, absolutely no one, can take them away."

He pulls me in for a hug then, and I cling to him just like I did when I was a boy. Back when this larger-than-life man was my hero. Back when he and Mum meant everything to my brothers and I.

My eyes blur and I squeeze them shut, realising how much I missed this. How much I missed him.

In a way, I guess I felt like I lost him too. He was devastated after Mum passed, and I was in too much pain myself to understand why he couldn't be there for us in the way I wanted him to. So I closed myself off, hardened my heart, and welcomed the numbness that came along with it.

I was determined not to let the pain win, not to let what was happening to my dad ever happen to me, and for that I needed to toughen up. Needed to stop being a kid. Needed to forget about love, feelings, and childhood dreams.

Then Alice happened ... and all caution and control went out of the window.

"Thanks, Dad," I tell him, clutching his back. "I really appreciate you telling me all this."

We break away, but he keeps his hands on my shoulders. "Just do me a favour, Sebastian. Don't ever let go of that girl. The worst things in life are regrets, especially the 'what ifs'. Trust me, you don't want to look back and think you missed out. That you lost the love of your life without ever really having her ."

"I won't," I whisper, and I mean it. I'm still scared. Terrified of what I feel, really. But my dad's right, I can't live a life full of regrets. Alice is the love of my life, and I won't let go when my every instinct tells me to take her. When my every cell's screaming at me to make her mine. I shake my head. "I won't ever let her go, believe me."

"Good. That's what I wanted to hear. You're a Hunter, son. Through and through. And us Hunter men never let go of what's ours. Besides, you deserve to be happy. That's all I've ever wanted for you." With that he gives my shoulders a squeeze and gets up, leaving me alone with my thoughts.

I shake my head and blow out a breath. We've never talked about our feelings before—particularly the unresolved, painful ones—and I have to admit I'm shaken to my core.

Sighing, I get up and walk towards the window. I slide my hands into my pockets and stare out at the blue sky, at the grey clouds parting to give way to a shining sun.

It seems I needed this. Needed to hear my dad talk about my mother like that. Needed to hear that he didn't regret her—didn't regret us—despite his loss and his pain.

Strangely, it felt like his blessing to me. Like the final push I needed to make a go of things with Alice. To keep her and love her the way she deserves.

Like I've been set free of some of the guilt I was harbouring inside me. Guilt that was misplaced, I know, but nevertheless real.

And I can finally breathe. I can finally feel the light calling to me.

***

The rest of the day goes by slowly, and I find myself counting down the seconds, wanting to see Alice again.

God, I can't wait to hold her and kiss her. To tell her how much I want her and how much she means to me.

And when it's time to leave the office, I'm so eager to get home, I almost run to the SUV. Almost.

Suddenly I feel like laughing, and not just any laughter, no, but belly-deep, crazy laughter. I squash it down, though, ignore the urge and concentrate hard on breathing.

Maybe I'm going insane. Maybe I'm losing my mind more the harder I fall for my girl.

I grin. My girl. I sure like the sound of that.

Staring straight ahead, I put everything I've got into maintaining a fast, but somewhat normal pace as we all cross the garage and the guys finish doing their sweep.

Ryan snickers beside me and then coughs, trying to cover it up.

I glance at the guards in front of us, but they all continue doing their thing. Professional, polite and just as qualified as Ryan is, they're a good team. The best. After all, it's no accident they came to work for me. Not when Ryan and I handpick all of our guards ourselves.

"Just say it," I groan, keeping my voice down as I send him a glare.

"No, man. I'm good." He shakes his head. "Too much testosterone ruling your brain. Not to mention you've picked enough fights for one day."

"Fuck off, Ryan."

"See? That's exactly what I mean. And it's not going to get any better until you fu—"

"Don't." I give him a pointed look and whatever he's about to say dies in his throat. Good.

"Sort ... I meant sort things out with Alice. 'Cause, bro, honestly, at this rate, I don't think we can take any more of your mood swings."

"We? Who the fuck is we, asshole?" I ask, giving him a shove.

He laughs. "Look, all I'm gonna say is that Alice is amazing, beautiful, and incredibly good for you ... and you're one lucky son of a bitch to have her. Not to mention a lot nicer and a lot more fun to be around since she's been living with you. But man, you become an absolute ass whenever you're upset with her or with something that involves her in any way. It's like you have a personality disorder or some shit."

"Just shut up and drive, Ryan," I grumble when we finally get inside the SUV, a black Porsche Cayenne with tinted windows. "And FYI, nobody asked for your opinion, OK?"

He grins at the rear-view mirror before pulling out of the parking space. "God, I really hope she takes you off my hands soon. Can't protect you against the mob of disgruntled employees when they finally murder you. Hell, I may even join them." He bursts out laughing, and I feel my own lips twitching.

"You'd be out of work and in prison, dickhead."

"Well, we can't have everything, can we?"

"I don't know, man, I feel like I have everything I'll ever need when I'm with Alice," I admit, deciding to finally open up about my feelings for her. It feels good. Feels right.

"Yeah, you have it bad, my friend. Never thought I'd see the day, but here you are, all fucked up over a girl."

"You're an idiot. You know that?"

"What? It's true. You'll see. That's what women do to men. They pussy-whip you into shape and then fuck you up until you don't feel like one of the lads any more. I'm telling you, pretty soon, you won't even want to go out with us. You'll be too busy to make time for your friends."

Laughing, I drag a hand over my face and then yawn. This has been one long-ass day for me.

"And why would I want to feel like 'one of the lads' when Alice makes me feel like 'the man'?" I ask, amused. "Not to mention I'd much rather spend my nights being 'pussy-whipped into shape' than go out with any of you ugly fucks."

Yeah, preferably on my back with Alice riding me hard.

Ryan bites his lip, clearly trying to stop laughing.

"Jealousy is unbecoming, Ryan, even for you," I drawl, deciding to mess with him.

"Nah. Haven't met a girl yet who has had that effect on me. Don't believe I ever will either."

"That's what I used to say. Now look at me."

"Shut up, you're being a dick," he grumbles.

My grin widens. Yeah, payback's a bitch, Ryan. Payback's a bitch ... and I'll be waiting for the day you fall. You can count on me, my friend.

You can count on me.

* * *

Getting up from the couch, I pour myself another whisky while I wait for Alice to come down. I finish it in two gulps and fill my glass again.

Usually, I don't drink this much, especially before dinner. But I'm feeling frantic—a mix of nerves and excitement dancing in the pit of my stomach—so I guess I truly am in need of liquid courage tonight.

Fuck, what is this girl doing to me? To my cool, my calm?

Taking a sip, I pace myself this time and walk towards one of the floor-to-ceiling windows near the couch. I can't stand still, though, and after only a few seconds, I end up pacing the floor, images of all the dirty things I want to do to Alice invading my mind until I'm ready to knock on her door.

Throwing my head back, I down the rest of my drink and close my eyes, letting the burn of the alcohol steady my nerves and calm my raging hard-on.

At least until I see her again. Until I touch her. Because, guaranteed, no amount of liquor will help me then. It never does.

Just as no amount of control will either. Particularly if she looks half as ravishing as I'm picturing her right now.

I pinch the bridge of my nose. I can't remember the last time I was this nervous about anything, this rattled.

But what if she's changed her mind? What if she doesn't want to give this a chance any more? Give us a chance?

We haven't seen each other since morning. I could hear the girls still fussing over her when I came in, so I went straight into my bedroom to shower, not wanting to interrupt. Now I'm regretting my decision.

She's not like other girls. Most definitely not like my usual conquests, who I could always charm with money and looks.

No, with her, I'll have to make an effort. I'll have to do something I've never done before—I'll have to romance her. Be so swoonworthy she'll have no choice but to melt in my arms.

Only then will she trust me. Only then will she truly give herself to me. She can't help it. She's a good girl. It's ingrained in her DNA.

Resisting the urge to pour myself another drink, I place the glass on the coffee table and go wait by the bottom of the stairs. I glance at the mirror in the hall and adjust my tie.

I'm wearing a dark grey suit, a crisp white shirt, and a midnight-blue tie to compliment Alice's dress. I know I look good. Handsome and sharp. All my life, women have told me I'm attractive, and even if they didn't, the hungry looks they throw my way would attest to that. Designer clothes or not.

Still, I can't stop fidgeting like a boy. Can't stop wondering if Alice will be impressed.

I've never dressed with someone in mind before, but with her, I want to please. I want her to want me just as much as I long for her to be mine.

Flicking my wrist, I check the time again and blow out a breath. What's taking her so long?

I slide my hands inside my pockets and stare at the ground until I hear it—the sound of high heels approaching the stairs.

A huge smile spreads over my face as I look up, and there she is.

"Holy fucking shit," I whisper as I momentarily forget how to breathe.

Even the fact that my trousers are tightening, trapping my hard-on painfully and pressing it against the zipper, doesn't faze me. I discreetly adjust myself. I bet if she knew what she was doing to me, she'd run the other way.

She looks ravishing. A wet dream as she starts making her way down the stairs and towards me. Her every curve is accentuated by the dress, her every movement so flawless and ladylike, I just want to throw her over my shoulder and finish what we started last night.

I owe Margaret a big thank you, that's for sure. This dress is sexy as hell.

You won't be disappointed, Mr Hunter, she promised. And as I let my eyes roam over Alice's body, letting them settle on her breasts—no doubt where they'll be glued the rest of the night—I have to agree, disappointment is the furthest thing from my mind.

"You look stunning. Absolutely stunning, sweetheart," I tell Alice as soon as she's within my reach, and offer her my hand to help her down.

Smiling bashfully, she takes it, and in that moment, I know without a shadow of doubt that there isn't a thing I won't do to keep that smile on her face. That I'd walk through fire to make her happy.

Worry and jealousy gnaw at my insides. Worry for all the shit I've ever done—the women, the fast life, anything with the potential to destroy what we have now. And jealousy because I won't be the only man to see her like this tonight.

"Thank you," she says. "You're looking quite stunning yourself, Sebastian. You're a very handsome man." My chest fills with pride, and I bend to kiss her cheek.

I like that she finds me handsome. Never cared before. My looks were merely a means to an end. But with her, it feels different. I want to woo her, sweep her off her feet, so it doesn't hurt that she likes the way I look.

My lips linger on her smooth skin as her breath hitches. And it's there again, the insane, out-of-this-world chemistry we share, igniting a blazing fire between us and making me almost lose my mind.

Fuck. I close my eyes and swallow hard. It never ceases to amaze me how strongly I react to this girl or how quickly she responds to me.

I rein myself in and kiss the smooth skin of her other cheek as it turns pink, absolutely loving the fact I can make her blush like this. Her lips part and her breath catches, and I have to stifle a groan.

Oh, baby, I want to kiss you too, believe me, but we need to take things slow.

She smells so good, though, strawberries and vanilla and her own personal scent, that I want to give in. I almost give in.

"Shall we go?" I ask, grinding my teeth together and taking a step back.

"Yes, of course. Sorry." She shakes her head a little, as if to clear it, and I grin like an idiot at having such an effect on her. God knows she has it on me.

Resting my hand against the small of her back, I guide her to the entry hall wardrobe and, like the perfect gentleman, help her with her coat and scarf before putting on my own.

She runs her hands down the front of her new coat. "It's so soft. So lovely," she says in wonder.

"Just like you," I rasp, brushing my knuckles along her jaw.

"Thank you, Sebastian."

I smile, loving how she says my name. But then she's looking down, avoiding my eyes, and I'm not so sure I like where this is going.

"No one's ever given me such beautiful gifts," she says in a quiet voice. "I'm not used to it. No one ... no one ever cared before."

My fingers slide under her chin, forcing her to meet my gaze just as tears start gathering in her eyes.

Shit, it cost me next to nothing to do this. Yet it means so much to her. "Now you have me to care. To be thoughtful and considerate of all your needs. To fulfil your every desire."

"Do I?" she asks, searching my eyes.

"Yes," I reply, and I've never been so sure about anything in my whole life. Her needs, her desires, they're all above mine. For as long as she's happy, I'm happy. "I'll give you anything you want, Alice. Anything your little heart desires. All you have to do is ask."

"I don't need material things to make me happy, Sebastian. The fact that you thought of me, that you wanted to make me feel special, that's what makes me happy."

Gobsmacked, I stare at her. I'm not used to women like her. With so much depth, so much emotion.

There's not a bad bone in this girl's body. No greed in her sparkling grey eyes, and I'm not quite sure what to say. I don't want to end up hurting her in any way.

"Let's go. We have much to talk about tonight." With that I reach for her delicate hand, entwining our fingers together, and kiss the back of it before leading her out.

* * *

Parked in the driveway, my dad's custom-made black Rolls-Royce limousine comes into view straight away, and Alice raises her free hand to cover her gaping mouth.

"You ... you didn't ... why?" she gasps, her steps coming to a halt.

I shrug. "Because I can. Because you're mine. Because I told you I'll always make you feel like a princess from here on out."

"Sebastian, this is too much," she says, turning to face me. "People will think I'm taking advantage of you, that—"

"Shh." I press my forefinger to her lips. "It will be a cold day in hell, sweetheart, when someone manages to take advantage of me. Besides"—I brush her hair off her face and enjoy how she shivers under my touch—"apart from my family, I don't give a fuck about what other people think. And as far as my family goes, the thought that I'm being taken advantage of won't even enter their minds."

Yeah, they know me only too well. The real me. The cold suit. The mean bastard who's always in control. The thought that I'm being conned by Alice would only make them laugh.

She's about to say something else, so I lift her hand to my lips and kiss it, distracting her. She shivers, goosebumps spreading all over her arms, and her pulse picks up.

Never breaking eye contact, I let my tongue slide across her silky skin as she looks up at me in a daze. Her lips part and she blushes, closing her eyes, her breaths coming in quick succession as she melts under my touch.

Fuck, she's so much sweeter, so much better than anything I've ever imagined. So much more than I've ever dared to desire.

In a heartbeat my good intentions are all but forgotten, and I pull her into my arms, my hand sliding into the back of her hair as I take her full lips in a deep, sensual kiss that leaves us both dizzy and breathless and totally high on each other.

Mmm, hard enough to cut through diamond? Check.

Leaking pre-cum like a faucet? Check.

Holding the girl of my dreams in my arms? Check. Check. Check.

My fingers twitch, itching to tear apart the wispy, delicate fabric of her dress. I want to bury myself in her, and for a moment I seriously consider dragging her upstairs to my bedroom.

I smile against her lips, already imagining myself ripping the sexy little dress to shreds, then her lingerie, then throwing her on my bed and plunging my aching cock deep inside of her.

"Sebastian," she moans, most certainly sensing my desperation, and I finally lose control, pushing my tongue deeper into her mouth. Fucking it. Possessing it. Just as I'm imagining fucking her with my shaft.

She tastes so good. Like strawberries and cream, and I can't resist her. Can't deny myself any more when all I want is to give in, to let go and succumb to this hunger burning me from within. So I feast. I devour. I fucking consume her. Her little whimpers and gasps only fuel my desire and spur me on, daring me to just take her, consequences be damned.

She shivers and grips my biceps, her fingers tightening through the layers of my clothes. God, she's perfect. So innocent and pure I barely manage to pull my mouth away, and when I do, she follows. Lips puckered, eyes closed, cheeks blazing pink as she silently begs me for more.

Jesus, I feel like a fucking beast. An animal. I just can't seem to control myself with her.

"Do you know what you do to me?" I whisper, pressing my forehead to hers. "Do you have any idea?"

"Mmm," she moans, and her tongue darts out, licking along my upper lip, slipping into my mouth, coaxing me until I can't fucking think straight any more.

"Alice," I rasp. "We need to stop, baby girl, or I'm going to throw you over my shoulder, take you back inside and fuck you hard and fast on the first surface I find."

She gasps, flushed. She wants me. Not as much as I want her, not possible. But still, she wants me, and that's already more than I deserve.

My eyes search hers. "You make me crazy, you know that? Make me lose control," I admit, watching as she bites her lower lip, trying to hide her smile. Little vixen.

Unable to resist the urge, I kiss her one more time—hard and fast—before lowering her to her feet.

"Do you need to go back inside?" I straighten her coat and scarf. "You know, to fix your hair? Your makeup and stuff?" I ask, trying not to sound too eager.

If she says yes, maybe I could make her come. Have a real taste of her right before we leave.

Just then her eyes widen and her mouth falls open in realisation, and I know she just caught on to me.

I go to grab her again, but much to my disappointment she pushes her hands into my chest. "We should go, Mr Hunter. I wouldn't want us to miss our table. Besides, I'm only wearing lip gloss. I'm confident I can fix whatever damage you've done to me when we get inside the car."

I grin. Yeah, she's onto me, all right, and she's not ready for whatever's going on in my depraved mind. Not yet, anyway.

Which makes perfect sense, of course, when I already knew she's still feeling insecure and undecided regarding our relationship. Our future. That's why I wanted us to talk, planned this night down to the very last detail, and then ... then I almost let my dick get in the way. I'm an idiot.

Especially when I know she's not like that. Not to mention she's way too important for me to fuck her on our very first date. She deserves better than that. She deserves better from me.

"Don't worry, sweetheart. We won't miss a thing," I promise, and, leaving one arm around her, I lead her down the driveway and to our waiting limo.

* * *

The chauffeur comes out and promptly opens the door for us. "Good evening, madam. Good evening, sir."

"Good evening," Alice and I greet, but I can tell she's embarrassed after realising we've been putting on a show for our driver.

I, on the other hand, am grinning from ear to ear. "Thank you," I add, feeling like the man of the hour as I help Alice get inside.

I follow her in and, after removing our coats and scarfs, put the privacy screen up.

"You OK, sweetheart?" I ask, finally turning my attention to Alice, only to find her eyes wide as she takes it all in—the flat screen TV, the cream leather sofas, the electric fireplace, the bar. I smile down at her, and, picking up her hand, I kiss it, feeling her heart rate go up when her eyes finally focus on mine.

There will be lots of firsts, baby. There will be lots of gifts. I'm going to spoil you, and care for you, and make sure no one ever hurts you again for as long as I live.

"Yes, I ... I'm OK. I just need to fix myself a little," she says, getting a compact mirror out of her clutch together with a light-pink tube.

I watch her intently as she fixes her hair and then her makeup. It's sexy. She's sexy, and watch is all I can do as she slides the new, shiny lip gloss brush ever so slowly over her lips.

My jaw slackens as visions of her doing the same with my cock assault my mind instead. Her pouty lips wrapping around my tip right before I push my whole length into the warm recesses of her mouth.

I imagine her plump little lips stretching and struggling to accommodate my girth, the pink gloss smeared all over my dick as she sucks me off, and it's almost enough to make me come.

Shit! Reaching down, I give myself a hard squeeze to relieve some of the pressure. Without my coat, though, and with the suit jacket unbuttoned, the big bulge between my legs is more than a little evident, and when I look up, I catch Alice staring at it, the lip gloss and mirror in her hands all but forgotten as her eyes stay glued to the sizable tent in my trousers.

What can I say? I'm a big guy. Big everywhere.

Laughter bubbles up my throat, but I squash it. She's not experienced. Probably one or two boyfriends at most, and, from the look on her face, much, much smaller than what I'm packing. She wouldn't appreciate the humour.

Also, now that the thought of Alice with other guys has entered my mind, my stomach doesn't feel so good. I grimace. The feeling is so hot and twisted, it's like acid burning me inside out. Filling me with so much rage, I might have to kill every poor fucker who dares to look at her tonight.

It doesn't matter. It's all in the past. I'm the one she sees now. I'm the one she wants. I can see it in her eyes.

I clear my throat, the small sound startling her out of her daze, and her eyes fly up to mine.

I shrug as I give her my best sexy look. "I've already told you I want you, Alice. I'm not hiding the evidence any more. I'm done with that. From now on we don't hide from each other."

Well, for the most part anyway. I still believe some secrets are supposed to be just that: secret. And it's my job to protect her from them.

She blushes furiously. "I did that to you?"

"You always do this to me."

She searches my face, swallowing hard. "It's ... big," she finally says, and this time I'm not able to contain my laughter.

"It's all for you, baby. Never been so hard for anyone in my life. Only you have such an effect on me." I'm serious. So serious, it's not even funny any more. All it takes is for me to think of her, smell her scent, and I'm hard as a rock in record time.

Embarrassed, she fidgets with her clutch, closes it and puts it in the seat across from us. "Does it hurt?"

"It can be painful, yes. The good kind of pain, though. Especially when you're this close."

"Is this all it is?" she asks, still avoiding my eyes.

I know what she's asking. What she's thinking. She's convinced I'll seduce her, take her to bed a few times and then break it off.

She has no idea the kind of power she holds over me. Or how fucked up in love I am with her.

I can't tell her, though. Not yet. Not until I find out exactly how she feels about me, so I do the next best thing.

"No, but I'm not going to lie and say I don't think about fucking you, because I do. Constantly."

Her eyes shoot back to mine, and if I ever had any doubts about this girl's feelings for me, I'm certainly left with none now. I can see her longing, her passion, her hurt from here. Maybe even love.

"In fact, ever since I laid eyes on you, I haven't been able to stop fantasising about all the dirty things I want to do to you ... with you." I slide one finger slowly down her arm, watching as she shivers under my touch, goosebumps appearing all over her skin.

"I want you, Alice. I want all of you. And I'm not going to make excuses because I want you as my lover. Not when I also want you as my friend, my partner, my confidante. Not when I want us to put our trust in each other. To laugh. To kiss. To fight and make love every night." I take her hand from her lap and press it to my cheek. "I want it all, Alice, and I want it with you. I'm falling for you."

"Sebastian ..." she whispers, her lips quivering as tears spill from her eyes.

I press a kiss to her palm and for a moment we stay just like that. Silent, unmoving. Staring into each other's eyes as I give her time to think.

I can't stand that she's crying, though. Can't stand to see her hurting, and after a while I can't take it any more.

"Baby, don't cry." I bring our foreheads together. "Please don't cry. I can't stand to see you like this." I know I'm acting like a caveman, a barbarian really, but I'm beyond-help obsessed with her.

Alice takes a shaky breath and her voice, usually so soft and melodic, comes out thick with tears. "I'm scared, Sebastian."

Shaking my head, I go to speak, but she places her fingers over my mouth, her touch so gentle that a sigh escapes my lips. It's been so long since I've been touched like this. So long since I've allowed someone to get this close to me.

"I'm scared ... because I'm also falling for you." She smiles sadly. "And because it's the last thing someone like me should do."

I'm flying so high that for a while her last words don't even register. "Baby ..." I kiss her temple, pulling her to me, breathing her in.

"You'll become bored, you know? Once the novelty wears off, you'll become bored," she murmurs into my chest.

Yeah, that's what I thought too, and now look at me. Falling head over heels for this sweet, precious girl.

And I haven't even fucked her yet. Imagine if I had.

"I'm just a regular girl, Sebastian. Simple. There's nothing special about me. You'll end up hurting me. Breaking my heart, and—"

"Shh. Shh." I hold her face in my hands, forcing her to look at me. God, she's gorgeous. So fucking beautiful, my heart clenches in pain. "Alice, I couldn't become bored of you even if I tried. You're all I think about. You're all I see. And I know I don't deserve you. That I'm bound to mess this up and upset you sometimes. I've never had a girlfriend and I don't really know what I'm doing here. But I'll never willingly hurt you, baby. I'll never use our closeness to harm you in any way. I give you my word. All I'm asking is for you to give us a chance … to give me a chance … and I promise you, if for whatever reason we don't make it, I'll look after you. I'll help you find another job. Whatever you need financially is yours. You'll never want for anything in your life."

A frown crosses her face and she shakes her head. "I don't want your money, Sebastian. All my life I've worked for what I have. I'm not like that."

"I know you aren't, but I want you to feel free when you're with me. I want you to feel safe. You're the first girl in the longest time to treat me as an actual person. A human being. Not a chunk of meat, a means to an end, or, worse, a bank account." I laugh humourlessly. "Not that it would make me want you any less, I'm afraid. I need you too much, want you too much to let something as small as morals get in the way."

We stare at each other, this underlying current passing between us, something so strong and sexual, I have to concentrate hard just on breathing. "Now say you're mine," I whisper. "Tell me you're mine, baby girl."

"I'm yours, Sebastian," she rasps, her fingers sliding into my hair. "I've always been yours, and that's what scares me the most."

Both fear and excitement flicker in her eyes, and then we're kissing and kissing. Our lips move together in what I can only describe as the sweetest kiss of my life, and I know she's right.

My sweet little thing is mine. Has always been mine.

Just like I've always been hers. Because it's written in the stars.

Chapter 9

Alice

With its nineteen-thirties decor and brown and gold colour scheme, the Glass Room restaurant is the perfect mix of luxury and boldness unlike anything I've ever seen, and I can't help my gasp as a smiling Sebastian guides me out of the lift.

The whole place has this soothing atmosphere that inspires nothing but calm and tranquillity wherever you sit. Fresh white roses and candles flicker at the centre of every table. Golden crystal chandeliers hang low from the ceiling. And it's all so beautiful, so sophisticated, it almost lulls me into believing I can relax. Almost.

Still, it's not the decor, nor the luxury, nor even the ambience that knocks the wind right out of me. It's the view. And what a glorious view it is when one finds themselves surrounded by floor-to-ceiling windows at the very top of the tallest building in London, no less, and with the perfect three-hundred-and-sixty-degree view of the city below.

I stifle a smile.

No wonder they cater to the finest, most elite members of our society. I mean, if I had money, I'd come here too.

Sebastian looks tall and gorgeous in his bespoke suit, Italian loafers and chunky, silver Rolex, and it's obvious we couldn't be more different if we tried.

I sigh and avert my eyes. Suddenly, I feel deflated. Not that I look anything other than amazing right now in my ultra-sexy dress and red-soled designer shoes. I also have good manners and know how to handle myself in any kind of situation.

But even if I look the part tonight, portraying the perfect illusion that I fit right in, I know in my heart that I don't. I don't belong in this world. His world.

And never will.

I'm falling for you, he said, and I so want to believe him. I really do. God knows I've fallen for him already and would like nothing better than for him to feel the same.

But old habits die hard, and I can't help but question why. Why would someone like him fall for someone like me?

Call it self-preservation, a defence mechanism … I don't know. What I do know is no one ever cared before. So why should he? What's so special about me that would make this beautiful, intelligent, accomplished, and richer-than-God man even take a second glance, let alone fall in love with me?

Insecure doesn't even begin to cover all that is wrong with me. And I know I have to stop. I know I'm sabotaging myself.

All this self-doubt and lack of self-esteem is holding me back, preventing me from living my life, and I promised myself a long time ago I wouldn't let that happen. That I'd no longer pay attention to the voices of the past.

Slap. "You little bitch! I regretted you as soon as I found out I was pregnant with you!" Another slap falls across my burning cheek as I beg her to stop.

"Mummy, please no more! Please!" I cry, but her furious expression is unmoving.

"You were a mistake, Alice. You took everything from me. My youth. My freedom. Everything," she snarls in my face, her hand tight around my hair, "and I'll never forgive you for that. Never."

I close my eyes, feeling sick to my stomach as I try to calm my racing heart. Suddenly I'm that little girl all over again.

I breathe in and out slowly, trying not to cry.

That day I realised my mother had no love for me. In fact, she loathed me. Something that worsened the older I got—or the older she got, I suppose.

"Alice." Sebastian tugs on my hand as the maître d' picks our menus up and begins to lead the way across the dining room.

Shaken, for a moment I just follow, not seeing or hearing anything as I try to shake the memories from my mind.

But then I see him—Sebastian—and he's looking right at me, telling me he has a surprise for me as we walk hand in hand, the excitement in his voice so strong it's almost palpable.

So I take another deep breath and let my eyes focus on him. On his smile. And before I know it, I find myself smiling back.

I smile because it's easy to smile for him.

I smile because he makes me feel happy.

I smile because he's irresistible to me. Especially when he's like this—carefree and fun, and looking his age.

Hmm, who am I kidding? The man's irresistible. Period.

Even in his darkest mood Sebastian Hunter does things to my insides I can't even begin to explain, making it hard to discern what I'm feeling when I feel so much for him.

I do love him, though. That much is clear. Desperately so. And I really do want to be with him. So much so, I'm trying to trust him. I'm fighting every self-preservation instinct in my body in order to give this a go.

Because you know you'd be a fool to waste this opportunity with him, says an insistent, annoying voice in the back of my head.

And for once, I'm inclined to agree.

So what if things don't work out? So what if we don't get married, have two point five kids and a house with a white picket fence? I have the chance to be with the person I love. The person I believe is the love of my life. Not a lot of people can say the same.

And I know this is all new. That this is all happening fast. But I also know in my heart that this is it. My great love story. The one that'll keep me warm at night in my old age. The one I'll treasure forever and carry with me in my soul to whatever chapter comes next.

The maître d' stops in front of a majestic spiralling staircase and, looking over his shoulder, instructs us to follow him up.

Ever the gentleman, Sebastian motions for me to go first, following close behind me with his hand securely wrapped around my waist.

I smile at his possessiveness. I like it. I like that he feels so protective of me. That he wants to touch me at all times and can't go long without having his hands on me, his mouth, his body ...

God. I feel my cheeks heat up and a sense of giddiness takes hold of me as I remember us together, my heart doing little somersaults in excitement as we reach the top of the stairs and another dining room comes into view.

Correction, a private dining room. And if I was impressed before, now I feel as if I'm about to faint from the gorgeousness of it all.

My feet almost falter on the last steps. My eyes widen as they take in just how beautiful and luxurious the space is, not to mention just as glamorous as the one downstairs, only a little smaller, a little cosier, and ...

"Wow. Oh, wow." I cover my gasp with both hands.

I can't believe he did all this for me!

Dozens and dozens of deep-red roses and golden metal lanterns are arranged throughout the room. A deep, sexy tune is playing in the background, and the glow from the chandeliers and flickering candles only adds to the sensual mood, making the whole thing seem so romantic, so magical, I have to fight back tears.

Dazed, I let Sebastian guide me by the hand to our table. The only table. Which has been strategically placed right in front of the main glass window with the chairs on either side of it.

The maître d' pulls out my chair, and I thank him, sliding into it. "Would you like to order your drinks now, sir?" he asks, handing us the menus.

Sebastian holds my gaze. "Yes. A bottle of Cristal, please. We're celebrating."

"Certainly, sir," he says, and then disappears.

I look around me, taking in the candles on our table, on the floor, and pretty much everywhere the staff could fit them in, and I almost giggle.

"Do you like it?" Sebastian asks, grabbing hold of my hand again, his thumb drawing patterns on my skin.

I shake my head, still trying to hold back tears. "I love it," I reply, my eyes going back to his. "It's beautiful up here. Everything is beautiful."

"Yes, beautiful," he drawls, whilst his eyes stay fixed on me. The heat in his gaze is so evident, so intense I can feel it down to my bones as the energy around us changes and becomes thicker with need.

I force myself to look away. My body's response to him is equal parts disconcerting, disturbing, and intriguing, and I don't quite know what to do with it.

He chuckles, a deep sound that sends shivers down my spine, and just like that I'm staring back at him. I can't help it.

He's the one who's beautiful.

"It's an amazing view," he continues, a smirk tugging at his lips. "I thought you'd enjoy it. I know I am." He bites his lower lip, and I blink up at him, enthralled. I feel as if I'm just waking up from a dream.

Out of nowhere, though, images of him bringing his dates up here and telling them the exact same things he's saying to me start playing in my head. The unwelcome visions make me scowl and pull my hand away from his.

"What's wrong?" Sebastian asks, but a waiter comes in at that moment with our bottle of champagne, and we're forced to wait until he leaves. "Alice?" he insists as soon as we're alone again.

"I was just wondering ... well, I think I'd like to know"—I flush red, I can just feel it—"if you've ever been here before? On a date, I mean?" God, why do I have to ask questions I don't really want to know the answer to?

"I've been here a few times before, yes. But only on business, and with my brothers and clients." He sounds way too amused by my line of questioning, and I can feel my blush spreading further, taking over my body as my embarrassment grows.

Way to go, Alice. Smooth.

He smiles down at me, his eyes twinkling. "What if I had, though? What if I'd brought someone else here on a date? Would you be jealous? Would you get angry with me?"

You think? "Maybe." I give him a small shrug as I play with the stem of my glass.

"To be completely honest with you, I've never taken a woman on an actual date. Not like this anyway."

I frown. Now I'm confused. How can he have the reputation of being a certifiable playboy if he doesn't date? "I don't understand. What do you mean, not like this?"

"I mean that I'd see a woman in a bar, a club or even a restaurant, approach her and eventually fuck her that same night—in a restroom, a hotel, it didn't matter. It was always cold and impersonal, just friction between two bodies, and afterwards we parted ways."

"You've never taken a woman to your house? To your bed?" I rasp, my throat dry with hope and incredulity.

And there I go again. Shit, what if he says 'yes' to this? What if he ...

I shake my head and look down at my plate. "Sorry, I have no right. I shouldn't have asked."

"Alice, look at me," he says, and my eyes rise at his commanding tone. "You're the only woman, apart from Linda or staff, who's ever been in my house. Not exactly in the way I wanted or imagined"— he smirks that sinful smirk of his—"but nevertheless, you're the only woman I've ever allowed into my space. My bed."

Mollified, I breathe out a sigh of relief.

I'm glad he never took them home with him.

I don't think I could deal with their past presence in the house. Particularly his bed. And I know I have no right to feel this way, that the jealousy I feel towards the women he's been with is irrational, but try telling that to my heavy heart.

Sebastian sighs. "Alice, you've nothing to worry about. The women before ... it was just sex. It meant nothing. They meant nothing, and I don't want that any more. I'm not interested in anybody else but you. Only you."

"I just want you to be sure about this. Sure you really want a serious relationship. That you won't miss your freedom."

"I want you, Alice. And I've never been surer of anything in my entire life."

"I won't be cheated on." There! I've said it, voicing one of my worst fears since I've fallen for him. "I won't tolerate it. I believe there's no forgiveness for that." Just the thought of him with another woman makes my blood boil and my vision turn red. So no, I'd never forgive him if he hurt me that way.

Sebastian smiles. "Oh, there will be no cheating, baby. Not from me, and not from you. As I said, I'm not interested. Not to mention that since I met you, the thought of being with another woman repulses me. Makes me feel physically sick." His smile turns dangerous then. "And you wouldn't cheat on me, would you, Alice? First, you're not the type. And second, you wouldn't want me to kill anyone. Because that's what I'd do. I'd kill your lover. I'd kill anyone who dared to touch what's mine. Who dared to touch you," he says, his gaze fierce and penetrating my own. A shiver goes through me. Who knew I'd like this possessive side of Sebastian so much. "So I'll say it again, and as many times as you need. There's only one woman I want, and that woman is you."

With my heart thumping hard inside my chest, I place my right hand on top of his. Heat creeps up my neck as I peer shyly up at him.

He flips his hand to engulf mine and slides his thumb over my wrist. "This is the first time you've reached for me on your own. At least since we've kissed." He brings my hand up to his full lips and kisses it, his eyes boring into mine. "Promise me you'll do it again. Promise me, Alice. Because I want you to touch me. I want you to touch me all the fucking time."

My core clenches and I press my thighs together in search of relief, finding none.

Oh, God. I swallow thickly. He's getting me all wet inside a restaurant. A public place, no less.

Yep. That's it, Alice. He's turning you into his personal slut, and you're letting him.

"You OK, baby?" he asks, a knowing smile on his lips. The devil. He knows exactly what he's doing to me.

"I want you to kiss me," I whisper, unable to fight the urge any more.

And judging from the look on his face, this is exactly what he wanted to hear.

His smile grows wider, predatory, as he gets us both to our feet, snakes his arms around my waist, and pulls me into his chest. 'Bound to You' by Christina Aguilera starts playing in the background, and he begins to sway us gently to the sound.

My lips part in anticipation, my core wet and pulsing as he grips the back of my neck, positioning me, trapping me in his arms just like I wanted him to. Just like I asked him to.

Then he's leaning in … closer … and closer … until our lips are almost touching, but not quite, his breath tickling my lips.

"That's good, sweetheart," he whispers, "because I want to kiss you too."

"Yes," I breathe, laying my hands on his shoulders, willing him to do it, but he still doesn't make a move.

Confused, I frown, and he chuckles, the sound low and deep in his throat. "Take it, baby. Take what you want from me."

And God help me, I do, hunger and need guiding my movements when I tug on his hair and finally pull him to me, showing him with all that I have, my body, my actions, just how much he means to me.

His lips slant over mine, warm and wet and ever so sweet, and I can't help but moan into our kiss. The connection and intimacy between us grows and transforms every time we do this.

Gosh, was it only yesterday that I was wishing for this? That I was crying into my pillow longing for this man?

My head spins, and I hold on to Sebastian for dear life.

"Alice," he groans as he loses control and deepens the kiss, his mouth devouring mine for a small eternity that never seems to be long enough. "Mine. You're mine," he growls against my lips, his eyes sparkling with a possessive need I feel deep in my bones.

He holds my face between his hands and kisses me, his thumbs dusting over my cheeks as I stare up at him.

"And you know I'm yours, don't you, baby?" He kisses me again. "Because you have me. Completely. So no more doubt, no more fear. From here on out we don't let anything come between us."

Breathless and panting, I nod as I let myself drown in those eyes. In the same electric blues that'll always have my heart.

"Say it."

"We don't let anything come between us," I whisper. And time stands still as we keep staring at each other.

The promise, the complicity we're sharing, like a cocoon around us, makes me feel as if nothing ever matters. As if nothing ever will ... and in that moment I'm owned, completely and utterly owned by him.

He touches his forehead to mine, his breathing ragged as it fans over my face. "Fuck, I can't wait to bury myself in you tonight, baby." My own breath catches, and he smiles before kissing my heated cheek. "As soon as we get home, beautiful ... and I won't stop until I'm spent," he promises—or warns, I'm not entirely sure any more, and at this point I don't even care.

Not when all my nerve endings feel alive with a constant pulse that draws me closer to him. Not when my days and nights begin and end with me thinking and dreaming of him.

"Breathe, Alice," he drawls before air rushes back into my lungs. I blink, my heart thumping loudly in my ears. "So innocent. Such a delicate, sweet girl, calling to the predator in me." He bites my lower lip, pulling it into his mouth, and then we're kissing again.

Kissing and dancing ... and completely consumed by what we feel.

* * *

My smile is huge when I see Sebastian returning to our table. He excused himself a little while ago, after dessert, to go to the restroom, and I've been mindlessly scrolling through social media while I wait.

Sebastian smiles back, but I can tell something's off. Even Ryan, who's following close behind him, seems agitated and on edge, betraying his usual steely expression.

"Is everything OK?" I ask as Sebastian slides back into his seat.

"Yeah, everything's good, sweetheart."

I frown. He's lying. "You seem ... upset," I insist.

He rolls his lips, looking away. "Bad business call, that's all. I just received some disturbing news."

"Would you like to talk about it? Maybe it'd help."

He shakes his head. "I ... I think I just need to leave. Do you mind if we go home?"

I stare at him. I don't think I've ever seen Sebastian this rattled. "Of course not. I don't think I could eat another bite anyway." I smile softly.

"Good. Good. Let's go then." With that he gives a nod to Michael—who's been watching over me during dinner—then rises to his feet and comes around the table to pull my chair out for me.

"Um, what about the cheque? Don't we need to pay before we leave?"

"Michael's taking care of it."

"Oh, right," I mutter, my head spinning.

Ryan's been on the phone this whole time, his expression almost as rigid as Sebastian's. Subtly I look around, looking for the reason they're acting so strangely, but I don't see anything out of order—or anyone.

Then it seems like we're in a race as we go from the private dining room, to the coat-checking counter, to the limousine waiting out front for us, with me noticing even more security around us than before.

"Sorry, sweetheart. I really didn't mean for us to leave like this," Sebastian says as soon as Ryan shuts the limousine's door and we find ourselves alone again.

Ryan jumps into the black SUV behind us and we all pull into traffic with two more SUVs following close by. I frown. Weird, I don't remember seeing them before either. But then again, my mind has been otherwise occupied.

Sebastian, the reason for my distraction, is still rambling apologies for the way we left. "Sebastian, it's OK. I really don't mind. I enjoyed dinner and our date." I shrug. "But to be honest, I'd much rather stay home, put on a good movie, and curl up on the sofa with you any time."

Sebastian sighs, seemingly more relaxed the further we move away from the restaurant, wraps his arms around me and pulls me into his chest. "Me too, sweetheart. Me too." He kisses my forehead, my temple, my cheek. Then his lips find mine, and all rational thought leaves my brain.

* * *

It's just past eleven p.m. when I enter the living room back at home.

Alone. And slightly more confused than I expected to be tonight.

A sigh escapes my lips and I pick up the remote to turn on the TV. Then I remove my shoes, throw my clutch on top of the coffee table and fall back onto the couch, remote in hand, stretching my toes in front of me.

We've only just arrived, and Sebastian and Ryan went straight into the study to go over tomorrow's schedule. Or at least that's what they want me to believe.

I frown, and, crossing my legs at the ankles, bite into my thumbnail as I try to make sense of things.

Something bad happened at the restaurant. I don't know what exactly, but it was upsetting enough to throw off Sebastian and even Ryan.

What I do know is that one minute everything was perfect. Sebastian and I danced, laughed, then danced some more. Had dinner and drank to our hearts' content. I can honestly say I don't remember a time where I've ever had so much fun.

A goofy smile spreads over my lips and I shake my head at myself. I can't help it. Everything was so magical. We talked so much. And I mean really, really talked this time—about us, and what we feel, and where we're going with this. And funnily enough, we never seem to run out of things to say now.

It's as if we've known each other for years, not weeks. As if we've been each other's company for a lifetime, not days.

Which is why it's even more disappointing that he didn't trust me enough to explain when I asked him what was wrong, making up that silly story about a business call. A story I might have been inclined towards believing a couple of weeks ago, but not now, not today.

Not when I've been living, eating, and sleeping under the same roof as the man, and know deep down in my gut that this is not him.

He doesn't get nervous over business, and apart from the Arthur fiasco, he doesn't get emotional either. So what the hell is going on?

I tap the remote repeatedly on my leg. Well, whatever it is, I do know better than to ask him again. With Sebastian the more you ask the less he tells you, so ...

It's just that it'd be nice to feel trusted, that's all.

Not to mention that right now I also wouldn't have to be out here—alone and bored—when we could've been working together on whatever is bothering him.

I sigh. This is definitely not how I saw our beautiful night coming to an end, that's for sure.

Restless and definitely bored, I throw the remote on the couch, stand and walk towards the window that overlooks the back gardens and the pool. I can see my reflection and I wrap my arms around myself.

I smile. I look well. Happy and healthy. Head over heels in love. My grin widens.

My, oh, my, what a difference only two weeks can make, right?

Especially when there's a very tall, very handsome, and totally virile beast of a man like Sebastian Hunter involved.

My fingers rise to my tingling lips, trailing them as the tantalising memory of us kissing invades my mind.

God, how will I ever get enough of him? Of this? Of the way he makes me feel whenever he puts his hands on me?

I shiver, excitement bubbling up inside me as something tells me that for as long as we're together I'll never have to worry about that.

I mean, the man kept kissing me throughout the night. His hands were always on me, his fingers lightly stroking my shoulders, my back, my thighs, or just simply entangled with mine, and I ate it all up, loving every single second of it.

He made me feel important, cherished. Made me feel like I was the centre of his attention. The whole time I spoke, he truly listened to me, listened to what I had to say.

What can I say? Sebastian's the perfect date.

Handsome, intelligent, funny, caring—the list just goes on and on, and somehow, I already knew he wouldn't disappoint. Didn't need a date with him to show me how incredible he is.

In fact, if there's one thing these past two weeks showed me time and time again, it's that he's everything I've been waiting for in a man, and that we are good together. Really, really good together.

First, we have amazing chemistry and companionship. Secondly, we make each other laugh. Constantly. And thirdly, we can talk about almost anything without ever feeling self-conscious or judged.

To be honest, the only problem we had was not knowing what to do with all this sexual tension between us. Which, obviously, is no longer an issue now we're an item and the awkwardness is gone.

Well, mostly gone.

There's still the tiny little detail that I'm a virgin ... and I haven't told Sebastian yet.

My eyes close in regret.

How will he react when I tell him? And what if he doesn't want me any more?

I don't think I can pretend. I won't know what to do. I mean, I'm not ignorant—I know how things work in that department—but I'm not experienced. I'm sure I wouldn't be able to fool a man like him.

And even if I did, then I worry he'd hurt me if he thinks I've done it before—and I'm too much of a chicken to put myself through something like that.

So no, there's no way around this. I have to tell him. I have to be honest with him.

I almost laugh.

The unfairness of the situation isn't lost on me when he gets to keep all of his secrets, whilst, yet again, I'm forced to tell him all of mine.

* * *

Strong arms wrap around me, pulling me against a very hard, very masculine chest, and immediately I'm surrounded by his scent.

Sebastian ... I take a deep breath, my eyes fluttering closed as I drop my head back in pleasure.

Mmm, he smells so good. Utterly delicious, and I can barely stop myself from jumping him on the spot.

Which sounds ridiculous, of course, considering it's coming from a virgin who half the time doesn't even know what to say to him, let alone what to do sexually with such a man.

My only defence is that I'm probably high on endorphins, and that I've never felt this way about anyone apart from him.

His lips fall to my neck, placing feather-light kisses all over my skin, and my core tightens. I swallow hard, trying to resist the overwhelming force of my desire.

Trying to resist him.

This just feels so right, though. So effortless. Like it's meant to be. Like we are meant to be.

And part of me just wants to surrender. Let him take whatever he wants and be done with it.

The other part, however, the damaged part, is not so keen on taking the risk. The thought of being intimate with someone just to end up being used scares me, terrifies me even, and I don't think I'm prepared for it. Not for a while at least.

Time ... I need more time to get to know him better. To learn to trust him.

Hopefully he'll understand. Hopefully he didn't lie to me just to get into my pants.

This is it, though. The moment of truth.

Inhaling deeply and with my heart thumping in my ears, I turn around in his arms, my eyes meeting his, only to find them already dark and heated with arousal. I swoon, my breath catching in my throat as I stare dazedly up at him.

Then those beautiful electric blues lower to my lips, and God help me, I lose the ability to put a sentence together.

"Sebastian," I try, but he's already pulling me to him. His head dips low as he brushes his lips over my temple, my cheek, the corner of my mouth, all the while whispering sweet little nothings to me. And I'm hooked, defenceless against his powers of seduction.

Then his lips are on mine, his grip on my hips tight, almost painful, ripping moan after moan from my throat. His hungry mouth is so possessive my whole body begins to tremble with the intensity of the deep, carnal kiss he's giving me.

The impressive bulge in his slacks becomes even more evident, hard and trapped between our bodies, leaving no doubt in my mind as to what he wants from me, what he desires.

Which is why I'm not expecting it when he pulls away and with a groan buries his face in my hair, his breathing ragged as he tries to rein himself in. Surprising me with tenderness and affection when I thought he was going to be rough.

Tears sting the back of my eyes, and I hug him closer to me.

"Alice," he whispers, stroking my back and breathing me in, and we stay just like that, holding each other close for what seems like forever.

In a daze, I feel him pull the pins out of my hair. The strands cascade down my back as he murmurs something about strawberries, I think.

I'm not sure. Can't be sure of much when he's gripping my hair like this. Like he owns me. Like I'm his.

Oh, and I want to be his. I want it with a passion I didn't know I had.

Then his mouth is on me again, his kiss hot and savage, almost violent as he claims my lips—and sparks fly. My skin tingles all over when he grabs my ass with both hands, lifts me into his arms, and I wrap my legs around him.

"Fuck, I want you so bad it hurts, baby," he whispers before biting my lower lip, sucking it into his mouth and trapping it between his teeth. His eyes burn into mine before he licks away the sting. "Please let me make love to you, Alice," he breathes, pressing feather-light kisses to my jaw, my neck, driving me crazy with need. "Let me show you how much you mean to me."

God, I want him to. I want him to so much I can barely breathe. "Sebastian, I ..."

His half-lidded eyes meet mine again. "Please, baby. I need you," he pleads.

"I need you too. I ... I ..." I shake my head and look away. God, I'm so stupid. I should've told him before. I should've ...

Sensing my distress, Sebastian walks us over to the couch and sits with me on his lap. "Hey," he says as he holds my face between his hands, his eyes boring into mine. "Talk to me. What's wrong?"

I bite into my lower lip nervously as I hold on to his forearms. "You might not want me any more once you know."

"Alice, I'll always want you. Now tell me, what's preoccupying that pretty little head of yours?"

If anything, he looks a little preoccupied himself, which only adds to my distress, making me feel even more anxious about opening up to him.

"I ... I've never done this before," I rasp, my heart beating frantically as I wait for him to say something, anything, but he remains silent, his eyes wide and staring down at me. I swallow hard. "Sebastian ... I've never been with anyone. You're ... you're the first guy I kissed."

A shaky breath leaves his lips, and all the while he's still staring at me, his body rigid as stone under my fingers.

"You're a virgin?" He finally speaks, and I nod, blushing furiously when I hear the words coming from him. "And I was your very first kiss?" I nod again, and to my relief he smiles, the realisation of what I just said turning his eyes smouldering hot. "And no one has ever touched you before me?" He repeats what I told him as if in a trance, and I'm so nervous, I begin to doubt my ability to read him.

Maybe I'm not reading him right after all. Maybe he's getting upset.

"I understand if you've changed your mind," I say, my voice barely a whisper, pain and embarrassment clogging my throat at the possibility of rejection from him. "I won't hold it against you."

He frowns, and I grimace. I just don't know what to think any more.

"Not a chance, sweetheart. And why would I change my mind? Why would I do such a thing?" His brows draw closer together as if he really doesn't know, and I huff out a humourless laugh.

"Because I'm not ready to have sex, Sebastian," I reply, my voice raw, betraying the depth of my emotions, my vulnerability. "I need time." I shake my head regretfully, knowing this is how I'll lose him, and lower my eyes to his chest. "I need to get to know you better ... I need to trust you, and you might not want to wait."

Of course he won't want to wait. Who'd want to wait for a virgin in this day and age? Silly me.

I sigh and push my hair out of my face. "I'm not experienced. I won't know what to do. How to please you. And I'm sorry. I'm so very sorry I didn't tell you before. I know I should've ... I know ..."

"Hey—hey, stop," he whispers, his thumbs caressing my cheekbones as he presses his forehead to mine. "Shh. I meant what I said before. What we have is not just physical. It's much, much more than that. You are so much more than that, Alice. You're my girl, and I want you to feel ready when I take you. I want you to feel good." His expression is earnest, and I know he's speaking the truth. "Baby, I can wait. I won't rush you, OK?"

I swallow the huge lump in my throat, my emotions still all over the place as my eyes well with tears.

I just can't believe how sweet he's being about this. How sweet he's being with me.

"OK," I breathe, pulling back a little to smile shyly up at him.

"OK," he repeats, giving me a smile of his own as he uses his thumbs to dry my tears.

Then our eyes meet and everything falls into place. My heart tells me it won't be long before I'm making love to this man anyway, and that I might as well take the leap now and get used to being more physical with him.

It won't do me any good if I'm this inexperienced when we do take the final step. Not to mention by then I want to feel more comfortable with him, relaxed. Something that won't be possible if I keep pushing him away.

"Maybe ..." I press my lips together, summing up all the courage I can muster and then some. It's not easy for me to talk about these things. "Maybe ... we could do the other stuff." I feel my cheeks heat up, but I persevere. "For now, I mean. Maybe we could do the other stuff for now," I rush to say, the words tumbling out of my mouth.

His bright eyes lock on mine, assessing, scrutinising as he slowly drags his hands over my arms, my waist, my hips. A sinful grin plays on his lips. "You're going to have to be a little more specific than that, Alice. You're going to have to tell me exactly what you mean."

Damn him. He knows what I mean. He just wants to hear me say it.

I take another deep, self-empowering breath.

OK, I can do this. I can tell him what I want from him.

"Kissing, touching," I say, looking at him through my eyelashes, embarrassed, excited. "I want you to show me. I want you to teach me what to do and what you like. All I need is a little more time before we take things further ... before we make love, that's all."

He smiles. "We can do anything you want, baby. Whatever you're comfortable with. You're in control. You set the pace, all right?" His hands massage my hips, and I begin to finally relax. "In order for this to work, though, I'm gonna need you to speak up. To be more open when we discuss sex. There's no place for shame in intimacy, only trust, Alice, and this is new to me too, so you're going to have to guide me. The last thing I want is to hurt you or scare you. I need to know that you're OK with whatever it is we're doing, that you're enjoying yourself."

"I know," I agree. He's totally right about this.

He gives me a look, and I smile. I can't resist. "What?"

He shakes his head. "I was just wondering, how the fuck does a gorgeous creature like yourself land in my lap still untouched? Innocent?"

"God, you're probably thinking I'm a prude, or worse, frigid." I cover my face with both hands.

He chuckles, pulling my hands away. "I'm not. And I can tell you right now you're not frigid. Or a prude, for that matter. If anything, I think you're the hottest, most passionate woman I've ever met." I smile, all the tension and anxiety from before leaving my shoulders at once. "Which is why I'm honestly curious as to why you decided to wait."

My eyes search his, but all I find is curiosity in them. "I just didn't want to be groped, you know?" I try my best to explain. "I wanted my firsts to be with someone special. Someone I could get to know better and have something meaningful with before taking the next step. I never met a man like that, though. Never felt a connection or wanted anyone until ... well, until I met you, really."

"Sweetheart ..." He presses his forehead to mine. "I'm sorry. I'm so sorry for the way I took your first kiss. Grabbing you like that, and ..."

"I'm not." My eyes hold his, and I give him a bashful smile. "I wanted it to be you, Sebastian. I wanted you to kiss me. I'm glad you did."

"I'm glad too, baby. Believe me. Still, you shouldn't say things like that to a man like me. I'm already way too happy with the fact that no one has ever touched you before me." He captures my mouth in a lingering kiss. "That no one will ever touch you after me." He kisses me again, softly this time, sucking on my lips before releasing. "I'm a selfish man, Alice. A possessive bastard when it comes to you. I'm pretty sure it'll upset you at some point."

I run the tips of my fingers over his smooth jaw. "I kinda feel possessive towards you too. So"—I shrug—"I guess I'll have no right to feel upset."

He grins. "I like that you feel that way about me. I want you to want me. To need me. Who knows, maybe it'll make you more understanding of my caveman tendencies and insane jealousy over you."

I laugh out loud at his pained expression, and after a while he starts laughing too.

"Come here." Sebastian hugs me to him, nuzzling my neck, and my eyes flutter closed. My heart is full and my mind finally at ease after the conversation we've just had.

The moment stretches between us and we stay just like that. The feel of his mouth on me makes me melt further into him.

"I want you to move into my bedroom tonight, Alice," he says into my shoulder, and my hands on his hair freeze, my heart jumping into my throat. What? What's he saying? "I want us to sleep in the same bed from here on out."

"Sebastian ..." The tension from before returns full blast, along with excitement and fear, and I find myself at a loss for words. I lean back to look at him.

"Sleep. I said sleep," he whispers, his breath brushing over my lips, making me shiver. "I just want to hold you while we sleep, that's all. But I want us in the same bedroom as of now. I need to be close to you. There's nothing else in this world I want more."

At his words, my body begins to relax and I breathe out a sigh of relief.

Jesus, I really have to stop thinking the worst of him.

Not to mention that being held by Sebastian while we sleep sounds like a dream come true.

"I ... I think I'd like that too," I rasp, and Sebastian gives me a radiant smile that has me melting all over again.

Then he gets up with me in his arms and carries me all the way up to my bedroom. "Get ready for bed, baby," he drawls, before giving me a quick peck at the door and placing me back on my feet. "Then come to my room—our room. I'll be waiting for you."

Dropping another kiss on my puckered lips, he turns and walks away.

I stare after him. My legs shake and my knees wobble as I drag myself inside, press my back against the door and exhale.

Dear God, what is this man doing to me? And worse, what the hell did I just agree to when I know perfectly well I have no power to resist him?

* * *

Nerves dance in the pit of my stomach as I walk up to Sebastian's door. My breath hitches when I find it wide open, with the lights inside the bedroom dimmed and the bed already turned down.

I swallow hard.

Sleep. He only wants to sleep.

I repeat the words I've been telling myself for the last ten minutes or so, praying I don't chicken out now. And that I can be strong. That I can be strong enough for a relationship with him.

Inhaling deeply, I look further inside.

My, oh, my ... My lips stretch into a smile. I can't help it.

Standing in front of the balcony door, Sebastian holds onto its frame, his ripped arms stretched over his head, emphasising all the hard muscles and crevices of his back. Low-cut black pyjama bottoms sit loosely around his hips. The light fabric showcases that fine, fine ass of his and his thick thighs, appealing to everything female in me. His feet are bare and his hair dishevelled, and my fingers twitch with a desperate urge to touch.

God, he's perfect. Mouth-wateringly perfect. Suddenly I want to lick him all over, kiss him all over, and call him mine.

The sense of ownership I feel is so strong, so animalistic and primal, I can't help but think I'm losing my mind.

Frozen in place, I can't even pretend when he finally turns and catches me staring at him. A satisfied smile spreads over his lips as his eyes slowly drop down my body before returning to my face.

"Miss Lake," Sebastian rasps, moves in my direction and holds out his hand to me.

"Mr Hunter," I reply shyly, my cheeks aflame as I place my much smaller hand in his.

He pulls me into his chest, his dark eyes burning with arousal as his other hand drops to my hip and he gives it a little squeeze. I shiver when he slowly brings my hand to his mouth and kisses it.

"Welcome to our humble abode." His thumb caresses my knuckles, and I twist my lips together to hide how pleased I am. Pleased, mesmerised, and to be honest a little shocked at how soft his tone and touch can be despite the intensity I see in his eyes. The sheer sexual need and hunger that's always present whenever we're close like this made me think he'd have a harder time containing himself with me.

As if reading my mind, he tightens his hold on my hip. His other hand falls to my waist and he presses me flush against him.

I gasp, and he kicks the door shut, a slow, lopsided smile forming on his lips when he turns us around and begins walking me backwards towards his bed.

"No escaping now, little thing," he murmurs, and I blink, feeling the heat of my own desire rapidly spread throughout my skin.

Before I have the chance to reply, though, Sebastian is picking me up in his arms and laying me down on the huge mattress. His gaze languidly travels down my body as my white, silky nightdress rides up my thighs, revealing my matching panties to him. "Christ," he growls as he climbs into bed with me.

He covers us both up with the duvet, and I stare up at him. I can't help it. His eyes glitter with excitement, bluer than ever as we finally lie together like this, side by side and with barely any space between us.

A few minutes pass and I know he's giving me time. Waiting for me to say something, give him a sign that it's OK. That he can touch me.

Words fail me, though, and as for signs, I'm not sure of what to do either. So I grab his hand and turn around, pressing my back to his chest and hugging his arm to me.

Tiny goosebumps break all over my skin and I release a sigh of relief when he gathers me up in his arms, pressing me to him, his hot breath making me shudder as his lips dust over the sensitive shell of my ear.

"Fuck," he groans, laying his palm flat on my stomach as he pulls me further into him. "You feel so good, baby." He kisses my hair, my temple, my cheek.

Oh, God. He feels so good too. Smells so good. I can't think.

Heat pools in my panties and sparks shoot up my spine as my nipples harden under my nightdress, and before I can stop myself, I'm turning around in his arms. Again.

I need to see him. Need to look into the tantalising blue of his eyes.

Our gazes meet, and I place my hand on his cheek, petting him, marvelling at the feel of his smooth skin and rough stubble under my palm.

Oh, he's gorgeous. So freaking gorgeous he could be a model, an actor, have anyone he'd like. Yet he's here with me. Such a sinfully beautiful man and he chose me. Wants me.

How on earth is a girl supposed to resist?

Sebastian covers my hand with his, and, closing his eyes, kisses my palm with such tenderness and affection a knot forms in my throat.

It's his thing, I notice—kissing my wrists, my hands, everywhere his lips can reach my skin since our conversation earlier in his study.

Meeting my gaze, he stares at me through half-lidded eyes and slides a hand into my hair.

I swallow hard, desperately trying to blink away my tears. Nervous, embarrassed, frustrated I won't be able to stop the waterworks once they begin.

But it is inevitable, I'm afraid. Since I'm the crybaby of crybabies and as sensitive as they come.

Which in turn makes me feel angrier, as I know I'm at a disadvantage here. The weak link. And, therefore, the one more likely to get hurt if anything goes amiss.

Sebastian presses his forehead to mine, his thumb caressing my cheek. "Do you even know how beautiful you are? Do you even understand what you're doing to me right now?" The sound of an anguished groan is the last thing I hear before he's kissing me fiercely and holding me even closer to him, touching me for what seems like hours, months, years.

His mouth only releases mine to trail kisses down my jawline, my neck, my chest, his hands sliding down my sides until he's gripping my waist, ripping moan after moan from me.

Drunk on him, I squeeze his broad shoulders hard, my blunt nails digging into the warm skin and rock-hard muscles contracting under my palms.

Christ, it's like he's made of stone. His frame is so big and strong a surge of excitement fills me as my hands slide down his thick biceps, his chest, the well-defined bumps and ridges of his six pack, the deep V going into his trousers. And it's still not enough. Not when I need to feel more of him. Need to touch and kiss every inch of this glorious man. So my hands keep going, exploring, moving to the rhythm of his breath and soft groans, until …

"Baby, no," Sebastian growls, catching my wrists. A grimace mars his beautiful face. "You're getting too close … and I don't want to lose control. Trust me, it's already a challenge as it is," he breathes against my mouth, and it's my turn to grimace as realisation finally sinks in.

Oh … oh!

Self-disgust and embarrassment take over, plus the sting of his rejection, and I swallow hard, feeling the burn of fresh tears in my throat. "I'm sorry. I … I wasn't thinking." Damn it, what am I doing? Not to mention I'm confusing the hell out of the poor guy—telling him one thing, doing another. Taking things further when I was the one asking him to wait.

"No, don't," he whispers. "I want you to. More than anything, I want you to. It's just that I was so rough with you before. Alice, I ripped your fucking top off."

My panties soak through at the memory, and my lips part, wanting his kiss. Wanting a repeat of that night.

Sebastian grabs my jaw, looking at me with wild, heated eyes. "Baby, stop looking at me like that. For once, I'm trying to be the good guy here."

"I liked it," I admit timidly. "I liked what you did to me."

"Fuck." He closes his eyes, his heart racing under my palms, matching my own furious pulse. Our eyes meet again, and I press my thighs together.

A predator. A dangerous, beautiful predator ... and I'm his prey.

"You're going to be the death of me, little thing. The fucking death of me, do you hear me?"

Still holding my jaw in place, he descends on me with everything he's got, his claim possessive and unapologetic as he ravishes me with his mouth. Taking what belongs to him, what has always belonged to him, body and mind, until I simply dissolve in his arms.

Chapter 10

Sebastian

A huge smile spreads over my face as I relish waking up with Alice's body pressed up against mine.

I take a long look at her, sleeping like an angel in my arms, and my heart clenches tight. Jesus! An involuntary groan escapes my lips and I bury my face in her hair, greedily taking in her scent as I hold my most precious possession, my girl, my love, with all that I have.

She smells so good. I stay just like that, listening to her soft breaths, delighted by the fact that from now on all my mornings could be like this.

Last night we stayed up for hours just talking and kissing, making out like two teenagers until we were both too exhausted to stay awake and fell asleep. It had been a long and emotional day. A rollercoaster. Nonetheless, a day I'll never forget.

The day this beautiful creature agreed to be mine. Agreed to put her trust in me and give this a try.

I grin, kissing her temple. Not that she really had a choice in the matter, or hasn't been mine from the moment my eyes fell on her, because she has. I just don't want her thinking I'm a brute who's forcing himself on her, which, of course, I am.

Except now her feelings matter. Her happiness is my own, and it's no longer enough for me to just take her.

No, I need her to give herself willingly to me. I need her to want this as much as I do. Even if the thought of taking her is just as appealing, at least to the caveman in me. The savage who's getting more and more restless, trying to take over at every turn and do the thinking for me. The psycho telling me to lock Alice up, to keep her. To not take into account if she wants this or even if she likes me or not.

She does, though. She does like me and wants me. It's written all over her pretty face. More than evident in her eyes, in the way her body responds to mine, to my kisses, my touch.

Shuddering, I gaze down at my innocent angel, my girl, looking as pure as she'll ever be lying beside me—hugging my arm to her breasts, her hand tenderly wrapped around mine.

And the need to corrupt her, to have her scream my name as she comes apart in my arms, intensifies. Gnaws at my insides until I free my hand from her light hold and cup one of the sweet mounds.

Fuck, her tits are perfect. The perky orbs not too big, not too small, just the perfect handful to drive me out of my mind.

Her nipple pebbles under my touch, my desire peaking, making me crazy, making me desperate until I can't fucking think any more. And I finally snap.

I need her, and I need her right the fuck now.

"Sebastian," she murmurs in her sleep, pushing her breasts into my palm.

I kiss her ear, sucking and nibbling on the sensitive skin, all the while rubbing myself on her, getting a wonderful friction on my aching dick. My other hand, which has been resting on her stomach, slides to her hip of its own accord, squeezing and loving her curves, making her moan.

But I don't stop there.

No, I can't. And with a tremulous exhale, I continue my descent, touching her thigh, her knee, until I find the hem of her nightgown and, hooking my thumb under the fabric, slowly begin to pull it up purposely baring my woman to me.

"Sebastian," she murmurs again, sounding a lot more like herself, and I know she's finally awake.

I smile and twist her nipple through the silky fabric of her nightgown, moving my other hand to the inside of her warm thigh.

She whimpers and her whole body turns rigid, reminding me to slow down. To be gentle with her.

"Shh, it's OK, baby," I whisper, my hand still on her thigh, massaging it, squeezing it whilst I continue to knead her breast, and soon she begins to relax again. "That's it, baby. That's it."

Mewling noises leave her mouth, and I trail kisses up her jaw, desperate to swallow the honeyed sounds.

Alice's eyes search mine through her long, doll-like lashes. "What are you doing to me?" she asks, her voice soft and her eyes glazed over with arousal, just like I want her to be. Just like I imagined.

"I'm showing you," I tell her, my own voice thick with lust before I take her mouth in an all-encompassing kiss.

Her legs part a little further, and I push my hand between her thighs, running the tips of my fingers over her panties as I swallow all her little cries.

Fuck! I groan into our kiss.

She's wet. So wet, it's seeping right through the fabric, moistening my fingers. Making me so bloody hard I start leaking precum like a faucet—turning my own goddamned trousers into a mess in record time.

But then she gasps, pressing her thighs together again, and I reluctantly break the kiss. "Baby, what is it? Is this too much? Is it too fast?"

She stays silent, her blush spreading as she hides her face in her hands.

"Baby?" Then it hits me. She's embarrassed. I keep forgetting how innocent my little thing is.

I smile. She really has no idea how hot she is. No clue that the fact she's soaking wet for me makes my dick grow that much harder, hungrier—excited for all the things I want to do to her, with her. "Alice, look at me."

Her eyes meet mine, searching, the blush still evident on her cheeks, and I have to take a deep, calming breath just so I don't end up grabbing her and kissing her again.

"Do you know how fucking sexy you are to me?" Her blush intensifies and I press my forehead to hers. "It turns me on, baby, that you're so wet for me. I fucking love it. Give me your hand."

She puts her hand in mine and, grinding my teeth together, I bring it down to my engorged cock.

She gasps, her eyes big as saucers, and it's almost too much. Her touch, the look on her face, her innocence.

And I know it's wrong, that her lack of experience shouldn't turn me on so fucking much, but I'm a bad man, a dirty man, and her virginity has awoken a possessive side of me I'm not quite sure how to rein in.

Shutting my eyes tight, I squeeze myself over my trousers with her fingers, trying my damnedest not to come. "This is how I like it," I murmur as I kiss her pink cheek, moving our joined hands up and down my shaft.

The barbarian in me revels in her dazed expression. Then our mouths are crashing into each other—lips sucking, tongues lashing, teeth clinking—lust burning us like a fever and making our movements desperate.

"God, you're so beautiful. You're the most beautiful woman I've ever seen," I rasp, touching our foreheads together as we both try to catch our breath.

"Touch me," she whispers, her arousal evident in her eyes.

"Baby," I warn, my voice husky and deep as my hand grips her inner thigh, kneading it, caressing it until she relaxes under my touch. Only then do I let my hand slide up.

By reflex she presses her legs together again, and I stop.

"Open for me, baby girl," I whisper, both of us panting.

She holds my gaze, and slowly, very slowly parts her trembling thighs. Fear and excitement shines in her eyes as she opens herself up to me, to my touch, and I cup her pussy without missing a beat.

"Alice," I murmur, my eyes glued to hers as I touch what's mine for the very first time. "Tell me you're OK. Please tell me this is OK."

She moans, and I inhale deeply, the heel of my hand pressing on her clit, stimulating and rubbing her through her panties as her kitten-like sounds trigger all kinds of wrong, delicious ideas to run through me, each dirtier than the last.

I smile with perverted delight as I watch her eyes begin to roll to the back of her head, her orgasm quickly building until I ease the pressure on her clit. She groans in frustration, her eyes pleading and her hips chasing, and it takes all my self-control not to tear her panties in half.

Gone. I need them fucking gone and out of my way.

Alice shudders in my arms, and I slide my hand up to her lower belly, trailing my fingertips over the seam of white lace there.

Slow. Take it slow, Sebastian.

Her lips part in expectation, and I smile before licking and sucking on them. My hand slowly pushes inside her tiny panties, brushes past her soft curls and finally meets her centre.

She gasps, her moans and whimpers filling the space. Her pussy is already slick and swollen with her arousal, and my mouth falls on hers, ravaging it, consuming it, conquering it in a hotter-than-hot kiss that has my blood pumping and my balls tightening to the point of pain.

Her submission, obviously, is the ultimate aphrodisiac to a man like me. Pure ecstasy rushes through my body, the look of pleasure on her sweet face intensifying my own.

"Fuck," I growl against her lips as the need to come becomes almost unbearable. "You feel so good, baby. So fucking lovely and soft. So warm."

I close my eyes, my dirty mind telling me to pull out my cock and shoot my load all over her delicious ass.

Hell, one day I'll have that too. I'll make her mine in every way known to man.

"You're mine. All fucking mine, do you hear me?" I hiss through my teeth, barely holding on to my sanity any more.

"Mmm ... yours," Alice moans, pushing her virgin pussy into my hand.

I kiss her gently then, letting our tongues meet and tangle before parting her folds and running my middle finger through her slit—spreading her wetness, massaging her labia, rubbing my way slowly up and down to her clit.

"Ahhh!" Her small body convulses and she cries out into my mouth.

I smile.

Mmm, she's so fucking responsive, my little thing. So fucking sensitive to my touch. And I have to say, nothing has ever felt so right or destined in my entire life.

"I want to feel you too," she murmurs, breaking the kiss.

God! I shiver, my weeping cock jerking and twitching in her hand.

I open my eyes and we stare at each other for an extended amount of time until I nod, push my trousers and boxers all the way down in one swift move and get them off with the aid of my feet. The expectation of having her hands on me makes me frantic, impatient.

Then her small, delicate fingers are touching me, skin to skin and wrapped tightly around my dick, and it's like I can finally breathe. My jaw slackens as I begin to thrust into her fist.

Her lips part and she licks them, and—"Fuck," I curse, my eyelids fluttering closed as I almost come in her hand.

I want those luscious lips on me. Around my cock, sucking me dry.

Opening my eyes, I find hers, hooded and heated with arousal as she looks up at me. She smiles, the little minx, feeling proud of herself, no doubt. "You're so big," she says before biting her lip. "And wet"— her smile grows bigger—"just like me."

I smirk, slipping my hand back into her panties and pressing my middle finger to her clit, circling it, flicking it. "Yes, baby. Just like you."

"Oh, God," she breathes, tightening her hold on me. "Is it good? Am I doing it right?" she asks when I take over biting her bottom lip.

"It's ... fucking perfect ... baby. You're ... fucking perfect." I struggle to get the words out, still thrusting my cock into her little fist. "Alice. Fuck," I whisper, dipping the tip of my middle finger into her entrance, so fucking tight and warm, my cock hums in appreciation. "Relax, baby. Let me in. Please, let me in," I beg when I feel her body turn rigid.

"It burns," she whimpers, her nails digging into my forearm.

I give her a soft peck on the lips and run the tip of my nose along hers. The overwhelming need to be tender with her is always present, and just as strong as the need to fuck her, if not stronger these days. "I know, sweetheart. That's why we need to get you used to it. I have to widen your pretty little pussy for when you take my cock." Kissing the tip of her beautiful nose, I add with a wicked smile, "And I want to make you come, baby girl. I want to make you cream all over my fingers."

She shivers, her cheeks coloured in the most alluring shade of pink I've ever seen as she opens her mouth to speak. "Sebastian ..." she starts, but then I'm kissing her, pressing my finger to her clit, and the words die in her mouth.

"Be gentle. Please be gentle," she whispers, looking at me with dazed, innocent eyes as soon as I release her lips. "I've never had anything in there before."

Holy. Fucking. Shit. This girl shouldn't say stuff like this to me. She shouldn't stir the possessive monster within.

The part of me that is more animal than man already.

The part of me that wants to tear her nightdress in half and claim her like a fucking savage.

I shake my head. Fuck, I can't hurt her. I won't hurt her. I want her trust, her love. I want her everything.

Gentle. I can be gentle with her.

Dragging my fingers through her wetness, I gently massage her clit, her folds, and her small entrance again. My eyes are glued to her face the entire time as I dip just the tip of my middle finger inside her.

I repeat this several times until her hips begin to rock against my hand. Her moans and incoherent words are music to my ears, arousing me and spurring me on—and this time I don't stop. No, I push all the way in.

Crying out, Alice lets go of my cock and digs her nails into my leg.

I still, not daring to move a muscle in case I hurt her. "Baby, you OK?" I ask, concerned, ecstatic, and so fucking turned on I can't even see straight.

Fuck, I almost exploded at the feel of her clenching on me. At the feel of her tight little pussy swallowing my finger.

God have mercy, but she's going to feel just like heaven when I finally take her with my cock.

"Yes," she whispers breathlessly, and I lower my head, kissing her on the lips. "I'm OK now. Please don't stop."

Her mouth falls open as I press my palm to her clit, slowly pumping my finger in and out of her. The sensations make her hips roll in time with my strokes.

"Fuck, baby. You feel so wonderful ... so tight and wet," I grunt out, feeling her fingers wrap tight around my cock, jerking me off again. Screwing my eyes shut, I let my warm breath carry my whispered words over the shell of her ear. "I can't wait to fuck you. Can't wait to breach your tight, virgin pussy with my big, swollen cock." Alice gasps, clenching hard on my finger, my dirty words eliciting even more heat to pour out of her in a rush. "Tell me you want that. Tell me you want me."

"Oh, God, please," she moans, and I go mad. In a flash, I rip the front of her nightdress, growling like an animal as I palm her beautiful breasts.

She whimpers, arching her back, her nipples hard little nubs against my hand. Her pussy is wet and warm as I fuck her with my finger, and I know she's finally surrendering to me.

"I want you so fucking much, Alice," I whisper in her ear.

"I want you, too," she murmurs, lost in what I'm doing to her, and I love it. I love that I can make her lose control this bad.

"I'm going to fuck you so good, baby. Fill you up so completely, we'll both see stars when you come on my cock."

"Sebastian ..."

Our lips crash then, our tongues meeting and dancing as we share the same air, the same breath. Our pants and moans fill the room.

And I'm close. So fucking close. But I need her to come with me.

"Come for me, baby girl. Let go," I command over her whimpers.

My voice is dark and raspy with desire as I pinch her pebbled nipple. And with a strangled cry, she comes, calling out my name as she trembles in my arms. Her little pussy spasms, rippling around my finger, my name still a prayer on her soft, wet lips, and I'm a goner.

My balls draw up and I spill myself all over Alice's hand, my mouth consuming hers as I coat her firm ass and thighs with rope after thick rope of my cum.

I shiver, waves of pleasure travelling up my spine, and just like the first time I came with Alice, it feels different ... special. More than anything I've ever experienced in my life.

It goes on forever. The pleasure. The release. The overwhelming need to be together like this intensifying every kiss, every touch, every word that comes out of our mouths.

Leaving us both spent and satiated and high on each other as we finally relax into the mattress and try our hardest to catch our breaths.

Burying my nose in her hair, I hold her close to me. Closer than I've ever held anyone.

Closer than I've ever allowed anyone to be.

* * *

Reluctant to break the spell, we end up spending most of the morning in bed. Our conversation is light and easy and our kissing never-ending as we make each other laugh. And the more we talk, the deeper I can feel myself falling for her.

She's funny, and not just in a ha-ha sort of way, but in a witty and charming manner. She's also an amazing person, my Alice. A beautiful girl with an even more beautiful heart.

I press my lips together to stifle a smile and hide my face in Alice's hair. Oh, boy, do I have it bad. Alice has me completely wrapped around her tiny little finger. Completely under her spell.

And the best thing about it? I don't even care.

I smile, and, grabbing hold of her small waist, flip her around so I can look directly at her face. The unexpected move is enough to make her squeal in surprise, and I laugh, taking her soft lips in mine just as her giggles begin.

And it's there again. The magic. The crazy chemistry between us. The energy and lust that always surrounds us. And I know—no, I'm sure—I'll do just about anything to keep her exactly like this: trusting and happy as she lies in my arms.

I force myself to break the kiss, pulling Alice towards me as I drop my head onto the pillow again.

We need to discuss contraception. I don't want to wear a condom with her. Don't want anything between us when I finally take her innocence.

My lips twitch at the thought. It will be a first for me too with a virgin. Not to mention I've never done anything without a condom before. Always made whatever slut I was fucking put one on me, even if she was only sucking me off.

Extreme? Then here's the shocker: never kissed any of them either.

Hell, haven't kissed anyone, really, since I was a teenage boy. Didn't feel the need, nor see the appeal.

Then Alice happened and that's all I can think about. Well, that and fucking her, having her skin to skin, feeling every ripple, every squeeze of her wet, warm pussy on my naked, swollen dick.

I'm getting hard again. Unbelievable. I just came like nobody's business, yet my cock doesn't seem to have gotten the memo.

Alice lays her head on my shoulder, her fingers drawing circles on my chest, and I will myself to relax. I need to be calm for this. Need to be gentle.

"Alice," I rasp. "Baby, I ... I want you to go on the pill. I'm clean," I rush to add, my fingers dusting down the smooth skin of her arm. "I never had unprotected sex, and haven't been with anyone since I got tested last time. Before I met you."

Yeah, got tested immediately after the Paris incident. On my first weekend back, in fact—afraid I'd shot myself in the foot after being with that ... with that ...

Shit, I don't even want to think about it. Not with my sweet girl lying in bed with me.

"I'm already on the pill. To regulate, you know, my periods," Alice says in her soft voice, and I look down at her, catching a glimpse of a nipple before she rearranges her ripped nightdress to cover it up.

My cock jerks at the sight and I want to tell her not to cover herself in front of me, not to hide, but I hold my tongue. I need to give her time. Need to be patient with her.

"Good. I don't want anything between us when I finally take you. Not even a condom." Smirking, I add, "I want to come inside you, Alice. I want to fill your tight virgin pussy full of my cum."

Her cheeks turn crimson red right before my eyes. Embarrassed, she hides her face in my chest. "I can't believe you just said that to me. God, the things that come out of your mouth are filthy."

I laugh unashamedly. "What can I say? I have a filthy mouth, and a filthy mind to go with it." She smells so good I can't resist shoving my face in the crook of her neck. Strawberries and fucking cream explode in my mouth as I lick and suck on her fragrant skin, and I can't have enough. I'll never have enough of this.

I feel her shiver, hear her moans, and thank God she's already on the pill. I know I won't have the presence of mind to think of condoms, or the restraint for that matter.

The need to claim her, possess her, overrides any logical thinking in my brain.

One more reason to be careful, I note. The last thing we need is an unwanted pregnancy. Or, worse, an unwanted baby.

I cringe, wondering if she even wants kids at all, my little thing. Probably. It's only natural she'd want what other women want. Marriage. Babies. A family of her own to look after.

Things I never wanted for myself.

What if I can't do it, though? Marriage, kids. The whole 'happy family' thing.

Would she leave?

Would she leave me for a dream?

* * *

Eventually, hunger drags our lazy asses to the kitchen.

"Can I help?" I ask Alice, not really knowing what to do. Cooking has never been my thing, but it's her thing, and there's nowhere else I'd rather be than here with her. Well, except maybe the bedroom, but I can always convince her to return.

"Sure. Who knows? Maybe you'll learn how to make something edible this time." She giggles, opening the fridge and looking inside.

"Edible is this hot little body of yours," I say, coming up behind her and pressing myself to her back. My hands are on her hips as I whisper into her ear. "I have half a mind to throw you over my shoulder and take you back to bed."

She shivers, and I pull her hair aside, trailing open-mouthed kisses up and down her neck. Her taste is divine on my tongue, and I lick the sensitive skin just behind her ear.

She mewls, letting her head fall to the side, giving me better access, even as she says in a breathy moan, "Stop, you're distracting me."

"I'm helping you cook breakfast," I drawl, right before taking a bite. Her whole body trembles and her nipples harden, becoming more prominent through the white tank top she's wearing.

"By grabbing me and kissing me every chance you get?" She tries to reprimand me, but her voice comes out weak, her desire evident in the rapid pulse of her neck as I lick it.

"Exactly." I chuckle and then turn her around, my lips falling to the tip of her nose as she wrinkles it up in a cute frown. "For which you should show more appreciation, Miss Lake. One might think you ungrateful with this kind of attitude," I admonish in a playful tone.

The look of incredulity on her face brings a wicked smile to my lips as I tighten my hold on her.

"Sebastian ..."

I attack her mouth then, my tongue slipping past her lips and teeth, despite her initial resistance—twisting and tangling with hers, licking it—and the way she responds, the way she kisses me back ... fuck, it drives me out of my mind.

Ravenous. I feel absolutely ravenous, and it's not for breakfast any more.

No, to hell with food! I'm taking my woman back to bed, where we should never have left.

My feet start moving us away from the fridge, our lips still locked in a frenzy.

All I need now is to break the kiss long enough to throw Alice over my shoulder and carry her upstairs. Then my stomach growls. Loudly.

You've got to be kidding me.

Alice giggles, breaking the kiss as she pushes against my chest.

"Mr Hunter, why don't you let me make you something to eat? As an apology, of course," she says with a cheeky smile as we both pant. "I should've been the first to recognise your expertise in the kitchen. I'm so sorry I failed."

Feigning a pained expression, I tighten my grip on her hips, not quite ready to let her go. "I don't know, you really hurt my feelings this time, Miss Lake." I shrug. "I guess it all depends on how sorry you truly are. That is, if you're even sorry at all."

"Why, of course I am," she says theatrically, a hand over her chest, drawing my attention to her breasts, obviously not aware I can see right through the flimsy fabric.

"Then take off your top and show me your gorgeous tits," I purr, licking my lower lip at the enticing sight.

"Sebastian," she reprimands, swatting my shoulder. "You're incorrigible!"

"Ow! What was that for?" I ask, pretending she hurt me. I also decide to keep the eyeful I'm getting to myself.

"For being a pervert." She pushes against my chest again, and I can't help but chuckle at her futile attempts to break free.

Taking pity on her, and sufficiently amused for now, I loosen my hold, finally letting her go.

"God, you're as strong as a bull. Jesus," she complains, out of breath, as she grabs hold of the kitchen island to steady herself.

"No one should be this strong, or tall, for that matter. It's not fair on other people."

I laugh out loud before grabbing my water bottle from the counter and taking a sip. "You mean it's not fair on little people. Right, shorty?"

I smirk, and she narrows her eyes at me. Her hands on her hips make her look so fucking cute, I almost lose my train of thought.

Oh, it's on, baby. Bring it.

"Maybe Shorty here won't feel like kissing a certain giant any more. What do you think about that, huh?" she threatens, a smug look on her face.

Putting my water bottle back on the island, I lean my hip on it and cross my arms over my chest. "I think Shorty has a smart mouth on her that's going to get her in trouble. Maybe even earn her a spanking or two if she doesn't behave." I smile menacingly at her right before I pretend to make a move to grab her.

"Ahhh! No!" she screams and turns around to run, giving me the perfect angle to slap her edible ass.

Her startled yelp makes me roar with laughter as I get her twice before she manages to escape.

"Now make me some food, woman. I need to keep my strength up for the spanking that's coming to you," I say, pointing at the fridge, sounding every bit like the damn caveman she already believes me to be.

Still laughing and rubbing her behind, Alice goes back to the fridge. I follow, wanting to resume my 'distracting' position, but the little minx is smart and this time she's ready for me.

"Take this," she says, turning before I manage to grab her, passing me the eggs and milk. Then she gets the cheese and mushrooms and tells me to put them on the island too. "You're in charge of the coffee whilst I make us the omelettes and toast."

"I can do more. Coffee doesn't take that long to make." I try to smile innocently, but with the threatening look she gives me, I'm pretty sure I showed the predatory signs she usually evokes in me. "OK, OK. Coffee it is," I acquiesce, raising my palms and backing away.

Five minutes later, I finish making our coffees and begin setting the breakfast area with everything we need. Fruit, orange juice, butter, a banana yogurt for me and a strawberry one for Alice, pastries, jam and fresh cheese.

Then I sit on the stool, on the opposite side of the island, and watch her. Just watch her. The happiness in her eyes, the smile on her face, the energy buzzing all around her.

She truly is in her element, and it's addictive to witness her love for cooking, her passion, her kindness. I shake my head with the goofiest smile plastered on my face.

"Here," she says, passing me the plates with our omelettes across the island.

"This smells amazing, sweetheart," I tell her, truly in awe of her and her talent as I put our plates on our place mats. "You're amazing, you know that?"

A shy smile forms on her lips, and I hold her gaze. I need her to see the pride in my eyes. Need her to see my faith in her.

"Thank you for saying that. It means a lot coming from you." The catch in her voice is raw and it reminds me yet again she's not used to taking compliments, much less having anyone take notice of her achievements. That has been obvious from the start.

Clearing her throat, she tries to disguise it, but the emotion is still there when she speaks. "I'll just get our toast and then we can eat."

I nod, wondering how such an innocent person survived such fucked-up parents. Contempt fills me and my blood boils all over again, something that's been happening a helluva lot since I learned all there is to learn about them. As well as Alice's past.

All it took was for my security team to do a little digging, hack into some medical records, and voilà, in no time, not only did they uncover more than enough evidence to back Dr Smith's suspicions that Alice had been abused as a child, but they also found evidence of a long and turbulent history of mental health issues affecting Alice's mother, such as depression, and substance abuse, namely alcohol, that affected her dad.

I won't bring it up with Alice, of course. Or pressure her into telling me anything.

I'll be patient. I'll follow the good doctor's advice and wait until she's ready to talk.

And when that happens—because it will happen, there's no doubt whatsoever in my mind—then I'll be here for her.

I'll always be here for her. No matter what.

Placing a plate with toast between us, Alice then hops onto the stool beside mine and picks up her mug. She smiles and takes a small sip of her coffee, then another and another, blowing on it, and I just about manage to wait until she picks up her knife and fork before I'm inhaling all the food on my plate.

Amazing doesn't do it justice. This is the best omelette I've ever tasted.

I grin and rub my full stomach when I'm finished. Then I reach over for my mug with my other hand, only to find Alice smiling up at me and with most of her meal untouched.

"What?" I smile back, unable to keep a straight face.

"You didn't even pause to breathe. I was worried you were going to choke."

Cheeky. I narrow my eyes. "Miss Lake, are you trying to be cute with me?"

She shakes her head quickly, trying—unsuccessfully, I must say—to stop the grin on her face from growing bigger.

"Well, you shouldn't worry, sweetheart. I already have a doctor and a tailor on standby for any food-related emergencies." I pat my flat stomach.

"A tailor?" A few more giggles escape her luscious mouth, and I can't help but stare at her. She's gorgeous. "Oh, I don't think you need to worry about your weight, Sebastian. Trust me. You're healthy and you exercise all the time. You're the picture of male perfection."

"Male perfection, huh? So you think I'm perfect?"

"I think you're perfect for me." She smiles shyly, and I melt at her feet.

"You're the perfect one, sweetheart. Believe me," I say, tucking a loose strand of silky hair behind her ear.

Our eyes meet and for a few seconds we stay just like that, locked in each other's gaze, both of us barely breathing.

"Um ..." I clear my throat. "I almost forgot. I wanted to ask you something. You come up with all your recipes yourself, don't you?"

Confused with the abrupt change to our conversation, she frowns. "Most of them, yes. Some I got from my nana, and others I change a few things here and there to make them my own."

"And when do you think you'll be ready to publish your work?" I ask her, deadpan.

Let's get this show on the road, shall we?

Blushing, she meets my gaze. "Well, as I told you before, that's my goal. My dream. But it's hard to find the time to work on it. That's why every chance I get I'm in the kitchen with my tablet, writing and editing my recipes as I cook." Her brows pinch together in another cute frown. "Being here with you, and off work, is actually the first time in years I've been able to do so much with it."

"Hmm ... perhaps you should consider not working for me, then."

She gasps and, at the shocked look on her face, I almost bite my tongue as I rush to explain. I'm a fucking idiot.

"I mean, I'd like to help you follow your dreams, sweetheart. Work on something you're actually passionate about. But for that to happen, we both know you need to fully dedicate yourself to your book, your cooking, and you have me now." I shrug. "I could support you, look after you while you write."

She shakes her head, her eyes wide and her lips moving even if no words are coming out. "Sebastian ... I ... Look, thank you, but I can't accept your help. I won't make any money for a while, and I won't take advantage of you."

"Sweetheart, I'd be the one taking advantage here. You cook, I eat. Honestly, I think I'm getting the better end of the deal."

"Not when you're the one buying all the food, paying all the bills ..."

"Seriously? You're worried about grocery expenses? Sweetheart, do you have any idea how much I'm worth? 'Cause I can promise you, it won't make the tiniest dent in my bank account."

She sips her coffee, looking uncomfortable with the conversation, but I don't care. I'm like a dog with a bone and I'm not letting this go until she says 'yes'.

"I know, but it makes me feel bad, Sebastian. Like I'm taking what doesn't belong to me. Besides, you're already giving me shelter and helping me until I can go back to work. I'm not taking anything else from you."

More like kidnapped and forced her into my shelter. Makes me feel like shit she thinks she owes me for helping her, when all the while I've been helping myself.

"OK, let's get some things straight," I start, raising one finger. "First of all, you're my girlfriend. You're not taking—I'm giving. Secondly, since you've moved in you've been looking after the house and cooking all these amazing meals for me, and I haven't paid you a single penny. And in third place, I want to help because I believe in you, in your talent, your gift. I think you'll be a huge success, and I want to be part of it. So, I'll ask you again, Alice. Let me help you. Let me make you happy. It will make me happy."

Yeah, I'm playing dirty, I know. But I'll beg on my hands and knees. I'll even make her feel guilty if necessary. What's important is that she accepts. That's all that matters to me at this point.

"God, you make it really difficult to say no." Her brows furrow further. "If I were to accept your help, you'd let me pay you back, right? Like, take a percentage of any money I'd make from the book?"

Well, fuck me sideways. Any other woman would've jumped at the chance I'm offering her. But not Alice. No, she's worried about taking advantage of me. Of me, for Christ's sake! Un-fucking-believable.

"If that's the only way you'll agree, then sure. I'll take a small percentage of the profits," I mutter, the words leaving a foul taste in my mouth.

It's not happening, sweetheart.

"That's the only way, Sebastian. I won't take advantage of you. I told you already." A stubborn expression takes over her features, and I have to stop myself from laughing as I pretend to agree. But if I want to make sure she accepts my offer, I have to be on my best behaviour.

"OK, agreed," I say, using my best business voice as I extend my hand for a shake. "Do we have a deal?"

She pushes her chin out and places her hand in mine. "We do. And thank you, Sebastian ... for everything." She holds my gaze as we shake hands, and I can't help but smile down at her.

"You're a tough negotiator. I'll give you that. Let's just hope you can keep it up until Monday," I say, not elaborating on purpose.

"Why? What's happening on Monday?"

"Well, for starters, you have a meeting with a very good friend of mine. A friend who's big in the book industry and is very, very excited to be meeting with you."

"What? Are you joking?" she asks, gaping at me like a fish.

I shake my head, grinning at her. "Nope. Not a joke. She's coming here on Monday, and her company does everything from editing, to design, to publishing."

Alice screams like a little girl and throws herself at me.

I catch her in my arms, holding her close. "I hope you don't mind, but when I told her about you, I had to show her some of your work. She didn't want to get your hopes up without being sure. Said there was no need to get you all worked up for nothing. It was funny, though, to see her face light up as she read through a few pages of your manuscript." I almost laugh, remembering Beatrice's expression again.

Alice stays silent, though, and that makes me feel anxious.

"Are you mad?" I ask, tightening my hold on her. "I know I should've asked you first, but in my defence, I was afraid you'd say no, and I couldn't just stand by any more when I have the contacts to help."

"I'm not mad," she whispers against my neck just as I feel the moisture of her tears. "I just can't believe you did all this for me, that's all. Thank you. Thank you so much, Sebastian."

"It's only the beginning, sweetheart. I plan on doing more … much, much more from now on. I'll do anything to make you happy."

"You already do, Sebastian. You didn't have to do all this."

My heart expands then, beating something fierce against my chest with all the love and pride I feel for this girl. Using the pads of my thumbs to wipe away her tears, I look down at her as she sniffles a little.

And I realise that I never stood a chance against such a wonderful creature. That there's no way I could not have fallen for this girl.

That there's no way I could ever resist her.

Shaken with emotion, I kiss her, pouring everything I feel into it, telling her with no words she's the most important person in this cruel and violent world for me. Telling her she's my one and only, my everything—her presence just as important as the very air I breathe.

"Now be a good girl and finish your breakfast, Miss Lake," I murmur, touching my forehead to hers. My lips brush gently against her mouth. "I have big plans for you, young lady."

"You have?" she asks breathlessly, squirming a little on my lap.

"I have," I rasp. Yeah, the hot and heavy kind. A re-enactment of what happened in the living room and on the couch the other night, to be precise. But I won't tell her that. No, I'll just jump her again when it's time.

I almost laugh. I feel like a teenager.

"Tell me more." Her eyes burn into mine.

I kiss her again, just a sweet peck on the lips. "No. It's a surprise."

"I wonder if I should like the sound of that?"

"You'll like more than just the sound, trust me," I promise, sitting her back on her stool and turning her towards her plate.

Jesus! I'm as hard as a rock already.

"Now finish your breakfast," I say between clenched teeth.

"Yes, sir, Mr Hunter." She smiles a playful smile, saluting me military-style before picking up her fork and digging into her meal.

I stare at her. She really has no idea what she does to me, my little thing. The desires she invokes in me, the deviant thoughts in my head ...

She's about to find out, though. She's about to find out everything that's worth knowing about me.

And I guarantee it's going to be one hell of a ride.

Chapter 11

Alice

Standing outside by the front door, Beatrice and I are still engrossed in conversation when her phone begins to ring.

"Sorry, Alice," she apologises, takes the phone out of her Prada bag and answers the call after one quick look at the screen. "Hello," she says, pushing her glossy brown hair out of her face as she frowns.

At five-three, with her big, expressive, chocolate-brown eyes and a body to kill for, Beatrice is a natural beauty and very difficult, I imagine, for most men to resist.

A thought that doesn't worry me in the least. I know if Sebastian had ever slept with her, they could never have remained friends. No, he would've pulled away from her eventually and she'd end up resenting him for it.

Not to mention, if that were the case, he'd never allow us to meet. Let alone have a professional relationship.

Rolling her eyes, Beatrice mouths, "The office ... again." I cover my mouth with my hand. This is getting ridiculous. They've been calling her non-stop the entire time she's been here.

"Of course, Eric." She smiles sweetly and then starts pulling at an imaginary rope around her neck as if she's hanging herself, her tongue sticking out for added effect. I can't help it, I start laughing.

God, this girl cracks me up. She really does. What can I say?

She laughs too, one hand covering her mouth whilst the other holds the phone away.

And funnily enough, it's in this precise moment, between our muffled giggles and our conspiratorial smiles, I realise just how much I don't want her to leave. Just how much I already like this girl. And that perhaps this business meeting is not just about business any more and I've made a friend.

I smile happily at the thought. But not too happily, since I'm also feeling a little bit guilty about monopolising Beatrice's time. All four and a half hours of it.

I cringe, embarrassed. Especially when I know she's being missed back at the office.

"OK. OK, I'm coming now, Eric. Yeah, calm down. I'll see you soon." She hangs up with a scowl. "It seems I have to go make an appearance. Eric, my so-called assistant, is 'close to a nervous breakdown and giving up on me'. His words, not mine." She shakes her head, and I press my lips together, trying to stifle a laugh. "Seriously, he can be such a drama queen sometimes."

Poor Beatrice. She really has her work cut out with this guy.

She huffs, dropping her phone back into her bag just as it starts ringing again. "Grrr, I'm binning this fucking thing, I swear," Beatrice growls, looking for the phone again, her bag propped up on her knee as she balances herself on a step, and I take a moment to look at her. I mean really look at her.

Beyond the beauty. Beyond the makeup and expensive clothes, the accessories and designer shoes. Beyond the business woman mask.

And the truth is, I really like what I see. Beatrice's funny. Smart. Easy-going.

So much so, it's almost embarrassing how sick I felt before she arrived.

God, I can't believe I even threw up. Just kill me now.

Beatrice cancels the call before hugging me tight. "Listen, Alice, just call me if you have any questions, all right? I wrote my personal number on the back of my card, so call me directly, OK?" Holding me at arm's length, she pierces me with intense eyes. "I'm serious, darling. Whatever you need. Oh, and let's grab coffee later this week. I'll text you the details."

I nod, smiling big and one hundred percent sure this girl and I are going to be great friends. I can just feel it. "Sounds good. And again, thank you so much for coming, Beatrice. It meant the world to me."

"Darling, I'm so excited about this, I should be the one thanking you." She smiles like the cat that got the cream. "It's going to be fucking amazing, trust me."

I laugh at her excitement. It's almost as much as my own. "Well, I hope so."

"Well, I know so, and I'm the expert. OK, I'm leaving. For real now." She hugs me again, then makes her way down the front steps and onto the driveway, calling over her shoulder. "Oh, and don't forget to send me the manuscript later on today. I want to read it in its entirety before I pitch it to my dad. He's the big boss, after all. Even if he always does what I want."

"I won't forget. Don't worry," I call, walking down the driveway as she gets inside her car.

* * *

Beatrice and I wave at each other as she drives off, and Rick, one of the security guys, instructs the others to close the gate as soon as her sensible BMW hits the road. He pushes his finger into his earpiece and then stands by the entryway as if to block someone from coming in, and I can't help but roll my eyes at him.

Ridiculous, really. As if something is going to happen at the gate. Almost as ridiculous as the amount of security at the house and around me these days.

Suddenly my mood takes a dive.

It's all Sebastian's doing, of course. None of the guys are to blame. Still, I can't help but feel annoyed. It feels like the more security I get, the more I lose of myself, of the person I am. Of my freedom.

I shake my head in disgust, and Rick gives me a sideways glance, probably wondering what has gotten into me. I'm too annoyed to act normal. Too angry to even make sense, let alone be nice like I usually am to them.

And Sebastian, well, Sebastian needs to calm the fuck down and get a hobby, because this is getting out of hand.

I'm about to turn on my heel to go back to the house when the screech of a car—no, two cars—roots me in place. My eyes widen and my jaw hangs loose as I get a little glimpse through the opening of the gate. Just a few seconds of colours and shapes before the two heavy doors crank closed, effectively blocking the cars and their drivers from my gaze.

"Get Miss Lake inside! Now!" Rick yells at Michael, my personal bodyguard, just as four other guards run towards the gate to secure it, prompting Michael to start moving my way.

"Rick, we should go check on them," I call, already taking a few steps down the driveway. "They might need help."

They didn't collide. It was more of a near miss from what I could gather. It has been raining nonstop the whole morning, and I think one of the drivers lost control, skidding on the wet tarmac and going straight toward our gate just as another car was driving past.

Thank God they both managed to stop just in the nick of time. Still, I'd like to see if we can help. Make sure nobody got hurt and all that.

"I'll go, Miss Lake, but I need you to go back inside. It's not safe."

I blow out a breath. "Rick, please ..." I start, but he cuts me off.

"Michael, take her to the house, now," he says with one of his sterner looks directed at me.

Well, no one's manhandling me. Not today, at least.

"OK. OK," I say, raising my palms at Michael as Rick steps outside the smaller gate, looking every bit the security team leader and big boss that he is. A couple of suited guys, looking very much like Michael and Rick, are already on the other side. "I'll go," I add, trying to catch another glimpse around Rick and my iron shield before he closes the stupid thing. But it's too late.

Damn it! I huff as the metal clunks closed again. Unbelievable. "Michael, just let me have a look. You can come with."

"Miss Lake, please. You'll get me in trouble."

"What's with the 'Miss Lake'?" I ask, looking at him. "I've told you to call me Alice."

Michael sighs, barely making eye contact with me. "Mr Hunter instructed us to solely use your surname when talking to you or referring to you. He also reminded us to keep conversation with you to a minimum and concentrate on doing what he pays us for—keeping you safe. So, I'm going to ask you again, Miss Lake. Please go inside. I'd hate to lose my job today."

"He did what?" I whisper, shocked beyond words. That jealous idiot.

Michael's brown eyes stay on the floor, his tall, bulky form straight as a ramrod as he keeps silent, and I shake my head.

Disappointed and a whole lot angry, I turn and walk back to the house. Disappointed because Sebastian's irrational jealousy is making him not trust me with the guards. And angry because I'm being treated like a defenceless child when all I wanted was to help the victims of a crash. A perfectly normal reaction, if you ask me. It's who I am.

"Sebastian, you big buffoon. You really need to lighten up," I mutter under my breath, closing the front door behind me and shrugging off my coat. My blood pressure rises when I remember I can't even go upstairs to sneak a peek at the scene outside because everything's happening too close to the gate. And of course, I won't be able to see anything no matter how much I stretch my little neck.

Huffing and puffing with indignation, I hang my coat back inside the wardrobe and remove my shoes. Then I rush into the living room where I pace and pace, my hands fisted at my sides.

Seriously, I love Sebastian, overprotective fool that he is, but this is too much. His jealousy, all this security.

And OK, OK, I get that he's rich and powerful, and that he has enemies who very much would like to hurt him, preferably through me, given a chance.

And now that it is official I'm his girlfriend and we've been seen out together, I understand I'm at risk too.

But this was different.

This was only an accident, for Christ's sake. Well, actually not even an accident, just a near miss.

Come to think of it, I couldn't even hear the usual arguing or shouting that's normal in situations like this. So, yeah, I guess they really are OK, and I'm just being ... difficult?

I don't know. I'm just not used to this. I sigh, looking around the grand living room.

All this luxury. The bodyguards. The twenty-four-seven protection and pampering. All this is new to me.

Not to mention being in a relationship and having to deal with Sebastian and his over-the-top protectiveness. A character trait that came as a total shock to me, if I'm being honest.

I mean, never in a million years did I imagine he could be so jealous. Or possessive. Or that he'd start scaring the living shit out of his guards because of it.

I shake my head.

Poor guys. Can't even hold a proper conversation with me for fear of getting sacked.

Try telling that to Mr Caveman, though.

He's overprotective because he cares, says a little voice in the back of my head.

I smile to myself despite my annoyance.

Well, I guess it's kinda sweet. Even if stupid at times. And I know he cares ...

I wouldn't be with him otherwise.

* * *

After a few more minutes fuming over Sebastian's obsessive behaviour and the security increase around me and the house, I decide there's nothing I can do for now.

This is new to Sebastian too—our relationship, us—and I have to let him deal with his feelings and fears in his own way until he calms down.

He's allowing me space to do the same, so why shouldn't I reciprocate?

I sigh.

I just have to be patient and give him time. Everything's going to be all right. And in the meantime, I'll just keep my opinions on security to myself. They're not doing anyone any harm, and Sebastian has enough on his plate as it is, what with work and his new position as CEO. Not to mention the problems with Arthur.

Going into the kitchen, I spot my phone on the counter and pick it up. There's a text from Sebastian.

Call me when Beatrice leaves. Thinking of you always. x

Always. Such a small word, yet it holds so much meaning. I smile so big my face nearly splits in half, and just like that all my previous thoughts dissipate.

I'm scared too, and trying to find faults in everything around me. I know that's what I'm doing.

I mean, who in their right mind would be complaining because they have a rich and protective boyfriend, right? Especially one they love and who takes such good care of them.

I should check in with him. He must be worried, wondering what's taking so long. My teeth sink into my lower lip and I text him back.

Hi, baby!
The meeting went well. REALLY WELL! You'd be proud of my negotiation skills.
xoxo

I press send, leaving out the incident at the gate. I'm sure Rick will tell him at some point anyway, and as I said, I don't want to get involved.

Putting the phone down, I blow out a breath and gather all the plates and mugs from the table, moving them to the sink to do the washing up.

Beatrice and I indulged ourselves with a few slices of cake, muffins, and a whole lot of coffee throughout our meeting. Another of Sebastian's great ideas.

"Are you sure about this?" I asked him, frowning. "It makes me feel like I'm trying too much."

He pulled me to him. "Baby, trust me. There's nothing like having a few samples of your product to finish up a sale. You'll be thanking me tomorrow."

"Sebastian, you got me this meeting. I'll be thanking you nonetheless. Even if I'm unsuccessful."

He gives me a sweet smile. "Impossible, sweetheart. Beatrice is a smart businesswoman; she won't let you get away now."

And what do you know? Not only was Beatrice well and truly impressed with 'my' initiative, I also couldn't be happier with the result. Or prouder for that matter.

Cake makes everything better, my nana used to say, and right now, it can't get much better than this.

My phone rings, making me smile, and I grab the dish towel to dry my hands. Naughty, naughty, Mr Hunter. I know for a fact he should be in a meeting at this very moment, hence the text.

"Hi, baby," I greet excitedly.

"Congratulations, sweetheart. I knew you could do it."

I grin at his faith in me. It's a novelty. No one's ever believed in me like this. And it makes me feel proud, special. Makes me feel like I could take on the world. "I couldn't have done it without you, Sebastian. Thank you."

"It's all you, baby. All I did was place a call. You're the one with the talent."

I clear my throat, flushed, excited, and a little bit emotional, to be honest. "What happened to your meeting?"

"Oh, um, we're on a toilet break, so I came to my office to call you."

Yeah, right. I shake my head. "More like you told everyone to have a break so you could go to your office to call me." He chuckles. "Sebastian, I texted you. You should've waited," I admonish, secretly glad that he didn't.

"I know, baby, but I wanted to hear your voice." Oh, be still, my heart. This man says the sweetest things. "Besides, they were boring me to death—"

Bang! The loudest sound comes through the phone, and I hold my breath.

"What the fuck do you think you're doing?" Oh, my, is that Luke's voice?

"What does it look like? I'm on the phone. Now get out."

"Is that Alice? Give me the phone."

"No. Get out, I'll be there in a few minutes. Hey!"

Confused by the bumping and grunting I hear next, I frown, looking down at my phone. "Sebastian?" I say, holding the phone back to my ear, my frown deepening when I realise the boys are actually fighting. "Sebastian?"

"Fuck!" someone growls, scaring the bejesus out of me.

Oh, God, who was that?

"Alice, it's Luke."

"Luke, what's happening? Why are you two fighting?"

"Well, first and foremost, can you bring your chocolate cake next time you visit, please? I miss it," he says, breathing heavily and on the move, apparently.

"You make your own fucking cake, you idiot," Sebastian sneers. "Now give me the fucking phone."

I pick up on more bumping and grunting and even a few smashing sounds, and then Sebastian is growling again. "Luke, I'm warning you!"

Luke laughs. "Your jerk of a boyfriend is about to go apeshit on me, so I have to be quick. Fuck, that was close! Listen, just ask him to go back to the meeting and call you when he's done, OK? This is probably the most important deal we'll make all year."

I go to reply, but at the thump, followed by Luke's moans of pain, I hold my tongue.

"You fucking asshole. I'm gonna break your fucking teeth," Sebastian growls, getting the phone back. I think.

"I'd like to see you try," Luke taunts.

OK, I need to distract my man. Knowing these two, they'll keep going until one of them is really hurt. "Sebastian, is it true? About the meeting, I mean."

"Don't worry, baby," he says, out of breath. "We all looked like we could use a break. I did us all a favour, believe me."

"Luke's right then, you have to go back."

"Only after you tell me you're happy with the deal."

"You're all I need to make me happy, Sebastian. No book deal could ever measure up to you," I reply, my smile growing wider.

"Well, you make me happy too."

"Yeah, and you two make me sick," Luke says. "Seriously, I think I just threw up a little in my mouth."

"I'm gonna kill you, I swear it," Sebastian growls.

"Baby, go back to your meeting. We'll talk when you get home," I insist.

"OK. I'll see you later, gorgeous. I miss you," he says.

Luke laughs. "You sound so fucking gay right now."

"Shut up or I'll shut you up," Sebastian threatens, and I snicker. It's like I can see him, his index finger pointed at his brother, his muscled body tense, imposing and ready for a fight.

God, hearing these two when they're like this, you'd never guess how much they love each other. How much they care.

"I miss you too," I tell him. "Say bye to Luke for me."

"Bye, Alice, and thank you," Luke says, raising his voice to be heard. "And don't forget about my cake."

I laugh again. "Goodbye, Sebastian."

"Bye, sweetheart. I'll see you at home," Sebastian whispers, ringing off.

* * *

I puff out my cheeks at the sight of the unmade bed and the tray of dirty dishes on the floor. Hell, I'd forgotten all about these.

I run my hands through my hair, pulling it into a ponytail, and walk further into the master bedroom, a sigh escaping my lips as I let out a humourless laugh.

Well, no time like the present and all that. After all, it was me who cancelled the cleaning crew so I'd have more privacy during my meeting this morning.

Bending, I pick up the tray and take it back to the kitchen, where I wash, clean and put everything away. Then I go back to the master bedroom, move the pillows to a chair and start making the bed.

I was so nervous and fidgety this morning, I couldn't even steel myself to do the most mundane of tasks. Good thing my gorgeous boyfriend decided to be extra-sweet and woke me up not only with his amazing kisses, but also the most romantic breakfast in bed.

I smile as I recall our makeout session this morning. How Sebastian was gentle and patient with me, how he showered me with endless support and attention. I sigh, my heart doing little flip-flops at the tantalising memory.

I'm the happiest I've been since I can remember ... and it's all thanks to this man. To the way he treats me and cherishes me, and helps me see life through a different lens.

Finished with the bed and feeling like the luckiest girl alive, I lie over the covers and hug Sebastian's pillow to my chest. I bury my face in the white cloth and inhale deeply. I still can't believe this is my life, that this is really happening to me.

Not that I want to rain on my own parade or anything, but I'm old enough to know that fairy tales are just that, fairy tales. And charming princes don't actually exist. Not in my life, at least.

I laugh bitterly, a sense of anxiety telling me to be ready, to prepare. Any day now I'll realise this is just a dream. A wonderful dream that will be taken from me like so many other dreams before.

"Sebastian," I whisper into the pillow, suddenly tired. Tired of running from what I want. Tired of hiding from what I feel. Tired of being scared all the time.

I've been surviving for so long, I've forgotten how to live.

Closing my eyes, I allow myself a few more minutes of despair, of doubt.

But then that's it, I decide. I deserve to be happy. I deserve to be loved.

I mean, why shouldn't I? What have I done that's so terrible that I should be punished into living my life alone?

Nothing, that's what. Absolutely freaking nothing.

So I push myself off the bed, throw the rest of the pillows on it and walk back to the kitchen. I just need to keep myself busy and not overthink things so much. Need to stop scrutinising every single little detail of my life and coming up with the worst possible scenarios.

I smile. What did Sebastian say? Oh, right, that I have one hell of an overactive imagination.

Well, he wasn't wrong about that, that's for sure. And it's about time I stop.

This is it, Alice, the crossroads. Either you take the road that offers you a chance at living—even at the risk of being hurt—or you continue down the same lonely road you've been on for most of your life.

One thing is for sure. You have to make a decision.

Be brave, be wild, but take charge.

Be your own woman from here on out.

* * *

"Are you done, sweetheart?" Sebastian asks lazily, his head on my lap as he watches the credits of a movie rolling up on the big screen.

"Five more minutes, baby." I run my fingers through his hair, having ignored him for most of tonight.

It's Wednesday, close to eleven p.m., and we've been perched on the sofa since finishing dinner almost two and a half hours ago. I'm working on my manuscript on a tablet.

Beatrice suggested I write down some of my memories. Just a few short stories to begin with about growing up and cooking with Nana, as well as any funny and interesting facts from when I lived on my own and came up with my own recipes. She happened to read a few of my older notes, where I included little tidbits of background information with whatever recipe I wrote, and she wants to bring that kind of connection to the book.

I grin, remembering her words.

This is amazing, Alice. Absolutely amazing. And your writing will feel that much more personal and intimate to the readers. Trust me. It will help us create a deeper connection and better rapport with them. We're talking a very long and healthy career here.

Not that she had to convince me or anything. The woman's a literary genius, and not only did I love the idea, I'm also loving writing about moments that are so special to me. Happy times when my nana and cooking made me feel good, hopeful even, about life and the future in general.

"Done," I announce, closing the cover of my tablet and letting out a long yawn. I stretch my arms and my back. "I'm all yours, baby."

Sebastian turns to face me, a slow smile forming on his lips as he looks up at me. "All mine, huh? I like the sound of that."

Not able to wait a minute longer to have his lips on mine, I lean down and kiss him, finding it unbelievable that I actually managed to get any work done with him around. "Sorry I made you wait for so long," I whisper, giving him a final peck on the lips.

Sweeping the hair off my face, he cups my cheeks. "Do you know how proud I am of you?"

Could this man be any sweeter?

Swallowing the lump in my throat, I simply tell him, "Take me to bed, Sebastian. I need to be close to you."

He nods and presses his forehead to mine. "I thought you'd never ask."

I smile, and, without another word he gets up, lifts me into his arms and carries me like a bride to our bedroom.

Chapter 12

Sebastian

I stare at the bathroom mirror, unable to wipe the shit-eating-grin off my face. It's only our sixth night together and already it couldn't be more perfect than this.

"What?" Alice mumbles around her toothbrush. I shake my head, and she smiles a cheeky smile. Then her eyes are crossing and she's sticking out her foam-covered tongue at my reflection in the mirror, and I chuckle as I bend over the sink. I choke on my own toothpaste, and the little firecracker laughs harder as I do my best to spit.

Oh, you're in so much trouble now, missy.

I grab her around the hips and throw her over my shoulder caveman-style, a low growl escaping through my teeth as I slap her edible ass and walk us out.

"Sebastian!" she screams, her squeals of joy and giggles making my grin grow as I slap her ass one more time and carry her through our bedroom.

"Take me back," she pleads, trying to twist out of my hold, toothbrush still in hand. "Take me back, I didn't rinse."

I throw her on the bed, my eager cock hardening as I stand over her. She's all curves and sex, her hot body barely covered by her flimsy white nightdress as she lies across the bed. And I'm having a helluva time controlling my libido.

Fuck, she's gorgeous. And I'm obsessed with her. With this bright and beautiful young woman who takes my breath away every time I look at her.

Who'll keep taking my breath away, I'm sure, long after we're ninety, in wheelchairs, and with diapers on our asses.

Alice looks trustingly up at me, the grey of her irises dark and stormy with her arousal. Evidence that she wants me.

Fuck, I want her too. I want her more than air, water or food.

As if knowing what I'm thinking, her smile turns radiant, her expression so tender and sweet my breath catches in my throat, making the pressure inside my chest increase.

It bloody hurts. Shit, could I have a heart attack at the age of twenty-five? Could I die? Because I'm starting to believe my innocent angel brought me back to life just to kill me for real this time.

Alice mimics my frown, looking so cute I just want to kiss her. "Sebastian, are you OK?"

"I just can't get over how beautiful you are, that's all. I'm a lucky bastard."

"I'm lucky too," she says, raising herself on her elbows. "You're gorgeous and kind. Charming and thoughtful, and you've been nothing but wonderful to me since day one."

"Is that so?" I ask, my voice raspy with guilt. I'm none of those things.

"Well, obviously I have to overlook your caveman tendencies and how you first kissed me." She shakes her head, a flirty smile on her face as she presses a tiny foot to my chest. "Cornering me and taking advantage of me like that. Mmm, so devious …"

Unable to keep my hands off her, I grab her ankle and raise her foot to my mouth, kissing it as I try to quench my desire, my guilt.

God, the way she was just looking at me. Like I matter. Like I'm everything she has ever wanted and dreamed of.

I close my eyes.

Yep, I'm officially a scumbag. A lying, manipulative scumbag who fights dirty at every turn.

I'm ashamed. So fucking ashamed of myself, of my behaviour. I turned into a person who has no boundaries to get what he wants. Who is rotten to the core. Whom I hate.

My chest tightens. Fuck! I practically abducted her.

Well, congratulations, Sebastian, you got the girl—for now, at least. Because if she ever finds out the things you've done …

I inhale deeply.

No, I can't lose this. I won't lose her. I may not deserve her, but I'll be damned if I'm letting her go.

"I'm glad you did, though," Alice continues, snapping me out of my guilt trip.

"Did what?" I ask, meeting her eyes, my hands still kneading her ankle as I wait for her reply.

She smiles. "Corner me, silly. If you hadn't, we wouldn't be here together like this. So I'm glad you did."

Taken aback by her response, I'm not sure what to say.

My sweet, sweet girl. If only she knew that's not all I've done.

"Sebastian, what's wrong?" she asks.

"Nothing, baby," I say, grabbing her other foot and pressing it to my chest, lying yet again. "Just have a lot on my mind, that's all. Work stuff."

She moans, dropping her head to the mattress when I suck her toe into my mouth, distracting her.

Her words still dance around in my head, tempting, tantalising, and I close my eyes, holding onto them.

If you hadn't, we wouldn't be here together like this.

Being the bastard that I am, I decide they go for everything I've done so far. Every wrong I've done her, every lie that brought us together, every sin exonerated just like that.

We belong together. And it's all that should matter, even if my conscience weighs heavy on me right now.

Alice, the light to my dark, my conscience, my heart.

I smile, kissing the silky skin of her ankle. Deep down, I'll always know that what I did was wrong, but if I want us to move forward, this is what I must do.

Maybe one day I'll seek redemption, tell her everything. Come clean … who knows?

But not now. Not when our relationship is so new and I'm still having to prove myself to her.

She'd leave me if she found out what an asshole I am so early on. A fucking disaster if there ever was one.

No. No, all I can do is be the man she deserves from now on—be good to her, for her. Be whatever she needs me to be.

"Hey, you've gone all quiet again," Alice observes, worry creasing her brow. "Anything I can do to help?"

"You already are. Your presence, your kisses, that's all the help I need."

She smiles. "Then I better kiss you right now, Mr Hunter," she rasps, whilst pulling out of my hold to go up on her knees.

Not daring to get that close to her until I regain some form of control, I take a few steps back, shaking my head as she opens her arms to me. "If I go near you right now, I'll rip your pretty nightdress apart with my bare hands."

"Oh, I ..." she stutters, bright pink covering her cheeks as her eyes lower to my crotch, stirring the predator in me. "Sebastian?" she whispers.

I swallow hard, the expression on her face making the tent in my trousers roar to be freed, and by the time her eyes return to my face, I have little to no control left in me. "Take your clothes off," I almost growl, half-expecting her to refuse, but hoping like mad that she doesn't.

So far we've only touched and kissed, and, not wanting to scare her or push her too far, I've been allowing our clothes and bedcovers to stay on.

But, goddammit, I don't think I can do it any more. I just don't have the strength to resist.

"Baby, I need to see you," I cajole, barely able to contain my excitement.

Much less believe my eyes when Alice slides off the bed—slowly, sensually—places her toothbrush on her nightstand and, standing before me, begins to lower the straps of her nightdress whilst looking up at me. First one then the other, her movements unhurried and delicate as the wispy fabric slides down her body and then pools at her feet.

I stop breathing. Sexy doesn't even begin to describe the enticing morsel. I lick my lips, mesmerised by the beautiful creature before me.

Visibly trembling, Alice covers her breasts with her hands, her cheeks still a lovely shade of pink.

"Don't," I command, holding her gaze. "Don't hide your beautiful body from me. Now show me what I want to see."

Aroused, she bites her lower lip as she obediently lowers her arms and lets her full breasts spill free.

I take it all in, my mouth watering at the sight. At the soft glow and smoothness of her skin. At the plump roundness of her breasts and small, rosy nipples, all pebbled and perfect and just begging to be sucked.

She's gorgeous. So fucking gorgeous she looks like she came straight out one of my dreams. And the way she keeps putting her faith in me …

I swallow hard, my eyes travelling down her body, caressing her flat stomach, pausing at her tiny waist and the cutest belly button I've ever seen.

"Fuck!" I mutter, giving in to the sensations and desire she always invokes in me.

She's so delicate. So soft. All curves and woman, my heaven and hell rolled into one, and I feel desperate. Famished. Crazy, wanting to rip those white, lacy panties off her round hips like a beast.

"The panties. Take them off," I instruct, my voice thick with need. My cock is hard as steel, pushing through the waistband of my trousers.

Blushing a deeper shade of pink, my gorgeous temptress hooks her thumbs into the sides of her panties and slowly wiggles out of them, letting them fall to the floor. Her eyes are glued to mine as she steps out of the clothes around her feet, lips parted, nipples hard rosy diamonds, pointed directly at me.

Growing impatient, I push down my trousers and boxers, getting rid of them in one swift move. My aching cock springs free, bouncing against my stomach, and Alice gasps.

"Alice," I rasp as she stares at it, her eyes big and round as saucers when they rise to meet my own.

She's an open book. Nervous, aroused, and so fucking beautiful she takes my breath away.

"I want you in my arms. I need to feel you," I say around the lump forming in my throat.

Her tiny nod is all the permission I need before I'm on her in two strides, holding her, embracing her. Tugging her closer to me as we breathe into each other.

I release a shaky breath, my skin breaking into goosebumps as I focus on the feel of her petite frame and naked body, all smooth and soft, finally pressed up against mine.

"Stunning. You're absolutely stunning, sweetheart," I whisper, my hands on her hips, possessive, demanding, gripping her in a bruising hold I have no control over.

She shivers, looking so vulnerable compared to me, I can't help the surge of adrenaline rushing through my veins at the thought of ruling her body. Of owning it.

Trapped in my arms, her palms flat on my chest, she already feels like a prisoner to my will. Mine to do with what I want. Mine to pleasure as I see fit.

And soon, very soon, I will.

Sweet as ever, Alice presses a kiss to my pectoral, her lips and right hand resting right over my heart. The gesture is so tender, so innocent, my throat constricts and tears burn the back of my eyes. I swallow hard.

"Baby," I whisper, cradling the back of her head and gently tugging on her silky hair until I'm staring into her eyes. Her lips pucker as she raises herself on tiptoes, offering them to me.

I bend, touching my lips to hers, my tongue slowly tracing the outline of her mouth. A world of emotions takes over as I give her the kiss I should've given her the first time.

Before long, though, we're kissing harder, hungrier. Our need for each other consuming us, charging the air between us. Urging us to fuse, to fuck. To come together as one.

Frantic, I lift her into my arms and take the final steps towards the bed, our lips still locked together in a frenzy as I lower her to the mattress and gently cover her small body with mine.

God! I didn't know it could be like this, that I'd feel like this.

Drunk on her, I plunge my tongue deep inside her mouth, my hand sliding up her side, inching towards her breast.

She whimpers, her nails digging into my shoulders when I cup the perky mound, her nipple pebbled and erect beneath my palm before I pinch it, first gently then hard.

"Mmm!" She thrashes, her quiet cries sending a jolt of pleasure down my spine. Spurring me on. Urging me forward.

And just like an addict getting his fix, I lose my mind.

I don't stop. I can't stop.

I continue to kiss her, tasting her and taking her lips until our burning lungs give out and both of us are on the verge of losing consciousness.

But goddammit—and call me crazy for it—even then I don't want to quit. Not now. Not ever. Not for as long as we both exist.

Dizzy, but nonetheless wearing a stupid smile on my face, I press my forehead to hers, our ragged breaths filling the space as we meet each other's eyes. And it's still not enough. I need more.

I'll always need more with Alice.

"Do you trust me?" I ask, twisting her nipple between my fingers.

"Yes," she replies, all breath and no sound. "Oh, God!" she mewls, clutching at my hair when I bite into her neck, sucking at the smooth skin. Marking her as mine.

I groan, wanting this woman so fucking much, I feel like I'm going insane.

Get it together. Just get it together, Sebastian.

More turned on than in control, I lick and nibble my way down to her tits. My mouth latches onto a rosy nipple just as I push my hand between her legs.

She cries out, arching her back off the bed as I press my middle finger to her clit. My eyes close momentarily when I feel how drenched she is. Stifling a predatory smile, I keep my touch light and the pressure on her slick clit almost non-existent, my mouth alternating from one breast to the other as I listen to her erratic breaths.

I'm torturing her, I know. Tormenting her, even. Deliberately taking her to the brink, only to leave her there hanging.

But all good things come to those who wait.

"Sebastian," she begs, her moans growing louder by the second, her body more desperate and heated, and I know she's ready for me.

She won't stop me now. She's too far gone for it.

With one last kiss to each nipple, I begin my descent. Worshipping her stomach, her hip bones, her legs, her feet. No part of her body is left untouched by my tongue or lips.

And by the time I kiss my way back up to her thighs, my mouth watering for her taste, she's a writhing, wet mess for me.

Barely coherent, I feel her thighs press closer together and I finally snap. "Open," I growl, forcing her legs apart, biting her gently. "Open for me, baby girl," I repeat in a softer voice, listening to her every gasp, every whimper. Watching as her delicate fingers clutch at the sheets and she quivers under my touch.

Nuzzling her, I enjoy all the pretty sounds she makes, my tongue following, licking her open for me. Lapping at her sweet juices and drinking her in.

"Oh ... oh, God," she breathes, sounding almost delirious now, making me smile. My male pride is only surpassed by the adrenaline coursing through my veins as I cover her pink, virgin pussy with my mouth.

She screams. She actually screams, my beautiful angel. The strangled sound sends jolts of pleasure down my body and straight to my dick.

And her taste ... Christ! Strawberries and fucking cream. Every fucking time. My girl's sweet all over.

Closing my eyes, I swirl my tongue around her clit, delve deeper into her folds, and then lick along her slit.

"Sebastian," she moans. The pink blush already tinting her chest, her tits, travels further up her neck, reaching her cheeks. Intensifying this never-ending hunger in me.

And then I'm lost. Lost in her taste, her scent. Lost in the moment that's been my fantasy for as long as I've known this woman.

Holding her trembling thighs down, I suck Alice's clit into my mouth, watching intently as she tenses under me. Her hips rocking and swaying, lifting with each flick and lash of my tongue. Her back arched, nipples taut and pointing up. The view before me is so decadent, so fucking erotic, I don't even know how I stop myself from coming.

"You taste so good, baby girl, I could eat you out for days," I murmur into her, reaching for my cock. The firm grip I give myself relieves some of the pressure, but not enough. Not nearly enough. "So wet ... always so fucking wet for me."

I lick her from clit to entrance, prodding at her opening before I push my tongue inside. Fucking her with it. Tasting her innocence. Touching her like this for the very first time.

She's small, insanely small, and so fucking delicious, it's a wonder I don't lose it right now. That I don't try to take her.

But then she cries out, holding me down, demanding her pleasure, and I almost lose the remnants of my meagre self-control. I grunt, my mouth enveloping her whole pussy as her breathless moans fill the space.

And I love it. I just fucking love seeing her like this.

Aroused. Unrestrained. With her small hands on me and her delicate fingers pressing me down. Her scent, her taste, and how she feels pressed up against me drive me wild.

Fuck, I love her. I just fucking love her.

This woman. This amazing, beautiful woman, who has me turned inside out, confused, and bursting at the seams with so many emotions, so many feelings, I don't know if I'm coming or going half of the time.

Giving myself one final squeeze, I replace my tongue with my middle finger. She's wet and primed and this time it slides right in.

I exhale deeply, relieved. I don't think I could bear to see her hurting tonight.

"Fuck, you feel so good, baby girl. So good and so fucking tight." I add a second finger, a harsh exhale escaping my lips at the feel of her channel clenching and pulsing like crazy on me.

She's close. I can tell.

"Watch me," I command. "Watch me as I make you come."

"Sebastian, please," she begs, our eyes locked together as I circle her clit with my tongue, pull it into my mouth, and suck the little button hard. "Ahhh," she cries, throwing her head back, every lash of my tongue taking her closer to the edge now, pushing her to the brink, making her fall apart.

My name is a prayer on her lips when she comes with a gasp.

Enthralled, I continue to lick and suckle her to prolong her orgasm, my eyes stuck to her angelic face the whole time until her body goes slack and she falls back into the mattress.

"Sebastian," she mewls, and I smile, finally withdrawing my fingers, knowing she's too sensitive now. "Oh, God," she breathes, pushing her hair off her face.

My smile grows wider.

'Oh, God' indeed, baby. And we're only getting started.

* * *

Still grinning, I crawl up her body, lavishing it with open-mouthed kisses until I finally reach her face.

My heart pounds in my chest as I seductively bite her chin, lick a trail to her mouth, and give her some of the sweet honey she just squirted all over my lips.

The act is so dirty, so unmistakably wrong, my dick throbs and my balls begin to swell, pushing yet more precum to leak out of my tip. "Mine," I murmur, holding the head of my cock to her crease and spreading my seed all over the little slit. "You are mine."

Alice moans, her hands sliding from my shoulders to my biceps, then slowly down my back to my ass. My skin begins to tingle the way it always does whenever her hands are on me.

I kiss her harder then, tongue, teeth and raw need dictating the pace, letting her know how much I want her—no, need her, even if deep down I'm still afraid.

Afraid to love her. Afraid to lose her. Afraid to let her in.

She kisses me right back, my Alice, raking her nails over my shoulder blades all the way up to my neck. Her fingers run through my hair, making my stomach tighten and my abs quiver.

Fuck, I do love her hands on me.

Sparks of pleasure shoot down my spine straight through my dick—my very hard, very eager dick—forcing a primal growl right out of my lips.

Ugh, we better stop. Otherwise I'm gonna grab her and fuck her, regardless of her being a virgin or not.

Covered in a fine sheen of sweat, both of us pant when we finally come up for air. My dick is so hard, I could probably cut through glass.

But tonight is supposed to be about her. Her comfort. Her pleasure. The discovery of her body, of sex.

So, with one last kiss to her luscious lips, I drop to the bed, pull her into my arms and lay her head on my chest. "You OK, baby girl?" I ask, kissing her forehead.

She looks up, her brilliant smile making my heart leap. I smile back, brushing her hair away.

I fucking love seeing her happy. Hell, I'll devote my entire life to putting this kind of smile on her face.

"That was amazing. You're amazing," she says in wonder, raising a hand to my cheek and kissing my jaw. "I didn't know it could be like this."

"Believe me when I say I didn't know either."

Her brows crease. "But you …"

"I know," I cut her off, not wanting an ounce of doubt to hang over her head. "But it was never like this, Alice. What we have is different, special." I pause, looking for the right words. "It transcends what is normally expected."

"Are you saying we're not normal?" she quips, and I laugh. This girl.

I shake my head. "I'm saying that what we have is extraordinary. That many people go through life without ever experiencing this kind of connection. This feeling. I know I hadn't … until you."

"It was magical for me, Sebastian," she says, her eyes sparkling as our gazes meet. "Because it was with you."

My chest constricts, tightening with so many emotions that for a moment it's hard to breathe. "It was magical for me too, baby." I tug her closer, kissing her softly. "It will always be magical with you. You're mine."

"Yours," she confirms, seeking my lips again, holding me tight, and my body instantly hardens. My possessiveness is at an all-time high as I grasp a handful of her hair, kissing her back.

* * *

"Sebastian," she whispers against my chest after a while, her breath tickling my skin.

"Yeah?" I say, my tone lazy as I caress her hip and lower back. "What is it, baby?"

"I … I want to taste you too."

I tense. My breath rushes out of my lungs and my hand tightens around her hip.

This girl is going to be the death of me. I swear it.

"Alice." I squeeze my eyes shut, my cock throbbing incessantly, pushing me to lose control. "Sweetheart, you don't have to do that," I say, not wanting her to think she has to reciprocate. Even if I'm hard as a rock and desperate for release.

"I want to. I want to make you feel good."

"You shouldn't say such things to me, baby girl. I'm not exactly a good guy." Holding her jaw, I lick her pink lips, already imagining them wrapped around my girth.

Swallowing hard, I press my forehead to hers. "I'm trying so hard to be good to you, Alice, but deep down I'm still an asshole. I'll always be an asshole. I don't want to scare you away."

She huffs out a frustrated breath. "No. I'm tired of hearing you say that. You're a good man, Sebastian. I know you are," she says, dragging her hand over my chest and down my abs. They quiver under her touch. "You're good to me." She lowers her mouth to my nipples, licking them stiff. "You've always been good to me."

I shiver, fisting her hair as she begins her descent down my body, convincing me with each flick of her tongue, with each kiss, with every sensual bite her tiny teeth leave on my skin.

"I want you in my mouth, Sebastian."

"Alice ..." I force myself to say. A whisper. A warning. A plea.

"Please let me."

I release a shaky breath. How could I ever think I'd resist her?

"I'm yours, baby. Do whatever you want with me," I rasp, obviously losing my mind. Yet surrender has never felt so sweet, so right.

"Will you guide me?" she asks, big eyes looking up at me. "I don't want to do anything wrong."

"Baby ..." I give her a pained smile, my desire and protectiveness taking over, as they always do whenever her innocence comes up. "You turn me on so damn much nothing you do could ever be wrong, believe me. Just follow your instincts. Do whatever feels right to you, OK? The rest will follow."

She nods, a mix of excitement and trepidation flickering on her gorgeous features as her hand wraps around my dick.

"Fuck!" I grunt out, my hips lifting off the bed to thrust into her fist. "Fuck, I love having your hands on me."

She licks her lips, her face right in front of my dick, and I stop breathing. The anticipation locks my jaw in place as her tongue comes out to lick a drop of precum from the tip.

I groan, a shuddering breath rushing out of me as she takes me deep inside her mouth.

Fuck!

She sucks me hard, her tongue swirling around the head of my cock like it's a damn lollipop, and my eyes begin to roll into the back of my head.

"Mmm, you taste so good, Sebastian," Alice half-whispers, half-moans after releasing me with a pop.

I inhale deeply, my breath ragged as I'm overwhelmed by my feelings. Overwhelmed by my love and equal desire for her. "God, you're going to kill me," I pant.

"Was it OK, though?" she asks, unsure.

Fuck me, how can she have any doubt? She's a natural. Can't she tell by looking at me?

"Baby, that was more than OK," I rasp. "Not to mention you with my cock in your mouth is the sexiest thing I've ever seen in my life." God, I almost blew my load from the sight of her alone.

She giggles, looking mighty proud of herself. Guess seeing me in this state is doing wonders for her confidence.

Well, what can I say? Ever the gentleman, I'm only too happy to oblige.

"Tell me what to do next. I want to make you feel good," she says, her expression still innocent no matter how much I defile her.

I almost growl then, my hips rocking in time with her fist as I tighten my grip on her hair and guide her back to my shaft. I want an uninterrupted view of this.

"Take me deep into your mouth, Alice. Suck me," I instruct.

Oh, and she does. And as I watch the head of my cock slide past her plush lips and disappear into the wet cavity of her mouth, I almost explode. My stomach quivers, my balls tighten, and I shut my eyes.

She has barely taken me into her mouth and I'm ready to shoot my load. My cock is in absolute blow-job heaven, in a state of pure ecstasy, and I can't hold on. I won't last.

Not when she begins bobbing her head and sucking me just right, taking me deeper and deeper each time. Her tongue is flat and pressed to the sensitive underside, her hand at my base working me in time with her mouth. Both building up the pressure, the tension, and igniting all my nerve endings to a point that even the rivulets of sweat sliding down my skin feel good.

"God, Alice." I sound like an animal, but she doesn't relent. Even when she gags a few times she doesn't miss a beat, my beautiful temptress.

Bright dots of light form in my vision, and I tighten my hold on her hair, guiding her to the pace I need, rushing towards the finishing line. "Baby, I'm there. If you don't want me to come in your mouth you need to back away. Now."

She moans around my cock, sucking me so hard my balls draw up.

"Alice! Fuck!" I growl, holding her down to my thrusting hips and coming in a rush inside her mouth.

She swallows me, eyes closed, cheeks pink, a look of pure pleasure on her face as my cock keeps shooting rope after rope of my cum.

"Holy. Fucking. Shit," I whisper, letting my head fall back to the pillow as I try to catch my breath. I'm spent, gasping for air, and mesmerised once again.

In a fog, I watch her crawl up my body and straddle my trembling hips. "Was that good?" she asks, seemingly very pleased with herself, the little minx.

I grab her around the waist and flip us both so I'm on top. I kiss her then, tasting myself on her. "Mmm," I groan into her mouth, the taste of us combined getting me hard all over again.

She moans in response, tugging me closer, her hands on my hair, her pussy, wet and warm, pressed up against my stomach, and I have to break the kiss.

God, I'm going to end up fucking her if we carry on like this.

Falling to my side, I pull her into my arms until we are facing each other. "Did that answer your question, baby?" I ask huskily, kissing her temple. "Or do you need me to do it again?"

She giggles, the sound music to my ears. "You're such a caveman."

"Hey, it's Mr Caveman to you." We both laugh, and I finally turn off the lights.

She kisses my pectoral and turns, cuddling my hand to her breasts as I embrace her from behind. Our usual sleeping position since we started sharing a bed.

I sigh, and her hold on me tightens. "I want you to know that I love everything we do together," she says, linking our fingers and placing a kiss on my hand.

I close my eyes, my heart growing impossibly large for my chest.

"Baby," I whisper, "thank you. You don't know how important it was to me to hear you say that." My throat constricts and I swallow hard. "I want you to always enjoy yourself, Alice. I want you to be happy."

"And I do, Sebastian. I am ... because I'm with you."

Burying my nose in her hair, I inhale deeply. A small smile tugs at my lips as her breathing slows down, and after only a little while, she's sleeping and soft in my arms.

I tighten my hold on her. We've come so far together, and in so little time.

My eyes close and my body begins to relax. Like, really relax. For the very first time, in fact, since I told Alice my first lie.

But her words today ... her words made me realise she's right. That if I hadn't done all those things, she wouldn't be here with me. At least not so fast.

No. It would've taken me longer in an office environment to convince her, to make her succumb, and that would've been a shame.

Every day, every hour that we spent apart already feels like such a waste, and I'm not prepared to miss out any more. I won't let us miss out any more.

We belong together, of that I'm sure. And now we'll stay together till the end.

It doesn't matter what I've done. It doesn't even matter how we started. Besides, I'll make sure Alice won't find out. Not until I'm good and ready, anyway, and know without a shadow of doubt that she'll forgive me. That she won't punish us both for my mistakes.

Sleep comes easy then, fast, and after only a few more breaths I give in, drifting off with my Alice safe and sound in my bed.

It will be all right. We'll be all right. I'll make sure of that.

Chapter 13

Alice

I startle awake with a gasp. An alarm is blaring throughout the house, and my heart is pounding so furiously I can feel its beat all the way up in my throat.

"Sebastian," I whisper, but he's already jumping out of bed and putting on his boxers.

His whole demeanour is hard and tense in the glow from the small mirror light I usually leave on in the bathroom. His movements are strong and sure. And a dark, dark energy emanates from him.

Wow, I've never seen him like this, but of one thing I'm sure. Sebastian Hunter isn't afraid. No, he's pissed.

Pissed enough to kill.

Picking up my robe from one of the lounge chairs, he moves like a tiger to my side of the bed. "Put this on, baby."

I'm already getting up, so he helps me into it and ties the knot around my waist.

"Come." He leads me by the hand in the direction of the lounge again and I tense, knowing the bathroom or even our walk-in wardrobe are much safer options here.

"Sebastian," I start, but he's undeterred, moving with purpose as he crosses the bedroom. Then, stopping in front of the shelves between the couch and the entrance, he pushes a light fixture to the side, revealing a control pad with numbers, and punches in a code.

What are you doing? I want to ask, but my adrenaline levels are sky high with my heart trying to drill a hole through my chest, and I can't talk. I can only stare up at him.

To my surprise the middle unit moves, sliding open like a door towards Sebastian, and he pushes me into a hidden room. A panic room. A luxurious panic room stocked with everything one could ever need.

"Stay here until I come get you. There's food, water, a bed"—he points to each item in turn—"the toilet, everything to keep you safe, OK? Just don't touch any of the electronics. I'll show you how everything works later."

I nod, and he tenderly kisses my forehead before he turns towards the door.

Wait, he's going to leave? As in 'leave me here alone and put himself in danger' leave?

Grabbing his forearm with both hands, I hold on to him for dear life. "No, don't go. Please." I'm not actually holding him back, our difference in size and strength allowing him to leave at any moment if that's what he wants, but I tighten my grip on him anyway.

"Alice, you'll be safe, I promise," he says impatiently.

"Yes, but you won't. How could you possibly think I'd be OK with that?"

His eyes turn softer. "Angel …" He presses his forehead to mine. "I'm sorry."

Picking me up, he carries me into the bathroom inside the panic room like I'm no more than a petulant toddler, places me inside the bathtub and removes my hands from his neck before quickly stepping back and locking me inside.

"No. Sebastian, no," I shout, running to the door and banging my fists on it, but he's already gone. Leaving me behind.

* * *

More than an hour goes by until I hear the door to the bathroom click open again.

I raise my head, which has been resting on my knees, my arms curled around my legs where I'm sitting on the floor against the bathtub. The position I've been in since Sebastian left.

I've been worried sick. About Sebastian. About the guards. About the kind of threat they might be facing. I'm a ball of nerves, ready to explode at any second. I take a deep breath, trying to keep a clear head. To hear him out. To understand why he left me here, alone and terrified, while he endangered his life.

"Alice." Sebastian crouches, now in black sweatpants and a grey T-shirt, his hand outstretched, I assume to touch my cheek.

"Don't," I tell him and rise to my feet, too pissed off to let him touch me just yet.

He releases a long sigh and pushes back the hair from his forehead. "You're angry." He straightens to his full height.

"No, I'm great. I love being locked up in bathrooms whilst my boyfriend chases criminals."

Sebastian's jaw ticks, but he holds his tongue.

My anger goes up a notch. "You're behaving like a madman, Sebastian. Surely you can see that. Especially when you lock me in a panic room, but have no qualms about putting yourself in danger."

His nostrils flare and I know I hit a nerve. "You know, most women would be thankful for what I did. But not you. You're never happy with anything, are you?"

"How dare you?"

"I dare because all I did was try to protect you," he shouts. "Yet here I am getting nothing but shit from you. Well, fuck this."

My mouth falls open. "Sebastian ..."

"Don't 'Sebastian' me," he shouts again, and I step back.

"Is the house now secured?" I ask, my eyes burning with unshed tears. Sebastian never shouts or loses his temper like this, and I need to get out of this room. I need to breathe.

"Yes."

"Do you know what happened?"

"Just some kids messing around. Throwing rocks over the wall and into the front garden."

I nod, turn and finally get out of the damned bathroom, cross the panic room in silence and go through the doorway that leads into the bedroom's lounge.

A large hand wraps around my wrist before I reach the bed.

"I locked you in for your own good, Alice. I needed to protect you. I needed to know you were safe."

I huff. Is he serious right now? "What about my needs, Sebastian? What about you staying safe for me?"

"Oh, for the love of God ..." Sebastian's hands rake through his hair before they fall to his hips. "I was safe, Alice. I didn't take any unnecessary risks."

"What's the point of you even having a panic room if you're not going to use it?"

"My dad installed it, all right? I've never actually used it until today."

"But you didn't use it, did you? You locked me inside and put yourself in harm's way."

"You're being dramatic," he says.

"And you're being condescending," I shoot back.

We stare at each other, both wanting to say more, but afraid we'll say something we'll regret. Besides, he knows I'm right. I know I'm right. So there's no point in continuing this discussion when it's almost four a.m.

I sigh and begin to pull my hair into a ponytail with a hairband I keep on my wrist. "Did you call the police?"

Sebastian nods. "They're already here talking to the guards. Ryan and I will speak to them last."

"OK." Turning, I go into my walk-in wardrobe to throw on some clothes. I'm sure the police will want everyone's statement and I want to be dressed for that.

"Where are you going?" Sebastian chases after me, grabbing my waist when I don't reply straight away.

I free myself from the loose hold and move towards the shelf where I keep my sweats and T-shirts. "To get dressed so I can give the police my statement."

Sebastian visibly relaxes. What did he think? That I was going to leave him because we're having a fight? "That's completely unnecessary," he says. "Seeing that you didn't leave the bedroom and didn't actually see anything."

That makes me frown. That and the fact Sebastian also said he and Ryan are going to speak to the police together.

"I thought Ryan was off tonight." I put on my grey sweatpants.

"He is," Sebastian replies slowly, and I stare at him.

"I can't believe you called the poor guy at this godforsaken hour, and on his night off no less."

"He's my head of security. That's his job. And he lives right next door. It's hardly a bother to him."

I let my robe fall to the floor and slide on a pink T-shirt. "It's a dick move, and you know it."

"A dick move?" Sebastian's cheeks turn red. "A dick move?" he repeats, and I grimace.

"You said so yourself, it was only kids messing around. Why would you need Ryan here for that? I just think—"

Sebastian glares at me. "Well, don't. It's none of your business," he sneers. "In fact, why don't you just go back to bed and try to get some sleep? You clearly need it."

My eyebrows pull up. "OK, first of all, you need to stop talking to me like this. I'm not your enemy, Sebastian. And second, do you really think I can sleep after all this?"

"Do what you want then. Just don't come downstairs. I don't want to be interrupted."

My face falls at his harsh words and I take a step back from him.

He reaches for me again. "Alice …"

"Don't you dare touch me right now, Sebastian."

"Fuck." He scrubs at his forehead, pinches the bridge of his nose, and then he's staring at me with pleading eyes. "I'm sorry. I don't know what's gotten into me. I didn't mean it, I swear. I …"

"Just go, Sebastian."

"Alice, please …"

"Just go."

He gives me another remorseful look, and I hold his gaze, my face impassive.

He releases a long exhale and leaves.

Seriously, what just happened? My lip trembles as I fall into the chair in front of the vanity.

God, I hate fighting. And I absolutely loathe fighting with Sebastian. But this was a fight I had to win. I can't let him walk all over me. He needs to respect my opinions, my intelligence. He needs to learn how to trust me. And it's up to me to educate him.

Hopefully, after tonight he'll understand. Hopefully, after tonight we can be true partners.

* * *

"He did what?" Linda asks, her mouth open in shock as she sits across from me at the kitchen table.

It's Saturday afternoon, just a little after two, and we're having coffee and scones at Sebastian's after spending the last two hours baking and making strawberry jam. As for the boys, they're at the office, where they've been working since the crack of dawn, including Sebastian's dad.

Unfortunately, with the Arthur fiasco they're all having to put in even more hours than usual. They've been working many nights now, and weekends too, trying to control the situation. Not to mention come up with new procedures and crucial changes to take the Hunter Corp to the next level—business- and investment-wise— and make sure, of course, that what happened with Arthur will never happen again.

Which is why they're still at the office today, going over the contracts with the new suppliers and solicitors, and meeting with the police after two of their senior managers were arrested yesterday in connection with Arthur's escape and the embezzlement.

So, yeah, it seems Arthur sank his claws way deeper than we'd initially thought. Hence the new contracts, new business deals, and even new staff.

But we all agreed. It is worth it—the blood, sweat and tears—if the end result is a clean house.

A reality that shouldn't take too long now the major negotiations are done and the boys are just in the process of fine-tuning the details, thank God.

Because of one thing I'm sure: the sooner they boot every last one of those leeches out of our lives, the sooner we can all begin to relax.

Well, all apart from Luke, of course. That boy is much too angry to forget, too mad to forgive. No, he won't rest until he brings Arthur and all his accomplices to their knees.

Linda pours more milk into my latte, and I begin to stir it. "He shouted at me." I relay the whole scary affair from last night, up to the point Sebastian lost his temper with me.

She shakes her head, scowling. "I can't believe he left you alone, put himself in danger like that, and then has the nerve to shout at you for caring."

"Me neither."

Linda puts her cup down after taking a sip, and places her warm hands over mine, which are freezing. "I'm sorry you had to go through such an ordeal, Alice. The whole situation must've been frightening. I can't even imagine."

I release a shaky breath, remembering the ringing of the alarm, the helplessness, the worry. "It was," I admit, swallowing the big lump forming in my throat. In fact, I've never been so scared in my life. "But I didn't see anything. Not to mention that as soon as the alarm went off Sebastian pulled me out of bed and locked me inside that damned bathroom, so I was never in any danger. Not really."

"Yeah, but you were by yourself. And if I know you well enough, which I think I do, you were worrying yourself to death about Sebastian and the guards." Our eyes meet, and Linda lets go of a long sigh. "That boy."

"It took him over an hour to come back," I rasp, hurt, crestfallen. "Can you believe it? And then he shouted at me."

"He must've been really furious to lose it like that."

I nod and pull away my hands to wrap them tight around my mug. I shiver, feeling its warmth seep into me and melt away last night's icy fear that's still gripping my heart. "He was livid, Linda. Even got Ryan to come over when we had four guards with us at the time."

"I don't get it," Linda says with a frown. "Hadn't the guys secured the house by then? And weren't the police on their way?" I nod, and her frown deepens. "Why call Ryan then?"

"My question exactly. Which prompted Sebastian to have another go at me, telling me to mind my own business and get back into bed."

"Men, my dear. They do and say the stupidest things when they go into full protective mode."

"Yeah, but to lock me in the bathroom, put himself at risk, and then just order me around like I'm some kind of airheaded girlfriend he can't trust? God, I felt like killing him in his sleep."

I gesture with both hands the act of strangling someone, and Linda bursts into laughter. "In his sleep?"

"Well, yeah. The man's way too big to kill when he's awake. Let's face it. I wouldn't stand a chance," I say with a shrug, and then we're both laughing.

"What about the police? You said they were here until late?" Linda asks, picking up her cup and taking a generous gulp.

"Mm-hmm, but Sebastian wouldn't let me speak to them, deeming it"—I deepen my voice to imitate him—"'completely unnecessary, seeing that you didn't leave the bedroom and didn't actually see anything'." I shrug. "Then he took them into his study with Ryan."

"God, what a night from hell. No wonder you're so tired."

"Yeah ..." I yawn. "Tired, mad—furious, really. God, I'm just so angry with him."

She chuckles. "Oh, the poor boy is just smitten with you, Alice. That's all. Doesn't know if he's coming or going half of the time. And he was only trying to protect you. You mean the world to him."

Her words tug at my heart and I shake my head. "I miss him. I don't like it when I'm mad at him."

"Then don't waste your time fighting that hunk of a man. Besides, why fight him when you can make love to him?"

Why indeed, Linda? Why indeed, when making love sounds so much more appealing?

My phone dings with yet another text from Sebastian. Another apology. He's been sending them all day, plus dozens and dozens of red roses with the most romantic cards.

I smile into my coffee.

Yep, making love is definitely starting to sound better and better by the second, even if I'm still angry at my savage of a man.

But what if we had died last night? What if we had died and never gotten the chance again?

* * *

I feel him before I see him. His warmth, his scent, his power over me, unmistakable and surrounding me just as he enters the kitchen.

God, he hasn't even touched me and already my body responds to him, to his presence, readying itself for his touch. I grip the kitchen island for support, goosebumps breaking all over my skin as the ache for him intensifies.

The need I feel—the want, the love—all twist at my insides, winding me so tightly that by the time he wraps his strong arms around me from behind and pulls me into his muscular chest, I'm nothing but a mess of nerves and desire for him.

Barely able to stand, I let my head fall back and concentrate hard on just breathing. A hard task when my body knows exactly what this man can do to it and now craves it like a drug.

He's just as affected, the hard bulge in his trousers growing and pressing deliciously against my back, his rapid breathing matching my own. I can even hear his pulse if I listen hard enough.

And when he slips his hand under my jaw and turns my head to the side, his breath hot and ticklish on my cheek, my neck, my collarbone—making me tremble, making me gasp under the feather-light touch of his lips as he licks and nibbles on this spot just behind my ear—I know in my heart that this is it. That the moment I've been waiting for is here.

I'm ready. I'm ready to give myself to him.

"Shh," he soothes, his breath so hot on my sensitive skin, I can't help but moan as my knees almost fold under my weight. "Shh," he soothes again.

Oh, my, this is sensory overload. Sweet torture. And I don't think I can take any more. Not when I need him to touch me. Really touch me and make me feel his.

Just when I'm about to complain, I feel him smile and pull my earlobe into his mouth. His hand skims over my belly, my ribs and close, so very close to my bra.

Please touch me. Please, I want to say, but I can't. I can't talk. I can only feel as I breathe heavily through my open mouth.

"I've missed you so much, sweetheart," he whispers before licking the shell of my ear. "I don't like it when we fight."

"I ... I missed you too." I want him so much I can barely think straight, let alone put a sentence together.

"Not as much as I did you, but I'll make you. I'll make you think of me every night and every day."

"I already do," I murmur.

He chuckles, the sound low and dark as he grazes my ear with his teeth, nibbling and licking before sucking my earlobe into his mouth. Again.

I melt into his touch and let my head fall further to the side, exposing myself to him. Giving him better access. He growls and drops his mouth to my neck, biting and sucking on it until pleasure and pain take over my senses, triggering a need like no other to course through me.

God, I want his touch all over me. I want his mouth and hands, and I want his cock in me.

I want him to own me. To take me. To make me his woman.

I want him to claim me as his.

He grunts, and I realise that's what he's already doing. He's marking me, his mouth branding me in a manner that only accentuates the primal need we both feel.

God, what is this man doing to me?

Because I certainly don't recognise this wanton woman. This crazy-with-desire female, burning with need.

"Forgive me," Sebastian rasps, and I almost cry, my whole body vibrating under his lips and tongue and searing kisses. He licks and sucks his way up and down my neck, pausing at my pulse point. "I should never have spoken to you like I did. Please, sweetheart, forgive me."

Moaning, I do my best to stay still as my nipples stiffen, my breasts heavy and swollen, aching against the lace of my bra.

"Only if you continue to kiss and touch me like this," I breathe. "Then maybe, just maybe, I'll forgive you."

"Mmm, demanding little thing, aren't you?" Sebastian laughs, but seems to sense my impatience, since his lips drop back to my neck and he begins to kiss his way up my jaw, my chin, his mouth leaving behind a wet, burning trail of kisses until his mouth captures mine and he covers both my breasts with his hands.

"Ahhh!" I cry into our kiss, my skin tingling, goosebumps spreading, and I feel as if I'm floating on air.

He groans, squeezing my breasts as his tongue tangles deliciously against mine, pushing me higher, sending me soaring, until I almost lose track of who I am. Until I almost lose track of space and time.

Sebastian pinches my nipples between his fingers and then soothes them with his thumbs. "Undress. Now. I want to taste you," he rasps, kissing my blazing cheek and nuzzling my hair as he smiles. "I want my mouth all over you, sweetheart. Starting with your beautiful tits and finishing with your virgin pussy coming all over my tongue."

My core clenches, spasming and soaking my panties as I screw my eyes shut. My already white-knuckled grip on the counter turns firmer just to keep me upright.

Seriously, how many shades of red can a girl go anyway?

Not to mention that his crude words should've made me cringe. Should've made me feel disgusted, but instead here I am, wanting and craving them with every single fibre of my being.

Slowly, he turns me around and, smiling wolfishly down at me, brushes my flushed cheek with his thumb. I stare up at him, transfixed. Again this mix of roughness and tenderness, of barely controlled need and kindness, like he can't decide if he wants to fuck me like a demon or make tender love to me all night.

"So beautiful. Such a beautiful, innocent angel."

I sigh, parting my lips for his kiss, and he slides his fingers into my hair, his right hand cradling the back of my head and nape, his left hand squeezing my waist.

"And I'm the devil who's going to steal you away." He grins. "I'm the devil who's going to cut out your wings and forever bask in your light."

His eyes lower to my mouth, his irises no longer blue but almost black with his desire, with promises of sex, of pleasure, and then his lips are on mine.

Yes! Oh, God, yes. Sin has never felt so right. So good. And neither have I.

Groaning, he kisses me until my knees buckle and I'm holding onto him for dear life. "Mine," he growls, already lifting the hem of my T-shirt until I'm standing in front of him in my purple lace bra. "Mine," he repeats with a dangerous sparkle in his eyes when he grabs my waist, and, as if I'm a rag doll, parks my behind on the island, getting between my legs.

I squeal, gripping his shoulders for balance, and he grins like a big, wild cat toying with its prey. A predator's grin, I realise, just before he buries his face in my cleavage and begins licking and sucking at the swell of my breasts.

I swoon. I can't help it. My moans fill the space as I pull on his hair to tug him even closer to me. Loving the way he sucks my nipples through the fabric of my bra, loving how he soothes each bite with a flick of his tongue. If this is hell and he's the Devil, I'll happily let him steal me away, let him keep me forever, if that's what he wants.

I almost laugh at how carried away I'm already getting, knowing perfectly well I need to stop thinking like this.

Just because we're together now doesn't mean it will last. Nothing does—nothing this good, anyway. Not in my experience.

And that's OK. I've made my decision and I'm determined to have my love story, even if it's a short one. To have the man I love and desire take me at least once, even if he doesn't love me back.

No regrets. No more fear.

I can't resist him anyway. Can't resist my need for him. No matter how much I try, I want him, need him too much to keep denying myself. So I'll give him this—my firsts, my heart, my love—and make these precious memories with him.

Besides, they'll be all I have one day. All I'll keep once our time is up and I'm all alone again.

"Beautiful girl." Sebastian's voice penetrates through the fog of my thoughts, and I drag in a shaky breath. He takes a step back, my bra dangling from his forefinger before he lets it fall to the floor. "Stunning. Simply stunning."

I shiver, my whole body quivering under his intense gaze, missing his warmth, his closeness, and before long my hands are rising of their own accord in an attempt to cover my breasts.

"Don't," he orders, catching my wrists. "Don't ever hide yourself or cover your body from me." His eyes are dark, molten with arousal, burning into mine, and it's all I can do as I stare back at him. As I stare back at my beautiful man.

"Mine." He steps forward, cupping my breasts, weighing them in his big palms. "These are mine. You're mine." He twists and pinches my nipples, all the while still staring at me. "If only you could see yourself through my eyes, sweetheart. If only you could see how beautiful you are."

My breath catches in my lungs, and he brushes his lips over mine.

"You're the most beautiful woman I've ever seen, all my fantasies and wet dreams come true, and I need you unashamed, Alice. I need you to share yourself with me. So no more covering. No more hiding. Can you do that, sweetheart? Can you do that for me?"

Overwhelmed by his words and the sensations he invokes in me, I nod, my grip on the counter so hard I'm sure my nails will break.

He smiles, looking sinfully handsome, mesmerising even, and then his mouth is on me—ravishing me, sucking on my breasts and nipples, kissing me with such passion, such want, I can barely breathe.

I feel completely swamped. Taken over by the intense ripples of pleasure spreading through my body all the way down to my toes. The tingling sensations covering my skin in goosebumps and raising all my hairs to stand at once. And it's all too much, too intense.

"Sebastian." I tug on his hair, whispering his name as he hums in approval. "Sebastian," I repeat, but he's undeterred, already kissing and licking his way up my chest until he reaches my face, and with a devilish smirk captures my waiting lips in an all-consuming kiss that vanquishes thought and doubt and even logic from my brain.

Dear God, he's going to devour me. And worse, I think I want him to.

I think I want us to go all the way.

Chapter 14

Sebastian

I kiss her like a man possessed, my hunger for this woman never satisfied, never sated no matter how many times we do this. Her sweet lips move just as eagerly against mine, reminding me of how good they felt wrapped tight around my dick. Of how they sucked the cum right out of me.

And I could come in my trousers just from the memory alone. I shiver, my cock throbbing and trying to punch a hole through my trousers. Wanting into her warm mouth, wanting to shoot my load down her welcoming throat again.

I've never been this hard for any woman. Only for her.

"What are you doing to me?" I whisper, my mouth still pressed against hers, unwilling to give up her taste, her sweetness.

Yeah, I'm pretty sure she cast some kind of spell on me, the little witch.

Opening her eyes, she gives me the most adorable smile and my heart, already beating like mad from everything we've done so far, inflates, growing too big for my chest.

My throat constricts as if I'm about to cry, and I don't know what to do, what to say. I feel so … protective of her. So irrationally wild.

I've only ever known lust. I was used to it. But this—wanting to take care of her, make her smile, make her happy and mine— what do I do with all this? With all these feelings and emotions fucking up everything logical in my brain?

Feeling out of control, I plunge my tongue deep into her delicious mouth, licking, savouring, and holding her as tightly as I can, and still the pain in my chest, the need for more, does not subside. Does not disappear.

I'm so fucked! Not to mention desperate. For her. For her love. Her touch. For whatever this tiny girl decides to dish out to me, and I can't hold on any longer. I need to let these feelings out. Need to show her that this is it. That this is us ... forever.

Holding the back of her head, I take her mouth again, giving her the most passionate, fervent kiss we've ever shared.

She quivers, her hands wrapping around my neck as she pulls me even closer to her.

I stifle a smile, pleased, my ego making me feel ten feet tall as I rip moan after moan from her throat. I'm a man on a mission, after all. My every action, my every touch, lets her know that she now belongs to me. That I'm hers. And that I'm not about to screw this up.

With our lips still locked together, I cup her ass and pick her up, making her squeal in surprise. She breaks the kiss, and I chuckle, bouncing her a little to make her laugh.

She does. We both do. And I want this.

I want this more than anything I've ever wanted in my life.

Staring into her eyes, I carry her to the living room and lay her on the couch, my body hovering over hers as I rain soft kisses all over her lips, her jaw, her face. "I'm going to taste every inch of you tonight. And you're going to take it." My mouth touches hers one more time, sucking on her delicious lips, and then I'm kissing my way down to her chest.

"I ... I ..." She moans, her cheeks glowing and flushed as I begin to suck her nipples with equal attention. "Ahhh," she cries out when I suck on them particularly hard.

"Such a good girl, aren't you?" I growl, moving to her stomach, licking it as it quivers with every stroke of my tongue and every kiss I leave behind. "And you want to be good to me, don't you?"

"Mmm, yes. Oh, God, yes." She's a mewling, writhing mess by the time I reach her shorts and, sliding my fingers into the waistline, begin to pull them down.

"So wet. Always so fucking wet for me," I say, sliding the shorts down her legs and over her feet.

I stare at her panties, trailing my fingertips over the moisture. The tiny bit of lace that matches her bra covers her so prettily that it's all I can do not to tear it apart.

I like it. I like it a lot, but I need it gone. Like yesterday.

I look up and find her gaze fixed on me. Waiting. Expecting. Both of us breathing hard as she gives me the 'come fuck me' look through half-lidded eyes.

My cock throbs and pulses in time with my heart rate, and I can't look away. Can't take my eyes off her face. I just love her so fucking much. That's why I'm trying so hard not to be a bastard, to take it slow, to take my time with her. To show her how precious she is. Show her she means everything now.

Taking a calming breath, I bend and bite her left hip bone and then her right, my hands finding her ass again and squeezing it as I run my tongue across her stomach, driving her wild.

I slide further down her body, kissing her through her panties. My thumbs hook into the sides of the sopping-wet lace, slowly revealing her pretty pink pussy to me as she gasps, her fingers fisting my hair.

I draw in a sharp breath. "Did you do this for me, baby girl?" I ask, running just the tips of my fingers up and down her perfectly smooth and hairless flesh. She shivers, raising her ass off the sofa to meet my touch. "Got your pretty pussy all nice and soft for my tongue to lick you?"

Her already pink cheeks turn crimson red, and I can't help it, I chuckle a little.

Still so innocent, my little thing. So prim and proper.

And I hope that never changes. Hope that I can always shock her with my words, my dirty promises. I love the effect they have on her.

After pocketing my souvenir—because yeah, I'm keeping the panties—I close my hands around her knees, pulling them apart. "I need to taste you," I tell her, my voice thick with desire as I lower my head and lick along her slit.

"Sebastian," she gasps, arching her back as her hands fly to my hair. "Oh, God!"

I groan, and, despite my best intentions of being gentle with her, I go mad, licking and sucking at her slick folds like a starved man, forcing moan after moan to fall out of her lips as I lose myself in her taste, in the way she feels.

She shudders, her thighs shaking uncontrollably under my palms. "Feel it, baby. Feel everything I do to you," I murmur, blowing my hot breath over her pink flesh. My eyes are glued to her face, watching her every reaction.

Ravenous for more, I push my tongue inside her impossibly small entrance, fucking her with my mouth the same way I plan to do with my dick.

She cries out, her walls clenching and spasming at the intrusion, and I almost come, my body so fucking ready to go off, I have to reach down and give myself a squeeze so I don't explode.

God, she's so tight. I can't wait to fill her. To tear through her virginity and finally make her mine.

Patience. You need to be patient, Sebastian. Don't scare her. Don't fuck this up.

"Sebastian ..." She whimpers again when I press my thumb to her clit, her hips rocking faster and faster in time with my strokes.

And I'm hooked. Addicted. I want—no, need—to have my fix.

Feeling her body tense, I apply even more pressure to her clit. My tongue fucks in and out of her urgently, demanding, pushing her until she unravels with a scream. "Sebastian! Oh, God, Sebastian!"

Fucking perfect. The most wonderful and purest human ... my person ... the woman of my life.

* * *

Alice

"I want you," I moan as I sink back into the sofa, slowly coming down from my high.

"I want you too, baby girl," he says, crawling up my body and kissing my mouth, letting me taste myself on his lips, his tongue.

"No, I want all of you. Please, Sebastian," I plead between pants as his thumb continues to stimulate my clit. "Take me."

Breathing heavily, he locks eyes with me then. "Sweetheart ..."

"Please." I meet his intense gaze. "I want you."

"Are you sure about this?" he asks in a husky, heated tone that sends thrills throughout my whole body.

My skin begins to tingle.

He wants this just as much as I do, I can tell. Maybe even more. He's just being careful with me.

"There's no rush, I can wait. I'll wait for you for as long as you need," he murmurs, in spite of the hunger I see in his eyes.

I nod, struggling to find my voice as he increases the pressure on my clit. All I know is that I want this too much. We both want this too much, and I won't deny us any more. "I'm yours, Sebastian. Take me."

He swallows hard, his Adam's apple bobbing as without another word he gets up, lifts me like a bride in his arms and carries me to our bedroom.

His eyes are two dark pools of desire as he lays my body right in the middle of the bed, making me feel like the most precious, fragile thing he has ever touched, ever held. My eyes water, a myriad of emotions making my heart implode and my body ache for him.

He straightens to his full height by the side of the bed, his eyes intense and hungry as they roam freely over my naked body. I squirm, resisting the urge to cover myself, and he smiles. Of course he smiles—he knows exactly what he's doing to me. Making me wait, aroused like this, naked and vulnerable, whilst he's fully dressed and in control. Showing me that I'm at his mercy in this bed. Showing me that he's in charge of my body, my pleasure, my needs.

As if reading my mind, he starts undressing as I watch. "You're so beautiful, I'm committing every single detail of you like this to memory," he says as he unbuttons his black shirt.

His hair is dishevelled and messed up by my hands. By what he did to me. And I stare, the butterflies in my stomach fluttering as his shirt drops to the floor.

God, he's all muscle and power with his broad shoulders, hard chest, and six-pack on display. This man has no shame, so sure of himself, so comfortable in his own skin.

And why shouldn't he be? With a face that belongs on the big screen, a body that every woman wants in her man, and a smile that should be illegal? The same sinful smile he gives me as he drops his trousers and boxers to the floor.

I shiver at the sight of his cock—his long, thick, and very hard cock. My skin breaks into tiny goosebumps as wetness pools at my entrance, my body preparing for him.

Gripping his huge member, he strokes it as he climbs into bed and moves closer to me. I swallow hard, my need for him, for what we're about to share so strong my throat constricts and for a few seconds I can't breathe. I can only stare up at him.

Slowly he covers my body with his, supporting his weight on his elbows as he settles his hips between my thighs.

By pure instinct, I wrap my arms and legs around him and pull him to me, gripping his shoulders so hard, I'll probably leave scratch marks all over his skin.

Then he's kissing me, the kiss ever so gentle and with so much affection, I can't help but tremble in his arms. "Alice, are you sure?" he asks as he searches my eyes.

I nod, unable to speak, the feel of him hard and pressing between my legs robbing me of my other senses. All I can focus on is how big he is and how much this is going to hurt.

"Tell me with words. I need to know that you're OK. That you want this," he insists, struggling, no doubt, to remain in control when all he wants to do is shove himself inside me and fuck me. The thought makes me shudder in fear ... and something else: arousal.

God, I must be going crazy. I'm a virgin. I need him to be gentle with me.

"I want you, Sebastian," I tell him in a breathy, shaky voice I don't even recognize as my own. "I always want you."

"Fuck, baby. I need you so much. Want you so much." He captures my waiting lips and the world outside our bedroom ceases to exist.

He rocks his hips, sliding his shaft up and down my slit, and I gasp into our kiss, my core clenching and desperate to be filled as the head of his cock rubs deliciously against my clit.

God, if he keeps this up I'm going to come. I won't be able to stop myself.

He moans and grunts as more wetness flows out of me, and, shifting his hips, pulls back a bit to press himself against my entrance.

I gasp again, ripping my mouth away from his as my whole body becomes rigid with nerves.

"Relax, baby, I don't want to hurt you," Sebastian murmurs into my ear, making me shudder as he sucks my earlobe into his mouth.

I close my eyes, taking long, deep breaths and willing my body to work with me.

"Kiss me," he whispers against my lips, distracting me from my fears as he takes my mouth in a sensual kiss.

A preview of what's to come, I realise, as he glides his tongue between my lips. I melt into the kiss, the knots in my stomach unravelling just before he pushes in.

"Ahhh," I cry out, breaking the kiss, my nails stabbing into his shoulders so hard, I'm afraid they'll draw blood.

God, this hurts. This hurts really bad ... and I'm so tight he's only managed to slide the head of his cock into me.

Fear grips me and a small voice in the back of my head almost begs him to stop.

He presses his forehead to mine, both of us breathing hard as he rocks his hips into me. "Kiss me, baby. Just kiss me," he growls, crashing his mouth to mine, demanding, possessive, making me burn and throb with need and desire for him.

I kiss him right back, desperately. My heart beats at a thousand miles per hour, wanting to be joined with him, wanting nothing more than to share this kind of intimacy with my beautiful man.

"You OK, baby girl?" he asks in a pained moan, his eyes so dark I can no longer see the blue I love so much in them. His lips brush against my own, and I can feel how much he's struggling for control. How much he's holding himself back so he doesn't hurt me. "Baby," he prompts, his face twisted with both pleasure and pain.

"Yeah, I'm OK. Just go slow," I whisper.

He smiles as he lowers his head to my breasts, sucking a taut nipple into his mouth.

"Ahh!" My back arches off the bed and I whimper, tensing up when the motion makes him slide further into me.

"Shh ... It's OK, baby. It's OK. I'll go slow," he soothes as he continues kissing me everywhere his lips can reach—my breasts, my neck, my mouth—until I slowly relax under him.

He shifts his hips and with shallow pumps begins to push himself inside me again. I try to relax, taking deep breaths through my nose, but my body resists, rebelling at the intrusion as it attempts to push him out.

He feels too big—ginormous—as he continues to press, and I truly believe that there's no way in hell I could go through with this if I wasn't so in love with him. My core spasms, pulsing in sync with my heart, which is hammering against my chest.

"Fuck. You're so fucking tight," he rasps, shuddering as he raises his lust-filled eyes to mine. "You feel too damn good, baby. And I'm a bad man." He tenderly kisses my forehead. "I'm bad because I know you're hurting, Alice, and I'm sorry. So very sorry, baby. But I can't stop myself. I just want you too fucking much to be so selfless."

"I don't want you to stop," I murmur. "I want you to make love to me, Sebastian." God, I think I would die if he stopped now.

"Yeah, you're going to kill me," he grunts out, sliding a hand between us to expertly massage my clit. His hips move around, rotating and stretching me out for him. "Guaranteed, you're going to be the death of me."

"Oh! Mmm!" Pleasure and pain become one and the same, and I mewl under his touch, my body softening and opening right up for him.

"Keep your eyes on me. I want to see you when I take your innocence." I shiver, and he grins darkly at me. "I want you body and mind, Alice ... and everything else in between."

His shallow pumps return and this time it's not so bad. The light pressure of his fingers on my clit, the feel of his strong body over mine, and the desire to become his help me further with the pain, making me relax under his powerful frame.

God, he feels so good naked. So manly and strong.

And he wants me. This huge, beautiful beast of a man wants me.

His face tightens in concentration as beads of sweat start to gather on his skin. He leans in, his eyes intense, and then with one sure thrust he pushes into me completely, breaking through my virginal wall and burying himself to the hilt.

I cry out, my nails digging into his skin as tears spill from my eyes and slowly roll down my temples.

He stills, not moving an inch, not moving a muscle as he lets me adjust to his size.

God, that hurt. It still hurts, and I feel way too full, too raw, my inner walls trying to expel the reason for the pain.

"I'm sorry. I'm so sorry, sweetheart," he murmurs as he kisses my eyes, capturing my tears. "You are so beautiful."

I shiver, clenching again, and he groans into my ear. "Fuck. You feel way too good, Alice. So fucking wet and tight, so fucking perfect." Showering my face with tender, loving kisses, he continues to whisper sweet, dirty things to me. Making me grow wetter. Making me feel like the most cherished girl on Earth. "You're so precious to me, baby girl. So very precious, and I can't stand to see you in pain. Are you still hurting, baby? Am I still hurting you?"

I bite my lower lip, wiggling my hips a little to test for pain, and he gasps. "Fuck, baby! I'm trying to be gentle here," he says in a strained voice.

"Sorry. I was testing for pain," I tell him with a small smile. Now that the pain is subsiding and the promise of pleasure is taking its place, I'm actually enjoying seeing him like this.

"The only thing you're testing is my limits. Fuck! You keep doing that and I'm going to lose control."

God, I almost want him to lose it. Almost want him to unleash himself on me, but this is my first time and I need him to go slow, need him to be gentle with me.

"The pain isn't so bad any more," I tell him shyly, my eyes firmly on his chin. "And you feel … good … inside me."

"Still so innocent. So shy. Do you feel innocent, though? Now that my cock is buried deep inside you? Do you still feel innocent, baby?" he murmurs, kissing my burning cheeks and then the tip of my nose. "I told you I'm a bad man, and I've been dying to take your virginity. Corrupt you for myself. Now I'm loving every second of it."

He pulls out a little and slides back in, his eyes never leaving mine as I gasp and contract around him.

Again and again he fills me, keeping his thrusts smooth and slow, until my hips rise on their own.

"Mmm." My core pulses to the feel of him inside me, moving in and out of me. The sensations push the pain away as pure pleasure begins to take centre stage.

I focus on him—my love, my heart, my everything—revelling in what he's doing to me, relishing every single second of it as I lose myself in him.

Sensing the change in me, he picks up the pace, moving faster and deeper than before, fucking me as he takes my lips in a ravishing, bruising kiss.

My hands tighten on his shoulder blades, my nails digging into his skin as the pressure begins to build. The tension is so unbearably hot, so wonderfully twisted, my insides melt every single time he pushes into me. Wave after wave of pleasure travels through my body, and my eyes roll to the back of my head.

"Alice ..." He wants to know if I'm OK. I can hear it in his voice.

"Don't stop, baby. You feel good. So good," I reassure him just before my mouth falls open in a silent O.

"Fuck, you feel amazing. We feel amazing," he pants, gaining momentum and fully thrusting into me now.

The sounds of our cries and our bodies moving together fill the room, and all I can do is hold on to him as he takes me with abandon, pushing me to the brink of orgasm with every pump of his cock.

"Sebastian," I cry.

"I know, baby," he murmurs against my lips. "Come for me. Come all over my cock."

He shifts his hips, hitting all the right spots and then some, and I scream, my body shattering into a thousand little pieces as he captures my lips in an open-mouthed kiss.

"Alice, fuck," Sebastian growls, breaking the kiss, his hips pistoning into me. "I'm going to come. I'm going to pump you full of my cum."

"Yes, God, yes," I moan, my core clenching at his words as more liquid heat spills out of me, welcoming and aiding his thrusts.

This is ridiculous. I just came apart in his arms, yet my body is already rushing towards another release.

"Fuck, Alice," he grunts out, his thrusts becoming erratic, his breathing shallow.

"Come inside me, baby. Please, come inside me."

He tenses, his muscles bulging and rippling under my fingers, and I feel him expand. "Oh, God," he groans and with one final thrust he comes, crying out my name.

It sends me over the edge again. The sound of his groans, the look in his eyes, the way he throws his head back, lost in his pleasure.

He's beautiful. Perfect.

And as he shoves himself deep inside me and fills me with his seed, as we rock into each other for the longest time, I can't help but think that our lovemaking is just as perfect as him. That this is so much more than anything I could ever dream of.

We lie entwined, a beautiful mess of tangled limbs, locked lips, and sweaty skin as we moan into each other's mouths.

"Fuck, I'm crushing you," Sebastian growls as he turns on his side, taking me with him. He's still inside me, our sexes still joined as he kisses my hair and holds me to him.

I smile, content, and we stay just like that, both of us silent and lost in our own thoughts, holding each other close.

"Are you OK?" he asks after a long while.

"Yeah, just a bit sore," I reply.

"I'm sorry."

"No, don't. It was wonderful. You were wonderful."

He releases a long exhale, as if relieved, a small smile on his lips. "It was pretty wonderful for me too."

"Magical?"

He laughs. "Yes. Believe me, it doesn't get much more magical than this."

"I'm sleepy," I say, yawning.

He holds the back of my head, stroking my hair. "Me too. That was quite the workout you just gave me." We both laugh, and I wince.

Ouch. I'm very sore, much more tender than I thought I'd be.

"OK, sleep, little one. You need to rest." Sebastian kisses my forehead and I snuggle further into him, both of us exhausted and content as we drift away into peaceful sleep.

I made the right decision after all.

I love Sebastian. I love him more than anything. And I was right in doing this with him.

Chapter 15

Alice

9.00 p.m. Charles' Mansion

Grey walls with white wooden panels surround the luxurious dining room. The glass table is ginormous, and the dark blue chairs match the couches and armchairs in the adjacent lounge. Two huge chandeliers hang low from the ceiling, sparkling like a thousand diamonds, and the food has been glorious all night.

The laughter rings loud around the table, and I can honestly say I'm in love with the whole of the Hunter family. They're all here—Charles, Linda, Sebastian's middle brother Luke, and younger twins Nathan and Mason, who are taking a break from visiting the Hunter resorts and hotels like their older brothers did—and already it feels like I've always been part of the clan.

A phone buzzes and Nathan gets up. Tall and built, he has striking blue eyes with a hint of green surrounding the pupils, and the same jet-black hair that all the Hunters seem to share. "Excuse me," he says mostly to me. He's been glued to that phone the whole evening. Something about a new hotel campaign he created for the Hunter Corp and a TV commercial being filmed tomorrow.

I'm still staring at Nathan as he moves further into the blue and cream living room when Mason says, "Sebastian is lucky I didn't meet you before him. I would have snatched you up so quickly, he'd never have had a chance."

I laugh. Mason is endearing and funny, the most relaxed of the Hunter brothers, the most jovial. He's Nathan's non-identical twin, and even though they're both gorgeous and still very similar in the looks department, they couldn't be more different if they tried.

Nathan is too serious, preoccupied with everything and everyone, whereas Mason seems to be laid back, sweet and acting more his age, which is mind-blowing since he's already a solicitor and is supposed to lead the legal team at the Hunter Corp starting next year when he comes back from his travels.

"You're sweet, Mason, and I'm very flattered. But I can't see myself with anyone but Sebastian."

"As I said, he's a lucky man."

"You better be careful, Sebastian. Your girl is creating quite the stir with your brothers," Charles quips.

Linda laughs, and Sebastian's head snaps their way. "Sorry, what?" he asks his dad.

Sebastian's distracted, nervous. Has been since we arrived, which makes me think that perhaps this dinner was a bad idea. That perhaps he's not ready for a relationship. Certainly not one with this level of commitment.

Shoot. I should've known better. I should've held back. But I was so excited to come here and finally meet everyone.

"I said that your brothers are completely enamoured with your girl. I'd be careful around them if I were you."

Charles and Linda laugh again, and Sebastian drops his arm over the back of my chair, caressing my shoulder before he kisses my temple. "I'm not worried. I already told them that I'll kick their asses if they even look at Alice the wrong way." He feigns a threatening glare at Luke and Mason.

Hmm, maybe he's just concerned about something at work and I'm projecting my insecurities onto him. Again.

Or maybe you're spot on and he just wasn't ready for this.

I stifle the need to shake my head. These ugly thoughts have a way of creeping up on me at the worst of times.

Mason chuckles and raises his hands in surrender, but Luke has to poke the bear. He wouldn't be Luke if he didn't. "Yeah, you don't want me looking at Alice the right way either, bro."

Nathan comes back to the table and falls into his seat with a sigh. He looks stressed, unable to relax. "Sorry about that, everyone. What did I miss?"

"Just Sebastian threatening Luke again," Mason tells him with a grin. "And us."

Nathan rolls his eyes at Luke. "You just don't know when to shut up, do you?"

"What would be the fun in that?" Luke replies.

"You're an idiot," Sebastian says.

"I learned from the best."

"Boys," Linda warns, but Sebastian only smirks and throws one of the yellow roses from the flower arrangement at Luke's head.

With a huge smile on his face, Luke catches the flower and, facing us, tucks it in his ear as he throws Sebastian a kiss.

Everyone bursts into laughter, including Luke, and finally dessert arrives with great fanfare. There's even a pudding one of the waiters sets on fire at the table. We all laugh and clap, our conversation growing in joy and volume again.

I look over at Sebastian as he talks to his brothers, sounding happier and more like his usual self, and I swallow hard, knowing what I have to do. Knowing that the tighter you hold onto someone, the farther they'll get from you.

We'll talk once we get home, and I won't be pitiful. I'll be brave and loosen my grip. I'll give him the time and space he needs. And we'll be better for it.

* * *

Sebastian

The steam around us is thick and warm as we stand under the shower. "Did you have fun tonight?" I ask Alice, snaking an arm around her waist and pulling her close to me. We just had dinner at my father's and came back home a little less than an hour ago.

She whimpers when I nuzzle into her neck and bite her. "I did. What about you?" she asks breathlessly, and I smirk. "You looked kinda nervous when we got there."

Clever girl, seeing right through me. As always.

I think about it for a few seconds, arriving at the conclusion that there's no point in denying it. "It's true," I admit, my hand skimming over her side as I wash my way down to her hip and give her a little squeeze. "I was a bit anxious when we got there." I kiss her ear, her cheek, her temple. "But I had fun, baby. It just took me a little while to wind down, that's all."

To be honest, it felt weird taking my girlfriend to have dinner with my family. At my father's house, no less. The very same house where I grew up. It messed me up a bit.

The whole experience made me feel way too grown up and responsible, not to mention protective over Alice. OK, more protective over Alice.

But my family can be a bit crazy and overwhelming at the best of times, and I never brought a girl to the family home before, least of all a girlfriend, so I wasn't sure how they were going to behave.

I guess it was the novelty of the situation and my lack of control over it that threw me off balance. Which is stupid, of course, because Alice already knew everyone except for the twins.

Which, again, should've made me relax. Reassured me that Alice was going to have a good time.

Instead I was a nervous wreck, the importance of my family's opinion to me way bigger than I realised.

Something that actually took me by surprise tonight. I never thought I'd need their approval. But now that I have Alice and she means so much to me, I desperately want them to love her and welcome her into our midst.

"Maybe this was too soon, Sebastian. The whole family dinner, me in the middle ... I don't know, maybe we should slow down."

"Hey." I hold her face between my hands, forcing her to look at me. "What are you talking about? You think I was nervous because I didn't want you there?" She blinks, and I sigh. God, that couldn't be further from the truth. "Baby ..."

"Sebastian, you never had to do this stuff before, and I worry it might be too much, too soon for you. I worry you might be feeling pressured."

"Fuck, baby," I murmur, pressing my forehead to hers. "I'm sorry I made you feel that way. It was never my intention." My hands glide up and down her back in a calming, soothing way.

Yeah, way to go, Sebastian. You're an asshole. An absolute asshole.

I close my eyes in regret, knowing there's no excuse for my behaviour.

"I just don't want you to feel pressured into doing conventional stuff," Alice continues. "Especially when you're clearly not ready for it."

"Ready?" I ask, leaning back to look at her. "Baby, I was ecstatic to have you all under the same roof. That's why I said yes to my dad's invite in the first place. The only thing I wasn't expecting is how much I want my family to like you, and you them."

"Are you sure that's all there is to it? I felt ... I don't know how to explain ... this sadness? Yes, sadness. It was like it was pouring out of you. Not the whole evening, just for a moment when we got there, but it made me think that maybe you didn't want to be there—or didn't want me to be there, perhaps."

My perceptive little thing. I should've known better than to think she wouldn't notice. She's too intuitive, too attuned to me to miss something like that.

"I was thinking about my mum," I tell her, my throat tight as I say the words out loud, making the hurt more real, sharper somehow, like the cold blade of a knife slicing into my grieving heart.

Still, I persist. Alice needs to know more about me, and I need to learn how to open up to her. "She would've loved to have been there tonight. She would've loved to have met you. She would've loved you if she met you. You remind me of her sometimes, you know? In the way you're so selfless and giving. In the way you take great pleasure in looking after the people you care about. And for a moment tonight, I felt like I was losing her all over again. Another missed opportunity, another important occasion where I couldn't share my joy with her. My happiness." I roll my lips, emotion gripping me. "I just wanted to show her my girl when we arrived."

Alice's lower lip begins to tremble and big, fat tears form in her eyes. "Oh, Sebastian ... I'm sorry. I'm so very sorry."

"Shh, it's OK, baby. It's OK, don't cry." My heart clenches. I never had anyone cry for me before, feeling my pain, unless they were in it with me, of course, and my parents don't count.

This is different, though. This feels like the kind of connection only true soulmates can share. The kind of connection that comes from falling in love and having your heart beat in someone else's chest.

She loves me, I realise. She really does love me.

All the raw emotions, the sharing, the never-ending craving for togetherness between us, be it physical or emotional or both at the same time, they're all signs. Alice loves me and all is right in my world.

I kiss her forehead and her cheeks as she clings to me tightly, both of us seeking comfort and closeness as we hold on to each other.

"God, I should've known, Sebastian." She shakes her head. "Instead, I behaved like the cliché girlfriend, being all insecure and selfish, thinking the whole world revolves around me."

I smirk at her choice of words. They couldn't be further from the truth. "Well, my whole world does revolve around you. So I can't really fault you for that ... can I?"

"Stop, I'm being serious," she admonishes in a weak voice.

"So am I. Now turn this delectable little derrière of yours around, so I can wash your hair." I give her ass a squeeze, making her giggle through her tears, and she turns around.

I pour shampoo into my palm, my eyes fixed on her shapely ass as I admire her from behind.

Fuck, I'm a lucky man. Luckier than I deserve, that's for sure.

I begin massaging her scalp, her nape, her shoulders, and she slowly relaxes into me. The feel of her and the little sighs and moans coming out of her gives me all sorts of ideas. All sorts of feelings. And a boner that will not go away no matter how hard I try. Not on its own, anyway.

I close my eyes. All I want is to hoist her in my arms and fuck her hard against the wall. Make her scream. Make her come until she forgets what an asshole I am.

Guilt fills me. It's only been five days since I took her virginity and we've been at it like bunnies ever since.

Well, apart from when she feels too sore, of course. Like now.

Which, again, is entirely my fault. But I just couldn't resist her.

She was looking so gorgeous and perfect in her little black dress when I got home this evening. Her hair and makeup done up, making her look all prim and proper, and only adding to that air of grace she always has. Fucking delectable.

I remember the sway of her hips, the warmth and sweetness of her lips when she kissed me hello, and fuck, before I knew what I was doing she was bent over my desk with that pretty dress of hers bunched up around her waist, crying out my name as I filled her from behind.

I bite my lip as the memory of me fucking into her tiny little pussy like an animal in heat invades my mind. My possession was so primitive, so domineering we nearly collapsed when we both reached our peak at the very same time.

"All done," I announce huskily, kissing the top of her head after rinsing the conditioner from her hair. My voice is barely contained as my mind keeps drifting to images of us fucking and conjuring up the sensations in my body to go with them.

"Thank you, that was wonderful," Alice murmurs as she turns back to face me, her lips turning upwards right before her eyes land on my dick and she takes notice of my predicament. "And now ... I think it's my turn to help you relax," she rasps.

Before I make sense of what she means, she drops to her knees in front of me, grips my cock in her delicate fingers, and takes me into her mouth.

I hiss and my hand drops to the back of her head, tangling in her hair as my hips shoot forward instinctively. A silent plea. An order.

Suck me. Take me deeper, baby.

She flattens her tongue and swallows me in, sucking me hard.

"Fuck, baby!" I pant, slamming my other hand on the wall and leaning into it. "Do you know how many times I thought about this? How many times I jerked myself off in this very shower to the fantasy of you here on your knees with my cock in your mouth?"

My grip on her hair tightens and she moans as she fixes me with her big, beautiful eyes.

Fuck! The sound travels straight through my cock and my balls draw up. "Fuck, yeah, just like that, baby girl. Suck me just like that."

I spread my legs wider as her free hand massages my sack, her touch tender but sure, pushing me to thrust into her mouth until I'm just short of fucking her face.

"Alice," I groan, nearing my release.

White spots form in my vision and with a final thrust of my hips I come, emptying myself down her throat.

"Alice. Oh, God, baby." The guttural sounds leave me until my mind goes blank, unburdened of thoughts and problems as I float consumed by pleasure and in a state of pure bliss. Something I can only achieve with my Alice.

Regaining some of my balance, I open my eyes as I slowly come back down to earth, only to find her looking up at me, still on her knees and with a smug smile on her lips.

I bend, and, holding her upper arms, effortlessly lift her to her feet. Then, sliding my arm around her waist, I hold the back of her head and kiss her.

"Mmm, you seem very relaxed, Mr Hunter," Alice murmurs against my lips.

"I am."

"Then my work here is done."

I turn off the shower and pick her up like a bride in my arms.

"Sebastian!" she squeaks, and I laugh.

"Shh. I'm taking you to bed, wench. You just got yourself another shift."

* * *

Later that night sleep evades me as we lie together in bed, my mind going around in circles, bringing me back to the same matter time and time again.

"Alice?" I murmur into her shoulder before I kiss her neck. "Baby?" My heart rate quickens, but I won't be able to sleep until I ask her this.

"Mmm?" she mumbles, hugging my arm tighter against her breasts.

I inhale deeply. "I know we haven't discussed this in detail, but ... I want you to stay. I want you to live here. With me. As in"—God, I'm messing this up already—"you don't move out when your book is published, but stay here on a permanent basis."

She says nothing, and I begin to panic, wondering if she'll hate me if I keep her here against her will. "Alice, baby ..."

She turns around then, looking just as beautiful and bewildered as I was expecting, and also a little shell-shocked, I think. I fold her in my arms.

"Sebastian," she whispers, splaying her hands over my chest and my thumping heart, "what brought this on? Has something happened?"

"No. Nothing happened. I just ... I just want to make sure that we're on the same page. That you don't think your stay here has a time limit. That our relationship has a time limit."

Her eyes move down, fixing themselves on my chest, and I know I hit the nail on the head. For her. For me.

We both keep acting afraid, still being too cautious around each other, and that needs to change. We both need to start believing.

Even emotional blackmail is not beneath me. The only thing that makes it OK, I guess, is that, blackmail or not, it is the absolute truth, and I couldn't have chosen a better time than this to tell her. To let her know exactly how I feel.

I slide my hand into her hair, pulling it back so she looks at me. Big, honest, grey eyes meet mine and my throat constricts. "Alice, for the first time since becoming an adult, I find myself rushing home just so I can see you. Just so I can spend any free time I have with you." She holds my gaze, and I swallow hard. "And I know it's not healthy, perhaps even a little obsessive. But all I think about is being with you, coming home to you. I can't help it. Because all I want is you. All I've ever wanted is you. So please don't take that away from me. Don't leave me now when I'm just learning how to be happy."

"Baby," she whispers, cupping my cheek. Her touch is gentle and warm on my skin, and her eyes so kind, so fucking gorgeous, that before I can stop myself, I'm blurting out more than I planned.

But as per usual, my little thing has a way of making me share. Show more than I've ever shown anyone.

"You know, I used to dread coming back here." I frown, remembering those days. It was a dark, dark period in my life, even if at the time I didn't realise it. "Before you, this house was just that. A house. A cold, empty shell where I came to sleep and shower until you burst into my life. Until I brought you here and you turned the place completely around."

I sigh, shaking my head. "I don't know how to explain it, but you gave me a home, Alice. You filled it with warmth, smells, and sounds. You filled it with life. And now I can feel you everywhere. All of your light and goodness taking over and pushing my ever-present darkness out. Just like you do with everything else you touch. Just like you did with my heart." Reaching for her hand, I place it on my chest again, right where she can feel the life she saved, the life that now belongs to her. "Don't you get it, baby? Home to me is where you are, wherever that might be. And bed or no bed, roof or no roof over our heads, I couldn't care less about where I live just as long as you're with me."

Barely able to breathe, I hold her gaze as she searches my face for the longest time.

This is it. I just hope she can finally see she has nothing to fear. That there's no doubt in my mind that this is what I want.

It seems to work, judging from the sweet smile she gives me and the rosy blush tinting her cheeks. "You don't play fair," she murmurs, pressing herself into me.

"I play to win, baby. Fair has nothing to do with it."

She laughs, the sound a tonic for my soul. "OK, then ... I'll stay. But only because I love your kitchen so much."

Her smile is infectious, and I can't help but laugh. "So, it's all about the damn kitchen, is it? Admit it. You only put up with me because you want my kitchen for yourself."

"Well, duh. Took you long enough to figure that out." She shrugs. "It's a damn good kitchen, Sebastian. What can I say?"

"Oh, really?" I ask with my best threatening voice, making her snort and push at my chest as my hold on her waist tightens, my cock growing impossibly large and pushing against my boxers at the sight and feel of her trapped in my arms, so small and fragile, and so utterly feminine as she giggles and pleads with me to let her go.

It calls to the darker side of me, the one that enjoys overpowering her. The one that wants her to submit.

"So, you want my kitchen, huh?" My tone is menacing, hiding none of the heat running through my veins. "Is that all you want from me?"

"Yes!" she screams in a fit of laughter, pulling at my hair as I growl and bury my face in her neck. Her pleas and giggles grow in volume as I bite and suck on it, my hands closing around her ribcage to tickle her. "Sebastian, stop. Please stop. It's you, just you ... you're the only reason I want to stay," she manages to say between laughter, her eyes shining and wet with happy tears, and then we're kissing.

And kissing.

The familiar pull of our lust for each other surrounds us and leaves no trace of laughter in its wake as we begin to make out like teenagers, not stopping until sleep weighs heavily on our eyelids and Alice yawns into our kiss. The sound is so kitten-like and her face so fucking cute, I can't help but chuckle as I give her a peck on the lips.

"Come on, you." I turn her on her side, her back to my front, and embrace her from behind. "Let's go to sleep, hey?"

"Good night, Sebastian," she replies.

"Good night, sweetheart," I whisper into her hair.

She sighs happily and, raising my hand to her lips, kisses it before returning it to her breasts, locking her arms around it in our usual sleeping position.

It makes me smile. She's always so sweet with me, so loving and kind, it makes my heart squeeze tight and grow larger all at the same time.

No one has ever been so good to me, so gentle. At least not since Mum.

And sure, I have my brothers and my dad, but it's not the same thing. We're all guys. All of us alpha males. We don't have it in us to show weakness. Especially in front of others.

It's different with the woman you love, though. It's not weakness, it's not shameful. It's just ... love.

Shaking my head, I'm amused by my change of heart.

That's it, Sebastian, you've been caught. The hunter finally became the prey.

I smirk into the darkness. Yeah, my brothers won't know what hit them, and I sure can't wait for Luke to be next. I'll be sure to pay him back double—and with a shit-eating grin on my face.

I chuckle.

"What's funny?" Alice asks with a yawn, already half-asleep.

"Nothing, baby. Just go to sleep."

She mumbles something about wanting to laugh too. Soon after, her breathing slows down, her slender body softening in my hold, and I finally relax, emptying my mind of all but the overwhelming sense of relief and pride at Alice's acceptance of living with me.

And not because of a business deal, not because it's convenient. But because she really wants to be with me.

I sigh and close my eyes as I succumb to peaceful sleep, one full of hopes, and dreams, and endless possibilities now that our life together can begin.

* * *

Unfortunately, it's not a dream that wakes me up in the early hours of the morning. It's not a dream that almost makes me jump out of bed ready for a fight. No, it's a fucking nightmare.

And as Alice's little body thrashes and her screams fill the room, raising all the hairs on my body, I have to take several calming breaths just to reel in my anger.

"No, Mummy, no. Please no more. I'll behave. I promise, I'll behave," she cries, her arms raised in a defensive position. My heart bleeds for her, a murderous rage seeping into every crevice of my being as I take in her hurt and gut-wrenching fear.

"Alice, wake up." I shake her gently, but her sobs and cries for help only intensify, piercing right through me as I grab her and sit up with her in my arms. I rock her back and forth as I would to comfort a child. "Baby, it's only a dream. Wake up. Please wake up. It's me, Sebastian."

With a final shriek, she comes out of it shaking. Her gasps for breath kill me as her eyes snap open and then focus on mine.

"Sebastian," she whispers, and with a sob that turns my blood into ice, she throws her arms around my neck, begging me to hold her tight.

I swallow the lump in my throat and envelop her with strong arms. Holding her to me, giving her everything I've got. Hoping that one day I can help her heal, believe that no one else will ever hurt her again.

Not for as long as I live.

"You're OK, baby. You're OK. I've got you. You're safe now, I'm here," I reassure her, tightening my arms around her and rocking her in my lap. Her nails dig into my shoulder blades like she's drowning and her life depends on it.

It's the third time this has happened since we started sleeping in the same bed. I never tell her what she says, though. Or what I already know about her past.

I swallow the rage, push it down. After witnessing the depth of Alice's trauma, I want her to tell me herself, to trust me. So I'm doing my best to wait.

I won't push her. She'll tell me in her own time. Or at least that's what I keep telling myself.

It takes a while for her to calm down, and when she does, she's embarrassed, and again trying to hide her pain from me.

Oh, no, you don't, baby. Not today. Not on my watch.

I hold her jaw and raise her face so our eyes can meet. I may not push her to tell me what happened to her, but I also won't let her hide it any more. Her pain is my pain now, and I'll gladly carry as much of it as she will allow me.

"I'm sorry. I'm so sorry," she sobs, her lower lip trembling and making the anger inside me burn brighter. She looks so scared and lost.

Fuck, I'm seeing red, wanting to lash out at what was done to her, but I can't. She needs me right now, and I have to be strong. I have to remain calm for her.

"Sweetheart, no," I whisper. "Stop apologising. You've nothing to apologise for. And most importantly, stop lying to me. You're a shitty liar, Alice. The worst I've ever known. And no amount of promises or excuses is going to convince me that this was just a dream."

She bites her bottom lip, looking guiltily back at me. Good. She should.

"I know they're memories, your nightmares." My eyes hold hers as she visibly shrinks in my arms. "You don't have to say anything. All I want is for you to know that I'm here. That I'll protect you and keep you safe, even if you can't talk to me." I lean in, and, kissing her softly on the lips, I whisper, "I won't push you, Alice. I'll never push you. I just want to be here for you. Just let me be here for you."

"Sebastian," she murmurs into my lips, her palms pressed to my cheeks as she tenderly kisses me back. "I don't know what to say. I ..."

I kiss her harder then, swallowing her words as unexpected tears spring to my eyes. My emotions are all over the place as I realise I'm hurting—and that I'm hurting for Alice.

Her pain, her sorrow. All the times she needed me and I wasn't there to protect her. All the time it took me to find her and make her mine feels like a knife in my gut. Like a hole in my soul.

"I love you, Alice. I love you so much it hurts," I tell her, my gaze locked on hers as I pull back a little. Her lips quiver, and I brush her glossy hair away from her face. "I've loved you my whole life, I think."

"And I love you, Sebastian. But you deserve better." Her tears finally fall and stick to her long, long lashes. "You deserve someone who's not damaged, who's not broken and can make you happy." Her tears moisten her cheeks before falling to her breasts, and I watch as if hypnotised.

I shake my head as I whisper, "No. No." I cup her face. "How can you say that when you're my whole world now? When your pain is my pain just as your happiness is my happiness? I love you, Alice, and nothing's going to change that."

"I'm scared. I'm scared that I won't be enough. That ..."

"Alice, you're perfect. Absolutely perfect. Everything I need. Just the way you are. Exactly the way you are. Besides, everyone's a little broken, lost, misguided. I mean, just look at me and my brothers." I lay us down on our sides, back on the bed, and we hold on to each other tight.

"What should matter is that we're good together. That we're good to each other. And there's no doubt in my mind that you're good to me. That you saved me, baby. At a time in my life where I needed saving the most," I murmur, tasting her pain and sorrow on her soft lips. "Now you're fucking mine, Alice. And there's no going back. At least not for me."

She shivers, her nipples hard little pebbles against my chest, and I begin to kiss her harder, deeper, wanting to erase any signs of self-doubt, of fear. Wanting her moans, her arms around me. Her body writhing beneath my own as I bring her nothing but ecstasy.

As if reading my mind, Alice mewls, "Then make me forget, Sebastian. Make me forget about the past. Save me." Her hands drop to my ass, pushing my boxers down. "I need you."

My face screws up in pure agony. I need her too. But she's sore, and I haven't prepared her. "Baby, no. I don't want to hurt you."

"You won't. I trust you. Now please, Sebastian. Take me. Make love to me," she breathes against my lips, breaking through the last wall of my resistance.

A savage growl breaks out of me and I kiss her as if my next breath depends on it, my hand pushing into her panties as I lose control. My selfish needs take over as I find her ready and slick and slide a long, thick finger inside her, then another, pumping them in and out of her as I swallow all of her cries.

Painfully aroused, I flip us both so she's on her back and position myself between her legs. The air crackles between us, and I shiver against her sex, too far gone to stop now. Too consumed by my own lust as I grab the sides of her panties and rip them apart, my movements rough and possessive, fuelled by the most primal need to make her mine.

Breathless and with my eyes fixed on my prize, I get rid of my boxers and force her thighs apart. My hips open her right up as I lower myself to my elbows.

"Alice," I rasp, watching her with a mix of adoration and perverted delight.

She nods her acceptance, and I press the head of my cock to her small opening and begin to push inside, our eyes locked the whole time as we breathe into each other's mouths. "Sebastian," she whispers.

"I know, baby. I know," I whisper back, brushing her lips with mine.

I keep working her, my hips stopping at nothing as I enter her with small, shallow thrusts. She whimpers, and I shiver, vaguely aware of her nails digging into my lower back.

"God, you feel so good, baby. So good and so fucking tight," I groan, savouring the feel of her tight little pussy clenching around me and struggling to take my girth.

She moans at my words, her jaw slack and her head thrown back as I bottom out and then freeze, letting her get accustomed to my size.

"Tell me you love me, Alice. Tell me," I whisper my command, my eyes closing as they roll to the back of my head.

I probably sound like a lunatic. But I can't help it. I need to hear her say it. Need to hear her say the words again.

"I love you, Sebastian. I will always love you," she murmurs, wrapping her legs around my waist. "Now make love to me. Please make—"

I don't let her finish, slanting my mouth across her lips. Then I grab her hands and hold them up by the sides of her head, anticipation filling me as our fingers entwine and I begin to make slow, sweet love to the only woman I want. The only woman I'll ever love for the rest of my life.

We come together as one. Our cries and the sounds of our coupling cocoon us as the slow buildup plunges us deep into release and the most intense orgasm of my life.

She loves me. She loves me and she's mine ... and I've never been happier. My heart is full and replete for the very first time since I was a kid.

"I love you, baby," I tell her, staring into her beautiful grey eyes.

"I love you," she says around her tears.

I swallow the lump in my throat. This is special. Truly special, and I couldn't be more thankful that it's happening to us.

Reluctant to pull out of her, I kiss her and then turn us on our sides, still joined in the most intimate of ways as we hold on to each other and wait for our heart rates to slow down.

After a long while my throat starts to feel scratchy, though, and I know I have to get up. "Are you thirsty, sweetheart?" I rasp, kissing Alice's temple, my body already regretting having to pull away, even if my throat is sore and feeling like sandpaper.

"Yeah," she replies with a sigh, followed by a little whimper when I pull out of her.

Sitting up, I reach for the bottle of water on the nightstand and offer it to her. Alice takes a couple of small sips and then hands it back to me. Parched, I drain half of it in no time.

"Drink some more, sweetheart. Come on," I cajole, passing her the bottle again, concern heavy on my mind, and not just for her thirst.

She's quiet, lost in thought, and I'm afraid. Afraid that maybe I shouldn't have touched her. Not when she was clearly so distressed. So fragile. Damn, what was I thinking?

I run both my hands through my hair. My only hope is that maybe our admission of love will make her share. That she'll let me in once and for all ... and I can finally begin to help her.

Even if I do for her only a third of what she's already done for me.

Chapter 16

Alice

"Thank you," I say, after taking a few more swigs of water and handing the bottle back to Sebastian. Who's watching me like a hawk, by the way, as if afraid I'm going to break down on him all over again.

"Come here, sweetheart," he murmurs, reaching for me and pulling me over his chest as he lays us back on the bed. I close my eyes and press my nose to his warm skin. He smells good. Like sex and sweat—and me and him. The perfect combination, making me smile wistfully and relax into him.

He loves me. He loves me, and he deserves to know the truth. It's not fair to keep him out any more.

And as scary as it may be, I have to tell him about my past. I have to show him the real me—because no matter how hard I try to leave that broken little girl behind, she's always going to be a part of me.

"Do you really want to know about my dream?" I ask in a small voice, my heart bleeding as I focus all my attention on him, on the feel of him and the steady, calming beat of his pulse. I close my eyes, willing myself to be brave.

He's real, he's mine, and he's not going anywhere.

"Only if you're ready to tell me, sweetheart. Either way, I'm here for you. I'll always be here for you," he says, his fingers trailing up and down my naked back.

I swallow the lump in my throat, my chest tight with pain and embarrassment at the dirty secret I've been carrying for so long. "I want you to know. You deserve to know."

He stays silent, his hand still caressing and tracing patterns down my spine as I continue in a tremulous voice. "It started out small, and she was always careful not to leave visible marks on my face, hurting me mainly where I was covered by clothes." The first of many tears spill from my eyes, falling onto Sebastian's chest, and it takes everything in me not to curl myself into a ball.

"I was young. Too young. And at first, I thought I was to blame. That I had been bad and made her angry. It wasn't until I became a teenager that I realised it wasn't my fault that she hated me, and that there was nothing I could do to make her love me again.

"Unfortunately, by then the beatings had also gotten worse and more frequent than I could cope with. She was quickly losing control and would often hit me until I passed out. Which landed me in hospital quite a few times." My voice quivers and I swallow hard, trying desperately to remain in control.

"To this day I still don't understand how she got away with it all—the lies, the acting." I recall her cruel words about her clumsy, uncoordinated daughter and her falls.

"Always with her head in the clouds, this one," she'd often say. "So accident-prone it's a miracle we don't have to come to hospital every day."

I grimace at the disturbing memory and the hurt it uncovers. "The doctors, the nurses, even my teachers, they never questioned her. And I was too scared, too ashamed to ever talk, to ever tell. And so it went on and on until I was finally admitted into hospital with a broken arm, a fractured wrist, and a big ugly gash on my head."

I pause, my voice breaking, and Sebastian curses under his breath. He tightens his hold on me, his heart rate no longer steady inside his powerful chest as I struggle to bring my emotions to heel.

"That was the last time she ever touched me," I continue, determined to let the whole truth out, as ugly as it may be. "I was traumatised and concussed, and the police finally got involved. She ... she made me tell them it was an accident. That I was alone when I fell down the stairs. But it wasn't an accident, Sebastian. She pushed me. Her own daughter and she just—"

"Hush, baby. Hush." Sebastian's voice quivers, like he's trying to hold off tears, and suddenly I feel as if a weight has been lifted off of me. Like I'm finally validated. As if the simple fact that someone else knows about my secret, my shame, makes me feel less crazy and surer than ever those things didn't just happen in my head.

That what I've gone through was real, and sad, and just as hurtful as the physical scars I have left.

"She doesn't deserve your tears, Alice. Just as she didn't deserve to be your mum," he murmurs, kissing the top of my head. He turns us on our sides so he can look at me, sweeping my hair away from my wet face. "Some people are just not wired right, baby ... and they should never have kids. It wasn't your fault, you hear me? None of it was your fault. You didn't do anything wrong to feel guilty or ashamed. Christ, you were only a child, sweetheart. Someone should've protected you. Someone should've stopped her."

I inhale deeply, letting the anguish out on the exhale.

He's right. I know he's right, but unfortunately for me she was also a very talented actress.

"She was never abusive in front of others," I croak. "Not even verbally. Quite the opposite, in fact. Especially around people she considered important in some way. And she was always the loving mother then, bragging about her 'wonderful little girl's' achievements to whomever she needed to impress. Sometimes she was even gentle to me. Like she used to be before she changed."

Why do I still let this bother me so much? Hurt me so much? Why can't I just let it go?

"I guess ..." I pause, trying to make sense of what it is I want to say.

"What? You guess what, sweetheart?" Sebastian prompts.

"I guess she couldn't damage the façade, you know? The picture-perfect image she built around herself and her family. It was all she had left."

"What about your father? Your nana? Did they know?"

"My nana didn't know, and I didn't have the heart to tell her. She loved my mother something fierce, much more than she ever did me. It would've broken her. I couldn't do that. Not to her. She was the only one who ever cared about me. I didn't want to hurt her."

"Sweetheart," he whispers, his face mirroring my pain as he touches his forehead to mine.

And finally, realisation dawns on me:

I can trust him. I can break in front of him, let the past tear me to pieces, and trust him to make me whole again.

I squeeze my eyes shut, thankful for this wonderful man.

I've never felt so safe. So strong. And it's all because of him. God knows nobody made me feel this way before.

Which brings me back to ...

"My dad knew," I admit quietly, sad I could never feel safe with him, that I could never trust him. "But he was always too scared and often too drunk to protect me."

A vision of my father staggering, with his eyes bloodshot and unfocused, forms at the forefront of my mind. It's an unsettling image and it makes me angry. He was weak and broken. Beaten by the life he led and his mistakes. And not even his family, his wife and daughter who he claimed to love more than anything, were enough to save him, to set him free. He just gave up one day and that was it.

"Sometimes she'd hit him too. He never raised a hand to her, ever. Not even to stop her from hurting him, to stop her from hurting me. I think he felt guilty for losing the business. Losing all our money and turning to drink. But that doesn't excuse my mother's behaviour. Doesn't excuse what she became. I never blamed him for it. There's simply no excuse for the things she did."

I remember the hate in her eyes, the weight of her hands on me, hitting me, hurting me, and a piercing pain slices through my chest. Many people go through the same difficulties, the same hardships in life, and they don't turn to violence. They don't hurt the people they love instead of protecting them.

"The beatings, the name-calling, the constant criticism ... It's like she took pleasure in making us feel worthless. And when my dad didn't care any more, she turned all her attention to me." I shrug. "After a while I believed her. I believed I was a failure, that I'd never amount to anything. I broke just like my dad did. Just like she'd said I would one day."

"Fucking hell," Sebastian murmurs. "You understand that there was something seriously wrong with your mother, don't you?

Fuck me, that kind of behaviour isn't normal, Alice. Surely she must've had some kind of mental health issue going on."

I nod, certain it was the case. That there was something seriously wrong with my mother.

He cups my face. "God, baby. You've been so strong. So brave. It's a miracle how someone could go through all that and still come out like you on the other end. A kind, gentle soul, a good and genuine person." Sebastian shakes his head. "You amaze me, Alice, you truly do. Every single day."

"I didn't feel strong. Or brave, for that matter. Some days I didn't even think I was going to survive. Some days, I even wished she'd just kill me and get it over and done with. After she ..." I swallow hard, and Sebastian folds me in his arms again. "After she pushed me down the stairs, she didn't touch me again. I was able to finish school in peace. It allowed me to maintain my sanity, or at least part of it, until I was old enough to find a job and move out. By then my father had already passed away, and my mother died four months after I left." My eyes flood with tears and a lump forms in my throat. "She ... she killed herself. Took all her sleeping tablets and ..."

Wracking sobs shake my whole body as I lose control. I know I shouldn't cry for her, for them, but I can't help it. Despite everything, they were my parents and I had nothing but love for them.

"You have me now, Alice. We have each other. Thank you. Thank you so much for trusting me and telling me all this." Sebastian's voice is hoarse and full of emotion, and my heart clenches tight, no longer mine, but his.

I nod, unable to speak.

Sebastian is so much more than I originally thought. So much more than the cold, always-in-control CEO once described to me.

Even him being the heartless, implacable playboy that all my female former colleagues were gossiping about seems far-fetched and ridiculous.

And yeah, he may have played those roles up until recently, but that's not who he truly is.

Understanding rushes through me like a tidal wave as I lean back to look at him. No, who he truly is has been hiding behind a mask. Behind the ruthless image people have of him. And I wonder why.

Why would such an incredible, good man go to such lengths to push everyone out? To keep everyone away?

He once said we're more alike than I thought, and the more I think about it now, the more I come to realise he was right. Like me, he was hurt when he was young. Like me, he did everything he could to protect his heart.

And even though our experiences are different, and our childhood and parents worlds apart, his mother's passing was obviously a very traumatic event for him, not to mention destructive.

I mean, look at the way it shaped him. At the way it nearly destroyed his family back then, his dad most of all.

I shiver. God, I can't even begin to imagine the loss they suffered. The grief.

When my parents died it was awful, and I mourned them both with a broken heart, but I couldn't bring myself to miss them or the memories they left behind.

For Sebastian and his family, though, their loss has to have been unbearable. Devastating. The kind of loss and pain that will consume you from within until there's not much left of your former self inside.

So I guess we truly are a match made in heaven ... and Linda was right. She often is.

A small smile pulls at my lips and a feeling of hope fills me. Yeah, maybe we'll be OK, me and him. Maybe we'll be OK after all.

"I love you, Alice."

My smile grows wider despite my tears. "I love you, Sebastian. I'll always love you."

* * *

Our lives are defined by moments. Moments that shape us and mould us into who we are.

Because of them I'll forever be cautious, but I'm no longer afraid. Life is what it is. It will beat you down and it will pick you up, and I'm ready for it. I'm ready to live.

Smiling, I take the last batch of cupcakes from the oven and place them on a metal trivet on the counter.

That makes a total of one hundred and fifty. I pick up the pastry bag and sit on the stool to continue decorating the cupcakes that have already cooled down.

Sebastian will take them to the office tomorrow. I'm trying a new recipe for my new manuscript, and the office staff is always happy to sample them.

As for my book, it's almost ready, with good prospects of being published in a couple of months, maybe less. I hunch my shoulders in excitement as a burst of energy runs through my veins.

I bite my lower lip. I still have to pinch myself every now and then to make sure I'm not dreaming.

I'm a writer, a girlfriend, and I get to cook all the time. God, could I be any happier? I sigh, closing my eyes, feeling thankful. Blessed. Bewildered.

Out of nowhere, but as per usual, a wave of pure darkness sweeps over me. A voice in the back of my head tells me the day I get used to being this happy is the day my whole world will come crashing down on me.

Fate will pull the carpet right from under your feet and—

I push the negative thought away. I inhale and exhale deeply, fighting through my panic, just like Sebastian showed me. Then I count to ten, do the breathing exercise again, and count backwards until I calm down.

Thankfully I'm getting better at this. My self-doubting moments are sudden, but definitely getting less frequent and strong.

He loves me. He knows me and he loves me. And nothing bad is going to happen to us.

I know this. I believe this. Especially since our talk the other night, and not just because we professed our love for each other, but because we've opened up. Because we made a conscious decision to trust and believe in one another despite risking our hearts.

We've changed. Our relationship changed.

There are no more walls, no more barriers between us. No more games, no more hide-and-seek. We love each other and nothing else matters.

Not our past, not our pain, not our fears—nothing, and I mean nothing, can keep us apart. We know the ugly, the rotten, and everything else in between, and we love each other better for it.

Everything feels even more real, intense, intimate. The way we talk, the way we touch, the way we kiss. And I wouldn't change it for the world.

He sees me, broken parts and all, and he wants me just the way I am.

My only regret is that I didn't tell him sooner. That I didn't put my trust in him.

But unfortunately, I held onto my mother's secret for so long, let it poison my soul and my heart for so long, I didn't know how to. I didn't know how to let him in.

It saddens me and infuriates me in equal measure that she had such a strong hold on me. That I allowed her to continue my torment when I was supposed to be free.

I realise now I was simply existing, just going through the motions. A spectator watching from afar as others lived.

Then Sebastian came bursting into my life, one beautiful explosion at a time, and everything changed for me. All my senses came back at once and for the first time in years, I wanted more, wished for more, and with such ferocity it shook me to my core.

I was terrified. Of him, of myself, of the way he made me feel. My heart was still so full of self-doubt and regret, I didn't know how to break free.

I didn't know the first step was to give voice to my story.

The burden was not mine to carry. The guilt was not mine to feel. Sebastian made me see this.

"But it's not enough for you to know it," he said. "You have to feel it. Own it until you are free."

And for that little piece of advice, I will forever be grateful to him.

What can I say? Sebastian Hunter is quite simply amazing. Not to mention loving, wonderful, supportive, and completes me in ways I could never have dreamed.

He made me whole again. Gave me purpose, hope, and now I can see a future for myself. A future for us together. Maybe even with a little family of our own. Perhaps a sweet baby boy with bright blue eyes who looks just like his dad.

A vision of a little baby, grinning a toothless grin in my arms, pops into my head. The image is so clear and strong it makes me gasp, my hands frozen around the pastry bag.

God, how I want that. How I want to share my life with this man, have babies with him, grow old with him. Do everything with him.

Overwhelmed, I press a hand to my chest as I struggle to contain my emotions. I swallow hard and pick up my glass of water to take a few sips.

We'd make good parents. I know we would. We're good together, we'd be good at this too.

My eyes close and my spirit soars, flying high at all the possibilities before us, even if my cheeks are burning at the thought of us making a baby together. No doubt in my mind that's something we'd be good at.

I smile dreamily.

Oh, the things he'd do to me. I can't even ...

I shake my head, feeling terribly hot all of a sudden.

That man certainly has a dirty mind and no qualms whatsoever in doing dirty things to me.

My smile grows dreamier, if possible, as I put the glass down, pick up the pastry bag and go back to doing the icing.

I truly had no idea it could be like this. The tenderness, the fire, the intimacy. That we could go from making passionate love on the kitchen counter, to laughing and joking like the best of friends, to fucking hard and fast on the bedroom floor because we didn't quite make it to the bed.

Good thing Sebastian had to leave earlier today to train with his brothers at the gym—well, kickbox the shit out of each other, more like it—so I was able to catch up on some much-needed, precious sleep. Even if I still woke up with him early in the morning to say goodbye, of course.

And honestly, how he finds the energy to train at that ungodly hour is beyond me. I'm proud of him, though. He's doing his best to spend time with his brothers and sticking to it.

They all are. It's been a collective effort for over two weeks now and hopefully it's only the beginning.

They're siblings, they should be close. They should be there for one another.

I believe this. Want it for them. So much so, I made it my mission. Even managed to convince Sebastian to invite the boys over for dinner a few times.

Something he wasn't too keen on doing at first, because he didn't want to 'share me', but now, I think he secretly enjoys having them around. I can see the glint in his eyes, the happiness in his smile whenever they're all together.

And the boys ... Well, with my food as bait, it didn't take much convincing at all to get them to visit. They do seem happier, though, all of them, now they get to hang out and see each other properly every day.

And me ... God, I'm just over the moon for them. For Sebastian.

I love them all dearly. Brooding moods, sarcastic senses of humour, difficult temperaments and all. Even those naughty, conspiratorial smirks they give each other whenever they're up to no good are growing on me. Especially since their 'mischief' is usually directed at Linda. Poor woman.

She gives as good as she gets, though, and doesn't let them get away with anything. I don't know how she does it. How she doesn't get sidetracked by their looks and wittiness. Because even I have to admit, they can be a bit too much at times.

They're just too similar. Too close in the looks department and otherwise.

All of them tall, and dark, and handsome—strikingly so. And with bodies that are simply God's gift to women and quite a few men alike. Intelligent and in control. Powerful yet mindful. And they always, always know exactly what they want, when they want it, and how to get it if they're so inclined.

It's scary really. And the way they're always in agreement and supportive of each other, even when perhaps they shouldn't be ...

I press my lips together. It's downright frightening. Particularly if you're at the end of their anger.

Yet it's in their differences my interest is piqued.

Take Luke, for example. He's playful, sarcastic, funny. Has a wonderful smile and even better laughter. A mask. A role he plays to make people relax. Since he's also too sharp, too intense not to take things seriously. Which tells me, out of the four siblings, he's also the one who's the most dangerous to cross.

Then there's Mason. Sweet, kind, a serial playboy. Smart, too smart and much too handsome for his own good, and incredibly sad. I can see it. I can see it clear as day in his eyes every time I look at him.

And Nathan ... now that man can brood like nobody's business. Intense, mysterious, and constantly preoccupied. A fellow worrier like me, and with some serious trust issues, I imagine.

And still any girl would be lucky to have them. These four possessive, overbearing, dominant males. These four brothers who, despite hiding who they truly are behind their power, couldn't hide their hearts and souls from me. Couldn't hide their kindness and generosity once I got close enough to see them.

Now there's only hoping for the right women to come along. For the right women to sweep the rest of the Hunter boys off their feet.

God, I hope so. I really do. And sooner rather than later. I'm worried about them, about their hearts ... and most of all about how lonely they all seem to be.

* * *

Heavy steps sound out in the corridor, making me turn towards the door.

"Hi, sweetheart," Sebastian calls as he enters the kitchen.

"Hi, yourself," I reply, breaking into a smile as he beams at me and undoes his tie. "You're home early."

"Hmm, I missed you." He smiles again, and I melt into a puddle even before he reaches for me. Which, of course, he does as soon as he crosses the room in a few strides, and I jump down from the stool I'm sitting on. "I can help you prepare dinner," he drawls, already grabbing my waist and pulling me in for a kiss.

"What about your meetings?" I breathe against his lips.

"Sharon's rescheduling them. I'm the boss, after all."

"Is that so?" I whisper, and he kisses me again, his tongue sliding through my open lips.

It starts off slow, his hands sliding towards my ass as he deepens the kiss. I moan, tugging on his hair, and with a low growl that rumbles in his throat, he squeezes my ass, his touch possessive, almost aggressive as his mouth begins to devour mine.

He pulls away reluctantly. "You want me, baby?" he asks, his tone playful as he looks down at me, but I can still see the sparkle of barely controlled desire in his eyes.

I smirk. I like this game. "About as much as you want me. But you need your shower, Mr Hunter. And I need my assistant ready and clean in about"—I look at my watch, pushing against his chest, only to have him tighten his hold on me—"twenty minutes, I'd say."

He laughs, and I know sex is the only thing registering in his deliciously perverted mind right now. "Join me," he rasps, throwing me that sinful smile of his that turns my brain into mush. "I think I'm in need of some 'assistance' myself before I'm able to offer mine."

"Oh, I think you're perfectly capable of handling it on your own, Mr Hunter."

"I don't know, baby. These slacks are giving me quite a bit of ... trouble. It'd be nice if you could, you know, lend a hand," he says, raising an eyebrow, and I look away, trying not to laugh.

Then I feel it—the huge bulge in his slacks, pressing into my stomach—and my eyes fly back to his face.

He winks at me. "Sebastian!" I snort, and slap his shoulder.

"What?" He laughs, kissing my burning cheek and jaw.

"You're incorrigible, that's what." God, he smells so good, tastes so good, it makes my stomach flutter and my knees feel like butter under me.

"Before I forget, sweetheart," he murmurs, "I have to work this Saturday."

What? "At the office?" I ask, and he nods guiltily.

Oh, now that's just sad, I wanted him all to myself this weekend. "OK," I say with a small pout, and he groans.

"I'm sorry, baby. We just need to complete this deal and then I'm all yours. You'll be sick of me with all the weekends I'll be spending at home. You'll see."

That makes me smile. "Promise?" I know I'm being a big baby, but I can't help it. I want to be with him all the time.

"Promise." He kisses me again and my knees almost fold under my weight. "Mmm, I'm going to have that shower now. You sure you don't want to join?"

I stare at him, deadpan.

"Hey, can't blame a guy for trying, right?" he murmurs before he dips his head and gives me another kiss. One that has me off my feet and hanging onto him like a little monkey when he straightens to his full height.

My legs wrap around his waist. What is it with this man and the way he kisses me? It's like I'm under a spell. Like it's all new and shiny and I've never been touched before, no matter how many times we do this.

He continues to ravish my mouth until we both come up for air, a naughty smile playing on his lips as he lowers me to the floor. Then, before I can even react, he grabs two cupcakes off the counter and is flying out of the door.

"Sebastian, come back here!" I shout after him, but he's already gone.

I put my hands on my waist. I can hear him laughing like a hyena as he rushes up the stairs.

Bad, Mr Hunter! Very bad!

I bite my lower lip and shake my head in amused disbelief.

Who would've thought Mr Intense and Brooding could be so much fun to live with? And playful, and sweet, and sexy, and beautiful ...

I sigh. God, I'm so in love with him it's disgusting. In fact, I suspect we're turning into one of those sickening couples no one else wants to be around.

I grab the pastry bag and sit on the island stool again, a shy smile playing on my lips when I remember the surprise I've got for him. I'm sure he'll love the sexy little number I bought for us tonight. The black, delicate teddy made entirely out of lace, racy and full of tiny little ribbons and bows he'll have to untie.

That is, if he wants to get to his prize at the end of the night. I chuckle, doubting very much my lingerie will survive after he's done.

Oh, well, you can't have everything.

My smile grows wider, my happiness shining around me like the sun. Especially when I know only too well that what I do have is already more than enough.

Chapter 17

Sebastian

Saturday, 10.00 a.m.

"Are you sure about this?"

The question is written all over my not-so-happy-looking brothers' faces when I open my front door, even if it's just Luke who dares to voice it.

"Hey, guys," I greet them all warmly despite my mood taking a dive. "Thanks for coming. I really appreciate this."

"I asked you a question," Luke grumbles, shoving me aside as he makes his way past the entrance.

"Yeah, answer the man," Mason adds with a smirk as he follows Luke inside. "And drop the act. We all know you're only being nice to make us work anyway."

"What are you on about? I'm always nice," I say innocently, knowing perfectly well what he means. Nathan stares me down—well, he tries, at least. "Come on in, Nathan."

He shakes his head, hands in his jacket pockets. "You're too young to do this. You're making a mistake."

Losing my patience, I grab the front of his T-shirt and pull him inside. "Listen, and listen hard, you fuckwits," I instruct, kicking the door shut with a bang. "Alice is the woman I love. She's the one I want to spend the rest of my life with, all right? She is it. And I did not invite you all here to talk me out of it."

"Well, someone clearly needs to," Luke replies indignantly. "You've gone mad, Sebastian."

I shake my head, pulling at my hair. "I don't have time for this. There's too much to do."

"Why didn't you hire someone again?" Nathan asks.

I release a frustrated groan. "I told you. I want Alice to have a night to remember and I want to do it myself. I'm not about to let some stranger do a half-assed job and make it impersonal for us. I want this to be special and I want her to know that I did it for her. And you are going to help me."

Mason shrugs. "I get it. It's romantic and shit," he says with a smirk. "And I like Alice. You have my blessing."

I give him a grateful smile. He always was the kindest of us all. Still is. A fact that has landed him more pussy than any of us other Hunters will ever get combined. And I'm not talking about the slutty ones either. No, he likes the good girls best ... and even I have to admit he can charm the panties right off of them.

Nathan rolls his eyes. "We all like Alice, Mason. That's not in question here. We're just trying to make sure Sebastian knows what he's doing, that's all."

"What about Dad? What does he have to say about this?" Luke asks.

"He was surprised at first, but he understands it's what I want. He's happy for me."

Yeah, the old man understands better than anyone how I feel. How I cannot waste any time with formalities and etiquette. He knows that what matters in the end is that Alice and I make each other happy. That I love her and she loves me. The rest is white noise, as they say. Means nothing.

"Jesus. Fucking. Christ." Luke says, letting go an exasperated sigh as he sprawls on the stairs. "You've only known the bird for all of six weeks. You can't be serious."

"Luke," I growl, but he continues.

"Well, I'm telling you right now, no woman is going to get me this whipped, love or otherwise. No pussy is worth it, not even Alice's."

Heat rises up my chest, my throat, and before I know it, I'm moving. My hands curl into fists as my eyes stay fixed on my target—Luke.

"You sure as fuck want to get punched in the face," Nathan grunts to Luke as he grabs me by the shoulders, trying to stop me from knocking the lights out of our brother.

Luke's eyes widen in shock and then realisation. "Shit! Sorry, man." He gets to his feet, hands up in surrender. My fists uncurl, but I still stare the fuck out of him. "God, you're so fucking sensitive these days."

I point a finger at him. "Just watch what you say." There's a warning in my voice, and I know he can see just how serious I am. "You know better than to talk about Alice that way."

"All right, all right. Let's all calm down. We're starting to sound a lot like pussies ourselves," Nathan accuses, looking straight at me when I turn around to face him. "What? You sounded just like a chick before, you do know that? 'A night to remember'? 'Special'? 'I did it for her'? Dude, you might as well have a vagina." He laughs. "And the same goes for you, Mason. 'Oh, it's romantic. I get it.' What the fuck, man?"

Laughing, I lock my arm around Nathan's neck and ruffle his hair. "What was that, you little shit?"

He manages to free himself and shoves me playfully in the chest. Yeah, not so little any more, is he? He's a grown man, almost as tall and big as I am.

I put my arm around Nathan's shoulders in a brotherly hug that he returns. We walk over to Mason—also all grown up and strong as a bull—and my other arm goes around him. I love my brothers, even Luke ... most of the time. "I have to stop treating you like kids. And seriously, thanks for coming today. It means a lot that you did."

They both smile up at me and give me a few manly pats on the back.

"I'm still not one hundred per cent sure about this, Sebastian," Nathan says. "But if it's what you want, you also have my support. I'm here for you and Alice come what may."

"Thank you, Nathan. That's good to hear."

"You've got to be kidding me," Luke complains, looking at us as if we've lost our minds. "It's like I'm stuck in a bad movie or some shit. What's next? We're all going to sit around in a circle, hold hands, and sing the fucking kumbaya?"

"Luke?" I call to get his attention.

"What?"

"Go fuck yourself."

"Are you putting us to work or what?" he grumbles, rolling his eyes.

"Yes! Yes, I am," I confirm with a huge fucking grin on my face, and we all move to the living room so I can tell them the plan.

* * *

Three hours later, I find myself in the kitchen with Luke, who's been cursing like a sailor at the electric mixer, the oven, and pretty much every other kitchen appliance since we got here.

The twins are still busy in the living room putting up the rest of the decorations. The twinkling lights, lanterns, candles, and so on.

And Ryan—after coming back from the florist and placing the flower arrangements in their designated spots—has been scattering rose petals on the candle path we created from the entrance hall all the way up to the fireplace, where I'll be waiting for Alice when she comes in.

I smile confidently. She loves that fireplace, and has told me on many occasions she finds it the most romantic place in the house.

So my plan is simple. Maybe even too simple for some ... but not for my Alice.

I know she'd want something intimate and thoughtful with just the two of us, as opposed to something fancy.

No pretence, no over-the-top gestures or swanky restaurants, because that's simply not her.

She's a romantic, a gentle soul who'll appreciate the effort I'm putting into doing all this myself much more than if I'd done something extravagant or expensive.

I smile, feeling quite proud of myself at the moment.

Everything is almost done. The bolognese sauce is almost ready, together with a homemade green-olive ciabatta bread I have in the oven, and the tiramisu is set and cooling in the fridge.

That should only leave me with the spaghetti when Alice gets home, which in return should give us plenty of time to talk and me to convince her to agree to my madness. Hopefully.

A sense of satisfaction fills me and I'm once again one hundred percent sure this was the right decision. Alice will appreciate that everything's being made from scratch—the bolognese, the bread, the dessert—all of it, using Alice's tablet and her recipes to make them just the way she likes.

She cooks for me all the time, the least I can do is cook for her on special occasions. And with the bolognese being her absolute favourite, well, that's got to earn me some extra points in the romance department, right?

I reach for the cleaning cloth in the sink, the happiest smile plastered on my face while I clean away the mess we made, barely recognising myself as I whistle to the sexy tune playing on the stereo.

Luke's still grunting and cursing at the mixer, though, since it seems intent on not cooperating. He nearly lost a finger chopping the tomatoes, and I almost killed him when he bled all over the sauce, which I obviously had to redo.

I relieved him of his duties as my assistant, and he unfortunately went on to find Alice's recipe for her infamous chocolate cake that has every single one of my brothers at her mercy. He's been attempting to make the damn cake ever since. 'Attempting' being the correct choice of word. I don't know exactly when or how he screwed up, seeing that Alice's instructions are easy to follow, but somewhere along the way he did. Big time.

From the look of it, I guess we're going to be having cake with a straw tonight. If we're lucky.

I laugh harder, looking at it. The whole thing looks more like a milkshake than cake batter.

That's why he's been blaming the mixer for the last hour or so. The blithering idiot. He hasn't realised he didn't add enough flour to the mix, and I'm having too much fun watching him struggle to tell him. I'm quite sure it won't be edible anyway, so why bother?

"How's the investigation at work going?" I ask with a shit-eating grin after catching him, and not for the first time either, throwing a disgusted look my way.

I don't remember ever being this happy. But it's like Alice has awoken this whole other side of me. A side I never knew existed.

I don't know. She makes me happy. A better person, a better man.

My life finally has meaning, purpose, and nothing, absolutely nothing—not even Luke and his foul mood—can spoil my bliss today.

He smiles big, his eyes sparkling with pride and something else. Excitement? "Good, really good. The hackers are following the money trail, and we now know the names of a lot of Arthur's accomplices from over the years. Once we organise all the evidence, we'll hand it over to the police."

"So you're keeping the police informed of everything?"

"Only what I deem relevant to their investigation. There are parts I'd prefer them not to know about."

"Which parts?" I ask warily. I don't want him getting in trouble with the law over this. Him or our team.

"That, as of yesterday, our hackers managed to get a big chunk of our money back, and have covered their tracks so well no one will ever find out. It will be virtually impossible to trace it back to us once they're done."

"You're shitting me." He shakes his head, a wicked smirk on his face, and I snort. "Fuck, I love it. I fucking love that. I just can't believe our luck." It has only been—what, a month?—since we found out about Arthur's betrayal, so the fact we've recovered a big part of the money is the best news we could get. "Well, I guess Arthur should've gotten some of these computer geeks to cover his tracks," I say before dissolving into laughter.

"Oh, I think he did. Fucking bastard. Ours are just better than his. Lucky us, though, we'd have been fucked otherwise. No money and no evidence to follow."

"That's good work, man. I knew you were more than capable of being in charge of the investigation, just as I'm sure you'll continue to do everything in your power to get justice for our family. I trust you, Luke. And I'll back you up with whatever decision you make." I grin menacingly. "Especially if the opportunity to get revenge on the fuckers presents itself. We pay our debts, brother. And right now, we owe Arthur and his accomplices a lifetime of regret."

"Yeah, we do, and I will. You have my word. Just leave it to me and I'll bring them down."

"Arthur is a sneaky son of a bitch, though. And very good at keeping himself hidden. My best guess is that he'll stay that way unless we make him come out."

"I know. That's why our best chance is still the money. We've already drained most of his accounts and we'll continue to do so.

If we take it all back and then some, he'll have nothing left, and maybe, just maybe, we'll get our chance at revenge."

I nod. Yeah, we'll put him where he belongs ... behind bars. Together with the rest of his minions and the lowlife thugs we'll make sure will be eagerly waiting for them.

"What are you doing with the money anyway?" I ask, curious. It's not like we're hurting for cash.

"That's the best part. We're giving it all to charity. Using the fuckers' names on the donations."

My eyebrows shoot up. I can't help it, I burst out laughing again. "Oh, that's brilliant, just brilliant. I love it. And you, my man, you're a fucking genius if there ever was one."

"Don't I know it." He chuckles. "Just don't worry about a thing. I'll let you know if I need you to step in, OK?"

I nod. I'm impressed. I always knew my brother was gifted, quite the ingenious boy growing up. But this? This goes beyond any of my crazy expectations.

Even the police are going to be thrown for a loop. Using their names on the donations ... I shake my head. Oh, well, it can't be traced back to us, so who the fuck cares?

I'm still chuckling when Ryan comes into the kitchen. "Hey, assholes, is the food ready yet?" he asks.

"Yep," I reply, a sly grin on my lips. "All except for the cake. Luke's still working on it ... or fucking it up, I suppose. It really depends on how you choose to look at it."

Ryan chuckles as Luke gives us the finger with both hands. "Anything I can do to help? I just finished with the petals and candles. You did the bedroom, right?"

"Yeah." No way was I letting anyone else prepare our room. That was my job, preparing the bed for my future wife. Wife. My wife. Mmm, I sure like the sound of that.

Looking up, I know I'm smiling like an idiot when I notice both of them frowning back at me.

"Jesus, you look like a fucking retard, man. What's wrong with you? And your shitty mixer doesn't work." Luke gives the mixer a few shoves as he swears some more at it.

I roll my lips, trying not to laugh. Yeah, I think he might be done with his milkshake now.

"He's thinking of Alice," Ryan says in a girlish voice, placing his hands over his heart and sighing.

Luke bursts out laughing at Ryan's antics and it doesn't take him long to join in on the fun. "Oh, Alice, my love," he says, making these annoying kissing sounds as he begins to move towards me.

I throw the kitchen towel at his face. "Fuck off!"

Holding the towel to his face, he continues. "Oh, baby, you smell so good. So fine." He takes a sniff. "Mmm, onions and garlic, my favourite."

Ryan and I are doubled over with laughter when Mason and Nathan come through the door and find their older brother making out with a kitchen towel. The confused looks on their faces send us right into another fit of chuckles as they take in the scene.

Of course, two seconds later they also crack up, with Mason even trying to steal Luke's newfound love and challenging him to a sword fight with a wooden spoon in hand.

I stare at my brothers, taken aback, my heart squeezing tight with all the emotions I'm feeling.

I missed this. I missed them. And it feels damn good to be able to laugh with them again.

Our chuckles echo throughout the kitchen and mingle with the good memories from our past, and this calm, this tranquillity descends over me as I realise it's not too late. For us, for our family, for the women who are supposed to come into our lives to love us.

There's still hope. There's still light ... and it's time we all grab it with both hands.

After enough playtime and banter to last us a good while, we all get to work doing different tasks around the kitchen, making sure we finish up before Alice gets back.

"Where is Alice anyway? And how did you get her out of the kitchen?" asks Luke from his place at the sink.

"I had Linda take her shopping. Alice has no idea we're here; she thinks we're at work today. Well, she thinks I'm at work today, so it's safe to assume she thinks you guys are too."

Luke's eyebrows draw together as he looks at the clock on the wall. It's getting late and I know exactly what he's thinking.

"Don't worry," I reassure him, picking up another bowl from the dish rack, drying it and placing it back on its shelf. "Linda is in on this. She won't bring Alice back until I OK it."

"You know what else Alice doesn't know?" Nathan remarks, a sly smile on his face. "The state her kitchen is in." We all laugh, and he shakes his head. "You're so dead it's not even funny, dude."

"That's why we're going to start cleaning now, you idiot," Mason tells him with a smirk as he hands him a cloth and cleaning spray.

Nathan groans, taking the cleaning supplies from Mason. "This whole romance thing is already killing me and it's not even my romance. And you fucking owe me. Big time. Don't you forget it."

I grin, ready to offer him my help when it's his turn to do all this, but before I can reply, Ryan's phone vibrates.

"Ryan," he answers, still chuckling at Nathan's obvious dissatisfaction. "Are you sure?" His voice hardens, barely holding in his anger, and I lock eyes with him.

He's pissed. Royally pissed. And my brows furrow further in question.

"They were followed again," he mouths.

Fuck. That gets my full attention, and I move closer to him.

"You managed to lose her? Good. Have you seen the car since then?"

My shoulders feel tense, my jaw locked shut as I grind my teeth, and by the time Ryan asks his next question, I'm seething and ready to kill.

"OK. OK. Did Alice notice anything?" He shakes his head no, and I sigh in relief. "Just keep your eyes peeled and don't leave Alice's side no matter what," he tells Michael before disconnecting the call. "That bitch again," he hisses.

"I'll kill her," I sneer, so mad I have to punch the tiled wall a few times just to regulate my breathing. The pain helps me regain control, though, bringing my balance back as I exorcise the rage.

"What's going on?" Luke asks, concern all over his features. The twins are quiet, but wearing the same worried expressions on their faces.

"The slut I fucked in Paris," I grunt out, running my hands through my hair as I exhale in frustration.

"What, the deranged one who thinks she's your girlfriend?" Luke asks, narrowing his eyes.

I nod. "She's been showing up at the same places I take Alice to. So far security has been able to stop her from approaching Alice, but this is the second time they've spotted her car following them."

"They? You got more security then?"

"Yeah. They're in a different car and out of sight. Alice is only aware of Michael. I don't want her to be frightened."

"You should tell her. She needs to know what she's up against. She'd be more careful if she knew," Mason adds, a frown on his face before he falls onto the stool next to Nathan.

I shake my head. "I don't want her to live in fear. It's bad enough she has one bodyguard with her at all times and an army around the house. I just"—I pinch the bridge of my nose—"I just want her to be happy, you know?"

Luke sighs. "Has the bitch approached you yet?"

"A couple of times, yes. Once in a restaurant restroom, asking me to fuck her. Then at the office. She booked a meeting, pretending to be someone else. Same story, wanting sex, saying she missed me. Both times Ryan and the guys managed to get rid of her without attracting attention, but it's getting harder each time. Her behaviour's escalating."

"And now she's going after Alice," Nathan whispers, rubbing his chin.

"She also made some threats the last time I saw her. Said she won't wait much longer until I get tired of my whore. That she'll have to get rid of her for me if I take too long."

"Shit. That's fucked up." Mason runs a hand through his hair.

"What about the police? Have you contacted them?" Nathan asks.

"We have. She already tried to ram the gates here at the house, and we're pretty sure she's the one who broke in the night the alarms went off."

Ryan crosses his arms in front of his chest, contempt written all over his features. He's still not sure how she got in that night, and he keeps blaming himself.

"We reported it to the police then, and gave our statements, but there's not much they can do right now. They spoke to her, of course, and they know there's something wrong with her, but so far, we haven't been able to prove beyond reasonable doubt she actually broke the law. And the background checks on her and her family haven't been of any help either."

"Fucking hell. Why didn't you tell us it was her?" Luke asks. "All this time we thought it was just a random burglar, and you knew all along?"

"I'm sorry, OK? I honestly thought she'd go away after we involved the police, and I didn't want to bring you into all this shit. But now ... well, now I'm not so sure she's going anywhere. And I need to keep Alice safe. If anything happens to her ..." I shiver, unable to complete the sentence.

"Nothing's going to happen to Alice, OK? We're all going to keep an eye on her and make sure she's safe. We'll also visit more, and take turns escorting her places," Luke states with the twins agreeing right behind him.

"We'll also need a picture of the bitch. We need to recognize her if she tries something on our watch," Nathan adds.

"Thank you," I say in a choked-up voice.

"You really love her, don't you?" Luke asks, understanding finally in his voice.

"I do. She's everything to me now. My whole world," I admit.

"OK." He meets my gaze with renewed determination. "Then Alice is our sister. She's family now, and we do anything for our family, don't we, boys?" We exchange a look—one that says more than a thousand words—and a lump forms in my throat. "We're your brothers, Sebastian. You come to us, you hear me? You may be the oldest, but we're a team. If someone messes with you, they'll have us to answer to." With our eyes still locked together, I nod, and he squeezes my shoulder.

"I still think Alice should know about this. Just tell her, man, she'll understand," Mason insists.

"I'll think about it, but not today." Yeah, today's definitely not the day for this. "Now, let's get this finished, hey? I want to ask the woman I love to marry me and I don't need a dirty kitchen standing in my way."

* * *

'Kindly Calm Me Down' by Meghan Trainor is playing on repeat in the background, and I'm so nervous that by the time I finish lighting the last of the hundred or so candles, my stomach's all tied up in knots. Yet I can't help the surge of excitement rushing through my veins as I stand and take in the scene.

Outlined by the metal-framed lanterns, the rose petals glow under the candlelight, giving the illusion of a grand red carpet stretching from the front door of our house all the way down to the living room. Forming a path. An enchanted path of dreams and promises that tonight, I pray, will lead my beautiful bride to me.

The guys sure did a good job, and I'll forever be thankful for this. Having them here with me today of all days has meant more than I'll ever be able to put into words.

I smile, remembering how they all took turns slapping my back and hugging the shit out of me before they left, and I'm glad. I'm glad I asked for their help. Not just because the whole place looks amazing and we managed to do every single thing on my list, but because we did it together. Because we can count on each other when it matters the most.

It makes me feel good, our reconnecting, this new relationship between us, and as much as it pains me to admit this—due to all the years we've lost while I was grieving—I was wrong to push them away.

I walk into the living room, where row upon row of twinkling lights hang from the chandelier, covering the whole ceiling in a golden veil of light. The effect is so stunning it takes my breath away.

Our very own night sky, showering us with stars—a reminder that even in the darkest of nights all we need is a spark, a little glimmer of hope to find our way back.

I inhale deeply. A spark, a little light, just like my Alice is to me.

I touch the tiny little bulbs that drape down the fireplace. They cascade over the stone wall, giving the impression they go into the roaring fire behind the screen. It feels magical, and intimate, and incredibly hot. It feels like us. It feels like Alice and me.

I shake my head at all the poetry and flowery shit I've been thinking since I opened my eyes this morning. This is so unlike me. So unlike anything I'd have done in the past. I laugh. So unlike anything I'd ever have done, period.

Now look at me: showered, freshly shaved and wearing a sleek black suit and tie with a crisp white shirt underneath, ready to take my place in front of the fire and wait for my bride-to-be.

I swallow hard, hoping like hell she likes this. Hoping she likes everything about tonight. Hoping she loves me enough to say yes.

My heart begins to pound almost painfully inside my chest, and I slide my hands into my pockets, feeling the precious red velvet box again. I rub it between my fingers.

What if I freak her out, though? What if she thinks this is too much, too soon?

Closing my eyes, I force myself to take a few calming breaths before the crackling of the fire brings my attention to its flames. They dance and sway, alluring and hypnotic, as they move in a rhythm I know only too well.

I can feel it even now. My need, my want, hot and smouldering, burning me from within. Leaving nothing in its wake but desire and the all-consuming love I have for my girl. Reducing me to what I truly am—a man in love. A man who's facing his worst fears for what he desperately wants.

A man with his heart in his hands, waiting for his destiny to come.

The front door opens and I hear the first of many gasps, I hope, coming from the hall.

I do my best to ignore the butterflies in my stomach as I turn around, and a small eternity passes before the front door closes again.

I listen intently, counting the seconds. My heart rate increases with each beat as Alice throws her handbag and coat into the closet, and I know it won't be long now until I'm down on one knee in front of her.

She walks into the living room, tears glistening in her eyes and flowing down her cheeks, and then comes to a stop. Her hands rise over her gaping mouth to cover a series of sobs.

An angel, a rare soul. My body stiffens at how stunning she looks tonight. The little black dress with matching knee-length boots does nothing to hide her assets from admiring eyes.

I lick my lips appreciatively, undecided if I like how the dress hugs her every curve in all the right places. Or how it makes her look just like a doll with the way it clings to her top half, wraps tightly around her tiny waist, and flares over those tight, feminine hips my palms and I have come to know so well.

We stare at each other, and the breath I was holding finally rushes out, leaving me depleted, hungry, starving really as we stay just like that, locked in each other's eyes.

God, she's beautiful. Much too beautiful and good for a man like me.

And I know I should feel bad. Should feel guilty for having such a lovely creature in my life when I did nothing to deserve her. But I don't. I can't.

I've been past caring about right or wrong from the moment my eyes fell on her. From the moment I decided she was mine.

And now all that moves me, all that matters is this overwhelming, primitive need to possess, to claim, to ravish her till the end of time. And even then, I can tell it won't be enough. I want to consume her, fuse her to me, breathe her in until we're one and the same. Until she fills my heart and annihilates any lasting sorrow.

"Come here, baby," I say huskily as I extend my hand to her, beckoning her forward. My heart beats a hole through my chest as she takes that first step towards me, then another and another, walking in a daze as she covers the distance between us and places her much smaller hand in mine.

"Sebastian," she murmurs, and I smile, bringing her hand to my lips, kissing it tenderly as I drop to one knee.

A sob rips from her throat, her free hand pressed to her chest, and I hold out the box that holds my heart inside. Offering her my ring, my life, my promise that I will love her and only her for all eternity. Forevermore, sweetheart. Just as it says on the inscription. Our love is too pure, too strong to die with us. It's a love so beautiful, so bright I believe it will go on living through our children and our children's children long after we are gone.

I swallow the lump in my throat and take a deep breath through my nose. This is it. You can do this, man.

"Alice, before you came into my life I didn't know how to love, much less that I was capable of loving someone like I do you. You showed me how. You taught me with your kind, beautiful heart that love is worth the fall, the pain and the many uncertainties the future holds. Now I'm lost without you and no future will ever make sense unless you are in it." I kiss her hand that's still secured in mine.

"You're the very first thought in my head when I wake up and the very last one when I go to sleep, and even then, I dream of you, of us and what our life together could be. You make me want and wish for things I never thought I deserved—a wife, a family of my own. Now it's all I can think about. With you. For us. I love you, my sweet little thing." I smile, undeterred by the nerves eating at my insides as she laughs through her tears.

"I love you more than life itself, so I'm giving it to you. You have me. You've had all of me since day one. So be mine, as much as I am yours, Alice, and make me the happiest man alive. Marry me. Be my wife."

She takes a deep, shuddering breath, overwhelmed, no doubt, and I hold mine as the turmoil of emotions boiling up inside me constricts my throat.

She looks deep into my eyes, her smile big and radiant despite the tears that continue to flow down her face, and I see her. I see my girl. I see her love, her passion and all the dreams she has for us. I see our happiness.

"Yes." Her voice is but a whisper. "Yes, I'll marry you," she repeats more firmly, and my heart almost leaps out of my chest, clenching so painfully my hands shake as I pull the ring out of the box and slide it on her tiny finger.

My ring. My bride. My wife.

We seal our promise with a kiss. Both of us laugh when she throws herself at me and I stand with her in my arms, spinning us around in circles until she's squealing with delight.

I'm flying high. So high I feel like I'm walking on clouds.

She's mine. All mine … and now she'll be mine on paper too. Legally, lawfully, rightfully mine for all to see.

My chest inflates with pride and something else. Need. Animal, fierce, primitive need unlike anything I've ever felt before.

I hold her close, my hands and body responding to the sudden urge to imprint myself on her.

"I love you so much, baby," I rasp, kissing the bare skin of her shoulder before I kiss my way up to her neck. "I just hope you know how happy you're making me." I lick the spot just behind her ear as she melts into me, her breath catching, making me smile when I feel her whole body shudder and soften against mine.

I just need a taste. Just one taste, I keep telling myself. My resolve to wait until after dinner wavers, shaken by every gasp and moan coming out of her mouth.

Then her hands tangle in my hair, pulling me closer, demanding my kiss, and our mouths crash, fusing us together as the last shreds of my control disappear.

Rationality and even common sense elude me and with every lash of her tongue, every pull of her lips on mine, I'm pushed into a state where I can't suppress the hunger raging inside me any more than I can stop the day from rolling into night.

"Wrap your legs around my waist," I command, breaking the kiss just long enough to growl the words before my mouth slants over hers again—insistent, wanting, taking everything she has to give.

She obeys, holding on tight as I lower our bodies to the plush white rug in front of the fire and slide a hand under her skirt.

"Fuck," I growl, the sound rumbling in my chest at the feel of her silky skin and the suspenders under my palms. Jesus, what is she trying to do to me? Because if her plan is to make me lose it tonight, she's on the verge of finding out just how rough I can be.

Ignoring Alice's little whimpers of protest, I pull away and kneel up between her legs. Anticipation makes my heart beat frantically as I lift the flared skirt all the way up to her waist.

Mmm, she's just too fucking sexy for words, too delicious for me to deny myself a bite or two ... or a full-on meal, in this case.

I smirk devilishly at her.

Yeah, baby, I'm going to fucking devour you.

But then again, she already knows that. Sprawled out before me in her nude stockings, black garter belt and panties—crotchless, no less—she knows exactly what she's doing to me.

"I'm going to eat you out until you scream," I rasp as I trail my thumb over her slit. She's soaked, her folds already slick and hot with her arousal as her eyes silently plead for me to fill her. "You're so wet, baby. So fucking wet for me."

"Sebastian, I—I need you," she gasps, shuddering when I circle her clit with my thumb.

"You have me, baby," I tell her, my chest tight and hurting with emotions I thought I could never feel. "You have me forever. I'm yours."

* * *

A long while passes until we find ourselves completely naked and satiated, still lying in front of the fireplace as we fall in and out of sleep.

"We need to eat," I murmur as my stomach rumbles for the fifth time in the last five minutes. "I'm fucking starving and I cooked us dinner to celebrate. It's in the oven."

"You did?" She laughs. "Wow, you really went all-out."

"Uh-huh. And the guys helped with the decorations. Even Luke pitched in. I wanted to do as much as I could myself, so only family was allowed to help."

She kisses my chest, smiling up at me. "It's perfect. I love it. I love it all so much."

"You're perfect. And I love you. I love you more than anything."

A tear rolls down her cheek. "Thank you, Sebastian. You made me feel like a princess tonight. I'll never forget it. I love you."

Another tear falls to her cheek, and another, and before I know what I'm doing our lips are crashing together again, the food a second time forgotten as I show her with my body just how much she means to me.

Chapter 18

Charles

After the world's quickest knock, the door to my office opens and Linda comes in with a smiling Alice trailing behind her. Linda closes the door. "Charles, look who's come to visit us."

I beam and immediately get up from behind the desk to meet them near the lounge.

"Alice, it's so good to see you." I bend to kiss her on the cheeks and then pull her into my arms. This girl already means so much to me. She's the daughter I didn't get to have. And the way she loves my son—so fiercely, passionately and unconditionally—makes me her number one fan.

Linda covers her mouth as tears fill her eyes.

I frown. What has gotten into her?

"OK, I'm going to go," Linda says. "Alice, please come see me before you leave."

A teary Alice pushes away from me to look at Linda. "No, don't leave, Linda. I'd like you to stay."

Linda nods with a sniffle, and I confess, I become a little nervous with the way they're both acting.

Then Alice is taking a deep breath as her hands reach for mine. "Charles, you are one of the kindest people I know. Giving, supportive. Both you and Linda have been nothing but good to me—honest, trustworthy. Becoming the only people, in fact, I look up to and truly admire. It made me realise that even before Sebastian my luck had already changed because I had you two in my life. Which is why I can't think of a better person than you, Charles, to walk me down the aisle to Sebastian."

Shit! My heart tightens and my eyes begin to burn with unshed tears.

Alice's shoulders bunch up and a few tears roll down her exquisite face. "I just can't imagine anyone else by my side who's more deserving of taking my dad's place, and if you say no, I'll just have to do it on my own."

Ha. I almost laugh. As if I'd allow that to happen whilst I'm around.

"Oh," Linda gushes, and I clear my throat, trying to hold it together long enough to give this beautiful soul an answer.

"Alice..." My voice breaks and I clear my throat again. "It will be my pleasure to walk you down the aisle to my son. It will be an honour."

With an audible gasp, Alice throws her arms around me and starts sobbing her little eyes out.

Fuck. I close my eyes, hugging her tight, trying not to sob like a baby myself.

She just makes me feel so special, this girl—and so very proud I am her first and only choice.

The knot in my throat tightens. I swallow hard, doing my best to regain some composure, some control before I'm able to speak. "No one can replace your dad, Alice, but I'd like to think that one day I'll have a special place in your heart, just as you already have in mine."

Alice shakes her head, sniffling. "We are so thankful for you, Charles. You're the best father figure Sebastian and I could ever have asked for ... and I'm sure you'll be an even better grandfather to any future babies we may have."

I break down in tears—I can't help it, hugging this kind, beautiful girl like a lifeline.

Linda is weeping. Actually weeping. I reach for her and embrace her too. And the three of us stay just like that for a while.

With a long, shaky breath, Linda is the first to break away from us. She collects the box of tissues from the coffee table and offers it to Alice and I. "I'm so glad I got to witness this moment." Linda hiccups as we all take a tissue from the box. "Thank you, Alice, for letting me stay."

"I'm glad you were here, Linda," Alice replies.

Then we're all drying our tears and blowing our noses in a mixture of laughter and sniffles, and I don't even care that they're seeing me like this. All I care about is that I got my son back, gained a daughter, and now I can barely wait for the day I'll be bouncing a grandchild or two on my knee.

I grin.

Yep, I can feel myself getting younger already.

God, this sweet, sweet girl.

It's a wonder how alone she was when she came to work for us. No family to stand by her, nobody to cushion her falls. Something that worried Linda and I in the beginning. We were about to set her up with Sebastian, and we didn't want either of them to get hurt.

Yet we both knew we had to do something. Sebastian was turning off his feelings, trying his damnedest to push everyone who loved him away. And we couldn't just stand by and watch him drown in his own misery.

I sigh, glad that our plan worked out and that Sebastian fell for Alice. Thankful that boy found some sense. It was a big gamble for us. The stakes had never been higher. And I confess I was a little afraid.

For a moment there I didn't think we were going to find the right woman. But then Alice walked right through our doors—all sweet, kind and strong personality with her mesmerising beauty and big eyes—and I immediately knew all of our prayers had been answered. I knew Sebastian wouldn't be able to ignore her no matter how hard he tried.

"OK, I don't know about you two, but I'm starving," Linda announces, moving towards the phone on my desk. "Plus, we should be celebrating, so coffee and cake are in order. Perhaps even a little champagne if you two are game."

I glance at my watch. It's four thirty p.m., and yeah, I for one could do with a snack and a drink. "I think that's the best idea you've had all day, Linda. Thank you."

With a few more chuckles, Linda starts placing the call to the catering department, and Alice and I move towards the plush cream sofas where we take our seats facing each other.

"It really meant a lot to me that you said yes, Charles," Alice says in her quiet, sweet voice. "I'll treasure this memory forever."

I fix my gaze on her. "And I meant what I said, my dear. It will be an honour." I roll my lips, choosing my next words carefully. I don't want Alice to think me negative or a fatalist. "Also, I want you to know that you can always come to me. Be it good or bad news, I'll always be there for you and Sebastian. Even if things don't work out between you. And I'm not saying this because I don't believe in your relationship—I very much do. I wouldn't support your wedding if I didn't. But I want you to know I won't ever take sides or turn on you. You gave me back my son, Alice, and I'll forever be indebted to you."

She blinks away more tears. "You don't owe me anything, Charles. I love Sebastian. I'd do anything for him. You don't have to feel responsible for me because my parents are dead."

"I know, but sometimes life happens and things don't quite go the way we envisioned them. I've lived through that first-hand. It's good to know that someone else is there for us. And I'm there for you, Alice. Linda and I are there for you."

Chapter 19

Alice

The alarm clock goes off and the sound of 'Diamonds' by Rihanna fills the room. I hit the big snooze button and burrow under the covers again.

I just need ten more minutes ... ten more minutes, and I'll get up. Something I always do before facing the world outside my bedroom. Not that the world is half as scary as before, but I still need a moment to prepare.

I hear whistling coming from the bathroom and smile into my pillow, closing my eyes again. Yeah, nothing is quite as scary when you have a man like Sebastian Hunter by your side.

My superhero. The Peter to my Gwen, the Tony to my Pepper. The best, most wonderful thing that's ever happened to me in my whole life.

Ten minutes later, I'm up and walking into the bathroom just as Sebastian is finishing his shave. He smiles broadly when he sees me and lowers the razor to the sink.

A white towel is wrapped around his waist, leaving his chiselled chest and rock-hard abs on full display, and I swallow hard, barely able to form words in my head, let alone speak. No matter how many times I see him like this, I just can't get used to it. Can't get used to how gorgeous this man is.

"Hey, beautiful," he says, taking me in his arms and kissing my lips.

"Hi," I say breathlessly, and he laughs, lifting me off the floor and sitting me up on the counter in front of him.

He places himself between my legs, my hands sliding down his chest as he kisses down my neck, my shoulder, my collarbone. "Did you sleep well?" he rasps.

"I ... did."

He kisses me on the lips again, his tongue reaching for mine, grazing it, caressing it, and I melt further into his embrace.

Sliding a hand between my thighs, Sebastian begins to rub his thumb over my slit, stroking me everywhere except where I most need it until I'm soaked and humming and he's pushing a finger into me—two, then three, pumping me hard.

"Ohhh," I moan, gasping for breath, shocked when he presses on my clit with his thumb and I come on his hand, my heart racing as I stare dazedly up at him.

Then he's pulling my nightdress over my head, releasing the towel from around his hips, and, grabbing himself firmly in his hand, enters me without missing a beat. I cry out, my nails stabbing into his back as he starts pushing into me.

"Always so tight," he groans. "So fucking tight and wet for me."

"Yes," I gasp, and for the next hour or so we stay in that bathroom—making sweet love on the counter, tasting each other on the floor, and fucking like animals in the shower—until I lose count of all the orgasms he blesses me with.

God, whatever did I do to deserve such a man?

* * *

Sitting at the breakfast bar, I smile dreamily as Sebastian places a plate of toast and scrambled eggs in front of me and then lowers himself into his seat.

A girl sure could get used to this—the food, the sex, the gorgeous man grinning at me.

After our rendezvous in the bathroom, we quickly showered, and Sebastian came down to prepare breakfast for us, leaving me alone to get dressed and put on my makeup in peace. A rare occasion without the usual morning rush or sexual advances from him. At least until I entered the kitchen, and he was on me again faster than I could breathe.

Sebastian picks up his fork and leans over for another kiss before digging in, and I can't help but stare, my smile growing wider by the second.

I blink, pulling myself out of my daze, and open my tablet to start checking my emails. There's one from Beatrice with a few questions regarding the book, to which I reply straight away.

I sip my coffee and start eating my toast.

One from Sharon, asking for my chicken quiche and carrot cake recipes. It's her grandson's third birthday party this weekend and she wants to bake everything herself. I smile, offering my help anyway, and, shovelling more food into my mouth, upload the Word documents from my files and quickly send them to her.

And then there's one from a 'well-wisher.3000' I don't recognize. Oh, it must be the church with questions about the wedding and stuff. My lips twitch and I almost snort, imagining Father John coming up with such a ridiculous name.

I open the email and it's like a cold hand wraps itself around my chest.

Dear Miss Lake,

If you really want to know the man you're marrying, open the documents attached.

My eyes instantly rise to Sebastian, my lips ready to form the words as I stare up at him, but I find myself not making a sound, my fingers trembling as I look at the screen again and with a deep breath open the first attachment.

Nooo ... God, no ...

My heart sinks and tears form in my eyes as I read the medical report from my first consultation with Dr Smith. The room spins.

I can't believe it. I just can't believe it.

My ribs keep getting tighter and tighter by the second with all the lies and deceit webbed around me.

Then I read some kind of contract dated the day after my accident, between Sebastian and my former landlady, Mrs Hayes, where she agrees to end my tenancy earlier, and not take me back under any circumstances, in exchange for a full year's worth of rent and an additional ten thousand pounds after signing an

NDA. And my whole world comes crumbling down, turning to dust beneath his feet.

Bile rises up my throat and I cover my mouth with my hand.

God, he did everything he could to bring me to this house, to keep me here. And I was so stupid, so naive, I believed him. I believed everything he said.

This is sick, though. Crazy and sick. I mean, no normal person behaves this way, falls in love this way, and I don't know if I can ever feel safe with him again.

My eyes flicker back to Sebastian and my whole body begins to tremble as a choked cry escapes my lips.

He's just so beautiful. So, so perfect, and I can't reconcile the thought he could ever do this to me.

"Alice?" he asks, reaching for me, but I jump out of my seat. I don't want him to touch me. Don't want to feel him anywhere near my skin.

Blinking through my tears, I throw the tablet in front of him. "Is it true?"

He reads through the documents before meeting my gaze. "Who sent you this?" he asks, his voice void of emotion and his face blank.

And just like that, I know it's true. I know he did all those things.

He's not defending himself, not contesting the information. No, he's Mr Cool, Mr Control Over Emotion, and all he wants to know is who told me so he can exact his revenge on them.

I take a step back, then another, and another, and he tries to reach for me again. "Don't touch me," I whisper. A look of pain takes over his features, his eyes pleading with mine.

I cry harder as my heart breaks into tiny little pieces. I feel like my soul is being ripped apart, torn in two right in front of him.

"I didn't know what we were then, Alice. I didn't know how to interpret what I felt. All I knew was that I had to have you. That I had to be near you at all times." He shakes his head, dropping his hands to his sides. "I messed up. I messed up really bad, and I'm sorry. I'm so sorry, baby, but if you give me another chance, if you let me ..."

"I can't do this," I sob, shaking my head as I take another step back. "I can't do this right now." My eyes flood, burning with even more tears as I turn and run towards our bedroom.

Once there, I lock the door and pick up a small suitcase from my walk-in wardrobe, then on autopilot begin to fill it with some of my clothes, underwear, and a few toiletries from the bathroom.

"Alice?" Sebastian knocks on the door. "Let me in, baby. We need to talk about this."

Why is he being so sweet, so considerate, when I know for a fact he can break down the door? Damn him and his mind games! Manipulative bastard. Wiping my tears angrily, I fasten the zipper of the suitcase and haul it to the floor.

He's playing with me, confusing me, tricking me into forgiving him without much of an argument or a fight.

My vision blurs and for a minute I have to hold onto the bed. Please, God, give me the strength I need to do this. Please, help me.

Breathing through the dizziness, I grab my suitcase and my handbag and walk to the door, opening it just as he's about to knock again.

"Alice," he rasps, panic lacing his voice when he sees me in my coat and shoes and pulling the suitcase behind me. "Baby, please ..."

God, I need to get away from him. I can't think like this. And I need to think ... I need to think very carefully about what I'm going to do.

"Let me go," I croak. "Please, Sebastian. I need time."

"You can't forgive me, can you?"

"Forgive what? That you lied to me? That you tricked me? That the entire beginning of our relationship was a lie?" I shout.

He lowers his eyes, and I take a deep breath, trying to calm myself down.

"I don't know," I tell him truthfully. "That's why I need some time away. I'm too angry, too hurt to talk about this right now—logically, at least."

He nods and reluctantly steps back. "Where will you stay?" he asks as I walk past him. "I need to know you're safe."

"Don't act like you're not going to send security after me," I throw over my shoulder. "I know you better than that ... I think."

He winces, but I turn away, walking out of his house, out of his life, perhaps even out of being his.

* * *

Sobbing under my umbrella, I press the buzzer again and again, praying that Beatrice is home and doesn't mind taking me in. At least for a day or two until I figure out what to do next. Money's not an issue. Sebastian made sure of that, transferring five million pounds into my account as soon as I left. I just feel so overwhelmed, though. I need a friend. I need someone to listen. God, what a mess.

My fingers tremble as I reach inside my bag for my phone. I knew I should've called before just turning up here, but I was so distressed.

"Sweetie? What's wrong?" Beatrice gasps, taking me in her arms as soon as she opens the door. She's wearing a bathrobe and a towel is wrapped around her head, so it's safe to assume I interrupted her shower. "Alice?" she presses, but I can only shake my head, my throat so tight no words can get past it no matter how hard I try.

"Come on, let's get you inside," she says, taking the suitcase and umbrella from me and, with one arm still around me, pulling me inside.

She leaves my wet items in the hall and takes me into a modern, beautiful living room—a calming space decorated with white furniture and grey sofas, green and yellow ornaments and throw pillows everywhere. The gas fireplace is on, along with an aromatherapy diffuser, and the lights are dimmed, just right for the mood I'm in.

Taking my coat, Beatrice throws a blanket over my shoulders and rubs my arms as she leads me to the couch. "God, you're freezing. Here, sit. I'll go get us some tea, OK?"

An hour later, we're both sitting on the couch, on our second cup of tea, and Beatrice is still shaking her head. "And that's all he said? That he didn't know what he was feeling?"

I nod, and she blows out a breath.

I told her everything. About the email, my fight with Sebastian, and the half-assed explanation he tried to give me.

"He said he didn't know what we were when he came up with the plan," I repeat what he told me with a shrug. "But he wanted to keep me close. He needed to be near me."

Beatrice frowns, and for the first time since we met, she avoids meeting my gaze. "What?" I ask.

"Don't get mad, but knowing Sebastian, I'm actually not that surprised he did something like this."

"What, that he lied to me? That he tricked me into his bed and into falling in love with him?"

"No, Alice. I mean I'm not surprised that once he fell in love he acted out of desperation. That he resorted to some panic-fuelled plan to lure you in instead of just asking you out like a normal guy would."

I shake my head. "That doesn't make any sense."

"Doesn't it? Think about it. He's never been in a relationship. He's been emotionally unavailable ever since his mum passed. And the first time he feels something is with you. A good girl by all accounts. A proper girl who just happened to land in his lap— vulnerable, fragile, and in need of a hero. Come on. He jumped at the chance, if you ask me. It's not hard to imagine what he was thinking." She shrugs. "A man like him is not used to being patient. Not used to losing control. So he panics, does what he does best in business and takes over your life. He objectifies you. Tells himself he's helping you, even if deep down he knows he's just helping himself. He explains away what he's feeling with lust, desire, avoiding any of his real feelings like the plague."

I shake my head. "I ... I feel used, dirty," I croak, wiping my eyes with a tissue and then blowing my nose. God, I fear my tears will never end.

"I know, sweetie. But if it's any consolation, I don't think he ever got the chance to actually use you before he was head over heels in love with you."

"I don't know." I don't know what to think any more.

"The man asked you to marry him, didn't he? It's not a game any more."

"Yeah, maybe ... but it doesn't erase the fact it began as one."

"True, your beginning will always be a little dark. A little tainted. But it's up to you now to make a choice. Will you let it rule your decision, or will you let the love you have for each other guide you?"

I swallow hard. "I don't know if I can forgive him."

"And that's OK. You need time and space to process all this." She puts one arm over my shoulders and hugs me to her. "Meanwhile, my house is yours for as long as you need it."

She touches her head to mine, and I throw my arms around her. "Thank you, Beatrice. Thank you for being such a good friend to us."

"You'd do the exact same thing for me, sweetie. Now let's get you upstairs to your room so you can get some rest."

***

The doorbell rings and I jump out of bed, my whole body trembling as I open my bedroom door a little to listen in.

Could it be him? Could it be that he finally came for me?

Apart from a few texts telling me he loves me and that he's thinking about me, I haven't heard from Sebastian in almost two weeks, and I guess I'm feeling a bit more anxious than I thought, having doubts if what he felt for me was even real.

I mean, if he loved me, shouldn't he be fighting for me? Shouldn't he be begging me to take him back?

"What are you doing here, Sebastian?" I hear Beatrice ask, and my heart almost leaps out of my chest. I breathe out a sigh of relief, pressing my forehead to the door.

"I need to see her. I've waited long enough. I've been patient. But I can't wait any longer, Beatrice. I'm going out of my mind."

Tears fall down my face and I smile with pure joy as I listen to him.

God, I miss him. I miss him so much I can barely stand it.

"I know, but she's not ready yet. And you can't rush her. You have no right."

"But I need to explain. I need her to understand. I love her. Hell, I've loved her from the very first moment I saw her."

My heart clenches, almost squeezing the life out of me, and I have to stop myself from running down the stairs to him.

"And she loves you, Sebastian, but you messed up. You messed up really bad this time."

He sighs heavily. "Will you at least tell her I came?"

"Of course."

"And Beatrice ... thank you for looking after her."

"You're both my friends, Sebastian. I just wish the circumstances were different."

I hear them kissing each other on the cheek and saying goodbye, and my eyes close in pain as I convince myself I have to let him go.

He still has a lesson to learn, and whatever I do now will set the way he'll treat me and respect me in the future.

That is if we still have a future together, of course.

Leaving the door ajar, I walk back to the bed and sit cross-legged against the headboard, a small pillow pressed to my chest.

Beatrice knocks. "Hey, can I come in?"

"Yeah, sure."

"You heard?" she asks, leaning against the bedpost, and I nod, smiling sadly up at her.

God, why does this have to hurt so bad?

"For all it's worth, I think he's really sorry, Alice. And he looks like shit. Like he hasn't eaten or slept a wink in all this time."

"Good," I reply, but it lacks the anger I felt before.

"You're not fooling me, you know? I can see you've forgiven him."

"Yeah, but I can't go back just yet, Beatrice. He won't learn anything if I do."

She laughs, and, sitting on the bed, pulls me into an embrace. "Yeah, let him stew for a bit longer, I say. But not too long, babes. Men like him don't have the patience. Not to mention the ball's in your court now. It's up to you to make the next move."

I nod. She's right. It's up to me now. He won't come here again, not until he's desperate, anyway. And after that, all bets are off, as they say.

So I better take control of the situation. Soon. Either summon him here or go to him, but I can't continue to make him wait.

Besides, enough is enough. Especially when it feels as if I'm punishing myself right alongside him.

My phone buzzes with a message and I reach for it. It's from Sebastian.

I'm sorry, Alice. I'm so very sorry.
I'll wait. I will always wait for you.
I love you.

There's a link to a song—'Little Do You Know' by Alex & Sierra—and I click on it, my face screwing up in pain as it takes everything in me not to go down and run after him.

Chapter 20

Sebastian

Rushing down the steps of Beatrice's terrace house, I walk straight into an old woman and her shopping bags.

"Jesus, watch where you're going," she shouts over the rain, which has now picked up with heavy drops falling down on us.

"I'm sorry. I'm so sorry," I stammer, helping her pick up her groceries from the pavement and put them back into the plastic bags.

I can't believe Alice still won't see me. That she won't let me explain. That she won't even reply to my texts, if only to let me know she's still mad.

I apologise to the woman for the hundredth time before she rushes off, and I proceed to walk blindly to the car again, my feet dragging and my eyes stuck to what I assume is Alice's window the whole time.

The same window I've been stalking since she came here, and Michael and his team have been guarding with their lives.

I feel lost. Like I'm missing a piece of myself, of my soul, and have no clue how to make myself whole again.

"I'm sorry, man," Ryan mutters as soon as I open the door to the Cayenne and get inside.

"Yeah, you and me both, mate," I rasp, shutting the door. "You and me both."

"Where to?"

"Home. Just take me home, Ryan." I run my hands over my face, scrubbing at my stubble before closing my eyes.

Who knows, she might still change her mind and come to me tonight.

I almost laugh at myself as I swallow the lump in my throat. Yeah, and hell will freeze over.

* * *

Friday ...

Two whole weeks since Alice left. Two whole days since my visit to Beatrice's, and already I'm going out of my mind. Not eating, not sleeping, not living. Not really doing much of anything except waiting for her to come back. For the first time in my life, not even work has been able to distract me.

"These Japanese fuckers are crazy, man," Luke shouts in my ear over the loud music of the club.

We're in the middle of negotiations with the Japanese to finally acquire a piece of land in Tokyo that'll be perfect for our second hotel in the area. A piece of land I've been wanting for well over a year, and now, no matter how hard I try, I just can't get excited about it.

"Just keep them entertained, Luke. And for the love of God, don't let them get into trouble. I'm going home after I finish this drink."

"No way. The night is still young, bro. Come on, we're just getting started."

Right on cue about a dozen half-naked girls approach the VIP section where we're sitting and perch themselves on every man's lap. A roar of laughter goes around our tables as well as the clinking of glasses.

We're at a very luxurious, very exclusive strip club in Soho tonight. Luke thought it would be fun for the Japanese—after a few hints from them, of course—and that it would cheer me up. 'Bring you out of your funk for sure,' as he put it.

Two girls start walking in our direction and I neck my drink before getting up. "Seems like too much fun for me, bro, so I'm gonna go."

"Come on, Sebastian, stay," Luke shouts, grinning as both girls sit on his lap instead. "Don't you want a piece of this?"

I shake my head and laugh. "Enjoy, gentlemen. I'll see you all on Monday."

"She won't be home waiting for you, you know. She's gone," he says, and I pause, knowing he's right. Bile rises up my throat as I turn without a word and find my way to the exit.

She may be gone, but I'll be damned if I touch another woman. There's only one Alice. There's only one woman for me in this miserable life.

* * *

Luke

I stare at Sebastian's back as he walks away from us, my jaw ticking in time with my pulse.

Something's not right. Something in his eyes, his expression—I don't know.

What I do know is that he shouldn't be alone right now. He hasn't been himself since Alice left, and to be quite honest, I'm afraid of his state of mind.

God knows what my brother will do if left on his own for too long.

"Where's Sebastian?" Mason asks as he and Nathan return with fresh drinks. And surprise, surprise, even more semi-naked girls trailing to our tables behind them.

I smirk and shake my head. "He left," I reply, shouting over the music as I slide my palms over smooth, feminine thighs, making both girls on my lap wiggle and giggle with delight.

They're gorgeous, both of them, hot and ready for it, just the way I like it, with one already kissing down my neck as the other wraps her hand around my cock through my trousers.

Nathan nods. "I thought as much when we sent over the girls."

"Maybe we shouldn't have come to a place like this," Mason says. "Maybe ..."

"Maybe you should check if your balls are still attached to your dick, huh, Mason?" I shout over the music again, and he grins, giving me the finger.

"Fuck you, Luke."

I laugh. "Oh, I will, little brother. I will," I say, giving the girls a little squeeze for good measure as an idea begins to form in my head.

And although it might not be what Sebastian wants, it definitely is what he needs right now.

"What if we take the party to him? Make him have fun like in the old days," I suggest.

"I don't think that's a good idea," Nathan says.

"And I don't think he should be alone right now. He needs us." Not that I get what he's going through or anything like that. I don't. And, hopefully, never will. Love is not something I'm interested in.

Still, Sebastian's not doing well, and I'm sick of pretending he is. Sick of this fucking 'guy code' and all the bullshit bravado attached to it.

Neither should have a place between brothers. Let alone between us, when we've seen each other at our lowest. When we've been to hell and back together after our mum passed.

"Luke's right," Mason says. "He shouldn't be left alone, Nathan. Not the way he's been acting lately."

Nathan blows out a breath, and with one last look between us, I gently push the girls off of my lap. Then I get up and turn to our Japanese friends.

"Gentlemen, gather round," I announce, already doing up the buttons on my suit jacket. "We're taking this party somewhere else."

* * *

Sebastian

One hour later ... 11.00 p.m.

"Good evening, sir," Rick greets me at the gate and then waves at the two cars with my security detail finally pulling up behind me.

"Good evening, Rick." I rev the engine and also wave at the guards.

I sure gave them a run for their money tonight with my new silver Bugatti Veyron. Well, Alice's brand-new silver Bugatti Veyron, actually—her engagement present to match the black one I got for myself—even if she refuses to drive it, poor baby, claiming she's too scared of it after almost crashing it on her very first drive. I smile at the memory and then grimace as pain lances through my chest.

"Everything OK?" Rick asks, and I nod, noticing for the first time he seems fidgety tonight.

"Yeah. You?"

"Yeah, just finished doing a sweep. So you can go right inside." He pauses, not meeting my eyes. "Oh, and there's a package for you in the kitchen."

I frown. "In the kitchen?"

"I think it's one of Alice's gadgets. Probably another pressure cooker or something like that, so ..." He shrugs, and I nod in understanding.

"Right. Yeah, I'll deal with it." With that I rev the engine again, park in the garage, and then go inside the house.

I'm dog-tired and so fucking ready for this day to be over, I'm contemplating going straight to bed without showering. Anything so I don't find myself breaking and entering and consequently getting arrested for kidnapping my woman back. I imagine the headlines.

Sebastian Hunter, billionaire and CEO of the Hunter Corp, nothing but a common criminal after all. The heir to the Hunter Corp resorts and hotels arrested last night after ex-fiancée calls police.

Yeah, the press would have a field day with me all right.

I'm just about to go up the stairs when the thought of having something important to Alice in my possession stops me on the very first step, pulling me in the direction of the kitchen. I wonder what she ordered this time? And if maybe, just maybe it will be good enough to lure her here, to bring her to me.

I sigh. Who knows? Stranger things have happened.

Not to mention that it's been two fucking weeks now and I'm getting pretty desperate. So much so, I don't know what I'll do if we keep going like this.

After walking down the hall and past the stairs, I push open the door to the right and make my way in.

I frown. The lights above the dining table and countertops are on, and so are the ones above the island and breakfast area, where ... I gasp, my eyes widening.

Where Alice is sitting with a steaming cup of tea between her hands.

The shock of seeing her again freezes me to the spot, where I stay just like that, unable to stop staring at her.

Maybe I'm seeing things. Maybe I'm losing my mind.

"Hello, Sebastian," she says, and I breathe out a sigh of relief.

She's real. She's fucking real and she's finally here with me.

"Alice," I whisper. "How ... how are you?" I swallow the tennis ball lodged in my throat.

She smiles sadly. "Better. Ready to talk, if you are?"

"Yes, of course. I ... I've missed you," I tell her, unable to resist, and her eyes begin to water.

"I've missed you too," she croaks, and in two seconds I'm by her side, pulling her into my arms, kissing her cheeks, her nose, her lips, kissing her all over as she holds onto me tight. All the angst, the heartache from the past two weeks is pouring out of me, and I don't know how to stop.

"Sebastian, we—we need to talk," she whispers breathlessly, after I take her mouth in a particularly long and passionate kiss and pick her up in my arms.

"I know. Fuck, I know," I growl, pressing my forehead to hers, resisting the urge to carry her up the stairs to our bed and just bury myself in her.

But she's right. We do need to talk. And so, with one last peck to her lips, I place her back on her stool and sit on the one next to hers. I lace our fingers together and kiss each of her knuckles in turn. "I'm sorry. I'm so sorry, sweetheart," I start, my voice thick and filled with regret as we hold each other's eyes. "I'm so sorry I hurt you. It was never my intention. I never wanted to bring you pain. I just didn't know what I was feeling. I promise. I didn't know I was falling for you."

I place both her hands in one of mine and caress her cheeks, doing my best to dry her tears. "And I know I acted crazy, irrationally even, doing all those awful things and lying to you. Using my money and power to pressure you into moving in and make you stay." My lips curl in self-disgust and I shake my head, looking away. The right words to explain my insanity when we met are failing me.

How do you explain to someone that they are everything? That they are your whole reason for living when you don't understand it yourself?

"But I just had to have you, Alice. I had to, because I couldn't go on living without you. Because I needed you in my life, in my house, in my bed." I look at her, my heart thudding in my ears.

"Back then, I was stupid enough to believe this thing between us was just lust, that it was something that would go away once we slept together. But after you were here with me, and we were living together, eating together, spending every free minute talking and getting to know each other, I soon realised that there was so much more to what I was feeling, to what I needed from you."

Alice nods, tears still streaming down her face. "Please say something," I beg.

She presses a hand to her throat. "It's hard to look past the fact that you lied to me. That you manipulated me and the people around us to get what you wanted. It scares me. That side of you scares me, Sebastian."

"And to think I never lied to a woman before." I laugh bitterly. "Never did anything like this before. Fuck, how can I make you believe me, Alice? How can I make you believe what I'm telling you is the truth?"

She closes her eyes. "I don't know, Sebastian. And it's not even that I don't believe you as much as my trust in you is not the same. I don't know if it will ever be."

My throat tightens because I know what she's going to say next. "No, baby. No. Wait. Please."

Her eyes open. "And that's why I think we should cancel the wedding. Maybe postpone it until next year."

I shake my head, frantic, scared she doesn't want me any more. "Baby, no. Please don't do that. Dad and Linda are still organising the wedding, they never stopped. Don't do that to them. Don't do that to us."

"Sebastian, I—"

"Stop being a pussy, Rick, and open the fucking gate." Luke's voice rings loud and clear throughout the kitchen and I swear under my breath.

Dear God, please tell me he didn't.

"Is that Luke?" Alice asks, confused, and I spring out of my seat and move towards the door. Knowing Luke, he's right outside along with my idiot brothers, the Japanese, and the fucking strippers from the club, ready to 'cheer me up' yet again. I swear I'll kill him if he messes things up for me and Alice now that she's back.

"Wait here and I'll go check on him," I instruct.

"I'll come with you."

"No," I say too quickly. "I mean, stay here. I think he's drunk. We were entertaining the Japanese earlier and he was drinking, so—"

Alice snorts. "Oh, my, I've never seen Luke drunk before." She jumps out of her seat and grabs her phone from her bag. "Sorry, but I'm not missing out on that."

Fuck, fuck, fuck. I'm going to kill him if the girls are here.

I scrub at my face before following Alice out of the kitchen and out of the front door. My heart beats frantically inside my chest as all I can think is that Alice is going to leave me as soon as we get to the bloody gate.

God, she'll probably think I've been partying and cheating on her the whole time she's been away.

"I'm sorry, sir," Rick says, but I shake my head. He has nothing to apologise for.

"It's OK, Rick. I think he's drunk." I pat his shoulder as I pass him, in a way also thanking him for helping Alice tonight, and he nods, stepping aside to let me go through the smaller gate.

Outside, Alice, who's hot on my heels, gasps and then snorts as I breathe out a sigh of relief.

Luke's holding a bottle of champagne, his upper body sticking out of the roof of a limo—the only limo in sight, thank God—as he opens his arms wide. Mason and Nathan wave at us through the open windows, and I finally relax, seeing there's no one else inside but the driver.

Looking down on us, Luke lets out a big laugh and sways a little to the sides. Gosh, were they this drunk when I left them at the club?

"Alice," he sings, and she laughs.

"Hi, Alice!" the twins say in sync, and she bursts out laughing again.

"Sorry if we're interrupting," Luke says, winking at me in a most exaggerated way—the idiot—"but we wanted to check if Sebastian was OK. He's being a bit of a party pooper nowadays."

Alice smiles sadly at him. "Yeah, I guess neither of us has been great company lately."

"They seem to be sorting things out now," Nathan says with only a slight slur. "What do you say we leave them to it?"

"Where are our Japanese friends?" I ask, suddenly concerned for our business associates as Alice begins taking pictures of my drunken brothers with her phone.

Mason grins. "Oh, we left them at Mariana's club. She's looking after them."

Mariana is the owner of Club X, a gentlemen's club. A place where nothing is too dirty or forbidden as long as it is to do with sex—consensual, of course—and where my brothers and I have been going for years.

Yeah, they'll be well taken care of, our Japanese friends. I have no doubts.

"Guess we'll be going there too, now we know you're in good hands," Luke says before he knocks on the roof of the limo and they start moving down the road. "Goodbye, Alice. I'm glad you're back. Be sure to look after our brother."

"I will." Alice laughs, waving at them.

"Bye, Alice!" the twins say in choir again as they also wave.

"Goodbye, boys. Have fun. Oh, and make sure you drink plenty of water tonight. And eat something."

I smile at her concern. Knowing she cares about my brothers warms my heart.

Still giggling, Alice turns to me and our eyes clash under the moonlight. My stare drills into hers as we both become serious again.

I want to kiss her, goddammit.

"Let's go back inside," I murmur, and, placing my hand on her lower back, guide her towards the house.

* * *

"Please tell me you're back," I say as soon as I close the front door behind us and we both stand in the hall.

Alice keeps her back to me as she wraps her cardigan protectively around herself. I fist my hands, frowning as I stop myself from wrapping her in my arms instead.

She's scared ... and she's scared of me, no less.

She takes a deep breath and turns with her arms crossed. "I'm back," she replies, and I can't help the exhale of relief that rushes out of my lungs.

"Baby ..." I go to move, wanting to touch her, but she holds out a hand.

"That said, you can't lie to me again, Sebastian. I won't allow you to treat me that way. I'm your partner—your life partner!—and I deserve your respect."

"I know, baby. I know."

"Promise me, then. Promise you won't ever lie to me again."

"I'll never lie to you again, Alice. I promise." And that's the honest-to-God truth. After all, omitting is not the same as lying, right?

Well, not in my world, at least. In my world it's a necessity, especially when you're trying to protect the ones you love.

I do love Alice, and I tell her as much. "I love you, Alice. With all of my heart, my body and mind, my very soul, I love you, and I won't ever let you down again."

Her hand falls as tears spring to her eyes, and before I can control myself, I'm rushing to her and pulling her into my chest, kissing her until we're both panting and gasping for breath.

Lifting her in my arms, I carry her up the stairs, down the corridor, and into our bedroom where we continue to kiss, touch, and rid ourselves of a few clothes as she relaxes in our bed.

I don't want her to think this is all I want, though, so I do my best to slow things down a little to check on her. Even if it's fucking torture on my dick and I feel as if I'm going to explode.

"Do you want this?" I murmur huskily against her mouth as she blinks up at me in surprise.

"I want you, Sebastian. I'll always want you."

I press my forehead to hers. God, it's so good to hear her say that again.

Her hands caress my cheeks as our eyes stay glued to each other's, and with that she seals our fates, because this is it for me. She is it, and I'm never letting go again.

Kissing her long and deep, I slowly get rid of what's left of our clothes and our fears until there's nothing between us except for our desire and the heat of our naked skin.

"I love you," I murmur into her ear, nipping at her earlobe before pulling it into my mouth.

She gasps, and then I'm licking down her throat, her shoulders, her collarbone.

"I love you." I suck at her beautiful breasts, her rosy nipples, her stomach, kissing her and marking her over and over again until she begins to unravel and beg sweetly for more.

That's it, baby. That's it. Let go. Be mine again.

Whimpering, she grabs my hair as I reach her navel, her pink blush spreading to her chest and her moans a constant sweet sound as if she can barely contain herself.

I grin, biting her right hip bone and sliding my tongue across her belly. I bite into her left hip bone, and she cries out, arching her back.

"Sebastian," she pleads as my shoulders force her legs further apart and I breathe in her scent, the flowery smell of her already driving me mad.

Intoxicated, I kiss one thigh and then the other, tasting her sweetness and saltiness there. God, and to think I almost lost her. That I almost lost this.

"Marry me," I say, wanting her more than ever. Needing her total surrender.

"What?" she gasps, and I lick her, my tongue delving deep into her little slit before pressing on her clit. "Oh, God."

"Marry me," I say again before lapping at a new wave of cream gushing from her tight entrance and onto my lips.

She cries out, her delicate fingers tugging harder at my hair as her thighs begin to tremble, and I stop.

"Sebastian, please."

"You know what I want, baby. Give it to me."

She shakes her head. "We ... we should wait. We should get to know each other better ..." I push a finger into her, licking at her folds, and her eyes begin to roll to the back of her head. "Oh, God. Yes, yes."

"Yes, you'll marry me?" I press as she begins to shake again, and I add yet another finger.

"Sebastian ..." Alice moans, and I start thrusting inside her, rubbing against her G-spot as my tongue swirls around her clit. "Oh!"

"Say it," I command as she rubs herself all over me.

"Yes, I'll—I'll marry you," she shouts, and I suck her little nub into my mouth, watching as her whole body turns rigid and she comes with a gasp. "Sebastian." Her face lifts towards the ceiling, her mouth open in wonder as nothing but bliss shows in her eyes.

I continue licking her long after her orgasm passes, stretching out her pleasure. Making sure she's ready for me. "You with me, baby?" I murmur, sliding up her body and pressing my cock to her small entrance.

Her hands fall to my ass and she nods. "I love you, Sebastian."

I push into her a little and she cries out, so incredibly tight it's like she's a virgin all over again.

Fuck, two weeks without sex and already she's trying to kill me. I smile, tenderly kissing her lips, swallowing up her cries. "I love you, baby. So, so much. More than you'll ever know. More than you understand."

With that I entwine our fingers and push further into her, my thrusts slow and deep as I pin her hands to the mattress and begin to move with purpose inside her.

"Mine," I murmur as I get lost in her, in us, reclaiming my woman, my one and only, my wife.

"Yours," she confirms, and I take her mouth as I continue to make love to her throughout the night.

Chapter 21

Alice

Saturday 3rd June, Charles' Mansion

It's finally here. My wedding day. The day where I become Mrs Sebastian Hunter. The day where I become Sebastian's wife ... and he'll become my husband.

My smile is so big my face hurts. I just can't believe this is happening. That I found the man of my dreams and get to spend the rest of my life with him.

"Oh, Alice," Linda says, one hand pressed to her chest as the other trails down my veil. She's looking at me with so much pride and affection, my eyes sting and I know I'm about to cry. "You look so beautiful, darling. Such a glorious bride." Her voice breaks, and with tears running down both our faces we embrace.

"Shoot, we'll ruin your makeup if we keep going on like this." She laughs as we put some distance between us, only to look at each other and hug again.

A few minutes and many, many more tears later ...

"Are you ready to see yourself, my dear?" I nod as Linda uses a tissue to pat my face dry. "Good thing I remembered to ask the makeup artist to only use the waterproof products on you. You're such a crybaby."

My eyebrows rise. "Right, because I'm the only one crying here," I counter, grinning.

"Don't be cheeky with me, young lady," she warns, but her voice is full of humour as she guides me to the huge mirror standing in the corner of the room.

Linda's been amazing. A true friend from beginning to end. And honestly, I don't know what I'd have done without her guidance. Her help. Especially with the wedding, since she and Charles organised the whole thing.

And I don't just mean the ceremony and the venue, even when I thought the wedding was off. She also hasn't left my side, and has helped me through every single little decision. Just like a mother would, at least the kind of mother I want to be. So I'm incredibly grateful she's here, helping me navigate through all this.

And hey, if Linda ever needs a career change, I think we may have found just the thing.

I swallow a laugh, remembering how no one wants to disappoint the petite woman or let her down in any way. In fact, watching her going about the place in full military mode, telling people what to do like she was born to organise weddings, has been the highlight of my stay and the most fun I've had in days.

Not to mention the reactions she gets. Including from me, Sebastian and his siblings, when all of us end up resembling a bunch of scolded five-year-olds after nothing more than a look or a purse of her lips.

We reach the mirror, and I can't help my surprised gasp. I actually look like a bride.

Never in a million years did I imagine seeing myself like this, or even getting married for that matter. But now, looking at myself in the mirror, I can't help but regret not having had that dream, because Linda is right, I do look beautiful … and I've always deserved to be happy.

I've always deserved better than what my mother gave to me.

I touch my dress over my stomach, and a soft smile spreads across my lips. I'm in love with this dress. The design—a floor-length princess cut—makes me look graceful and tiny in all the right places. Especially with the fitted bodice hugging my torso like a second skin, whilst the chiffon skirt feels soft and light against my hips and appears so flowy I'm fighting the urge to spin.

I've tried it on before—many times, actually—and I loved it then too, but somehow it feels different today. I feel different today.

Maybe because I have all the accessories on—veil, shoes, jewellery. Or maybe it's because I'm getting married to the love of my life in less than thirty minutes. I don't know. But whatever the reason, I feel wonderful, and this dress feels perfect for me.

I look at myself again, taking in the strapless corset set in a sweetheart neckline, the layer of intricate see-through lace that was applied directly over it in a bateau neckline. The delicate lace both covers and shows the swell of my breasts, my shoulders and back—maintaining a romantic, modest look for the ceremony, but still with hints of sexy here and there.

I touch the pastel-pink belt that's showing off my tiny waist and release the shaky breath I was holding.

Yes, this is my dress. I'm a bride. And Sebastian is marrying me today. I smile goofily. Bloody hell! I'm getting married today!

"Oh, darling, you look exquisite, ethereal. Almost like you don't belong in this world." Linda fusses over me, adjusting the simple chiffon veil that's pinned to the back of my hair, which has been styled in a soft and loose updo, allowing some of the curls to escape. "Poor Sebastian won't even know what's hit him when he sees you coming down that aisle."

My gaze goes back to the mirror, and once again I'm shocked at what stares back at me. My eyes look huge and sharp, with different shades of grey, making them pop and look a thousand times brighter. Smoky eyes, the makeup artist said, telling me she was going to give me a romantic and natural look to complement my beauty rather than mask it. She was going to keep it simple— blushing, kissable bride cliché guaranteed.

Well, she was true to her word, I'll give her that. Apart from my well-defined eyes, a bit of blush on my cheeks and some lip gloss on my lips—which look very kissable indeed, even if I say so myself—I look like I'm barely wearing any makeup at all.

Still, I look like the best version of myself, the best I've ever looked. So perhaps Linda is right, and my already sex-crazed groom will be in for a treat. Let's just hope his self-control is on point until tonight, though. I'm not entirely sure I can deny him if he tries to take me.

I bite my lip in excitement, a shiver running down my back.

"Oh, that boy will have a very hard time keeping his hands to himself all right. So it's up to you, little missy, to keep him on a tight leash after the ceremony. You hear me?" Linda gives me a chastising look, and I nod, aware she's still upset about yesterday. More specifically, about catching Sebastian coming out of my bedroom in the middle of the night.

I almost smile despite myself, the memories from last night rushing over me as I feel the heat rise from my chest all the way up to my face. Christ, with the rushed way Sebastian had to leave me last night, unsatisfied and still wanting, we'll be lucky if he doesn't kidnap me as soon as the ceremony ends.

"There she is! How's my lovely daughter-in-law today?" Charles booms from behind us, and I turn, feeling so much love for this good, kind man that I can't help it when my eyes tear up all over again.

He takes my hands in his big palms. "Alice, my darling girl, you look exquisite. Absolutely stunning." He engulfs me in his arms. "You're God's gift to us, little one." He kisses my head. "Breathing life into Sebastian like that, making him happy again. You gave us my son back. You brought him back to us, and for that I will always be thankful. And you, my precious girl, you will always be loved."

"I love you all so much," I tell them in between sobs. "You're the family I've always wanted to have."

Linda's hand covers mine just as Charles' arms tighten around me. "And you do, Alice," he says gruffly. "You have all of us now. We're family."

* * *

The first notes of 'Canon in D' by Pachelbel ring loud and clear throughout the open space, and we begin our walk down the red-carpeted aisle. The sun is shining and the sky is clear, much to my relief, and my eyes sting as the violins and cellos announce our presence to our guests.

Pastel-pink and white roses cover the entire gardens, with thousands of shining, twinkling lights on every tree branch and every plant, creating a magical and almost otherworldly ambience around us.

And it's only noon. I can only imagine how beautiful it will all look shrouded in darkness when the sun finally goes down.

I glance over at Charles in a tux, standing next to me, my arm in his and our hands firmly entwined. I'll never be able to repay him or Linda for what they've done.

Everything looks wonderful. Amazing, really. And the more I take it all in, all the grandness that surrounds us, the more emotional I get.

I'll always remember this day. I'll remember it for as long as I live.

The guests all rise, their smiling faces and kind eyes greeting us as we pass them by, their nods encouraging.

And then I see him ... Sebastian. Standing in a black tuxedo, just like a supermodel in a photoshoot, looking so handsome that my chest constricts and I forget how to breathe.

I try to smile through my tears, still watching him. I couldn't look away if I tried.

Not when his jaw clenches hard, not when his Adam's apple bobs convulsively up and down and he fixes his stare on me. I shiver. Those electric blues I love so much burn into me with such intensity, such want, my entire body vibrates and my skin tingles, ready to combust with all the heat he's sending my way.

"We're almost there, darling. You're doing great," Charles whispers, interlocking our fingers together and tightening his hold on me, mistaking my shaking for anxiety.

Sebastian's eyes stay glued to mine, his smile calling me to move faster as I make my way down the aisle.

The girls, Beatrice and my friends from the office, take their places opposite the groomsmen, Ryan and the Hunter brothers, all of them looking gorgeous and smart as they stand on either side of the makeshift altar overlooking the lake. And everything becomes even more real, scarier.

My breaths turn shallow then and I feel the cold sweat that has been forming on the back of my neck finally slide down my spine.

Maybe it's a sign. A premonition of sorts that not everything will be a bed of roses for Sebastian and I. Especially since our worlds couldn't have been further apart before they crashed.

Or maybe it's just my nerves getting the best of me. A simple physical response to fear. The fear of losing this, of losing him.

Not that it matters anyway. Because just then we reach Sebastian, and when he smiles down at me the whole world disappears, the way it always does when he looks at me like this.

The hold this man has on me is so strong, I'm barely cognizant of his dad and him shaking hands before they embrace. Or of Charles kissing my cheek and placing my hand in Sebastian's before he steps away.

No, I'm too busy staring at my beautiful groom, my eyes watering as I swallow a sob of relief to be joined again with him.

"God, you're beautiful. Breathtakingly beautiful, sweetheart." He licks his lips and mine part, my body immediately reacting to his. "Screw it," he growls, and next thing I know he cradles the side of my face, snakes an arm around my waist, and without further delay slants his mouth possessively over mine, taking it in an all-consuming kiss that both pacifies and ignites the ever-burning fire in my heart.

I can hear the guests cheering him on, but by the time he releases my mouth, I don't even care. I'm under his spell. Lost in a haze where I can only see him.

Let the first day of our lives together begin. The first of many, I pray.

Father John clears his throat. "Are we quite done now, Mr Hunter?"

Sebastian chuckles, his eyes never leaving mine. "Oh, I don't think I'll ever be done, but I'll behave. I promise. And sorry, Linda. I just couldn't resist," he throws over his shoulder, eliciting laughter from our guests.

"Crazy boy." Linda's voice is barely audible, followed by her and Charles' low chuckles ... and then the ceremony begins.

"Dearly beloved," Father John says, but I can barely pay any attention. I only have eyes for my man and the infectious smile on his face.

Before long, though, it's time for us to say our own vows, and I take a deep breath.

"Sebastian, you are my soulmate," I start shakily as our gazes stay fixed on each other. "You're the love of my life, my partner, and my very best friend. And the only reason the world is finally starting to make sense."

I smile, my eyes clouding over with tears. "Loving, intelligent, handsome, and kind, you're everything I could ever have hoped for in a man. And you always make me laugh." My grin grows wider as I watch Sebastian's lips turn up.

"Even when I'm upset or in a bad mood, you always manage to find a way. And I adore you for it. You make me happy. More than I ever thought possible." My voice catches, and I fan my face in an attempt to stop the tears. But it's no use and the dam breaks as big fat tears begin to stream down my cheeks.

"Baby, I love you." Sebastian bends and kisses my forehead as he uses the pads of his thumbs to dry the tears.

"And I love you ... so much," I say in a raspy, shaken voice. "I love you more than words can ever say." I swallow the golf ball in my throat. "You complete me, Sebastian. You make me whole. So today I promise you my heart before our family and friends. I promise you my all to make you just as happy as I am. I promise you my love, my body and mind, and everything else in between until I am no more."

With trembling hands, I slide the wedding band on his finger, our smiles so big I worry our faces might split. And then it's Sebastian's turn.

"Alice, my stunning and beautiful bride," he says in that soft voice I've come to realise he uses only with me. "I fell in love with you from the very first moment I saw you. Dizzy and with the queen of all migraines, you were still the most beautiful woman I'd ever seen." I laugh, and so does he and everyone else who knows our history.

"For all who don't know how Alice and I met, let me clarify that it happened right after Alice had an altercation with her desk. A physical altercation, no less. That the desk won. Leaving Alice concussed, confused, and with me in the aftermath." He shrugs, and roars of laughter erupt from the crowd. "And now here we are. You, about to get a free meal out of the mishap. And us, getting married and making forever promises to each other."

His eyes glint and he adopts a more serious tone. "Promises I intend to keep and honour until my dying breath. Because I love you. I love you more than life itself, Alice. You're my whole world, and I will dedicate the rest of my days to showing you what that means. To showing you that our love is one in a million, and that you and you alone hold in your hands the key to my heart. So today I promise you in front of our family and friends that I'll protect you and keep you safe. That I'll take care of you and our children, that I'll love you and respect you, and that I'll never let you go—never let us go—for as long as I live. For as long as our souls live."

He slides the wedding band on my finger and drops a kiss over it, the gesture so tender and romantic that when he pulls me against his chest and covers my lips with his, he takes me by surprise. Me, the guests, our priest.

"Ahem. Ahem. Well, I now declare you man and wife," Father John announces, "and you may continue to kiss the bride."

Sebastian lifts me clean off the floor into his arms just as our audience roars and breaks into applause with a few whistles in the mix.

Chapter 22

Sebastian

What the...?

My heart starts hammering against my chest and I pray to God my brain is playing a trick on me. Because it can't be. It can't be Cassandra Oakes—that crazy bitch—I just saw dressed as one of the waiters, serving champagne to our guests as she makes her way to us. To Alice. My body turns rigid and I begin to sweat under my tuxedo.

Cassandra is unaware I just saw her, though, and I look away, doing my best to keep it that way.

Alice and I are being congratulated and taking post-ceremony photos with our family and friends. So I have to be subtle, careful.

My eyes find Ryan, and I signal Cassandra's presence to him as discreetly as I can. But I'm angry. So fucking angry right now.

How the fuck did she make it this far? Security is tight today, with triple the guards. And still, she's here.

I continue to smile nonetheless. Smiling at the cameras. Smiling at our guests. Smiling at Alice, whom I'm praying is too distracted by our happiness to notice anything.

I look over to where Cassandra is again, in the midst of the crowd in the garden, and witness the moment Ryan and Luke intercept her. They talk for a while, but all I can see is that she's getting more and more agitated. Shit, she's going to make a scene.

My temperature rises and my breaths quicken as I wait for the imminent disaster.

Suddenly, there's a muffled scream and Ryan is dragging Cassandra out as he covers her mouth with his hand. Luke follows them, carrying the tray of champagne. The crowd parts, looking a bit shocked as Cassandra struggles against Ryan's hold, and I feel mortified. Not to mention terrified someone's going to recognise her.

"What was that? What happened?" Alice asks, looking as shocked as everyone else.

"I'm not sure," I lie. "Probably a paparazzo. I'll have to go and find out as soon as we're done here."

She frowns. "Oh ... how, though? How did they get through security?"

"Good question. One I intend to ask my dad's guards, believe me." Ryan's not on duty today. He's here as my best friend. One of my groomsmen. Not that it should matter. It shouldn't affect the guards or the way they do things.

We go back to taking photos with the guests as if nothing has happened, but as soon as we're done, I tell Michael not to leave Alice's side, and I go in search of Ryan and my brothers inside the house.

I pull out my phone and there's a text from Luke. We're in Dad's study.

I sigh, not looking forward to this conversation in the least, and turn in the direction of the study. When I reach the white door, I knock.

"It's Sebastian," I say through the thick wood. The lock turns and, to my utter displeasure, I'm looking at Cassandra Oakes.

Ryan, Luke, Nathan and Mason are also inside. "Guys," I say to the twins, "why don't you two go back to the party and keep Dad and Alice entertained? Also, maybe make an announcement saying our unwanted guest was a pap. It'll appease our more sensitive friends and nip any rumours in the bud."

"You're sure you don't want us to stay?" Nathan asks, glaring at Cassandra, and I nod. I don't want the boys to witness what I'm about to say. They're young and impressionable, and this is a side of me they haven't seen. I don't want them to think less of their big brother.

Always the more sensitive, Mason rises from the couch. "I'll keep Alice company, don't worry," he assures me. "Nathan can make the announcement and distract Dad."

I nod, and Mason begins to pull Nathan by the arm towards the door. They leave, and I inhale deeply for the first time since spotting Cassandra almost thirty minutes ago—the longest thirty minutes of my life, with the exception of when I fucked her in Paris.

I stare at the she-devil. She looks pitiful. Her makeup is ruined, her hair is messed up. Tears are running down her cheeks and her uniform of red vest and black trousers is dishevelled from struggling with Ryan.

"What were you hoping to achieve by coming here?" I ask coldly.

She shakes her head. "You're making a mistake, Sebastian. You're confused. I had to stop you. We belong together—"

"Oh. My. God. Not this again," Luke growls, pulling at his hair as his nostrils flare. "I can't take it any more. The woman's completely deranged."

I'm a bit more desensitized, seeing as I've heard all of Cassandra's psychotic babble before. "I'm going to say this one last time, and then I'm done being patient with you. Leave us alone. Get help, Cassandra. You're sick. You need a doctor, not me."

She giggles. "I'll never leave you, my love. You know that. You and I are destined to be together."

I look at Ryan. "Have you called the police?"

"They're on their way," he replies.

"They won't hold me for long," Cassandra says. "They know you're having a relationship with me and that I'm only trying to warn Alice."

"OK, Cassandra, I don't think I've been explaining myself right so far. So, let me be clearer. You will leave us alone once and for all. Or the privileged, luxurious life you're so accustomed to is gone. For starters, I'll destroy your father's career. Make sure the well is truly dry." I smile wickedly, and Cassandra visibly begins to shake.

"My father's a good man."

"I don't care, and by the time I'm through slaughtering his reputation, no one else will either."

Cassandra's eyes move nervously around the room to Ryan, then Luke, and then settle on me again. She licks her red lips, and for the first time ever, she looks scared. Not for her father, I'm sure, but for herself. Because make no mistake, I'm serious as shit. And if she continues with this, I won't stop until her life as she knows it is over. Especially when we've already reached out to her father several times to stop her and he ignored us.

"I understand," she says.

"Good. Then let's not do this again. I want you gone and I want you to stay gone this time. It's my last warning."

She nods, and I turn to Ryan. "Let me know when the police arrive so I can give them my statement."

"Will do," Ryan confirms, and I leave the study with Luke following close behind me, a deep sense of relief filling me. I think this time I got to her. I really got to her.

Luke squeezes my shoulder as we walk side by side back to the party. "You did the right thing, Sebastian."

"I know." I frown. "This is not the kind of man I want to be, though."

"I only see a man protecting his family."

I nod. "Still, I hope this is the last of it. The last time Cassandra's name is of any matter to us. The last time I have to threaten someone. I want to be better, Luke. I want to be better for Alice."

"You already are, brother. In my eyes, you already are."

* * *

Alice

I laugh out loud as Sebastian sways us around the dance floor to the sound of 'If I Ain't Got You' by Alicia Keys, our first dance as an official married couple.

"Ahhh," I scream, my laughter turning into a girlish giggle when Sebastian lifts me into his arms, kisses me on the lips, and then spins us around in circles until I'm hanging onto him for dear life.

He just came back from talking to the police and pressing charges against the paparazzo who broke in, and I was afraid the whole thing would spoil his mood. I've never been happier to be wrong.

"You take my breath away every day. Did you know that?" he asks, his body exuding the same kind of strength and male dominance he has with everything else he does as he kisses me before lowering me to my feet. His gaze is filled with such wonder, such light that my throat tightens and my eyes water as I shake my head. "Well, you do." He resumes our slow dance.

"Although today, I have to admit, your effect on me is stronger than usual. But I'm only human, and I just can't get over how stunning you look, how alluring. A divine creature sent from another realm to bewitch me, if I ever saw one. Too good for the likes of me, that's for sure." He smirks. "But then again, you've always been too good for me, haven't you, Alice?"

When the first tear escapes my eyes, he catches it with his thumb. The adoring smile he gives me makes me swoon. "I love you, Alice, now and forever. I will always love you."

"I love you, Sebastian. You're the best thing that's ever happened to me. I'm lucky to have you. To have your love."

With that he lowers his mouth to mine, kissing me. "I'm the lucky one, sweetheart. Trust me," he breathes, and I slide my hands into his hair, pulling him to me, kissing him back, forgetting everything and everyone around us as I lose myself in him. As I lose myself in us.

* * *

"You've made an old man very happy today. I hope you know that," Charles says in his deep and now slightly hoarse voice as he throws his arms around us, hugging us to him.

I nod, a smiling, tearful mess as he looks down at me with nothing but love in his eyes.

"Oh, don't cry, Alice." He rocks me back and forward and kisses the top of my head, but my tears continue to fall.

We just left the dance floor. I've already danced with the whole Hunter clan, including the 'father and daughter' dance with Sebastian's dad. And now that the music has changed to a slightly less romantic beat, we're taking a break to catch our breaths.

Charles clears his throat. "So, have you two been giving any thought as to when I can expect my first grandbaby? You know, to keep me healthy and fit."

My mouth falls open at his cheekiness, and Sebastian bursts out laughing into his drink. "Yeah, you'd spoil them rotten, and end up digging yourself an early grave, more likely," Sebastian jokes.

"Don't listen to him, Alice. You just concentrate on giving me a grandbaby or two to keep the old ticker going, all right?"

Sebastian chuckles. "Oh, we're playing the guilt card, are we? Have you no shame, old man?"

"Hey, watch it. You may be a married man, but I'm still your father, Sebastian."

"Just ignore him, sweetheart. There's nothing wrong with his ticker or any other vital organs you need to concern yourself about ... yet," Sebastian says threateningly, just before they lock eyes and both of them burst out laughing again.

An hour later and after a few more rounds on the dance floor with Charles and the boys—including two of their very handsome and equally rich American cousins—Sebastian and I dance some more and then start making the rounds, doing our best to chat a little with all the guests. A task that is proving more and more difficult with Sebastian stealing me away every chance he gets, sometimes even carrying me off into a different room entirely or hidden corridor just so he can touch me and kiss me without restraint, both of us making out like two teenagers in lust in all the dark corners of his childhood home.

That is, until our escapades almost get us in trouble with Linda again when it's time to cut the cake and we're nowhere to be found.

"I'm telling you, man, she's fuming," Luke says after coming to our rescue yet again, just like he did last night.

"I'll handle it."

"I don't know, she looked about ready to use that cake knife on you for ambushing the bride. Again."

Sebastian just grins. "Don't worry. I'm still her favourite. Just follow my lead."

The guests all laugh when Sebastian enters the room fireman-style with me giggling over his shoulder. "OK, OK. No need to panic. I'm bringing my lovely bride back so you can all have some cake."

Linda points the knife at Sebastian. "You are incorrigible, young man."

"I know. I know, and I'm terribly sorry, Linda. But I can't help it. I'm just too in love with my beautiful bride." He raises his voice, addressing the crowd. "And it's my wedding day."

Linda visibly melts under Sebastian's uncharacteristic display of sweetness. I smile, holding my laughter in as everyone gushes, with even a few prolonged 'ohs' and 'awws' from the women.

He has them all eating out of the palm of his hand.

"Oh, just—" She shakes her head, defeated. "Just put Alice down, and get over here."

After the cake is finally served and we're all talked out, hugged out, and exhausted, we take a final walk around the garden with the wedding photographer and her team for the last set of pictures and recordings for the video. I swear my cheeks are hurting so bad, I won't be able to smile again for at least another year.

"It'll be worth it, trust me," we're told over and over by the boisterous, thin woman with the camera who guarantees not only that the pictures are looking amazing, but that we've been able to capture the very essence of the day.

I laugh. I sure hope so, given the number of pictures we had to take and the small fortune I'm sure she's being paid.

We keep going until it's dark, and I was right. With all the twinkling lights and lanterns spread throughout the garden, the whole place looks amazing. Like our little slice of heaven here on earth.

So once all the photos are taken, we end up lingering in the garden long after the photographer and her team go back inside. We don't talk as we walk, though. No words feel necessary, and as Sebastian sits on a bench with me on his lap and we hold onto each other tight, I know he feels the same.

This sense of happiness and completeness. This sense of connection and belonging.

This feeling of being right where you need to be, with the person you need to be with ... for the rest of your life.

Chapter 23

Alice

"Welcome home, Mrs Hunter," Sebastian says, right before he lets go of my hand and, bending, lifts me into his arms with ease.

I squeal, delighted he's being so traditional—even if only for this last part. My arms wrap around his neck and I can't help the huge smile that takes over my face as I stare up at him.

"Welcome to our life together," he continues, the excitement in his voice telling me everything I need to know about this man, about the love he has for me.

Then he's crossing the threshold, his lips brushing mine, and I can barely hold on to my tears. "Welcome to our house," he murmurs between kisses. "Our family."

I swallow hard, my emotions all over the place even as my eyebrows wrinkle in question when he doesn't put me down.

He smiles. "Oh, the only place I'm letting go of you, baby, is our bed. And even then it's only so I can get you naked and fuck you right after I finish making love to you."

I shiver, absorbed by the electric blue of his gaze. His smile grows wider, darker. The kind of smile I can only associate with a sinner.

Then he's kicking the door shut and walking us towards the stairs, carrying me all the way up to our bedroom.

The mood around us is thick and heavy as with every second our arousal grows into need. A necessity so primal, so animalistic, I can barely breathe.

God, he looks so happy like this. So young and sexy. And before I know it, my eyes water and a lump forms in my throat, my feelings raw and pulsing with a life of their own as they render me speechless. Cut open. That's what he does to me. His ability to get me to feel, to get me ready and eager, my emotions and desires focused on wanting him. And with just a look or a few of his words.

It scares me, confounds me even. Mainly because I don't understand it. Don't know how he does it. How he has such power over me, or I over him.

But such is love, right? And who the hell knows anything?

Kissing me, Sebastian lays me down on the bed as his strong body descends on mine.

"Sebastian, the dress." I push against his chest. "Sebastian, please, help me with the dress first. I don't want you to ruin it," I plead as he continues to kiss me.

After several hours of making out, grinding and touching, I'm more than ready for the next step, and I'd really like to change into my lingerie—the special nuptial set I got us for tonight specifically.

"Are you sure you don't want me to keep going, baby? I'll make it worth your while, believe me."

I swat him playfully across the chest. "Behave, Mr Hunter." I give him a fake disapproving look, and he gets to his feet.

"Naked it is then," he announces, making me laugh.

He offers me his hand and pulls me into his arms. Then he's turning me around, finally assessing all the tiny little buttons on the back of my dress. "Fuck me. I'm assuming this thing doesn't come with a zipper?"

I shake my head. "Nope, no zipper, I'm afraid," I answer, glad to have my back to him so he can't see my impish grin.

"You've got to be kidding me."

"I'm sorry, baby." Except I'm not. I'm enjoying torturing my big, impatient man.

"We'll be here all night. There's at least thirty of the tiny fuckers to go through."

"Forty," I correct, right before I scream with a giggle. "Ahhh! Nooo!" I jump up and wiggle, trying to no avail to break free from Sebastian as his big hands slide across my ribcage and tickle me mercilessly.

"Ahhh!" I scream again, but his arms are like steel, the muscles tense and rippling as he secures me against his chest.

"I know you think I can't see you, but I can tell how fucking pleased you are with yourself." He pulls my earlobe into his mouth, and I melt into him, goosebumps spreading all over as he holds me prisoner to his will. "Naughty girl, you just keep on adding to your transgressions. Pushing me so I'll finally take you across my knee," he whispers, and my breath hitches in my throat. I can just imagine him doing it, touching me that way.

"Soon, baby. Very soon," he promises in a dark tone. "But not tonight. Tonight, I'm going to be too busy fucking my wife. Sinking my cock so deep inside her we won't be able to tell where one ends and the other begins."

Stepping back, he finally starts working on the buttons with purpose, a few curse words leaving his mouth every now and then as they slip his big fingers.

"Sebastian, please, be careful," I plead when I feel him struggle with the tiny pearls again. "I love this dress so much and I'd really like to keep it." As is, I mentally add, not wanting to stress him out even more.

Chuckling, he plants a kiss where my shoulder meets my neck. "Don't worry, sweetheart, I have no intention of ruining your dress. You, on the other hand ..."

I gasp and the minutes stretch as he works in silence after that, the wait doing nothing to quench my desire. As if in slow motion, he pushes the delicate lace down my shoulders, kissing a path down the exposed skin as he lazily uncovers me to him. The dress flows freely, sliding down my body like silk until the fabric pools at my feet and he helps me step out of it.

The sharp intake of breath and hissing between his teeth tells me he's looking at my bum. At the skin just between my upper cheeks, peeking through the cut-out heart on my lacy white panties.

Grabbing my hips, he turns me around and presses me to him, his hands covering my ass possessively as I raise my palms to his chest, enjoying every groan, every ripple of his hard flesh quivering under my fingertips.

"Jesus. Fucking. Christ," he whispers as he takes in my bustier. His stare bores into me with such fire, I feel like actual flames are licking at my skin. "What the fuck are you trying to do to me?" He almost sounds like he's in pain, his face contorted in a grimace, and I love seeing him like this. Love the fact that he loves my lingerie, an all-white bridal ensemble with just enough lace and sexy to drive him wild. And for once, I have to say, he actually looks as tormented as I feel. "No angel should look like this." He runs his tongue over his lower lip, and I shiver, knowing full well the effect my appearance is having on him.

The pure and innocent look he loves so much taunts the devil in him. Taps into that kinky, perverted side of his he's been trying so hard to get under control.

Seductively, he lets his fingertips trail over the top of my bustier, exactly where the fabric meets skin, forcing another moan to fall out of my lips. My nipples pebble, stiffening further against the almost-see-through lace of my cups, begging for release, for his attention, for his mouth on me. "This is one hell of an invitation if I ever saw one, Mrs Hunter. You must want me to go mad, teasing me like this."

My core clenches and I press my thighs together.

"Jesus," he growls, closing his eyes. "I'm so hard for you it hurts, Alice. I'm going to do whatever the fuck I want with you tonight, and you're going to let me. You're going to let me devour you. Understand?"

Something flashes in his eyes when he steps back from me and begins undressing. Something dangerous, something primal, something wild.

My stomach tightens, my mouth watering at the sight of him when he slowly shrugs off his shirt. The bulging muscles ripple and contract with his every movement, every breath, freezing me in place.

I watch as if hypnotised as he peels off layer after layer, uncovering his magnificent, Greek god body before me until his cock springs free, hard and thick as it slaps against his stomach.

My breath hitches.

He smirks and moves closer again, this time beautifully naked when he reaches for me. His hands are strong and sure as he grips my hips, hooks his thumbs under the sides of my soaked panties, and pulls them down my legs and off my feet.

I moan my need, my core clenching and unclenching with anticipation, clit throbbing as my eyes lock with his, wanting, pleading, begging for his touch, his kisses. For him to take me and do whatever he wants with me.

Sebastian straightens to his full height, one hand grabbing hold of my hip again as the other cups my face. "Mmm ... I think first and foremost, my beautiful and delicate wife, I'm going to give you my tongue. Going to lick you before I make slow, sweet love to you tonight." He runs his thumb over my burning cheek, then down my jaw, and I lean into his touch, desperate for his affection, his love. The gentler side he only shows when he's alone with me. "And when I'm done with slow and sweet, I'm going to fuck you. Hard. I'm going to bury myself in you so deep, I'll turn your every moan into a scream."

His thumb dusts over my lower lip as his mouth hovers over mine, our lips almost touching but not quite. I breathe hard, staring up at him.

"You're my wife now, Alice. My wife. My everything." His eyes search mine. "My confidante, my lover, my slut. Everything I'll ever need in this life. And I'm going to worship you like the goddess you are. Like a queen at my side."

With that he crashes his mouth to mine, slides his arms around my waist, and pulls me flush into his body.

Yes. I sigh when his full lips envelop mine, my plans to change into something more nuptial for him falling into oblivion as I melt into his arms. The kiss goes on forever before I manage to gather my thoughts.

"Sebastian." I push lightly against his chest until he reluctantly breaks the kiss. "I have something special I'd like to wear for you tonight," I say, and bite my lower lip nervously at the desire I see in his eyes.

"Something special, huh? Something more special than this?" He squeezes my naked hips, lifting me and rubbing me up and down against his length.

I moan as the sensation melts my insides, pleasure like no other shooting up my spine.

"Mmm. Too bad I can't fucking survive any more 'special surprises' tonight. Particularly if they're anything like this." He glides a hand over my bustier. "Virginal, sexy and white?"

I blush and stifle a whimper. Don't know why I'm still so shy around him, considering everything we've done so far, but there you are.

He gives me a lopsided smile with a touch of wicked as he says near my mouth, "We'll save it for a special occasion, all right? Another special occasion. Just put it on when I tell you to. Can you do that for me, baby?"

I nod. I actually don't mind that at all. I had a feeling he wouldn't have the patience to wait anyway. That's why I put so much thought into choosing what to wear under my dress.

So I put on my best 'come get me' expression and whisper in a sexy, low voice, "I'll do anything and everything for you, husband."

That seems to seal my fate.

His eyes close, his nostrils flare. And when he looks down at me again, his entire demeanour is sex. Want. And pure unadulterated lust.

He descends on me, ravishing, devouring, consuming. His desire burning through my body so hot it scorches me all the way down to my soul.

Then he peels off the rest of my clothes and, laying me on the bed, makes slow, sweet, passionate love to me until I swear it feels as if we're one and the same. Just one being. Our souls twisting and curving tightly around each other as he does everything he promised and more, so much more than I could ever dream. And I come over and over again, falling apart in his arms until he finally chases his own release.

His grunts and searing kisses push me over the edge one more time as he roots himself in deep, coming with me, coming inside me, pouring himself and his heart as I give myself to him completely.

It's one of the most intense experiences of my life. Everything I could ever wish for my one and only wedding night.

Happy tears spring to my eyes and fall down my temples in rivulets. "Sebastian," I breathe.

"I know, baby. I know," he breathes back. Then he presses his forehead to mine, his grip on my hands tightening, and we kiss.

A kiss that lasts for hours on end, it seems. His body is still hot and hard inside mine as we hold onto each other close, the closest we've ever been, and he begins to move again.

* * *

"Sebastian?" I murmur, moving my head from his chest to his shoulder so I can look up at him. We're both still lying in bed, basking in the afterglow of our lovemaking as we hold onto each other.

"Mmm," he groans back with his eyes closed, and I smile. He just sounds and looks so relaxed right now.

Which makes it the perfect moment to ask. He always opens up more when he's like this.

"Why do you think you became so cold?"

His fingers pause caressing my naked back. "What do you mean, baby?"

"I mean before we met. Before me."

His jaw ticks and suddenly his eyes are boring into mine. "What's brought this on, Alice?" he asks as his fingers resume their hypnotic movement up and down my spine.

I close my eyes, embarrassed. I should've asked him about this a long time ago. Definitely before our wedding night. "Just a few comments at the party today."

"Right." He sighs. "Well, I told you about my mother and how I didn't handle her passing so well."

I nuzzle his chest and then kiss it, thankful he's not closing off on me. "Yes, I know. I was just wondering if it was more than grief that made you act that way, that's all."

Something like trauma or fear, perhaps? I want to say, but don't. For some reason I can't. Maybe because I have a feeling he doesn't quite know it himself.

"Why? What are you thinking?" he asks, and I look away.

"I don't know. I'm just trying to understand."

"Don't think too much about it, Alice. And don't waste your sympathy on me either. I was a spoiled, selfish little prick. Then my mum died, and I became even worse. Told myself I needed to push everyone away, that I needed to be alone so I could deal with my pain. God knows I was hurting a lot back then and needed the time and space. Problem is, after a while, it just became easier to keep acting that way. Easier to be a bastard rather than work on my issues and care again."

I nod. "It's just that I keep hearing about how cold and detached you were. How controlling and manipulative. And I, well ..."

"You never really saw that side of me," he offers.

"Yeah. Well, except for the controlling and manipulative part." I give him a knowing look. "But not the rest of it, no. And certainly not to the extent people describe."

"No, not with you. And certainly not since you, Alice. Truth is you made me feel again, baby. You made me feel in a way I hadn't felt in years. It's like before you, all I had was this numbness inside me. This hole. And yes, sometimes I felt detached and isolated. I was cold, and cruel, and the control factor quickly became one of the most important things in my life." He takes a slow, deep breath. "It became the only thing I actually liked about my life. Until my eyes fell on you.

"Then I realised I wasn't really living any more, and that nothing, absolutely nothing else mattered if I couldn't have you by my side. That nothing could ever compare to you and the way you made me feel. So ... I pulled my head out of my ass, stopped behaving like a bastard and a control freak, and despite my dominant tendencies, I am now a much nicer and tamer version of myself."

"'Tame' is definitely not a word I'd use to describe you. Not when you scare the crap out of everyone you meet." He laughs, his chest rumbling, and my grin becomes wider. "'Beasty', I think, is a much better fit. Has a much better ring to it too. And is one hundred percent accurate. As well as 'controlling', 'domineering', 'bossy', 'intimidating', and sometimes even 'cunning' ... in and out of the bedroom." I go on, emboldened by his good mood.

"It seems you have me pinned down, Mrs Hunter, but I assure you it's different with you. I am different with you. I'm not saying I don't like to dominate, command, or bend others to my will, because I do. I wouldn't be in the position I am today if it didn't give me a rush. And yes, they're all just other forms of control I still very much enjoy practising and don't see myself giving up, least of all with you, Alice." He gives me a wolfish grin.

"But now I need more ... I need you. Your love, your compassion, your tenderness. I crave it like a starved man. I crave the sex, the intimacy, the closeness we share. I crave our relationship, the connection between us, your friendship, your support. I don't even know how I lived before. How I managed without you, without these things. And I know I act crazy sometimes, but there's just so much I want to do to you, with you, I don't even know where to begin."

"I think you're doing a pretty good job so far," I say shyly, smiling into his chest before I press my lips to the smooth, hairless skin.

He laughs out loud, running a hand over my hair. "Oh, you do, do you?"

"Uh-huh. It is my humble opinion that you are the best lover in the world," I tell him playfully, yet also honestly.

"I'm your only lover, sweet girl."

I smile. "Not every woman needs to shop around to appreciate a good thing. Besides, I could never imagine myself with anybody else. You're the only one for me."

"I'm probably going to sound like a selfish prick for saying this, but when you told me you were a virgin and I realised I was going to be your first, I couldn't help but feel happy. Ecstatic, really. Not to mention incredibly proud that you had chosen me. That you were going to give yourself to me that way." Our eyes meet, his heated and full of desire, and mine filled with tears.

He brushes the hair off my face. "It was important to me too, Alice. Life-changing. And I want you to know that I'll cherish that moment forever. That I'll cherish you and your love, and that no matter what happens between us, I promise to never forget. To never stop loving you. I promise to never forget to remember us."

I swallow the huge lump in my throat. "I love you, Sebastian. I love you so, so very much." I hiccup, overwhelmed by the love I have for this man.

Holding my face in one hand, he tenderly kisses my lips and then the tip of my nose.

"See how I have a difficult time imagining you being cold or cruel to anyone? You're always so sweet to me," I say.

"But I was, Alice. I was. And not only was I closed off to other people, I was closed off to my own feelings, my own emotions. I was determined to keep them at bay. To not let myself be guided by them."

He shrugs, and I stay silent, not knowing what to say. We stare at each other for a long moment, and then Sebastian sighs, resigned, I think.

"You have to understand it was only us guys in the house when my mum died. And we all grew distant without her. All of us too busy, I guess. Too consumed, trying to find our own way to grieve and cope with the pain. So I did what I had to do to survive. I turned off my feelings. And I never looked back."

I swallow hard, my eyes watering. "Baby ..." My heart breaks for him as I picture him as a young boy, alone and confused, going through that kind of loss and pain. It's enough to screw anyone up.

I grieved my parents and they weren't even half as loving or caring as his mum. So I can only imagine how he must've felt after losing someone so special.

"I'm so sorry you've suffered. That I wasn't there for you." I cup his cheek, petting his face. "It makes me wish I'd met you sooner. Maybe I could've been your friend back then. Maybe I could've helped you or at least comforted you in some way."

He blows out a breath and shakes his head. "I would've been too afraid. I had enough trouble dealing with all the emotions you stirred up in me when we met. I can only imagine myself as a teenager panicking and pushing you away. I would've hurt you, Alice, and myself in the process. I have no doubt about that."

"Afraid of what, Sebastian? Why would you push me away?" I don't want to press, but I feel this is important. Come on, baby, talk to me. Let me in so I can help you. "You think you were pushing others away so you wouldn't feel? Or was it because you wanted to punish yourself? Because you didn't want them to feel for you? What were you so afraid of, Sebastian?"

I don't want to hurt him, but I also need to be sure the thoughts that made him act so badly in the past are well and truly gone. Sebastian may not realise this, but he was self-harming, closing himself off like that, and I worry that without help he might fall into the same pattern again.

He exhales slowly, and kisses my head. "Yes, sweetheart, something like that. Now that's enough of the heavy stuff."

He moves and I find myself under his strong body again. "Sebastian!" I yelp and giggle as he leans in and moulds his lips to mine.

All giggles die in my throat when his tongue enters my mouth. The slow dance and erotic motion makes my stomach quiver and sparks shoot up my spine.

I know he's trying to distract me. He doesn't want to talk about it. Not yet, anyway. And that's OK, I won't push him. I know he was and still is frightened of letting people in.

I just think it's important for him to share and understand, maybe even come to terms with some of his fears.

I think he felt abandoned by his mum when she passed. He thought that if he let anyone get that close again, they'd have the power to hurt him. Especially if they, for whatever reason, also left.

However, he's making such good progress, the last thing I want is for him to feel pressured and go back into his shell.

He'll tell me eventually. Let me in when he's ready.

In the meantime, I'll just have to keep an eye on him. Make sure he knows how much he's loved and wanted.

He's going to be OK, though. We're going to be OK.

Wrapping my arms around Sebastian, I pour all my love into the kiss, letting him seduce me, letting him infect me with his lust.

Flipping me so I'm lying on my stomach, Sebastian then grabs my hips and pulls them up. "On your knees. Ass in the air. I want to take you from behind." His voice is commanding, sexy, and so goddamn husky, I can't help but shiver all over.

Then he's pressing the head of his cock to my entrance, his hold on my hips bruising as he pushes into me a little, forcing me open before plunging himself inside.

I cry out, my knees lifting off the mattress with the force of his possession.

Oh, my, he wasn't kidding. He really is going for hard.

I brace myself, my legs shaking uncontrollably as he reaches the very end of me, and I almost climax.

"Fuck, Alice," he whispers, breathing harshly. His right hand glides up and down my back to soothe and calm me down. "Are you all right?"

I nod with a moan. He's not able to do this often, but he's just been inside me and with me still wet with both our fluids, he just about managed to fit.

I feel so full, though. So deliciously stuffed. And as the burning pain begins to subside and the pleasure pushes me to a new high, it almost becomes too much, too perfect ... and exactly what we both need, I think, right now.

Sebastian rotates his hips, trying to loosen me up, his hand still gliding up and down my spine. "That's it, baby, take it. Take my cock like the good girl you are."

I whimper when his hand wraps around the back of my neck, and he pulls his thick length almost all the way out only to push back in, in a deep, punishing thrust that has my core spasming and my clit throbbing for more.

I cry out again, pain and pleasure mingling together once more in this perfect moment in time.

"I'm going to fuck you now, wife. I'm going to fuck you as if you're my slut," he groans, his thrusts coming harder. "I'm going to drill into your tight little cunt until you're gushing all over my cock."

With that, his hips start moving harder, deeper, and soon he's pounding into me. His cock pistons in and out of my channel so fast my mouth falls open and my eyes roll to the back of my head.

God, I can't even keep up. Can't do anything except stay still and take it. My moans and whimpers rise in time with my pleasure as I behave in an unrecognisable way. As I behave indeed like his slut, his whore, everything he'll ever need and want, like he said.

"Sebastian! Oh, God, Sebastian. Harder, take me harder," I cry, feeling the pressure build as my man grabs my hips with both hands and begins to fuck me with abandon, ripping my eighth orgasm of the night right out of my body as if the first seven didn't happen at all.

"Come on, Alice, give it up. Give it to me, baby," he orders, panting in time with his thrusts. "Come for me."

Shutting my eyes tight, I feel my core clench violently, squeezing around his shaft like a vice as I explode into one of the most intense orgasms of my life. Legs trembling, toes curling, I'm even screaming as he continues to pound into me, fucking me straight through my climax. His big shaft prolongs and intensifies the sensations until I can no longer control myself and liquid heat comes pouring out of me.

"Such a good girl, gushing all over my cock as you come for me. Soon I'll be fucking a baby into you, Alice. Spilling my seed deep inside you until your belly grows round."

"Mmm," I moan, his words spiking my arousal to a whole other level I don't even understand.

"Fuck, you're so hot." He slides a hand over my sex and begins to rub my clit furiously between two fingers. I start to quiver.

"I'm close, baby. So fucking close," he groans. "Come with me, Alice. Come with me while I pump you full of my cum."

"Sebastian!" I'm close too ... again. My hips move in time with his fingers, my ass pointing up as he takes me faster and deeper. His brutal thrusts grow urgent and more erratic as he nears his release.

Then, with an animalistic growl, he shoves his whole length into me and calls out my name in a breathless groan. The sound barely registers over the cries of ecstasy being ripped out of my throat as my core clenches, spasming and rippling, milking him of every last drop of his cum as my own orgasm takes place.

White sparks form in my vision, and he takes my mouth in a feral, deep kiss, still emptying himself in me.

"Fuck, baby, you're going to kill me," he murmurs, out of breath, already pulling my exhausted body up and against his chest. He embraces me from behind as he pants and kisses my neck, his half-hard cock still twitching inside me. "You drive me fucking crazy, you know that?"

"Mmm, I guess we're even then. 'Cause you do the same to me."

He chuckles, the sound a deep rumble in his throat and chest, sending sparkles down my entire body. My nipples peak and my skin tingles with renewed desire.

"Happy wedding night, sweetheart. Was it everything you dreamed of?" He smiles into my neck before sucking on it.

I laugh. "Happy wedding night to you too. And no, it wasn't. My smile grows wider. "It was more. So much more than anything I could ever dream. I'm lucky to have you, Sebastian. You make me happy."

"No, you make me happy, Alice. More than anything in the world. Especially today, when you walked down that aisle in your wedding dress, taking me as your husband ..." He takes a deep breath. "You've made me the happiest man alive. I hope you realise that." He grips my jaw and turns my face to him. "I love you," he rasps, and then he's kissing me and kissing me until yet again, I'm nothing but putty in his arms.

Chapter 24

Alice

Placing the blusher back on the dressing table, I apply some calming cream to my hair and just a dash of shimmering light-pink lip gloss to my lips. I smile at my reflection in the mirror. I look good. And I'm never, ever happy with my makeup when I do it.

Hmm, maybe it's because I'm feeling so relaxed. My smile grows wider and I turn to look at the balcony and the incredible view of the beach beyond. Yeah, I'm sure that's what it is.

Then again, 'relaxed' may just be the understatement of the year, seeing that for the past four weeks, I've been living in nothing but bliss since arriving in beautiful Jamaica.

Sebastian owns a beach house near the Hunters' resort in Ocho Rios, and that's where he whisked me away for a surprise honeymoon. Taking me to paradise in more ways than one, if you know what I mean.

Which reminds me, where is that delicious husband of mine anyway? He wasn't in the room when I came out of the shower, and that was at least half an hour ago.

"You ready, baby?" Sebastian asks huskily as he enters the room, only to stop in his tracks as soon as his eyes fall on me.

I smile and mentally high-five myself as I slide my lip gloss into my purse. "Yeah," I reply in an equally husky tone, slowly turning and walking over to him.

He stays silent as he watches me.

I'm wearing a white, strapless summer dress—cinched at the waist, with a flared skirt and sexy as hell—my nude wedges and a little matching purse. My hair is soft and wavy, my makeup natural, and judging from my husband's stare, I'm pretty sure I'm already having the desired effect.

"What about you? Are you ready?" I ask.

He nods, and then swallows hard as his eyes stay riveted on me. Too bad he's going to have to wait. I was promised a romantic dinner at the resort tonight, and I'm intent on collecting.

Not that we're lacking in that department, obviously, what with all the late-night strolls on the beach, the candlelit dinners on the terrace overlooking the sea, and the sex ... God, the sex. My heart begins to thump, and I have to remind myself to breathe just thinking about it.

Still, we've been far too wrapped up in each other, and apart from the occasional long drive, a couple of excursions, and the few times we've been to swim with the dolphins, we haven't left the house nearly enough, so it will do us good to go out on a date.

Besides, we're going home in two weeks. We better get used to being social again.

His eyes continue to drop down my body, hungrily taking me in, and I shiver under his gaze. "You look far too delectable, Mrs Hunter," he says, pulling me into his arms and kissing me on the lips. "I'm beginning to regret taking you out already."

I laugh and slap him playfully on the shoulder, all the while secretly enjoying his possessiveness over me. "Stop being silly. Besides, you look pretty yummy yourself, and you don't hear me complaining."

Dressed in dark jeans and a black, long-sleeved T-shirt, my husband is a picture of male perfection. Yummy face, yummy body, yummy everything, and I'm never going to complain.

This time he laughs too, the sound rich and throaty as he throws his head back, making my heart rate go up a few beats.

"OK, you little perv. Stop ogling me and we'll go," he replies, and presses one last kiss to my lips. Then he grabs my hand and pulls me out of the bedroom.

We walk out into the large corridor lined with clear glass, black metal pendant lanterns hanging low from the ceiling, and once again, I'm struck by the beauty of this house.

Which, of course, is nothing short of amazing. The huge mansion is a state-of-the-art modern building with high ceilings, one-way glass walls, and a wrap-around porch and upper balcony with breathtaking views of the gardens, the pools, and the private beach at the back. That, by the way, is inaccessible, unless someone uses a boat or the entrance through the house. Heaven!

The inside, again, is just as gorgeous, and beautifully decorated with soft fabrics—all pastels, whites and creams—light grey hardwood floors and white furniture throughout. Simple, yet stylish, and our very own sanctuary since we've arrived.

"Where are the boys?" I ask when we get outside.

Sebastian opens the door of the black Porsche 918 Spyder for me. "They're following us in the SUV." He smiles, helping me in. "I feel like driving tonight." With that he closes the door and rounds the car, slipping into the driver's seat.

He turns on the ignition and revs the engine, looking at me, a mischievous smirk on his face. I squeak and he does it again before he floors it out of the driveway and I'm thrown back into my seat, my giggles and screams mixing with his chuckles.

* * *

Magnificently bright, the resort's reception is in the shape of an octagon with white walls, flowy drapes hanging from its cathedral-high ceilings, and sandstone flooring throughout.

There's also a lounge with a garden in its centre and a wide variety of stores all around. And on the outside, the guests can find a wrap-around terrace where they can enjoy drinks from several bars. It's like something out of a movie and designed to make you feel like a superstar.

Hand in hand, Sebastian and I go down the few steps from the terrace and start making our way towards the restaurants and entertainment buildings—which contain a cinema, a theatre and a club.

"Mr Hunter," Joe, the resort manager, calls, intercepting us near the main pool, which is still busy with a group of young men drinking.

Sebastian looks down at me apologetically. "Sorry," he mouths, and then we're turning and facing a very out-of-breath and sweaty middle-aged man who barely resembles the Joe we've come to know and love, as he so often is the one who brings our meals to the house. His white shirt is untucked on one side and his tie is missing, very unlike his usual OCD self.

"Mr and Mrs Hunter, I apologise, but we had a small kitchen fire in the barbecue restaurant. We'll need to find you another venue for tonight. Perhaps the seafood or Italian restaurant? Whatever you like."

"Oh, my God, was anyone hurt?" I ask.

"No. No. Just the chef's pride." Joe laughs awkwardly, and I give him a compassionate smile. Joe always jokes when he's nervous. Poor guy.

"What about the damage?" Sebastian asks. "Was there a lot?"

I spot the restroom to my right. I'm desperate for a wee, and these two will be talking for a while. I look up at Sebastian. "Baby, I need the loo. I'll be right back."

Sebastian nods and signals Michael, who's standing to the side with Ryan, to follow me to the restroom.

I make my way to the small white building in the garden, use the toilet and wash my hands before coming out. I see Michael straight away waiting across the footpath. He's on his phone, probably talking to his mum. His baby sister, Winter, who's only nineteen, just had a double mastectomy and reconstruction earlier this week, due to carrying the BRCA2 gene, and naturally he's been worried sick about her.

I start to make my way towards him, eager to hear about how Winter is doing, when an arm curls around my ribs and pulls me into a hard chest. The scent of beer attacks my senses and I have to fight the urge to vomit just as much as I have to fight the urge to panic.

"Hello, gorgeous," a throaty voice slurs near my ear, and my stomach somersaults. I throw a look over my shoulder and see a tall, blond young man with red cheeks and bloodshot eyes. Shit, he's drunk. Really drunk, and doing a terrible job at keeping himself—and me—upright.

"Michael," I shout, but he's immersed in his call and doesn't hear me. Shit! "Let me go," I order Drunk Guy, pulling at his hand whilst still trying to get Michael's attention.

"Feisty." Drunk Guy laughs. "Hey, everyone," he calls to his friends, who are equally hammered and laughing. "Look at the beauty I'm going to fuck tonight."

His hips roll, and that's it. I know I have to be the one who saves myself from this animal.

With a shout, I bring my heel down with all my strength on Drunk Guy's sandaled foot and stab my elbow into his lower stomach, just like Sebastian taught me in the self-defence lessons he's been giving me since we've arrived. The man releases me with a curse, and I quickly step away from him.

"Alice." Michael rushes me, pushing the man backwards and putting himself between us. "Fuck, I didn't see you come out. I'm sorry ..."

A loud noise of something hitting the floor—a table, I think—makes me look back just in time to see an infuriated Sebastian rushing towards us. Then, quick as lightning, he grabs Drunk Guy by the throat and starts punching him repeatedly in the face.

"Sebastian, no. Stop," I plead. But he doesn't listen. He's lost in a world of rage.

"Mr Hunter, I've got this," Michael says as he tries to get Sebastian to stop.

"You've done enough," Sebastian growls at him, actually growls, like some kind of feral animal, forcing Michael to step back.

Ryan reaches us just then. "Ryan, stop him," I shout, frantically pointing at Sebastian. "He's going to kill the guy."

Ryan nods and goes to grab Sebastian from the back. Sebastian is quicker, though, and, as if he's expecting it, drops Drunk Guy to the floor, turns and punches Ryan in the face.

Ryan falls on his back, and I yell at the top of my lungs, "Sebastian! Help!"

In an instant Sebastian's wild eyes find mine, just as I knew they would. He's breathing hard, ready to attack, to hit, to mangle, clearly not thinking straight. "Sebastian," I whisper, and then Ryan and

Michael are on him, finally managing to grab him and subdue him, each gripping a thick arm as he struggles against their hold.

Sebastian's eyes find mine again. He knows I only yelled to distract him and he looks positively betrayed.

Well, bring it on, Hunter. 'Cause if it's a fight you want ... it's a fight you're going to get.

* * *

A few minutes later, we're all standing somewhere in the middle of the resort, still near the main pool. The sun has just set, and all the lights around the beautiful, exuberant gardens and stone paths have come on, a gorgeous sight I'd be thankful for on any other night.

"Fucking let go of me," Sebastian snarls at Ryan and Michael as they both turn to me for guidance.

Joe, the resort's manager, is standing by in case he's needed again. He immediately got the resort's security to take Drunk Guy to the infirmary, and also called the chief of police—his cousin—to press charges against Drunk Guy and his friends for being intoxicated and disorderly and upsetting the other guests. Joe assures me they'll be sent home tomorrow as soon as they're sober and that Sebastian won't be in any trouble with the law.

As for me—well, I'm still in shock, I guess, as I nod at the guys and they finally let go of Sebastian.

I've never seen him so angry or acting so violent, and my mind is still reeling. All those times we talked about us and the kind of life we want to build, about our future and everything we'd still like to achieve, play on a loop in my head.

Images of us laughing and swimming, of us sunbathing and making long, passionate love on our beach only add to the feelings of hurt and disappointment weighing heavy on my heart right now, and I don't know what to think. All I know is that this brute, this savage I see in front of me is nothing like the man I love.

And I want him back. I want the beautiful, tender man I know he is to come back to me now.

"All I'm saying is that you didn't need to punch him, Sebastian. You could've just pushed him away," I continue as calmly as I can, still trying to reason with him.

"What do you mean I shouldn't have punched him?" he yells, his face twisted in anger. "The son of a bitch had his paws all over you."

"He grabbed my waist, Sebastian," I shout back, finally losing my temper. I've had it up to here with his bad attitude. "And he was clearly drunk, not thinking straight. You, on the other hand, were sober, and didn't need to be so aggressive. Not to mention that Michael had the situation already under control." I glance at Michael so he doesn't talk. Sebastian doesn't need to know he was on his phone. The way Sebastian's acting right now he'll probably sack Michael on the spot.

"Are you listening to yourself right now?" Sebastian snaps before pointing a finger at me. "You're my wife. Nobody gets to touch you but me."

I roll my eyes at him and cross my arms. "You're behaving like a caveman and making a complete fool of yourself. All I'm saying is that he was drunk, and I'm not going to condone unnecessary violence. Not even for your sake."

His jaw thickens. "Maybe you liked it. You do seem to enjoy all the male attention directed your way." My mouth drops open in shock. How dare he speak to me like this? "Is that it, baby?" he sneers. "Did you like his hands on you?"

"Sebastian, that's enough," Ryan says, placing a hand on his shoulder, but Sebastian shrugs him off and takes a step towards me.

"Do you like having other men look at you? Touch you? Is that why you're defending the fucker?"

Tears well up in my eyes, blurring my vision, and I'm only half-aware of my actions when my hand falls across his face.

Slap!

The sound is loud, deafening, and my lips quiver.

"How's that for violence, Hunter? Is this what you wanted? Is this what you wanted from me?" I cry, and without any further thought, I turn in a rush, storming off, just as the angry tears begin to roll down my cheeks.

I need to get away. Need to get away from him. Dinner be damned. I can't even look at his face, let alone have a meal with him.

My dramatic exit only lasts five seconds, though, before the brute grabs hold of me again. He throws me over his shoulder and crosses his luxury resort from one end to the other with me kicking and screaming at him. His manner is calm and collected, even relaxed as he greets the guests and many of his employees on the way. Some even wave and smile, commenting on how romantic we look, and that 'for sure we must be newlyweds'—as if what he's doing to me is perfectly normal, and not the act of an insane man.

"Grrr ... seriously, what the hell is wrong with these people?" I mutter under my breath, my body spent and limp from fighting him as we finally approach the car and he makes me get in.

Because there's absolutely nothing romantic about the way I want to kick my husband in the nuts right now. I can promise you that.

Sebastian starts the car, and I look away, staring out of the window for the entire drive. The silence between us is stifling, though, so thick it feels like a whole other entity in the car.

It grates on my nerves. That and the fact he still hasn't apologised. By the time he parks the car in front of our home, I'm fuming with anger.

Determined to make it inside the house before him, I undo the seatbelt in a jerky move and push open the door. I just want a chance to calm down. To collect my thoughts before he gets in my face again.

But, of course, I should've known better, and before I'm even clear of the car, he stalks after me, grabbing me like the caveman he is and again throwing me over his shoulder.

I cry out in shock, fighting him and punching his back, screaming bloody murder as he walks up to the front steps of the house. His pace is fast and sure, his energy dominant and unfazed by my struggling as he carries me inside.

Even now, he doesn't falter, the bastard. Doesn't stop stomping on my heart as it bleeds. As it breaks into a million tiny pieces after what he said to me.

He hurt me. He really hurt me this time. And now I'm simply too mad to forgive. Too wounded and disappointed in him to ever forget.

He enters our bedroom and with no preamble throws me on the bed, climbing right after to pin me down to the mattress, imprisoning my wrists, dominating me as he holds my hands above my head and crashes his lips to mine in a punishing, bruising kiss. His voracious mouth setting me alight until I finally stop fighting him. My struggles are soon replaced by my body writhing and offering itself to him. Surrendering. Surrendering to the all-consuming love I will always have for this man.

I begin to tremble. Wanting him. Needing him. Wishing that the hot, carnal kiss he's giving me will never come to an end.

"I hate you!" I whisper as soon as he breaks the kiss, the anger of what he said to me morphing into just plain hurt as I look up into his eyes.

"I'm sorry," he rasps, his breathing all over the place as he touches his forehead to mine. "I'm so sorry, sweetheart. I just ..."

"You hurt me," I sob, and he lifts his head to look at me, his face falling with guilt.

New tears roll down my temples, soaking my hair and the pillow. "You hurt me, Sebastian," I repeat, wanting him to acknowledge my pain. I can't have him do this again. I won't stand for it.

"I know, baby. I know," he whispers. "And I've never been so ashamed." He shakes his head. "I should never have said those things to you."

My heart squeezes painfully, breaking that little bit more at the regret I hear in his voice.

God, I don't want to fight with him.

"No, you shouldn't have," I agree, my voice small and my lips trembling.

"I ..." He shakes his head as if frustrated and then opens his eyes again. "I ... lost control, Alice." He sighs. "Seeing that motherfucker's hands on you made me want to kill him. I can barely stand it as it is when I see other men gawking at you. This time something just snapped, and when I got over the rage I'd ... I'd already said those God-awful things to you." He presses his lips to my forehead. "You must know I didn't mean any of it, Alice. I love you and I respect you more than anyone else. Please, forgive me."

He's tripping over his words, and I know he's nervous, which for him is unusual. And a little disconcerting, I must add.

I inhale deeply. "You need to work on your jealousy, Sebastian. You can't treat me like that whenever someone says or does something inappropriate. It's not my fault, and I have no control over it."

He nods. "I know that. I do," he insists at my raised eyebrows. "It ... it just felt like you were defending the asshole at the time, and before I knew it ... well, I was losing my shit."

"I'd never defend that kind of behaviour, Sebastian, but I also can't agree with the violence you displayed. First, the guy was drunk, and second, you could've just pushed him away."

"No, the fucker deserved it. Believe me, he'll think twice now before grabbing another innocent girl like that, sober or drunk."

I roll my eyes. Seriously, this man can be as stubborn as a mule.

Suppressing the urge to call him a Neanderthal, I counter, "You're missing the point. Women covet you all the time. Even throw themselves at you in front of me. What am I supposed to do? Beat them all into a pulp? Punch them?"

"Of course not." His brows knit together. "I don't even look at other women. They mean nothing to me. I only see you. I only want you."

"Exactly! It's the same for me. So all you've accomplished tonight was to behave like an idiot in front of everyone ... and hurt your wife in the process."

"You're right. I am an idiot," he drawls, pulling off the best 'puppy eyes' look I've ever seen and making my heart melt on the spot. "An idiot who's completely and utterly in love with his wife. An idiot who's very, very sorry he hurt her. An idiot who's going to do his best to make it up to her."

"I guess that's a start. You may continue," I instruct, and he smirks, obviously pleased with the effect he's having on me.

"Well, what else can I say except that I don't deserve to have such a gorgeous, wonderful, intelligent woman by my side," he goes on, and I have to bite down on my lip to keep myself from laughing. "And that I promise to do nothing but grovel, spoil her, and worship at her feet until she's ready to forgive me."

"Only until she forgives you?" I question as a smile spreads over my lips.

"You little minx. You know what I mean." He tickles me, finally letting go of my wrists, making me giggle while he laughs and showers my face with kisses. "I'm truly sorry, though." He raises his head, and his expression is earnest, all traces of laughter gone.

"I never meant to hurt you, Alice. I love you too much for that. I love you more than anything."

"I know. And I love you, Sebastian. But you can't do this again. Please, don't do this again."

"I won't, baby. I promise." His eyes hold mine, and I know he means it. Stupid, stupid man. If I didn't love him so much ... "Now it's your turn," he adds, a wicked smile playing on his full lips as his eyes bore into mine.

"My turn for what?" I ask, confused.

"To apologise," he says, deadpan.

I frown. "But I didn't do anything." What's he talking about? Is this because I slapped him?

"Just what you always do."

"What do you mean?"

"I mean that you make me crazy," he growls, dropping his head to my neck and biting me sensually as I shudder under his touch. "I mean that you make me behave like a caveman, an animal, all the fucking time."

Giggling, I relent. "OK! OK! I'm sorry, I'm sorry. Please forgive me."

He laughs and lifts his head to look at me, his expression changing from playful to intense in a matter of seconds. "Oh, baby, you should know by now that's not how you're going to apologise to me. You're a temptress. A stunning, beautiful temptress who was put into my life to drive me insane. So, no, you need to truly repent. Show me how sorry you really feel."

The atmosphere changes, turning the air heavy and charged, and my pulse picks up. "How should I apologise then?" I ask, all breath and no sound.

He smiles darkly, making me shiver. "I think it's time for some discipline, Mrs Hunter. You've been misbehaving for quite a while now, and your punishment has been long overdue." He leans in, his lips brushing against my ear. "Now go and put on your sexy lingerie. The one I told you to save for a special occasion."

Oh, God! I almost forget how to breathe, my brain turning to mush when I realise what he intends to do to me. Yet my panties are drenched and my core clenches desperately at the sudden empty feeling inside me.

And as he turns me, leading me towards the bathroom so I can change, I don't resist. I don't mutter a word because deep down I know I want this. Deep down I know I'll take whatever he's willing to give.

I love this man. I love him, and he loves me ... and nothing we do together can ever be wrong, bad. As long as our love is at the forefront of all our fantasies.

* * *

Ten minutes later, I step nervously out of the bathroom to find him sitting on the side of the bed. I bite my lip.

God, he really is a gorgeous specimen. All broody, intense, and wild, not to mention gloriously naked. He's undoubtedly the most beautiful man I've ever seen, and my mouth can't help but water at the sight.

Our eyes meet across the room and we silently stare at each other. I'm wearing the white silk babydoll and matching panties I bought for our wedding night, and Sebastian looks positively feral as his hungry eyes drop down my body to my toes and slowly come back to my face, devouring every single inch of me like I'm food and he hasn't been fed in days.

I shiver under his stare, goosebumps scattering all over my skin as I wait for his next move.

He's already in full dominant mode, hard and thick between his legs, his erection engorged and leaking precum, and I know he's not going to be gentle with me. No, tonight is all about him taking his pleasure. Taking my body and making it surrender to his will. Making me surrender to him, to his needs, however dark and twisted they may be.

A little frisson of fear mixes with my arousal, sending a rush of excitement through my veins, and I feel myself getting wet, my body preparing for his impending onslaught.

His jaw thickens and he swallows hard, and I know he's just as affected. Just as in love as I am, and just like that, my nerves begin to fade. Replaced by the same red-hot, uncontrollable need that has brought us together—the same need that'll keep bringing us together no matter how hard we try to keep apart or how mad we are at each other. I know that now.

The pull is just too strong between us. Too ingrained in our cells. Just like the need to breathe, it can never be ignored.

"Come. Stand between my legs," he commands, his voice husky.

I begin to move in his direction, my confidence building with every step at the reverence I see in his eyes.

Then he's gripping my hips, his large hands positioning me just so in front of him. "Beautiful," he rasps. "You look just like I imagined. A virgin, pure and innocent, and ready to be sacrificed."

His words send a new surge of excitement to my core and just like that I'm dripping wet. My sex is swollen and throbbing, nipples standing at attention, and I know he knows I'm more than ready for him.

"You won't be needing these," he says, a predatory smile playing on his lips as his fingers hook into the sides of my panties and he pulls them down to my feet.

He helps me step out of them, and I cling to his shoulders, my legs barely holding my weight. My centre is wet and glistening with my arousal, left in plain sight for him to see.

He hisses approvingly, and, running his hands up and down my legs, takes a sensitive nipple into his mouth, sucking it through the silk of my babydoll as he grabs my behind. I gasp, my own hands flying to the back of his head, tugging at his hair and holding him close as I lose myself in him, as I lose myself in the sensations setting my body aflame.

"Sebastian," I moan, and his touch turns rougher, violent even, as he gets more and more worked up. "Oh, God," I moan again, and he growls into my flesh, his mouth latching onto my other breast, making me pant, making me squirm.

Yeah, I've died and gone to heaven because this man is a freaking god in bed—a sexual beast, a deviant—and I'm the lucky gal who gets to have him all to herself.

Too soon he's pulling away, though, and just as I'm about to complain, he runs his thumb over my slit.

Holy hell! I convulse, whimpering as I almost come undone.

His jaw falls slack and he lifts his eyes to look at me.

Oh, he looks so hot like this. So freaking turned on. And I want him. I want him more than I can bear.

"Nice, very nice. Such a good girl you are," he drawls. "All wet and ready, and mine to do with as I please." He slips his middle finger into my channel, pumping me gently as his eyes stay riveted on me. "And you do want that. Don't you, baby? You want to please me? You want to get fucked by me?"

My mouth falls open, but I can't speak. I can only breathe as he adds yet another finger inside me and continues to stroke me deep, my nails digging into his skin.

"Mmm, yeah, I think you do want that. I think you want me to shove my big, fat cock into this tight little cunt of yours and fuck you raw."

Oh, God, what is this man doing to me?

He laughs, the sound deep and low in his throat, and I shiver. My core tightens and spasms uncontrollably around his fingers as I almost come again from his words alone.

He flicks his hand, finding that special spot inside of me, and my legs begin to tremble. He doesn't relent, though, his strokes turning faster and deeper, getting me so close to the edge all I need is one more thrust, one more push of his clever fingers, and ... and ...

Nooo! I almost cry when he removes his fingers to bend me over his knee, one strong hand pushing most of my upper body to the mattress.

I whimper, and he chuckles, brushing my hair aside. Positioning me so he can look at my face, and I can see his.

Oh, shit! We're really doing this, aren't we?

My heart begins to thump in my ears, my breathing coming in pants, and I begin to shake when I see the hungry look in his gaze.

Dear God, I think he's going to devour me.

"Yes, you're such a good girl indeed. So well behaved," he says, his hand rubbing my ass cheeks in a gentle yet weirdly hypnotic way, and my hips begin to sway, rolling on his thigh like a wave. "Which makes me think that perhaps it's time I help your inner bad girl come out. Let her play a little. Who knows, maybe next time I want to be bad, you'll want to be bad with me."

His fingers dip between my thighs, and I jerk under his touch, my hips rising and falling as if they have a mind of their own.

And if his other leg wasn't wrapped tight around my own, holding me securely in place, I'm sure I would've fallen off his lap.

Chuckling, he presses a big hand between my shoulder blades as he continues to massage my clit, my entrance, and before I know it, I'm lost in him again, desperately chasing the orgasm he so bluntly denied me when he pulls his hand away.

Slap!

I hear it before I feel it. Like a slow-motion affair, a movie where you are given a few precious milliseconds where nothing can touch you or hurt you until reality sinks in. And, oh, boy, this time reality comes with a sting.

A sting, a bite, and I scream as I bury my face on the bed. My fists tighten in the sheets as another three consecutive slaps land on my innocent ass.

Holy Mother of God!

He stops and starts rubbing my smarting cheeks, all the while whispering words of endearment until all I can feel is a tingling sensation where there was only burning before.

Doesn't stop the tears from erupting, though. Or the confusing feelings of betrayal and arousal twisting me up inside.

Um, maybe I can't do this. It hurts, and even if I do love the dominant side in Sebastian, I'm not so sure I can handle the pain.

"Shh ... shh, baby girl," he coos as he dips his fingers into my folds, and to my absolute horror I'm soaked, drenched as he easily slides two of his fingers inside me.

How? How can this be? How the hell am I still getting aroused by this?

He pumps me hard, fucking me faster and deeper than ever before, and I find myself pushing back, seeking the hard, punishing thrusts of his hand. My desperate moans and heavy panting shock me the most as I barely recognise myself, especially when he pushes a third finger inside me.

"Fuck, yeah," he murmurs, building up speed, his breathing just as heavy and laboured as mine.

Then he's pulling away again and his hand falls open on my behind, landing another four consecutive slaps as he alternates between each cheek.

And this time, to my surprise, it's not so bad. It doesn't sting. It doesn't bite.

In fact, it feels kinda good—hot, even.

And as his fingers push into me again, thrusting and rocking me hard, I should probably feel embarrassed, ashamed by how wet I am for him and how much I want him inside me, but I'm too far gone at this point and completely under his spell.

Truth is this man can do whatever he wants to me, and I'll always come back for more. He's my whole world, just as much as I'm his.

And yes, he's kinky, domineering, and a bit rough around the edges, but he's mine. Mine to keep, mine to love, mine to cherish ... and I wouldn't have it any other way.

Time stands still as he continues to smack my ass and my pussy lips, alternating with massaging my clit and penetrating me with his fingers, and all my inhibitions melt away, disappearing one by one, one slap at a time. My desire rises and soars with each strike of his hand, each stroke of his fingers, until somewhere along the way my core clenches and rippling waves of pleasure steal my sanity away. My orgasm is so intense I very nearly faint.

"Fuck!" Sebastian growls, grabbing me by the waist and throwing me on the bed.

I giggle, bouncing on the mattress, my brain slow and relaxed, my sex still spasming and tingling from the mother of all orgasms, and then his hands are on me. Turning me, placing me on my hands and knees before he grips my hips and impales me with his cock.

I whimper, gasping for air, but he's too frantic, too desperate to join us and keeps pushing into me, so I do my best to relax.

God, he's never been so rough with me, so utterly sexual, but now he's given me a taste, I don't want him to ever stop. Don't want this to ever be over.

It feels way too good, too right, the burn reminding me of our very first time together, sending a new gush of arousal to my core.

"Sebastian," I cry as he slides in deep. His whole body trembles as he sheathes himself in me and releases a guttural sound.

He's breathing hard, his grip on my hips tightening to the point of pain, heightening my desire. Taking it to a whole new level I don't even understand.

But, by God, I needed it, needed this. Needed to see him lose control and finally own my body like he wants to, like he needs to, giving me all of himself in return.

Shuddering, he pulls almost all the way out and then sinks back in deep, making us both cry out at the intensity of his possession.

"I'm going to fill you up so good, baby girl. I'm going to give you all of my cum," he growls low in his throat as he hits all the right spots in this position. Again and again, he pulls out and plunges back in, going deeper than ever before, rubbing incessantly against my G-spot, fucking me so hard, so good, I can barely breathe.

"Come for me," he orders as he finally lets loose, his pants getting louder and quicker as the bed starts to shake and hit the wall with force. "Come all over my cock, baby."

And I do. God help me, I do. And it's explosive and soothing. Like fire and ice, hell and heaven all rolled into one. A sin and a kindness as my core squeezes him tight, clenching and spasming around him, and I let go with a scream.

Oh, sweet Jesus!

My eyes roll to the back of my head and I feel as if my arms might give up, but he doesn't relent, doesn't miss a beat as he continues to thrust into me, intensifying my climax, driving me wild with more and more need.

So full. So good. This is fucking. Pure, unadulterated fucking, and I'm glad he's doing it with me. His wife, his slut ... his everything.

"I'm going to put a baby in you, Alice," he grunts out, and my core clenches hard, gripping him with renewed desire. "You want that, don't you?"

"Oh, God, please." More than anything, I want his baby in me. I want us forever united in the miracle of creating a life together.

Lowering one arm to the bed, he bends over me and kisses the back of my neck. "You want my cum, sweetheart?" His breath is harsh, heated against my skin, and my whole body begins to shake.

"Yes ... please. Please come inside me, husband," I whisper, so lost in my pleasure I can barely speak.

"Fuck," he grunts and sinks his teeth into me, biting me right where my neck and shoulder meet, his other hand moving towards my clit.

Still sensitive from orgasm, I squirm, trying to get away, but he holds me in place. It's too much, though. Too many sensations running through me, and I can't ... "Sebastian, no, please."

"Again, baby. Again," he pants.

"I can't. It's too much. Sebastian, it's too much," I try, pleading with him, but he doesn't stop, doesn't listen, and soon his fingers are matching the crazy pace of his hips pistoning into me. Fucking me so hard, so fast, that I can't help it when I explode again with another scream, my whole core gripping him so tightly he can barely move an inch. "Sebastian. Oh, God, Sebastian. Aaahhh."

"Mine! You're fucking mine!" He thickens inside me and warm spurts of his cum hit the mouth of my womb. The sticky mess slowly slides down my sex and thighs as he keeps emptying himself in me. "Fuck. Oh, fuck, Alice! Baby!"

"I'm yours, Sebastian," I whisper. "I'm yours, baby."

We collapse on the bed, his arms around me, holding me close as we try to catch our breath.

"I'm yours too, Alice," he whispers, smiling into my neck as he kisses it, his wicked tongue licking the sweat off my skin.

My eyes close and I inhale deeply. I've never felt so happy. So complete. He's being himself with me, his beautiful, rugged self, and I can't wait for him to show me more.

I know that with each day that passes I'm getting closer to him, and even if he's still keeping things from me—which I know he is—it's only a matter of time before he lets me in. Before he trusts me and sees that I'm here to stay.

Because of one thing I'm sure. I'll never leave him. No matter what demons or fears still haunt him, whatever he's done in the past, I love him, and I've faith in him. In us. And in our strength to deal with whatever comes our way.

Yawning, I turn to face him, only to find him smiling lazily down at me.

"Hi," he rasps, and I smile shyly back at him.

"Hi." I trace his lips with my fingers, and he leans in to run his tongue through my open lips. "You feel spiky." I cup his cheeks, my thumbs caressing the coarse skin.

"And you feel good," he whispers into my lips. "I love you, Alice."

"I love you, Sebastian."

Our eyes lock, and then he's kissing me and kissing me, his lips slow and sensual over mine, and the whole world disappears until it's just me and him again.

Us, and the unconditional love we'll always have for each other.

Chapter 25

Alice

Staring at the pregnancy test in my hands, I smile so big I'm afraid I may end up with permanent damage.

Oh, Sebastian's going to be over the moon when I tell him.

My man was determined to get me pregnant the entire time we were on our honeymoon, asking me to stop taking the pill on our very first night in Ocho Rios, and telling me how much he wanted me to have his baby. How much he wanted us to be a proper family.

I shake my head, remembering how sweet he was. How earnest when he said nothing would make him happier than us having a child of our own. And OK, he's said stuff like that to me before, but never outside of the bedroom and more along the lines of dirty-talking to sex me up. So this time I knew something had changed.

I knew that if he was discussing it with me and asking me to stop taking the pill, he was serious about it. Which is ridiculous, of course—crazy, really, considering we just got married and how short a time we've known each other, but just like that everything else became secondary.

My worries, my fears ... unimportant. Because in that moment I was sure that not only had I found my true soulmate, I'd also found my true partner in life. My true love.

In all honesty, I'd been thinking about us starting a family ever since the day Sebastian proposed. I've always wanted to be a mother, and now I have him in my life my hormones have taken over my brain. He's just too sexual, too dominant. And he has such an effect on me that he can turn me inside out with nothing but the look in his eyes.

Of course, the fact that I can't stop imagining a little miniature of my husband in my arms doesn't help matters either. And I know we're young, that it's too soon, but I can't help myself—especially now I know he wants the same.

I place the test on the bathroom counter and turn on the tap to wash my hands. It dawns on me that the reason I've been feeling so off ever since we came home two weeks ago is probably because of the pregnancy.

Bloody hell, no wonder I didn't know what was wrong with me, could never quite put my finger on it. All I knew is that I couldn't relax, couldn't sleep. Not to mention that my anxiety levels went straight through the roof as soon as Sebastian went back to work.

So much so that when I started having nightmares again and feeling unwell, I didn't pay it any attention, thinking it was just an upset stomach or maybe some virus I picked up during our travels.

I grab a towel to dry my hands. It wasn't until yesterday I realised I was also late. And I'm never late. Never.

Pregnant. I'm frigging pregnant.

A goofy smile spreads over my face as I find myself remembering a few of our many baby-making attempts, blushing at the memory of Sebastian spanking my ass. God, that was hot. Like out-of-this-world, incredibly hot, and it wouldn't surprise me if he got me pregnant that night.

In fact, I'm pretty sure we would've needed at least three different kinds of contraceptives if we wanted to prevent a pregnancy that time.

My smile grows goofier. I can't help it. I just can't wait to see his reaction. I touch my still-flat stomach in awe, my feelings all over the place, going from terrified to overjoyed, from worried to excited … and so, so happy, I don't know what to do with myself. I laugh out loud, overwhelmed by my emotions.

"Thank you, God," I whisper. "Thank you so much for this blessing. Thank you for my husband and my baby. And most of all, thank you for giving me a heart strong enough to love again."

Because I do. I love again.

I love my life and this new crazy family of mine. I love my man and our unborn child.

And I vow to always protect them, to always defend them until the day that I die. Until the day I am no more.

Smiling through my tears, I stare at my reflection in the mirror, heart hammering inside my chest.

Now all I have to do is tell my beautiful husband the good news ...

My stomach somersaults with barely controlled exhilaration ... And I think I already have a pretty good idea of how I'm going to do that.

* * *

Ugh, of course he had to be late this evening!

Frowning, I look at my watch again. It's already eight p.m., almost twelve hours since I took the test, and I've been more hyper than an addict on crack.

I've cleaned, cooked, polished, and even ironed, and now I'm in the bedroom, further busying myself by putting our clothes away.

Sebastian is stuck in a meeting, and according to Angela—his new, middle-aged, happily-married secretary, who called to let me know—it looked like it was going to take them at least another hour or so. That was over two hours ago.

My hands begin to shake and I almost drop all of Sebastian's shirts on the floor after missing the rail. I'm so anxious to tell him the news, I feel like I'm about to have a heart attack.

Just then the door to our bedroom opens, and I sag with relief. I hang all the shirts in a row and spread them out before turning towards the exit of Sebastian's dressing room.

He's already there, one shoulder leaning on the door frame as he stares down at me. "Hey, sweetheart. Sorry I'm late." I can't help but stare back at him, all the air rushing out of my lungs.

Mmm, my beautiful, sexy, intense man.

He looks tired, though, drained, and despite my anxiety and earlier annoyance I find myself smiling back.

"It's OK." I walk over to him, stand on my tiptoes, and, stretching my arms, slide my fingers through his hair. "You're home now, that's all that matters."

Our lips touch and what was supposed to be a peck on the lips turns into a full-blown kiss. We both groan, and Sebastian pulls me further into him, gripping my bum possessively as he loses control.

I giggle and try to pull away, but he's unstoppable now, and with a growl starts kissing down my jaw, my neck, my collarbone, and then finally my breasts.

My eyes flutter closed. God, he's in that mood tonight. The one where he doesn't care about anything except getting what he wants. And momentarily I forget all about my plans.

Then his mouth is back on mine, his tongue and lips devouring my very soul, and my knees almost fold. "Mmm," I start to moan just before remembering myself.

Grow some backbone, Alice. Stop this.

Reluctantly, I push my palms into his chest. "Go have your shower, baby. We can continue this later."

He tightens his hold on me. "I know. But I don't want to."

"Sebastian ..."

"Mrs Hunter, are you implying I smell?" He sounds offended. Except the slight curve of his lips is a dead giveaway he's playing with me.

"Well, you've smelled better." I raise both my eyebrows in challenge, and he grimaces.

"Oh, the pain!" He presses a hand to his heart, shaking his head dramatically. "How could you? How could you hurt me like this?"

I laugh. "I'll hurt you a lot more if you don't get that hot, perky ass of yours into the shower now."

"So, you think my ass is hot, huh?"

"Sebastian," I sigh. "Dinner is ready, and ..."

"Shhh. No, this is interesting. What else do you think is hot about me?"

"Let me stop you right there, mister. I know what you're doing, and there will be no funny business before dinner tonight." I struggle uselessly against his hold.

"But baby, business—funny or otherwise—should always come before pleasure. It's the responsible thing to do." He sucks on the skin of my neck, and my knees begin to tremble.

Then his hands are on my behind, his strong arms lifting me clean off the floor as he buries his face in my breasts, and I can't help my moans when he sucks my nipples through my blouse.

Of course, he sees that as a green light and starts moving towards the bedroom. The bed.

"No. No. Put me down, you deviant," I shout as I begin to struggle, but he only laughs and starts lowering us to the bed, his hips between my thighs as his hands wrap around my wrists.

"You're putting up quite a fight today. You want me to make you, baby?" His hips push against my sex, sending sparks of pleasure all over my body. The thick, hard bulge in his suit trousers rubs me so perfectly, I don't want him to stop, much less go anywhere.

Shoot, how the hell am I supposed to stop him now when all I want is to let him have his dirty, wicked way with me?

I stare at his beautiful face—take in his bright blue eyes, the long, thick lashes, straight nose and strong, square jaw, and those lips ... those full, beautiful lips that make my toes curl and steal my breath away every single time we kiss—and I almost give in.

God, he's gorgeous. So gorgeous, it's unfair.

And the bastard knows it too, smirking devilishly at me as I swoon like some kind of lovesick schoolgirl. He thinks he has me.

"You want me to make you like I did on our honeymoon, baby? You liked that, didn't you?" he asks, and if by some miracle my panties weren't already ruined, I'm pretty sure they're beyond saving now.

God, yes, I want it. I want him. But I know I can't, at least not until I tell him the news.

The way he is now, he won't give me a break until I pass out in orgasmic bliss in the middle of the night, and then what? My surprise will be ruined.

I shake my head. "What I want is for you to take your kinky self to the shower and then have dinner with me."

He frowns, scanning my face. "What's wrong, sweetheart? Are you mad at me?"

"No, baby. Of course not." I don't want him thinking I'm mad at him, it'll ruin the whole mood. "It's just that I slaved in the kitchen all day and I really want us to have a romantic dinner tonight."

This is true. I did slave in the kitchen all day, preparing a very special meal for one of the most important nights of our lives—the least he can do is have dinner with me, right?

"I'm sorry, baby, and please don't think I don't appreciate what you do. I'm your biggest fan. I'll always be your biggest fan. It's just that I go crazy when I see you, and then ... well, this happens."

I bite my lip. This man really knows how to kill me softly with words. "I know. And I love that you want me so bad, but right now, I'm in the mood for some romance. So slow down, cowboy, play your cards right, and maybe, just maybe, you might get lucky tonight." I give him a cheeky smile and slap his behind. "Now get your gorgeous self into that shower, and when you finish come join me downstairs."

He smiles big at my compliment. "Yes, ma'am. I'll be quick." With a peck to my lips, he jumps off me and the bed and rushes to the bathroom.

My eyes close shut and I fan myself.

Stage one completed. Now onto the second part.

* * *

"Can I open it now?" Sebastian asks for the hundredth time, eyeing the beautifully wrapped silver box I placed at the head of his place mat.

I smile over the rim of my glass. We just finished dinner, and the whole meal he's been studying the box intently, asking me several times already if he can open it and what it is.

"You know, most people would think a billionaire doesn't get this excited over a little gift." I take another sip of my orange juice, trying not to laugh at him.

Seriously, he's such a kid when it comes to presents, and the excitement on his face is something else entirely.

"Well, they'd think wrong. And I never get presents apart from my dad and Linda, so ..."

What? "Why?" I ask surprised, and a little bit shocked, I must say. Surely that's not right. He knows a ton of people.

"The same reason you just pointed out. I'm a billionaire. People don't know what to get for someone like me. They think I wouldn't be happy with something small or inexpensive." He shrugs and rolls his eyes as if the idea is absurd to him.

"But you would." It's more of a statement than a question. I can see clearly that he would. Although I'd still like to hear him say it.

He nods. "Of course I would. It's the thought that counts, not how much you spend. Especially when it's something meaningful and sentimental."

"You're a good man, Sebastian Hunter. I'm glad you didn't lose sight of what's important just because you have money." I kiss the tip of his nose, and he gives me a bashful smile.

"Sooo … can I open my present now?"

"I think I'll go get us some tea first," I taunt.

"Oh, come on," he whines. "Alice?"

I get up and walk away, a mischievous smile on my lips when I turn my back to him. I'm quite enjoying this.

"Fuck it, if that's how you want to play it, I'll just open it while you're gone," he threatens.

"Don't you dare, Sebastian. I mean it. You'll have no sex for a week," I throw over my shoulder.

A few minutes later I come back to the table with our steaming mugs to find him shaking the small box next to his ear. "Tsk, tsk, tsk. Such a naughty boy," I admonish in spite of my smile.

"Can I open it now?" He cocks his head to the side, his eyes pleading with mine.

I shake my head. He looks adorable, and I can't help but laugh when he pulls me onto his lap.

"Sebastian," I giggle, and he tickles my ribs as he bites into my neck with a growl. "OK, OK," I concede, wrapping my arms around him and dropping kisses all over his cheeks. "You win. You can open it."

He smiles a beaming smile, and I can barely breathe as he annihilates the wrapping paper in seconds and shakes the closed box with my pregnancy test next to his ear again.

His eyes shine, making him look so happy and boyish, I make a mental note to once in a while surprise him with a little something, just so I can see this expression again.

Then he's lifting the cover, and it's my turn to barely contain my enthusiasm. He gasps and his eyes widen before they snap back to mine. I smile broadly and touch my palm to his cheek.

"You ... is this ..." He swallows hard, his eyes still searching my face. "Are you pregnant?" The emotion in his voice is so strong it brings tears to my eyes, and I nod, unable to speak.

His lips stretch and he breaks into a radiant smile—a smile so big that for a second I worry he might be the one who ends up with permanent damage. "We made a baby?" His eyes glisten with tears, bringing a lump to my throat.

"Yes, our baby," I whisper, smiling through my tears when suddenly his mouth is on mine, his hand at the back of my head holding me exactly the way he wants. The deep groan in his throat and the way his tongue possesses mine commands me to give him what he needs.

And I get lost in him. Lost in his kiss, in the way he holds me against his body, in the way he takes what he wants from me.

I taste the salt of our tears, the love we have for each other, and I melt further into him. I feel so cherished right now, so unbelievably safe. Utterly loved by this big, strong, wonderful man, and it's overwhelming.

Sebastian loves me, wants me, and now is going to be the father of my baby, and I have no words that could possibly describe the kind of happiness I feel.

Then he's getting up with me in his arms and rushing towards the stairs. "Sebastian, the dishes." I giggle against his lips.

"Tomorrow. I'll do them tomorrow. Right now, I'm taking what I was denied when I got home this evening."

"You have a one-track mind, Mr Hunter," I tell him, laughing. "One very dirty, very filthy one-track mind indeed."

He laughs too, and, bouncing me in his arms, takes the stairs two at a time. "Mrs Hunter, you have no idea ... but don't worry, tonight I'm going to show you exactly just how dirty and filthy my mind can be."

* * *

"You think I'll be a good father?"

"The best," I tell him sleepily as we lie in bed facing each other, our fingers intertwined as we bask in the afterglow of our lovemaking.

"What about me? You think I'll be a good mum?"

He nods, his eyes glinting under the dim light of the bedside lamp, and my heart rate picks up. "The best, sweetheart," he murmurs, using my words.

Then he's nudging my chin and his lips are pressing against mine, kissing me softly, gently, and with so much affection I melt under his touch. He caresses my hair, my neck, my cheek.

"I'm just so happy, Sebastian." My voice trembles as I desperately try to control my tears. But I'm just too emotional, too hormonal to hold them in.

"Me too, baby. Me too." He rubs his nose along mine as he tucks my hair behind my ear. "And for the record, you're already the best mother I could ever wish for our children. In fact, you're the only woman I could do this with."

Our eyes lock, and I feel so overcome with emotion for a moment I don't know what to say. Except that I feel the same, exactly the same, and that this baby is a testament to our love. A rare, beautiful love that most people can only aspire to have.

"I'm scared, though," I admit. "We're going to be responsible for this tiny, innocent life, and I'll never forgive myself if anything bad happens to it."

"Alice, you're the most caring, loving person I know. There's absolutely no doubt in my mind that you're going to be a great mum. Our baby is lucky to have you, just as I'm lucky to have you in my life."

I give him a bashful smile. I needed to hear this from him. Sebastian is my rock, my anchor. The only person who can feed or break my confidence now.

"Our baby is lucky to have you too." I kiss him on the lips. "You're good and strong." I kiss his chin and press my body to his until his arms wrap around me. "Loving and protective." I nuzzle his jaw before burying my face in his neck. "And I know she'll always feel safe with you around. Just like I do whenever I'm in your arms. You're going to be an amazing dad, Sebastian, I know you are."

"She? Isn't it a bit early to know for sure?"

"I know, but since I found out I'm pregnant all I can picture is a baby girl. Which is weird, actually. Because when we were trying, I kept imagining a boy, one who looked just like his dad. A little miniature of you." Sebastian laughs, and I giggle into his chest. "What? You're gorgeous. And you looked super-cute in all your baby photos. Can you blame me?"

"A little princess, then," he sighs, sliding my hair over my shoulder. "Daddy's little princess. Hmm, I wouldn't mind that at all. I could do with some more tenderness in my life. I know I can be a bit rough around the edges. Another beautiful, sweet girl might be just what I need to soften me up, at least when I'm at home." He chuckles. "I'll be outnumbered, though, so I'll need lots and lots of love and kisses to make up for it."

Oh, that's sweet, and the way he says it has me already imagining him bouncing our giggling little girl in his arms. Yep, I can just see her, all tiny, and in a pretty, girly dress, being held by my very tall, very strong hunk of a man.

"You're amazing, you know that?" I cup his cheek, and he covers my hand with his big palm. "And such a good man."

He shakes his head. "No, Alice. I'm not. I've done some terrible things in the past. Made some really bad choices. You're the only good thing about me. And now our baby too, of course."

"Don't. No one has ever been so good to me. No one." I don't like it when he talks like this. When he puts himself down. Why can't he see what I see? Why can't he see how good he is? "Even before you knew me you were kind to me," I insist.

"Only because I wanted you. Because I wanted something from you. You know that," he says grimly.

"And I've forgiven you. Because I know you loved me then, because I know you love me now, and because I know you're a good man. You were only a little lost, your intentions a little misguided."

"I was a miserable fuck, Alice. Selfish, cold, even cruel at times. But I'm trying now. I'm trying to be better for you. I want to be the man you deserve." Sadness flashes in his eyes, but I hold my tongue and let him continue. "I was lonely before. You coming into my life showed me that. And I thank God every day that you did. Because now I have you. I have purpose."

I nod, swallowing the lump in my throat. "You do. Now and forever, baby," I promise.

He smiles, and some of the sadness leaves his eyes. Yet I can't help but feel there's something still bothering him.

"Yes, now and forever, both of you." He rolls so he's on top of me, kissing me until I'm gasping for air. "And nothing has ever felt so right, Alice. So meant to be."

His lips slant over mine just as he slides back into me. And as my beautiful husband begins to make love to me again, I do have to agree.

Nothing has ever felt so right indeed.

Him, our baby, our future together, they're all that matters now, and I'll do anything, absolutely anything, to keep them safe, happy, unharmed. Even if I have to sacrifice my own life.

Chapter 26

Sebastian

Snapping out of my daydreaming, I find that all eyes around the table are fixed on me, their expectant expressions waiting for my decision.

Shoot. I turn to Luke, searching his face to gauge what my reaction should be, and if his smile is anything to go by, these people just gave us one hell of a presentation. Double shoot.

I smile in return, giving them the usual, "We'll let you know once we've made our decision," and we all leave the conference room.

Fuck, I must've missed at least the last thirty minutes of it. I rub my forehead in frustration as I walk along the corridor and then cross the waiting room in a rush. It's been a long and difficult day, and to be quite honest, I just want to go home to my babies.

I smile, and, sliding my hands into my pockets, can't help but think about my young and beautiful wife. God, I desperately miss her these days, barely able to make myself leave the house in the morning, let alone concentrate while I'm at work.

She's pregnant—twenty-six weeks and counting—and looking so fucking radiant, I can hardly stand to be away from her.

I picture her. Picture her round belly that is growing bigger every day, stretching to accommodate our child, and a lump forms in my throat.

It's a fucking dream come true. A dream I didn't even know I wanted, and if I had trouble keeping my hands to myself before, now she must think I'm some kind of sex maniac with the way I keep reaching for her.

I cover my mouth with my hand, slide it slowly down my chin and rub at my stubble. I probably sound like a fucking perv with a thing for pregnant women right now. Except I'm not. Never even looked twice at a pregnant woman before.

But with her, with my Alice, God, she drives me wild. Fucking crazy whenever my eyes fall on her.

Which is bad. Which is really bad. I was already all kinds of obsessed with the girl, and then she goes and gets pregnant with my seed … Fuck.

And OK, OK, I was the one who instigated the whole 'let's make a baby together'. More like convinced her to let me put a baby in her belly, but I was desperate to make her stay, to tie her to me in the most unbreakable bond known to man.

Now I'm fucked. More dependent on her love than ever before. Lusting over her like some kind of lovesick puppy, when all the poor thing is doing is making sure that our baby is safe, that it's growing healthy and happy inside her little womb.

God, surely it's not normal to want, to need your wife so fucking much. And shouldn't this obsession of mine have simmered down a little by now? Now that she's here. That she's mine. Mine by love, by marriage, and now by carrying my baby for everyone to see. So shouldn't I see an improvement on my affliction? Shouldn't I be granted a reprieve?

"You asshole. You didn't listen to a fucking word in there, did you?" Luke follows me into my office and closes the door behind him before walking up to my desk.

I'm not in the mood for his shit right now. Turning to him, I raise both my eyebrows as I give him my best serious-corporate-shark look to intimidate him.

I just need Angela to finish the minutes, and I'll know exactly what happened in the presentation.

Of course, Luke doesn't need to know that. He's only fishing, trying to have a bit of fun riding my ass.

"I don't know what you're talking about."

"Oh, please. Don't insult my intelligence, Sebastian. You were miles away. And sighing, for fuck's sake." I try to stifle my smirk, and he rolls his eyes. "Seriously, what the hell is wrong with you, man? And where the fuck are your balls? Because only a chick sighs that fucking much in public, all right? It's embarrassing."

"Fuck off, Luke. You're pissing me off."

"You know she loves you, right? The girl is smitten. God only knows what she saw in you, 'cause it sure wasn't that ugly mug of yours that did the trick."

That makes me snort. "What? The same ugly mug that looks exactly like yours, you mean?"

"We both know I'm the prettiest out of the four of us," he says smugly.

"Prettiest, huh?" I let out a bark of laughter. "Now who sounds like a fucking chick?"

He chuckles, obviously pleased he made me laugh. "Come on. Let's take a seat, Sebastian. Talk to me." He grips my shoulder, giving it a firm squeeze, and leads me to the plush sofas in the seating area. "OK, now tell me, what the hell is going on with you?"

I stare at him, assessing how much I should tell him as he waits for me to spill the beans. I mean, where do I even begin?

"I'm fucking scared, all right?" I finally admit to it out loud for the very first time. "With the baby coming, I keep wondering if I'm going to be a good dad. It's terrifying. Actually, no, it's petrifying, knowing that you're going to be responsible for another life. What if I screw up? What if I screw up so bad, I fuck up the kid's life?"

"Don't take this the wrong way, but isn't that normal? I mean, I'd be shitting my pants if I were in your shoes." Luke gives me a smile, and I shake my head, my fingers running through my hair and pulling at the ends.

Not helping, Luke. Not helping.

"Hey, you know what else that tells me, right?"

"What?" I snap.

"That you're going to be a brilliant dad, an amazing dad. Come on, only a shitty motherfucker wouldn't feel scared, wouldn't have concerns. Don't you see?"

I inhale deeply. That actually makes a lot of sense. In fact, it's how I see things every time we discuss Alice's fears and worries. So why can't I see things the same way when it comes to me? "Thanks, Luke. I ... I think I needed to hear that."

He nods. "What else is eating at you, though?"

I frown, unsure if I should continue. But when all I see is real concern in my brother's eyes, real worry in his expression, I decide to just let it out once and for all. To release my biggest fear into the world. "What if I lose them?" I whisper.

He frowns. "What do you mean?"

"Exactly what I said. What if I lose Alice and the baby? What if they get punished for my sins?" I sigh, defeated. "What if like Mum, they get punished instead of me?"

"Is that what you think? That death is punishment? That Mum was punished somehow?"

My haunted eyes meet his. "I don't know. I just don't know any more. But yes, that's what I thought back then. That's the only thing that made sense. That Mum was being punished because of us."

His frown turns deeper. "Why because of us? What did we do that was so bad to deserve such a thing?"

"Come on, we were all little shits back then. Spoiled, entitled, out of control. And Mum was too good, too pure to deserve what happened to her." I shrug. "I just figured it couldn't be her fault. It had to be because of us."

"Now it finally makes sense. The way you behaved. The way you turned off your feelings and pushed us away. Not only did you blame yourself, but you blamed us as well." Luke fixes me with his stare, and I drop my head in shame, my eyes clouding over with tears. "God, Sebastian. Death isn't about punishment. You go when your time is up, that's all. And there's nothing you can do to stop it either. To delay it. All you can do is live your life to the fullest as best you can."

I nod, still unconvinced.

"Sebastian, nothing is going to happen to Alice or the baby. You need to believe that, otherwise you'll drive yourself insane."

"I know." I bite into my thumb, a lump lodged in my throat.

"Perhaps it's time you see a therapist."

"Don't—"

"No. You don't. You should've seen one years ago when we were kids. But you said no and Dad respected your wishes. Now I'm asking you to see one for Alice, for your unborn kid."

I shift in my seat uncomfortably. "I don't think I can. You know I don't believe in them."

"I didn't either, Sebastian, but it helps. I promise you it does. It also won't erase what happened, and it's hard work. And it sure as fuck won't cure you of being a jerk." He smirks. "I mean, look at me. But it helps you deal, you know? It helps you understand yourself and your fears better. Who knows, it may even help you with your unnatural obsession with your wife."

It's my turn to smirk. "Oh, nothing can help me with that, brother. You'll see when it's your turn. One day you just fall and don't even want to get up any more."

"Shut up, man. Are you trying to curse me?"

I laugh. "Hmm, maybe that's something you should discuss with your therapist. Your fear of commitment, of women ..."

"Fuck off. I love women. All women, obviously. And commitment isn't something I'm interested in."

I nod, smiling. "Uh-huh."

He grabs his wallet and pulls out a card. "Here. My therapist's number. Just give him a ring and try it for a little while. No pressure. You'll like him, though, he's a nice guy and a big supporter of our charities."

"I thought you said he's a therapist."

"He is." Luke smiles. "He just happens to be a rich one."

I blow out my cheeks, tempted to say no. To do what I always do in the end and deal with things on my own. Except I'm not on my own any more, am I? And this is not just about me. It's about my family. So maybe I should try it and see what good comes of it.

"OK, enough of this shit," Luke snaps, interrupting my troubled thoughts. "All this talk about feelings and being in touch with one's emotions can only be taken in small doses."

I shake my head, and with a smile shove the business card into my jacket's inner pocket. I'll give the matter some more thought when I'm alone.

"What? It's dangerous. Next thing we know we're growing vaginas between our legs and cuddling after sex." He fakes a shiver, and we fall into a fit of laughter over his stupidity.

"You're an idiot, you know that?"

"Did it help, though? You know, talking and shit. Did it make you feel better?" he asks, and surprisingly, I note that it did. The irrational fears and worries are still with me, but at least I don't feel like I'm drowning in them any more.

"Yeah, it did," I answer truthfully, swallowing the lump in my throat. "Thank you, man."

"No problem. Have you told Alice about any of this?"

"No. Everything with us happened so fast, and we've had so much going on, I've just kept pushing it back."

"You should tell her, Sebastian. In fact, you should tell her everything. Have all this stuff out in the open so both of you can figure it out. Together."

The way he says 'everything', I know he's referring not only to the way I feel, but also the accident, Cassandra and the danger she represents.

I nod. "Yeah, I will. I just need to find the right time. She's pregnant and has enough on her plate, she doesn't need my shit too."

"I don't think she'll see it that way. But in the meantime, you have me if you need to talk, OK?"

"I appreciate it, Luke. And ... I'd like it if we could do this again. I ..." My voice quivers, breaking a little on the last words, and I press my lips together, not sure of what else to say without sounding like a total pussy in front of my younger brother.

"Yeah ... I think I'd like that too. I miss you, big brother."

I get up and without thinking pull him into a bear hug.

I love my brothers. Always will.

And as we embrace, our bond stronger than ever, I make a promise to myself.

The Hunter brothers will be a united front again.

The Hunter brothers will be a force to be reckoned with.

* * *

Later when I'm lying in bed with Alice, I do try my best to find the words to tell her everything. Everything about my fears, my doubts, and even the issues we've been having with Cassandra.

Problem is, I'm getting awfully distracted with a certain hot little ass, wiggling and rubbing itself incessantly against my dick, making it increasingly harder for me to concentrate on anything other than the friction.

I smile knowingly into Alice's hair. My little wife is horny as hell tonight and doing everything she can to get me to jump her.

Which usually is an instant affair, I admit. Since I'm so consumed with my own hunger, I don't even stop to think.

Except now that I do, I realise she's been initiating sex a lot more often than I've ever given her credit for, my little temptress. And not in an obvious way either, no, but more like: 'Oh, I didn't do anything. I was just lying here looking all pretty and hot, and you just attacked me.'

Basically what she's doing right now.

I smirk.

Well, well, and here I was thinking I'm always the instigator. A fucking sex fiend molesting his beautiful, sexy wife, and it turns out she has also been playing a part in it, seducing me and driving me crazy until I'm out of my mind.

Yeah, no wonder we've been having so much sex lately.

Leaning in, I keep rubbing her baby bump with both hands as I breathe in her ear, "Is everything OK, sweetheart?"

"Um, yes," she murmurs, confused, I think. "Are you OK?" she asks, and I swear, I have to bite my lip hard to keep myself from laughing.

"Uh-huh." I swallow a chuckle. "I'm good, baby. You, however, seem to be a little tense tonight. Restless." I kiss her temple. "Is there anything you need, perhaps?"

"Nope," she answers, giving me some of her sass, the little vixen. My lips twitch as I break into a broad smile.

Oh, she's getting angry now, and she's way too cute when she gets angry with me.

I should probably feel used being manipulated like this. For my body. For sex. Too bad for me, I don't have an ashamed bone in said body or the will, for that matter, to even try to say no to my girl.

"You sure, sweetheart? 'Cause whatever it is, I'll give it to you. I'll always give you what you need," I whisper darkly into the shell of her ear.

She shivers, wiggling her ass again, and it takes all of my willpower to just keep taunting her like this. But tonight, I need her to ask me.

I need her to beg me for it. I need to be sure that she really wants this. Just as bad as I do.

Trailing soft kisses down her neck, I bite gently into the tender flesh of her shoulder before kissing my way back to her ear.

"Sebastian," she whispers, making these sexy, mewling sounds that go straight to my dick.

I grunt, her heat crashing through me like a wave, and I have to close my eyes for a second, barely able to think. "You have to tell me what you want," I pant. "You have to ..."

"I ... I want you, Sebastian," she says, her voice all breathy and needy. "I'll always want you."

Fuck, I'm so hard for her. "Be more specific." I pull her earlobe into my mouth.

"I want you inside me," she murmurs, and I inhale deeply, enjoying the sweet scent of strawberries and vanilla on her skin, the way she tastes under my lips. She smells so good, my little thing. So fucking pure and innocent.

Pushing my hips forward, I rub my erection between her ass cheeks. "Is this what you want, baby? You want me to put it in?"

"I ... yes. Please," she gasps when I cup her sensitive breasts. They're larger now with the pregnancy—still lovely and perfect, but very tender—and she begins to pant as I gently knead the mounds.

"Say it. Tell me to put my big, fat cock in your little pussy and fuck you hard, deep, until you're coming and gushing all over my shaft. These exact words. I want to hear them."

I lightly pinch and twist her nipples and she cries out. "Sebastian, please. Just ..."

"No!" I crash our lips together in a heated, messy kiss.

I feel ravenous, completely and utterly ravenous. Hungry for her. Hungry for more. But I still need to hear my filthy words coming out of her innocent lips. Still need to hear her beg me for it before I lose myself in her. In us.

"Say it," I order as soon as I dare to release her, her sweetness still in my mouth.

"I want you," she starts as she nervously licks her lips. Our gazes lock and she keeps her voice soft as she tells me what I want to hear, her face blushing a lovely shade of pink. "I ... want you to put your big, fat cock in my little pussy and ... and fuck me hard, deep ... until I'm coming and gushing all over your shaft. Please, Sebastian, I want you to take me—"

I don't let her finish. I don't even try to control myself as I pull her chin up and consume her lips.

"Baby girl," I moan between kisses, finally feeling like I'm not forcing myself on her. Fuck, I feel ten feet tall—my ego as a man, her man, close to bursting, and my heart full of pride. "Let me get you ready then."

"I'm ready," she says urgently, like she can't take another minute without having me inside her. "Just take off my panties and take me, Sebastian. Now."

Jesus. Fucking. Christ. I do love it when she's desperate like this.

Growling, I rip the side of her panties and pull her top leg up, laying it over mine. Then I hurriedly lower my boxers and position myself at her entrance until I'm pushing in. Both of us groan and pant as I enter her slowly, taking her with small, gentle thrusts that push me further and deeper into her.

She trembles, her little pussy clenching and spasming convulsively around my cock, trying to fight the intrusion but having no choice but to adjust to my size. It's still near impossible to enter her roughly, particularly at the very beginning of our coupling, so I always keep it slow and sweet whenever we start.

I'm big, she's small ... and I fucking love it. I love that she's so tight around me.

Especially now she's pregnant with my child—a feeling so primal, so ingrained in my being, that it's like coming home every time I slide into her.

Fully sheathed, I pull halfway out and push back in, my arms wrapped tightly around her, one hand on her belly, the other on her breast. Perfect. "You OK, baby girl?" I ask, panting as I kiss her cheek.

"Yes," she moans, and then whimpers, her eyes closing as I pull and twist her erect nipple. "Now fuck me, Sebastian. Please fuck me hard." She turns her head, and we kiss—lips wrapping, tongues twisting, teeth clinking.

"I love you, Alice," I murmur against her lips, thrusting into her a little harder, a little deeper as I find a steady, delicious rhythm and begin to make love to my beautiful wife.

My hand slips from her belly to her clit, and she gasps. "I love you, Sebastian."

Our eyes meet and a shiver goes through me. The intimacy and connection between us makes me feel more loved than I ever thought possible. More wanted than I deserve.

And as we both shudder and come together in an earth-shattering climax, my arms tight around everything that matters to me, I can honestly say:

I have never felt more complete in my whole life.

I'm a lucky bastard, blessed, and it's about time I let myself enjoy it.

Besides, I've already gone and done the unthinkable, booking myself an appointment to see Luke's shrink. So I guess that's it ... I'm finally ready to be done with the past and am getting the help I need.

Which makes me think maybe I shouldn't tell Alice.

After all, if I'm getting things fixed, why worry her with any of it?

Chapter 27

Alice

Nine weeks later ...

Michael and I are coming out of the hospital when I notice a young woman dry-heaving near the door to my right, one hand on the wall holding her weight, and the other rubbing her belly. She's pregnant, the poor thing, and obviously still suffering from morning sickness despite the size of her bump.

I shiver as I recall my first trimester. This morning sickness business is no joke, and whoever decided to call it that clearly has never been pregnant themselves.

Suddenly the woman sways on her feet, and I jump. "Michael, help her," I shout, pulling on his sleeve and pointing at her. He's quick, thank God, and before I know it, he's holding her up.

I breathe a sigh of relief, pressing a hand to my chest, and slowly make my way towards them. Slowly being the operative word these days. I'm dragging my feet so much a snail could beat me to them.

"Hi," I pant, already out of breath when I finally reach them. "Do you need us to call someone?"

"No. No, I'm OK now. You can go. Thank you," she groans, and it's obvious she's still unsteady on her feet.

Glancing at Michael, I can see he's also reluctant to let her go. "I'm Alice and this is Michael," I say in an effort to make her relax. I'm not comfortable leaving her like this.

"Anna. And thank you for stopping, really. I didn't mean to be rude. It's just that I wasn't able to eat anything this morning, and when I felt sick ..." She shakes her head, shutting her eyes. "God, I almost passed out. I could've seriously harmed my baby."

"Hey, stop blaming yourself. It's not your fault," I say sympathetically as I rub my own bump, and she gives me a small smile. She's pretty—chocolate-brown eyes and hair, great skin, full lips—and seems so nice I can't help wanting to help her.

"How far along are you?" she asks.

"Thirty-five weeks. You?"

"The same," she says, her smile getting brighter. "God, it really is nice to meet you. I just wish it was under better circumstances."

"Me too," I reply, laughing and extending my hand to her. She takes it, and I know what I have to do next. "Look, maybe we should try to get you something to eat. Do you think you can manage?"

"I could try, I guess," she says, pulling her hand back and sounding reluctant all over again. But I'm not about to give up.

"Good. 'Cause I was just telling Michael we should try the new coffee shop around the corner."

She smiles, clearly catching on to my game, and, looking at Michael and I in turn, says, "Thank you. You and your husband are really nice."

"Oh, nonsense, and Michael's not my husband. He's ... um ..." I hesitate, and Michael throws me a warning look. "He's my husband's friend, a family friend," I lie, not wanting Anna to know I have a bodyguard. At least not yet, as it might make her uncomfortable—and, oh, yeah, it's also bloody embarrassing.

"Sorry, I just assumed since you're here together," she says, pointing at the hospital behind her.

"Right. We should go," Michael mutters. "Do you feel more stable on your feet now?"

I smile. He really is such a sweet guy. Not to mention hot with his dark looks and incredible hazel eyes. But overall, he's kind, and it's been a tremendous blessing to have him around. Especially at times like this, when I'm having so many appointments and Sebastian is stuck at work all the time.

"Yes, thank you. I'm feeling much better now."

At the coffee shop, Michael gets our decaffeinated lattes and some really yummy sandwiches and pastries, and we find a nice table at the back where we begin our little feast, the conversation pleasant and easy the entire time as more than two hours go by. Which is crazy, I know, but it's not like I know anyone else who's expecting, at least not anyone I like, and it feels amazing to be able to finally talk to someone.

"So, Anna, are you also a patient of Ms Roberts'?" Michael asks when I finish telling Anna all the recommendations I've been given on morning sickness so far.

"Uh, no. I'm seeing someone else."

"Oh, and who's that?" Michael pushes, and I give him a pointed look, kicking him under the table. I know exactly what he's doing. Sebastian told him to screen everyone who comes near me, and like a good boy, he's fishing for information. Yeah, he's worse than Rick and Ryan put together, this one.

I won't allow it, though. It's hard enough for me to make friends, being shy and whatnot, not to mention the security detail following my derrière everywhere I go. I won't let him scare Anna away.

"Mr Thomas," she tells us, a big smile on her face. "He's not as popular as Ms Roberts, I'm afraid, but he's been brilliant so far. I'm very happy with him."

"And that's all that matters," I say, giving Michael another dirty look. He's embarrassing her, and that's the last thing I thought he'd do. Frigging Sebastian.

"To be honest, I didn't care about who I saw, as long as they were good and I felt comfortable with them. Name and prestige were never important to me."

"Oh, me neither. Of course, that said, Sebastian, my husband, doesn't quite share the same opinion. He must've screened and interviewed every single obstetrician in the city until he was a hundred percent sure I was being seen by the very best. Thank God I actually like the lady, you know what I mean?"

"Aww, that's sweet," she gushes, and I snort.

"More like embarrassing. But he was so worried, I really couldn't stay mad at him."

"He sounds like a keeper if you ask me."

"I know, and he is." I shake my head, pushing the hair off my face with one hand as I'm suddenly overcome with emotion, my eyes clouding over with tears. Damn these pregnancy hormones! "In fact, he's been nothing but wonderful. I couldn't ask for more. A doting husband, an amazing dad, a good, honest man who's over the moon for our baby's arrival. What else could I ask for?"

She nods in agreement. "You're lucky. When I told my ex-boyfriend I was pregnant, he couldn't run fast enough. Said he didn't want a serious relationship, let alone a baby, and that I was on my own if I chose to keep it." She blows out a heavy breath. "I knew he had commitment issues, but never thought he'd actually run away from his responsibilities, you know?"

"He doesn't deserve you," I tell her, reaching for her hand and giving it a squeeze. "Seriously, he doesn't, Anna. And look, I know we've only just met, but I can already see you're a bright and courageous young woman, not to mention beautiful and kind. It's his loss if he doesn't see that."

"Thank you, that's very kind of you to say." She gives me a sad smile. "And deep down, I know you're right. It still hurts, though, being rejected like that. Also, I'm all alone in the city and it can get pretty scary at times. But I know I'll be fine. I have my baby now to think about. New priorities, and the little one has to come first, right?"

"Right." I count my blessings, my chest tight.

"He's a wanker," Michael pipes in with a scowl. Right before he begins to give us a piece of his mind about assholes like Anna's ex-boyfriend and what he'd like to do to them, making us both laugh as he talks murder out loud.

All the while, though, I keep thinking about Anna and her situation. About how lucky I am.

Christ, her ex is such a loser. What a bastard. And this poor girl ... I can't even imagine what she's going through right now. And there I was, complaining about my overprotective husband when he's been nothing short of amazing—perfect, really, since he's been there for me every step of the way. Supportive and affectionate. Caring and patient despite my new grumpy, hormonal self.

So yeah, I'm definitely lucky.

I have the man I love by my side. A wonderful, loving family backing us up. And I still get scared all the time. So how's Anna supposed to do this on her own?

I can't help but worry myself sick about her, her baby, and the uncertain future in front of them. And that's when I know in my heart that I have to help her. That I have to do something, otherwise I won't be able to live with myself.

"We should exchange numbers, Anna. I'd love it if we kept in touch. We could maybe do some shopping together for the babies, or just meet for coffee and stuff, just to talk?"

Anna bites her lip nervously. "You don't need to do that, Alice. I'll be fine."

"I know, but I'd still love to be friends. I don't have any girlfriends who are expecting, so it's not like I'm doing you a favour." She looks at me with a small smile on her face, hope shining in her eyes before I continue with a shrug, acting like it's no big deal. "We could spend some time at my place today, get to know each other. What do you say?"

Her whole face lights up like Christmas. "I'd love to! But only if you're sure I won't be intruding."

"Nonsense," I tell her, putting all the enthusiasm I can muster into my voice, and tug on her hand. "Now let's go. We have a lot of time to make up for, and an ice cream cake in my freezer waiting for us."

* * *

Later that evening ...

Sebastian pats his ripped, naked stomach with a laugh. We're in the kitchen, sitting at the island, our mood light and relaxed.

My gaze drops down his torso, which is looking more and more muscular each day, thanks to all the extra training he's been doing with the lads, and I let myself simply enjoy the view. No restrictions. No shame.

"Seriously, this lasagne is the best I've ever had, sweetheart," he continues, unaware of my new deviant tendencies. "Hands down the very best." Our eyes meet, and I give him a warm smile before

I let my gaze drop to his hard stomach and the big bulge between his thighs once more.

But what can I say? Wearing only his black pyjama bottoms, the kind that hang loose on his hips, the man keeps diverting my entire attention to all things naughty and wrong, and I can barely wait to get him in bed, let alone inside me again.

"Alice? … Alice?"

"Huh? What?" I ask, coming out of my daze.

"You spaced out on me. Again." His eyes zero in on my mouth and I forget how to breathe.

My own lips part and I lick them in anticipation. Crap, I can't even pretend to be cool these days. Not when these raging pregnancy hormones are responsible for my libido and most of my functional brain.

He winks at me, the bastard, still toying with my inability to act to this day. Then he's standing and before I know it, he's holding my chin between his fingers. He kisses me, dominating me fully as he licks and sucks on my tongue. I moan and my whole body begins to burn, vibrating for him, wanting nothing else but to surrender, to give in … every last inch of me.

His tongue touches mine again—teasing, caressing—once, twice, three times, and then he's pulling away. I follow, stretching my neck, lips puckered and eager. Begging, wanting, needing more, so much more from him. But he only chuckles, drops a quick peck on my lips, and, picking up our plates off the island, walks away to the sink.

Wait, what? I blink, startled and breathless as it takes me a moment to recover.

"Um …" I clear my throat, forcing myself to snap out of it. "Do you want tea?"

"Yeah, please," he replies whilst doing the washing up, and although I know he's as crazy about me as I am about him, I can't help the little twinge of embarrassment about the way I always respond to him. Want him.

With a sigh, I turn on the kettle and get the tea bags and mugs for our tea.

"I've made a friend at the clinic today," I begin, getting the sugar and spoons next and placing them all on the counter. I want him to hear about Anna from me. Maybe that way he'll understand her friendship is important and ease off on the background checks and the twenty million questions I know he'll want to ask her once they meet. "Her name's Anna and she's pregnant. Thirty-five weeks along, just like me."

"That's nice, sweetheart," he replies without turning. "Is she a patient of Ms Roberts' too?"

"Um ... actually no, Anna's seeing someone else. A male doctor, I think." I laugh nervously, throwing a glance his way. Damn it, I can't remember the name. Why can't I remember the name? I'll have to ask Anna tomorrow. What I really need is for him to just be my husband right now and not go into full bodyguard mode. "Anyway, she's lovely, and we had loads in common straight away. So I invited her over and we spent most of the afternoon here."

"I'm glad, baby. It's good you're making new friends, especially one who's also pregnant and going through the same things. I sometimes worry you might be feeling lonely, you know? You spend too much time by yourself."

"You do?"

"Of course I do."

I smile broadly. "Well, I'm not, baby. Lonely, I mean. And I have my cooking and the book, and now all the baby planning to keep me busy."

"I know, but that's all work. What about fun, hobbies?"

"I already have you for fun, and you wear me out as it is."

He laughs out loud. "Feeling cheeky tonight, Mrs Hunter? Or is your smart mouth trying to get you in trouble again? 'Cause I have just the right medicine for it."

"Take your mind out of the gutter, Hunter. There'll be none of that tonight," I say, and whip his ass with the kitchen towel before quickly running away. Well, as quickly as I can these days anyway.

"Hey, now you're really asking for trouble, young lady," he warns, splashing me with water from the sink.

"Ahhh," I scream, still giggling as I move further away, all the way to the other side of the kitchen island where I sit waiting for him.

It's funny, but since I told Sebastian I was pregnant, we've started having dinner here, in my spacious, beautiful kitchen, instead of the dining room. It's like with the baby coming I finally came to terms with my fears, my insecurities, my disbeliefs, and accepted that this is also my house. My domain. That it's OK to want to change things, change routines—like having our meals in the kitchen when it's just the two of us. OK to feel excited when turning the bedroom across from ours into a nursery in preparation for our baby's arrival. Because I'm turning this place into a home. Our home.

Basically, accepting once and for all that this is really my life and I deserve to be happy.

My heart lodges in my throat and I blink away tears, my eyes firmly on Sebastian.

And I am happy, aren't I? Happier than I ever thought I'd be. Happier than any person has the right to be.

Sebastian dries his hands and gets our drinks from the counter before taking his seat next to me. "So tell me more about this new friend of yours," he says, taking a sip.

I smile back, glad he's not interrogating me. "She's super-nice. We got on really well, and I'm teaching her how to bake. She wants to learn for the baby, so ..."

"Oh. You must really like her then?" he asks, and I nod. "And was Michael with you the whole time she was here?" I nod again. "Did he scrape the pans?"

"Mm-hmm." I grin. "And I made hot chocolate, so Rick was in the kitchen as well."

Sebastian chuckles. "Figures. Can't say I blame them, though. You make the best hot chocolate and cakes. You make the best of everything."

Emotion fills me and I look away, overwhelmed by the affection and pride I see in his eyes.

Holding my cup with both hands, I blow into my tea, and that's when I remember. "Oh, can you believe Anna is having the baby on her own?"

Sebastian frowns. "You're joking, right? Why? What happened to her fella?"

I sigh. Ain't that the million-dollar question?

"He left her," I reply sadly, and, taking a deep breath, tell Sebastian everything, making sure he understands that I want Anna to be more than just an acquaintance. I want us to be friends, and if at all possible, I want to help her and her baby.

"You're too good, Alice, too much of a kind soul." He holds my hand in his, his thumb rubbing my knuckles. "And I know you want to help this girl, but please promise me you'll be careful, OK? Some people are just bad, and they'll try to take advantage of you."

"I'll be careful. Besides, Michael is around all the time—you have nothing to worry about."

Sebastian gives me a look that says it's his job to worry, and I grin. "We're going shopping tomorrow for baby clothes, and then we'll come back here to bake."

"Then I think I'd like to meet her. If that's all right with you, of course? Maybe together we can find out what else we can do to help her."

I smile so big my cheeks actually hurt. "You're the best, you know that? And you can meet her tomorrow if you want. I'm just worried she's very shy, and might feel uncomfortable if she knows you'll be here."

"I'll pretend to surprise you by coming home early. How's that?"

"Perfect. And thank you. You're the best husband a girl could ever have," I tell him, throwing my arms around his neck and kissing him all over his face.

Chuckling, he puts his arms around me and hoists me up into his lap. "I know. I'm also the most handsome, the most intelligent, the best lover and dancer ... What can I say? I'm just that wonderful."

"You are, but don't let it go to your head. I'd hate to add 'conceited prick' to the list."

Sliding an arm under my knees, he takes me with him as he gets up. "Hmm, let's go to bed. All this talk about 'heads' and 'pricks' is giving me ideas."

"What do you mean 'with all this talk'? I only said it once."

"Don't worry about it. When we get to our bedroom you won't be saying anything, and we'll still be on the subject."

"You're incorrigible, Mr Hunter." Giggling, I lay my head on his shoulder and let him carry me to our bed.

Chapter 28

Sebastian

"Someone's had a good night," Ryan mutters, watching me through the rear-view mirror as I take my place at the back of the Cayenne.

"Just shut up and drive," I bite off, pulling on my seatbelt and trying like hell to get rid of the goofy smile that's been plastered on my face ever since I woke up this morning.

I look like an idiot in love, I know it. Trouble is, I just can't seem to stop.

Last night keeps playing in my mind. The touch of her smooth skin against mine, her sweet scent driving me wild, the feminine curves of her body—a body that was made to fit mine—making my fingers tingle and my cock rise even now.

And finally, her company. Just her company. The reason I feel human again, the reason I feel happy to be alive, the reason I feel at all.

Jesus, you have it bad, Sebastian. You have it really bad.

"That good, huh?" Ryan asks as he pulls out of the driveway, a wry smile still stretching his lips, making me laugh, even if I look away to avoid his eyes.

Yeah, that good, Ryan. But there's no need to tell you that. It's written all over my face.

"We'll need to leave the office earlier today," I tell him, purposely changing the subject. "So can we please focus and stop fucking around? We'll have to get started as soon as we get there."

"OK, OK. I'll go and get us some breakfast then. We can have it in your office, how's that?"

"Actually, that's a great idea, thank you." I check my emails to get a head-start.

"It's the least I can do, boss," Ryan says, and my eyes rise to meet his. He never calls me 'boss'. Ever. Unless ... "I figure if you're leaving earlier today, maybe you didn't get enough smooching time with Alice after all. But don't you worry," he says in a sickly-sweet voice. "I'll make sure you get plenty of it tonight."

Yeah ... unless he's pulling my chain. The idiot.

"Fucking hilarious," I go to say, but then his lips pucker and he starts making these kissing noises at the mirror, and I can't help it, I burst out laughing with him. Stupid git.

"The fuck, man?" I punch his shoulder from the back. "How old are you? Eight? I swear, I'm going to sack you."

"Yeah, you won't, though. You love me way too much to sack me. Enough to smooch with me, I reckon. Trouble is, you know I'd kick your ass if you tried."

"Watch it, fucker," I growl, punching his shoulder again, both of us still laughing like idiots. Just like we used to when we were kids.

It feels good. It feels right, this happiness. This feeling of belonging exactly where I am. Of love freeing me from within, clearing away my doubts, my burdens, my self-hatred, letting me finally be me.

And once again, I have to thank Alice. Her patience, her kindness, her heart.

She's the one who freed me. Who stripped me of my defences. Who broke away my walls and made me finally see sense.

Who made me put all the cynicism and negativity I had in my heart behind me, and gave me the strength to start making a real life for myself. A life where I get to have her, her love, her innocence ... her light cancelling out my darkness.

She's good. Too good for me, that's for sure. Too good for this world.

Which reminds me. "Alice invited her new friend over again," I say to Ryan, and he and I exchange a more serious look in the rear-view mirror.

He knows I'm concerned about this. I want—no, need—this woman checked like yesterday. I told him so late last night when I texted him.

Ryan frowns as I continue. "Apparently they're going shopping and then doing some baking back at the house. So I thought maybe it's time we meet this mystery woman ourselves."

"Yeah, Michael mentioned something along those lines when I spoke to him. And before you ask, I already gave him shit about not doing a background check. He knows better than that. Unfortunately, he still didn't have her surname, otherwise I would've gotten the ball rolling myself."

I nod, pinching the bridge of my nose, and then sigh. "Well, we'll need to get it today. I'm not comfortable with a total stranger hanging around Alice."

"Me neither, man. Me neither. Not when our Alice is so innocent. So kind."

I smile at Ryan's choice of words, knowing he truly sees Alice as family now. And to my surprise, no jealousy overcomes me, not when I can see how precious she's become to all of us.

"We'll get her details today, trust me," he reassures me.

"Just tell Michael she's not to go inside the house or anywhere near Alice without providing him with her surname." I bite my thumb as I think. "Maybe even some photo ID for good measure. Oh, and we'll have to pretend I came home earlier to surprise Alice. Apparently, this Anna girl is shy, and Alice is concerned she'll feel uncomfortable knowing I'll join them."

"I'll call Michael to let him know." Ryan smiles wickedly. "And don't worry, I'll keep him on his toes after yesterday."

"Just make sure he stays close at all times. I don't want to upset Alice, but I won't take any risks as far as her safety is concerned."

"We'll keep her safe, Sebastian. I promise. Just let me do my job."

"We can't take any chances, Ryan. She's too gentle a soul. She wouldn't know if she was being taken advantage of, not until it's too late, and I'm not about to let that happen. Not on my watch."

"She's smart too. And tough, you know that."

I nod. "I do." My little Alice may be innocent, but she's not naive. She never was. "Still, better safe than sorry."

Our gazes meet, an agreement passing between us before I go back to checking my emails on my phone.

I can't concentrate, though. Not when Ryan keeps sucking on his lower lip, his eyes flicking to the rear-view mirror every couple of seconds to look at me. Telling me something's wrong with this picture. "What? What is it?" I ask.

"We haven't heard from the psycho bitch in a while. Not since your wedding, anyway. I don't know. It makes me uneasy." He scratches his head, and I frown. "It's just a feeling, but my gut keeps telling me something's wrong, that she must be lurking around, waiting in the shadows to strike."

"You think she'd send someone to befriend Alice? Get close to her just to harm her?"

"It's a possibility. Definitely something we should consider."

I hadn't even thought about the crazy bitch, but now that Ryan mentioned her, I can think of nothing else. What if it's her? What if she's out to get blood?

"At least we know the girl isn't the bitch herself," Ryan continues, and I force my attention back to him. "Michael's description doesn't match her features—that's something, I guess."

"Did you show him her picture?"

"Yeah, and he said they look different, thank God. Different hair colour, different eyes, even skin tone, and of course this girl's pregnant. As pregnant as Alice. The real deal." His eyes flick back to the mirror. To me. "Still, Anna could be friends with the slut or be on her payroll to get close to your wife."

"Fuck," I breathe out as fear grips me by the throat. "Ryan, whatever this is, we find out today. In the meantime, Michael can't leave Alice's side."

"You know you should tell her, right? Alice is smart, but if she's not aware of any threats it makes her more vulnerable, easier to get to. You're putting her more at risk by keeping her in the dark."

I sigh. He's right. I should've told her. I should've told her from the start, but I was too scared of her reaction. Still am.

"I'll tell her tonight," I finally agree, and he nods in that familiar, quiet way of his that always makes me smile.

I just hope we can overcome this. That Alice won't be so disgusted with me or my past that she'll run out screaming, never wanting to see me again.

Who am I kidding? I wouldn't want to see me again.

* * *

The rest of the day is a whirlwind of back-to-back meetings, phone calls, and endless problems coming my way. It's so bad, Luke ends up offering to take my place at the last meeting, so I'm able to leave earlier than I initially planned.

I think I was driving him crazy, anyway. I'm worried. Really worried. Especially since the external cameras at the house haven't picked up this girl's face and Ryan still hasn't managed to find out a single thing about her. Even after Michael got her full name—Anna Morley—and date of birth when Anna first arrived at the house.

It's mind-boggling, but nothing has come up, no information whatsoever.

And it's winding me up, eating at my insides, until Luke pushes me out of the office, telling me that if this was his girl, he wouldn't have come to work today—no, he'd personally be following and watching her like a hawk with his own bodyguard.

I smile, 'cause that sounds a bit extreme. But, hey, that's Luke for you. Intense, overprotective, and over-caring, even when you don't want him to be.

However, this time, I fear he may be right. And if any of our concerns are true ... fuck, I almost wish I was as crazy as he is.

Problem is, I'm also trying to be considerate. I'm afraid I might be overreacting, behaving too much like the caveman Alice has complained about in the past. It's something that upset her then, and I'm sure will upset her now. So I'm really giving it my all here not to act like an asshole.

"I'll call Michael. We should let him know we're almost there," Ryan says from his place at the wheel, startling me out of my thoughts. We're on our way home now, back in the SUV. "Sebastian, it will be OK. The rest of the security detail has been shadowing them all day and they're parked just outside the house if Michael needs them."

I nod. "Put him on speaker."

"Hello." Michael's joyous voice comes through the speakers in the SUV.

"Hey, Michael, we're almost at the house. How's everything?" Ryan asks.

"Good. The girls are in the kitchen now and having a great time. It's been a really good day so far."

"Where are you? Are they near?" I ask.

"No, I stepped into the study to take your call. Oh, and I remembered something Anna told us yesterday. She said she's a patient of Mr Thomas. I forgot to tell you, Ryan, sorry."

I close my eyes, the lump in my throat swelling so much it almost stops me from speaking. There's no obstetrician with that name at the hospital. "Are you sure that's the name she said?"

"Positive. I kinda had to put some pressure on her to tell us. Got a death stare from Alice and everything."

I don't have a good feeling about this. Why would anyone lie about their doctor's name? "Michael, go to my desk and open the first drawer on the right. You'll find a hard-copy list of all the obstetricians that work at the hospital. Tell me if you see that name in there," I instruct.

"We're almost to the house, Sebastian. She'll be fine," Ryan says, looking regretfully over his shoulder at me.

"Fuck, I don't see the name," Michael states. "I'm not liking this. I'm going back to the kitchen."

"Stay glued to Alice," Ryan orders. "And don't forget to be nice to Anna. We don't want her suspecting that we know anything."

"Yeah, don't worry. I'm going ..." Suddenly there's a hiss, then a groan and a loud thump on the line followed by deadly silence.

My eyes fly to Ryan, and he curses under his breath, then puts a finger to his lips to silence me and disconnects the call.

What the fuck just happened?

My head begins to spin. "Fuck, fuck, fuck," I yell, punching the door repeatedly. "Fucking step on it! Now!" I scream, going out of my mind with worry, rage, fear, terrified of whatever punishment the universe has decided to throw at me.

My body begins to shake, trembling so bad my teeth clatter, so I clench them instead. I'm so out of my depth here, I can't help but lose control for a minute. I hold my head in my hands.

Please, God, please don't let anything happen to my babies. Please, please, please. Oh, God, Alice.

"Anna doesn't know we're close. She doesn't even know we're coming," Ryan says. "Michael didn't say anything to give us away, even if she was listening in. She thinks she has time. That will work to our advantage."

"What does this bitch want?" I sneer, covering my face and rubbing at my eyes as a migraine starts to form. "I swear, if she touches one hair on my wife's head, I'll kill her. I don't give a fuck that she's pregnant. I'll fucking end her."

"Sebastian, listen to me," Ryan says over my voice. "We're two minutes away. We need a plan." I nod, sucking in precious air as our eyes find each other's in the mirror. "I don't want to go in guns blazing. So let's keep this just between us. Just us two, and keep the bodyguards out. Last thing we need is to spook this woman into losing her shit, especially with Alice in there."

I nod again. He's right. We have the ability to remain calm and in control under the worst circumstances. We've proved it in the past. So it'll be just the two of us, Ryan and I, against whoever this is. I just hope we're not too late.

"Good, I'll call the others and let them know," he says. "They'll stand down until we get there. Sebastian, we got this."

* * *

As I walk into the kitchen, I see Alice sitting stiffly on a chair. Tears are running down her pale cheeks and her arms are wrapped protectively around her belly. She's scared, my poor baby, but otherwise unharmed, and I can breathe better already.

I'm here, baby. I'm here. Everything's going to be OK.

Her eyes grow big the moment she sees me, a flash of hope shining in them. I almost smile.

She's strong, my girl. Stronger than I ever gave her credit for.

A fake strap-on baby bump and a dark wig lie on the table before her. There's also a syringe and different-coloured vials next to it, and standing behind her ... No! Fuck, no!

Cassandra.

Her eyes are brown instead of blue and her skin looks darker, like she's wearing some kind of heavy-duty makeup, but it's her.

My stomach turns and I almost puke my guts out right then and there. The anger and hatred I have for this woman makes me want to kill her with my bare hands.

"What is the meaning of this? What are you doing here?" My whole world is being threatened, yet my voice is steady when I speak, as cold and in control as ever. As harsh and unforgiving.

Cassandra's lower lip trembles. "She tried to steal you from me. She bewitched you. I'm only taking back what's mine."

The kitchen knife glints then as it catches the light, and I freeze, panic taking over my senses when Cassandra presses it harder against Alice's side.

At the same time, I notice Alice's hand as she twists it, moving a pencil into an upward stabbing position before she looks me directly in the eyes.

Oh, God, I'm going to lose them. I'm going to lose the woman I love, my unborn child still growing inside her. My worst nightmare and fear all rolled into one.

I take a deep breath. I've got to calm down. One wrong move and the bitch goes for Alice's belly, taking from me the two beings I love most in the world.

And I can't let that happen.

I won't let that happen. I'll die first. They're all that matters. They're all I have, and I'll fucking die to protect them.

I look at Alice, subtly shaking my head no. Silently begging her to do nothing and sit tight. I've got you, baby. I've got you.

"Cassandra ..." I put some warmth into my tone, giving her the sexy, slow smile that has landed more women in my lap than I can count. "We both know what you really want, so why don't we go into my office and talk? I'm sure we can work something out."

The involuntary gasp she releases tells me she was not expecting this, and for a moment she's lost for words, her hands shaking.

This is good. I'm throwing her off.

Alice on the other hand looks murderous, eyes narrowed and ready to shoot daggers at me. She's not liking my tactic. Not one bit. And even if it's all pretend and I'm doing it to save us, I can't say I blame her. I'd feel exactly the same.

Cassandra smiles. "You still want me, don't you? I knew it." Delusional bitch. Then her lips twitch and just as quick her expression is twisting in anger. "Fucking slut!" she snarls beside Alice's ear, pulling on her hair until Alice releases an ear-splitting scream. "You could've ruined everything, getting between us like that. Stealing him from me."

I stare at the knife, my muscles wound up so tight they ache. "Cassandra," I say, but she ignores me and continues with her babble.

"You know, at first I thought the bitch was tricking you," she says, a scowl disfiguring her face, "but now I know she really is pregnant with your child."

I can see Ryan in my peripheral vision as he goes around the conservatory and comes through the kitchen's back door, moving silently as he approaches Cassandra from behind.

Alice squeezes her eyes shut as if she can't take another second of this, more tears rolling down her face and chest as her arms tighten around her bump.

I love you so much, baby. Just hang in there a little longer. Please.

"You're right. I made a terrible mistake, and I'm sorry," I say, picking up where Cassandra left off. "But in my defence, I didn't know what I was doing. I guess how I felt about you scared me. I've changed, I promise. And I won't be making the same mistake again."

"Oh, darling, that makes me so happy. You don't know how many times I wished you'd say that," she gushes, her voice sweet again.

I inhale deeply. "I've also missed you. Missed being alone with you. But you have to give me that knife before we can even attempt alone time, Cassandra. Don't want my guards to get all angsty over nothing, now, do we?"

"Knife?" She lifts the knife to look at it as if she'd forgotten it was there. "I don't think so. I have … I have to kill her, Sebastian. Don't you see? I just have to—"

Turns out that's enough of a distraction as Ryan comes up behind her, reaches for her wrist and, grabbing it in a bone-breaking grip, shakes it until the knife hits the floor.

Cassandra screams, struggling to no avail, howling profanities and threats as he twists her arm around, presses it against her back and, grabbing her by the throat, finally drags her away.

Thank fuck! I release the breath I was holding, my chest heavy and my head spinning as I move towards Alice lightning fast. The need to hold her and kiss her is almost unbearable as I kneel beside her and wrap her protectively in my arms.

God, I could've lost her today. Tears threaten and I hold her as tightly as I can, the force of our embrace so strong, so powerful, so full of love it takes me a whole minute to find my voice again. "I'm sorry. I'm so sorry, baby girl. Are you OK? Did she hurt you?" I manage to push past the lump in my throat.

Alice shakes her head, her tiny little fists holding onto my shirt as she sobs into my chest.

It breaks my heart. And again, I'm sorry. So sorry she had to go through something like this. Sorry I was such a cold, miserable bastard in the past. Sorry I was so fucked up then, I allowed this crazy woman to come into our lives.

"She didn't hurt me. I'm OK."

"And the baby?"

She shakes her head again. "The baby is fine. We're both fine ... I think."

Burying my face in her hair, I breathe in her scent before exhaling a sigh of relief. "I'm so sorry, sweetheart. I'm so sorry," I tell her again and again, my throat constricting the whole time I open my mouth to speak.

"Who is she, Sebastian?" Alice finally asks, pushing into my chest to look at me.

I shake my head, but loosen my hold a little, giving her some space, although not fully releasing her. I can't. I need to feel her, reassure myself that she's real, that she wasn't taken from me.

Still, shame eats at me when she looks straight into my eyes. Shit.

I look away. "I slept with her before coming back from Paris," I push out, regretting that night forever. "It was just the one time, just like the others. But also a terrible mistake."

God, how I wish I didn't have to tell Alice any of this. My eyes close and I inhale deeply. "She was, I don't know, behaving oddly right after we were done, and then downright unstable when I asked her to leave. Acting like we were together or something. Like we were a couple just having a row. It was disconcerting, to say the least." I frown as I remember.

I chance a glimpse at Alice. She's quiet, my girl, real quiet, but at least she's still listening to me.

"When I came back, she started showing up here, at the office, all the places I was taking you with me." I sigh. "Then it was just you she was after. At one point it got so bad, she even tried to break in."

Alice's jaw drops and her eyes widen as she looks up at me. She's in shock, I think.

"That's also when we decided to involve the police," I continue. "We kept reporting her, and after she crashed our wedding, I threatened her and she finally stopped, disappeared off the face of the earth, and we believed that was the end of it." I take a deep breath, trying to calm myself down as I slowly release it. "And, Alice, baby, I know I should've told you. I know I should've been honest with you, but I was scared you wouldn't forgive me. That you wouldn't want to look at me again."

Alice's face is impassive as she holds my eyes. "So instead, you decided to keep me in the dark. To keep yet another secret from me. Something you promised, you swore you wouldn't do."

"I'm sorry." My head drops in shame. "I'm so sorry, sweetheart. It was wrong of me. I should've told you. I ..."

"Damn right you should've told me. I would've been more careful if I'd known, not to mention smart. And I would have forgiven you, you big dope. It's not like you could possibly have known she'd turn out like this."

I swallow hard. "I knew she wasn't just another regular girl. I knew there was something wrong with her, and that's precisely why I chose her." I cringe at how this is going to sound. "Back then, she was just my type. Fake, shallow, unhinged, greedy enough to try to use me and stupid enough to get used by me." Alice goes quiet again, and I begin to panic. "And I know I sound like a right asshole, a bastard really, but the truth is ... I was afraid. Afraid I'd fall in love one day. Afraid I'd meet someone wonderful and become trapped by them—by marriage, kids, by the promise of forever when I was so sure forever didn't exist."

"God, that's awful. Just awful, Sebastian," she whispers, struggling to get free, but I don't let her go. I can't. I'm afraid she'll disappear on me. "Why are you with me then? Why are you here?"

"Because I love you," I rasp. "Because one day I met that wonderful someone I was so afraid of, only to realise I shouldn't have been afraid at all. In fact, I should've been searching for her." I press my forehead to hers, instantly calming my racing heart. "Alice, don't you see? You make me whole. You and this baby mean everything to me. And even if this only lasts long enough to tear me open and cut out my heart, so be it. I'd rather have you and lose you than not have you in my life at all."

"But you didn't want this. You didn't want us. What if you end up regretting me? Resenting your life? What if this becomes too much?"

"Never. That will never happen, you hear me? In fact, my only regret is that I didn't meet you sooner. Every day we spent apart feels like a waste of time. Time we could've had together." I smile, pulling her close. "You tipped my whole world upside down, Mrs Hunter. I didn't have a fighting chance. Not when I saw this tight little ass of yours up in the air"—I give her bum a good squeeze—"and heard you cooing at that stupid computer from under your desk."

She frowns, and then bites her lower lip, and I know she's trying to stop a smile. And although it's a small one, I'll take it. Any smile is better than none. "Always the charmer, aren't you?" she asks.

"What can I say? I was done for before I even saw your beautiful face," I joke, and she finally laughs.

I exhale and relax a little. Especially when I hold her even closer, and she doesn't resist.

"Why didn't you want to fall in love, Sebastian?" she asks after a while, and I sigh. "Is it because of your mum?" she guesses, but I don't reply. I can't. "Why can't you let go of the pain? Why do you feel so much guilt, Sebastian? It's not normal. She's been gone for years."

I shake my head, not wanting to discuss it. Not wanting to talk about any of this.

"Sebastian, please. We have to talk. You have to tell me—"

"Because I was in the damn car with her, OK?" I whisper-shout. My eyes go back to hers, and I release the shaky breath I was holding. "Because I survived and she didn't."

Alice gasps, covering her mouth with one hand, and my face screws up in pain. "Losing her ... it broke something inside me. And after seeing my dad struggle to even get out of bed—his suffering so bad it almost destroyed him, almost destroyed us—I didn't want the same for me. I didn't think I could handle any more pain."

She nods, tears sliding down her face. "You've been hiding, haven't you, my love?" she asks, cupping my cheek.

I close my eyes at her tender touch. "Yes." I swallow hard. "But you found me."

She has. She truly has.

And now only she can see the real me, reach into my dark heart and make it beat. Because my heart beats only for her. For this tiny, beautiful girl who keeps saving me at every turn.

Holding her neck with one hand, I bend and kiss my wife, tasting every part, every nuance of the sweet flavour of her mouth, letting her wash over me, cleanse me of my self-hatred and my sins, of the guilt still eating at me.

"Can you forgive me?" I ask.

"Always," she whispers into my lips. "I'll always forgive you, Sebastian. But this is about more than just forgiveness. This is about trust, and unfortunately you keep betraying mine." Her eyes fill with even more tears. "I just don't know where we can go from here."

Fearful, I begin to stutter. "Alice, please ..."

At the sound of someone clearing their throat, we both turn our heads to the side.

"Cassandra's tied up in the security room, and the police and paramedics are on their way," Ryan informs us.

"And Michael? Is he OK?" Alice asks.

"I found him passed out in the study and placed him in the recovery position. I think the bitch drugged him, but we won't know for sure until help arrives. He'll be all right, though, he's a tough guy."

Alice nods, her trembling hand covering her mouth. She's pale, paler than I've ever seen her. And that's when my worry escalates. "We need to go to the hospital. We need to make sure you and the baby are all right," I insist, and to my surprise she just nods again, her expression grim.

Five minutes later, Ms Roberts is nothing but accommodating when I make the call to her private number, agreeing to fit us in straight away and give Alice a complete check-up, including bloods and an ultrasound.

To be honest, I think she's doing it more for my sake than Alice's. I know I'm behaving like a madman. But who can blame me? I almost lost my wife and baby today.

I'm still on the phone when Alice groans and bends over, hugging her bump. "Alice, what's wrong? What's the matter, sweetheart?"

"I don't know," she cries. "It hurts, it hurts really bad. Oh, God, my baby. Please, not my baby."

Helping Alice to the sofa, I get her to lie down and describe what's happening to Ms Roberts, who in turn instructs me to stay on the line, wait for the paramedics, and ask them to take us to her as soon as they arrive. "I think the baby might be coming, Mr Hunter," Ms Roberts says in a tight, urgent voice, making all kinds of alarm bells go off in my head.

Fuck! I run my shaky fingers through my hair. It's too soon, way too soon for the baby to arrive, and I can't help but wonder if this is it. If this is the moment I've been dreading all my life.

If this is the moment I lose them ... and, like my dad, I have to pretend to survive.

Chapter 29

Sebastian

As it turns out, Ms Roberts is right, and Alice is indeed going into labour. So it's nothing short of a miracle the paramedics are already on their way.

Thank God for Ryan and his quick thinking, that's all I'll say. That guy can keep a cool head when most men just crumble and break. Myself included.

I can't even talk to the authorities when they get to the house. Too focused on Alice. Too scared to make sense. Once again it's Ryan who steps in, assisting the police with their questions and investigation until they finally make the arrest—taking that she-devil into custody and once and for all out of our lives.

As for Alice, she's never looked so small or so frightened, her fragile form curled and racked with so much pain she looks like she's going out of her mind with fear.

"It's too soon, Sebastian. It's too soon," she keeps saying. Her moans and cries turning into prayers as the paramedics rush us into the ambulance and shoot out of the driveway. "Please, God. Please not my baby. Please don't take my baby away."

My heart bleeds as I hold her, murmuring to her the entire time they drive us like maniacs to the hospital. My own fear taking a back seat as this basic, most primal need to protect her takes over my senses, letting me be her rock, her shelter whilst I pretty much crumble inside and, of course, shout and curse at everyone else like a madman. Starting with the paramedics and continuing with the nurses when we finally arrive. It's so bad, I'm sure our obstetrician has to stop herself from hitting me a few times.

"You need to calm down, Mr Hunter. Alice is doing fine now, and the baby's just coming a little earlier, that's all," she says as soon as she finishes checking Alice's vitals and we hear the baby's heartbeat.

Caroline, our midwife, is also there, reassuring us. Calming Alice and I down all through the waiting and the hard times, up to the point where Alice is ready to push, her contractions at an all-time high.

Then, as Caroline had previously explained, it's indeed a fast ride, with me feeling powerless the whole time. Alice is amazing, though. My strong and beautiful wife who's doing everything she can to deliver our baby safely, even when all I can see is agony in her stunning grey eyes.

She was almost fully dilated when we arrived, so there are no painkillers or injections they can give her. News she took pretty well, since that's what she originally discussed and arranged with Ms Roberts as part of the birth plan.

As for me, that's when my brave façade fell and I finally cracked, dry-retching and vomiting a few times until I had nothing left in me. Nerves and fear making me so sick, I thought I might pass out.

If I could, I'd take her place. Gladly go through the whole thing if it meant not seeing her in pain. But that's not how these things work, and the worst is yet to come, as I'm about to find out.

"Grab onto her shoulders," Caroline shouts over Alice's screams. "Now pull up her right knee to help her bear down," she instructs, pulling Alice's left knee up.

I follow her lead, even if I'm shaking like a leaf.

"Alice, we're going to need you to push now, honey. You can do this. We'll be with you every step of the way."

"You're doing so good, Alice. Just listen to what Caroline and I say," Ms Roberts instructs.

Alice nods, crying so much, though, it feels like I'm being stabbed in the heart. Her perfect face covered in sweat and tears as she screams and yells her little lungs out.

"I love you so much, baby. You're doing so well," I keep murmuring into her ear, encouraging her every single time she bears down and tries to push our baby out. "Almost there, sweetheart. You're almost there." I kiss her lips and her wet brow.

I myself am drenched in my own sweat and both our tears. My heart breaking as for the longest time, Alice's laboured breathing and grunts are the only sounds in that room. And then ...

Then it happens. The most beautiful sound in the world.

Our baby cries.

"Congratulations, you have a beautiful baby girl!" Ms Roberts announces as she and the nurses examine and clean up the baby. "She's doing well, and her vitals are good, so you've nothing to worry about."

I close my eyes, thanking God. I feel faint. The sheer happiness and relief rushing through me in this moment is indescribable. And the love I have for such a tiny being is so strong, so deep, I can feel it in my bones.

It means everything now. She means everything, right alongside her mother. Alice, my eternal love, my soulmate.

Tears fall down my cheeks as I embrace Alice and hold onto her tight, kissing her passionately, kissing her gently, kissing her over and over again as we both laugh and cry at the same time.

"Thank you. Thank you so much, sweetheart," I keep murmuring as she sobs into my mouth. "I love you so much. I love you and our baby so much."

Our baby. Our baby. It still sounds surreal. We've made a perfect, healthy little baby, and now she's here.

Then Caroline places the little bundle on Alice's chest, and we melt all over again. She's tiny, the tiniest baby I've ever seen. Her head is the size of an orange, and her body so little she looks like a doll.

Alice kisses her forehead and caresses her cheek with a shaky finger, and a lump forms in my throat. My eyes watering all over again as I marvel at it all, my mind still reeling at the perfect little human we've made and brought into this world. At my wonderful wife, who I know I'll never deserve. At our life together and our happiness so far.

And for the first time, I understand. I understand my purpose in life now that this little girl is here.

For as long as I live my job is to protect her, to protect her mother. I'll never get lost again. I'm finally on the right path, and I'll be damned if I ain't gonna stick to it.

Reaching out, I gently touch my daughter's tiny hand with my index finger. She's so small. Such a defenceless and fragile little thing. An innocent.

And in that moment, despite the sweetness of it all and the beauty of the emotions I'm experiencing, I'm sure of two things.

One—I'll kill without hesitation to protect my wife and daughter.

And two—I'll lay down my life for either of them.

Too soon, though, Ms Roberts is interrupting our little moment. Telling us Alice still has to push the placenta out and also needs stitches.

"Now, if Daddy could hold the baby, we'll be finished with Mummy in no time," she says, looking at me.

So I get up, quickly kiss both my wife's and baby's foreheads and pick the little one up, wonder washing over me as I sit back on a chair by Alice's side and finally hold our daughter in my arms.

A magical moment if there ever was one.

A magical, picture-perfect moment right before hell descends on us.

* * *

"Mr Hunter." Caroline and her calm voice are trying to pierce through the white noise in my head. But I can hardly hear her. "Mr Hunter, look at me," she repeats as I shake my head.

My eyes are glued to my wife's, watching as they turn dull and out of focus, her eyelids fluttering closed as she loses the battle with death.

The previously calm and professional staff begins shouting, moving in a frenzy around Alice under Ms Roberts' rule.

"She's haemorrhaging!"

"Quick, she's losing consciousness!"

"Get him out of here!"

The words keep bouncing off the walls, making my head spin, and once again Caroline is there. "Mr Hunter, I'm going to take the baby now," she says, lifting my screaming daughter from my arms and passing her to another midwife. "Don't worry. That's Jenna, one of our best. She'll look after the little one," she assures me, tugging on my arm as she tries to get me to stand.

I rip my arm away from her.

"Alice," I bellow, my voice drowning out all the other noises in the room. The numbness that until now had choked me disappears, replaced by chaos and fear. So much fear. "Help her. Please help her. Do something!"

No, dear God, no. Don't take my Alice. Don't take my love from me.

I hug her fragile frame, sobbing and screaming uncontrollably right up to the point where I feel a prick in my neck and everything turns dark.

* * *

When I come to, I'm no longer in the delivery room. I'm in the private bedroom where Alice and I were admitted when we arrived. Where she's supposed to be resting after delivering the baby. Our baby.

"Alice," I murmur, looking around. "Alice."

"They're still working on her, Mr Hunter," a calm voice says from my left-hand side.

A young nurse smiles at me as she continues to check my drip. "Don't worry, she's in good hands. They deal with this type of complication all the time."

"What type of complication?" I croak, my mouth dry like the desert.

"She was haemorrhaging," she replies, pouring water into a cup before adding a straw and holding it to my mouth. I drink greedily, my head still spinning from whatever they injected me with. "That sometimes happens when women deliver the placenta. The uterus stops contracting and blood vessels bleed freely if not sealed or tied. That's what they're doing at the moment."

"So she's having surgery."

The nurse looks at me with pity in her eyes. "I'm afraid so, Mr Hunter. It was the only way to stop the bleeding."

I huff out a sigh. "I see. And my daughter?"

"She's doing well and has already had a couple of feeds. We don't want her overtired when Mummy offers her the breast." The nurse takes my temperature and then my blood pressure. "In the meantime, I'm gonna ask you to stay here. You'll have more privacy to recover, and Alice will be brought here as soon as she's stable enough."

Right, not to mention it'll be easier to control and sedate me again if push comes to shove.

I nod. There's no point pretending they aren't right anyway. Besides, if they do have to drug me that can only mean one thing. I shiver, my mind refusing to even go there.

God help me, I'd probably welcome the drugs then.

"Good. Now, this is the buzzer here," she says, placing a remote on the bed. "Press it if you need me. My name's Sarah, by the way."

With another pitying look, she turns and finally leaves.

Alice. I close my eyes, letting the first of many tears roll down my temples. The last memory I have of her haunting me to no end.

Please, God, don't let it be the end. Please. It will crush me. I won't survive.

It doesn't matter if she never forgives me. It doesn't even matter if she never takes me back. All that matters is that she's OK. That she and the baby make it. I'll never ask for anything again.

I cover my face with my hands.

Never in my life have I ever felt so afraid, so terrified. Not when my mum died. Not when my dad's grief got so bad it felt as if we'd lost him as well.

Not even when my own grief changed me and froze me and destroyed the happy, carefree boy I once was.

Minutes pass where I allow myself to wallow in my pain. To feel, to cry. To cleanse my soul of any remaining clutter and filth from the past.

I won't let it hurt my future again. I won't let it hurt my life.

Because that's what Alice has become—my future, my life— and I'll never keep anything from her again.

I promise, baby. No more walls. No more secrets. From now on I will trust you with my heart.

Turning to my side, I get up and pull the cannula out. I can't stay still any longer. I have to do something.

Despite the throbbing headache and the needles stabbing at my eyes, I make my way into the adjacent bathroom where I empty my stomach of the little water I've drunk, dry-retching and heaving for the longest time until I've nothing left in me. Not even tears.

My nightmare is real after all. And I woke up right in the middle of it.

My therapist will be proud, though. I haven't broken down completely, and I've been dealing with my feelings and emotions a lot better than in any of our sessions.

After splashing some water on my face and brushing my teeth with the complementary stuff on the sink, I go back into the bedroom and outside only to be ushered back in. I pace the floor relentlessly as I wait for news, tearing at my hair.

An hour passes. An hour and one minute. Two minutes. Three ... and I can't wait any more. I'm out of desperate prayers, out of promises. And the bedroom's so eerily quiet it's making me feel insane.

I open the door and step out into an equally quiet corridor that leads straight into a luxurious ward. Even the swankiness of the place is adding to my stress. I've always found the hotel vibes more reassuring than the harsh clinical settings, but it doesn't offer me an ounce of comfort now.

I rub at my eyes, frustrated. And to think it had all seemed so nice when Alice was here. The fancy artwork, the plants, the fresh flowers everywhere. Everything designed to look expensive from the medical equipment to the furnishings to the fucking stone tiles on the floor.

At least I can do this, I remember thinking. At least I can provide them with the best possible care.

Fuck!

"Any news?" I ask the nurse sitting at the nursing station, as I've been doing nonstop for the past hour or so.

She shakes her head, her smile sad as her eyes meet mine above her computer screen. "Not yet, I'm afraid."

"Well, can you call them? Is there someone who can go check?" I ask, finally losing my temper.

"Mr Hunter, please." Sarah's voice comes from behind me as the nurse in front of me visibly relaxes, her eyes still fixed on mine. "Come on, let me take you back to your room."

Are they afraid of me? Do they think I'd harm them?

I had to be sedated and brought up here, didn't I? So who can blame them for being scared now?

Realising this, I nod to the nurse, silently turn on my heels, and let Sarah shepherd me back to my and Alice's room.

"Is there anything I can bring you?" she asks as I go in.

I shake my head. I've no more words. No more patience.

"Just try to stay calm, Mr Hunter. They're doing everything they can to help your wife."

I stare at her, my eyes burning. With a sigh, she turns and is just about to close the door behind her when the door flies open again and the nurse from the nursing station comes rushing in.

"They're moving your wife to the recovery room, Mr Hunter. She's stable and Ms Roberts is on her way up to see you now."

Her misty eyes meet mine and I swear my knees give out.

Alice!

Chapter 30

Sebastian

Three months. It's been three whole months since Lily was born, and she keeps getting stronger every day. Not to mention cleverer, the little munchkin, and just as beautiful as her mum.

I swallow hard, my throat constricting the entire time I look at my daughter's face.

She just looks so much like Alice. The same delicate facial features, the same angelic expressions, the same smile that cuts through my heart every single day.

As if she can sense my melancholy, her tiny hand shoots out and grabs hold of my finger, making me smile. She gurgles, and my smile grows wider, the usual feelings of love and elation overfilling my chest.

My flesh and blood. A mix of Alice and I together wrapped in a tiny little bundle of joy. A testament to our love.

Lily gurgles again, and I laugh, watching as milk dribbles out of the corners of her mouth.

She's feeding well, my little princess, and all the time too. So much so, I swear the kid probably dreams about boobs. Why else would she smile so much during naptime, hey?

I snort. I almost want to say she's more obsessed than I am, but I know that's not true.

"What's so funny?" Alice asks as she rocks Lily back and forth, a soft smile stretching over her lips.

We're all in the nursery, the room just across from ours. We had it remodelled and redecorated just before Alice gave birth to Lily, thank God.

And now, painted in a soft grey to go with the white furniture and the pastel-pink furnishings—which, according to Alice, are a must-have if your baby is a girl—it's the warmest and cosiest room in the house.

And, of course, now it's also my favourite.

Sitting on the light-grey ottoman, I watch as she breastfeeds Lily in a matching rocking chair by the window. She looks stunning in the sunlight. Ethereal. Unreal. And I can't help but stare at her like the lovesick puppy I've become.

"Just our daughter's obsession with boobs," I reply, a sly smile forming on my face as I let my eyes drop down slowly to Alice's breasts, her hard nipples.

Christ, I'm such a deviant.

Alice giggles as she tenderly pets Lily's head. "You think she's obsessing now? Wait till she's thirteen and wants to grow boobs of her own to impress the boys."

I make a face. "Don't. I'll end up locking her in her room until she's thirty."

"You know I won't let you."

"Guess I'll be buying a hunting rifle and a flaying knife, then," I threaten, half-joking, half-not.

Alice laughs out loud. "You'll do no such thing. Besides, not all girls turn hormone-crazy and start chasing the boys. I for one was a late bloomer, wasn't I?"

She was, my little thing. And that's exactly why I have to be even more careful with our girl.

She's too much like her mother, too similar, too sweet. An exact copy of Alice.

"Oh, I'm not concerned about Lily's hormones," I say. "It's the fucking boys I'm worried about. She already looks so much like you. I'm sure she'll be just as gorgeous as you are."

I groan, my lips pressed in a tight line right up to the point where Alice pinches my pectoral.

My mouth drops open in feigned shock. "Ow," I cry, trying to continue the charade, but then our eyes clash and I burst out laughing.

Alice giggles and pinches me again, and I shake my head. "I'm fucked, aren't I? Shit, I'll probably end up in prison by the time I'm forty, right after I beat the crap out of some fifteen-year-old with a bad case of acne and an eager dick."

Ding-dong.

Just then the doorbell rings and I sigh. "They're here," I murmur as I reluctantly stand.

Alice's smile is radiant when I look back down at her and bend to kiss both my girls on their foreheads, distracting Lily, who lets go of the nipple to smile back at me, milk sliding from her little mouth down to her chin.

God, she's cute. So cute, it hurts to look at her. Suddenly a huge lump takes up residence in my throat.

Yep, she's going to get anything she wants from me, the little princess. I know she is.

Who am I kidding? She already has Daddy wrapped tight around her tiny little finger, the little munchkin.

Alice wipes the milk off Lily's chin, all the while cooing at her and singing her praises. She's such a good mum, my Alice. The best I could ever hope for, and the way she is with Lily ... I shake my head, fighting back tears. God, what an amazing woman I have. What an amazing mother to our kid.

And to think I could've lost her. Lost all this. I close my eyes, willing myself to calm down.

The memory of that woman threatening Alice will forever haunt me. Not to mention what happened at the hospital later that same day, when I thought I'd lost Alice, when I thought I'd never see her, touch her, or hold her in my arms again.

I shiver. It's something I'll never be able to forget. Something I'll never be able to forgive myself for. How can I when I was the one who brought that horrible, crazy woman into our lives?

With the 'crazy' now being quite official, since Cassandra has been properly diagnosed and committed to a psychiatric hospital while she waits for her trial. The same hospital where she'll probably serve her sentence for the rest of her miserable life.

A fucking light punishment if you ask me. According to the police, she's been linked to several other open cases of stalking and harassment thanks to her prints and DNA now being in their system.

Also, the 'accidental' overdose that killed her ex-boyfriend three years ago? Yeah, not so accidental after all. Not when she was the one drugging him and poisoning his food for over a year.

And then there's Michael, of course, the poor bastard, who the paramedics brought back just in the nick of time, defibrillating the shit out of him right here at the house.

Cassandra had somehow managed to get her hands on some pretty powerful drugs—including morphine and oxycodone, plus the general anaesthetic she injected Michael with—leaving no doubt as to what her intentions had been.

At least I hope there's no doubt to a judge and twelve of her peers.

He made a full recovery, though—Michael, I mean—and at his insistence was back at work after only two weeks. And yes, he's back as Alice's guard, and no, I was not fucking happy about it.

I still think if he had taken the usual precautions none of this clusterfuck would've happened in the first place, so I was quite reluctant to give him his job back. Unfortunately for me, Alice wouldn't let it drop, going on and on about lessons learned and second chances until guilt consumed me and I finally caved in.

What can I say? I've never been a hypocrite. And I couldn't very well ask for Alice's forgiveness when I myself wouldn't give it to Michael.

He, however, has been the perfect employee ever since his return, proving to be more of an asset than a liability time and time again, and working his ass off together with James—the new bodyguard I hired for Lily—to ensure both my girls stay safe.

So, yeah, maybe Alice was right about him.

I already warned her, though. One more strike and he's out. There'll be no more second chances from me.

Stroking Lily's cheek, I watch on as she latches onto her mummy's breast again. Then I bend and kiss Alice. "I love you," I say, looking deep into her eyes. "I love you both so very much."

"I love you, Sebastian," she replies breathlessly as she pulls me in for another kiss. "We both love you so, so much." She smiles against my lips.

"Mmm, I wish we didn't have to do this family lunch thing," I grumble, and Alice's smile grows bigger.

"Don't be grumpy. And tell them I won't be long. I'm sure Lily will doze right off without you to distract her."

I smile back, stealing yet another kiss. "I'll see you in a bit then."

With one last lingering look, I finally turn and walk away, taking the stairs two at a time as I hurry down to our waiting guests.

In the back of my mind my conscience is still weighing heavy on me, though. I have a lot to prove to Alice. As her husband, as the father of her child, but most importantly as her partner. Her best friend.

Which is why I've been working harder than ever at improving myself. At going to therapy and talking to her about all the twisted shit that goes on inside my head.

No more secrets, no more walls, and hopefully with each word, with each act of love and honesty that shows her my true self, my worth, I'll be closer to restoring the trust and faith she once had in me.

I'll be closer to being the man she deserves.

* * *

"Hey, bro," Luke says as soon as his eyes land on me. "How are you?"

Everybody's here—my dad, Linda, and every single one of my brothers, already seated and waiting in the living room.

I embrace Luke first. "Hey. Good." Then Dad and Nathan. "Sorry, guys. I really meant to get the door."

"No worries from us, but if I were you, I'd steer clear of Penelope for the next hour or so." Mason pats me on the back.

"Yeah, she was pissed, man. Going on and on about nobody liking dry lamb and overcooked potatoes," Nathan adds.

Bastard. He thinks my new housekeeper's hilarious. Plus, he loves the fact that she's old, bossy, and doesn't hold anything back. Especially from me.

"And rightly so," Linda pipes in as I bend to kiss her cheeks. "Imagine if you had to cook for all of us and answer the door simultaneously," she continues, pulling me in for a hug.

I chuckle, suddenly finding myself the recipient of so much affection. "I know, I know. And I'll talk to Penelope later," I promise.

Maybe I'll buy her some flowers too. To go with my apology and all that.

She's already doing us a solid by working on a Sunday, her day off—I wouldn't want to aggravate her by behaving like an inconsiderate asshole.

"Oh, stop giving him such a hard time." Dad puts an arm over my shoulders and pulls me closer to him. "Can't you see he was with his girls?"

"Where are they anyway?" Linda asks, looking around.

"Yeah, I can't wait to see my niece. I've been missing her like crazy these past few days," Nathan gripes.

"What do you mean, 'past few days'?" Luke says in outrage. "You only just saw her on Friday. I'm the one who hasn't seen her all week."

I laugh. This is a common occurrence now—them fighting over Lily, and Alice and I trying to keep the peace.

I look over at my brothers, take in their angry expressions and deep scowls. Who would've thought they'd come to love a baby so much, hey?

"Alice will be along shortly," I say. "She's just finishing feeding Lily and putting her to bed."

They're still at it, though, the boys bickering like an old married couple with my dad joining in. Mason is the one who complains.

"Oh, man, I really wanted to see the little munchkin," he whines, and I shake my head.

"You will ... later," I tell him, narrowing my eyes at him. "When she's up and awake and not a minute before. Understand?"

Mason and Nathan have gotten into the habit of disappearing and then returning with a very sleepy and confused Lily in their arms. Which usually results in a hellish night for both Alice and I when the norm is for our baby girl to wake up once, maybe twice, for a nappy change and a feed. Other than that, she sleeps well, and so do we.

"I'm warning you, Mason. If you or Nathan wake her up just so you can hold her, so help me God, I'll have both your heads on a silver platter for Alice."

"I'll help," Ryan offers, raising his hand from his place on the couch where he's watching the news, a huge grin on his face. "Hell, I'll even bring my own axe to play."

"Oh, come on, you two," Mason pleads. "Like Nathan and I would do such a thing."

Out of the corner of my eye, I catch Nathan gesturing something to his twin, and I turn on him like the Devil himself. "I'm serious, Nathan," I warn as I point a finger at him. "Don't you fucking dare."

"What? I-I didn't do anything," he stutters, raising his palms defensively and backing away.

I keep moving with him, my finger still pointed at his face, my expression still murderous. Right before he gasps as his foot catches on the rug and he goes down with a thud, landing mostly on his ass.

The whole room turns silent as we all stare at him sprawled out on my living room floor. Then Linda and Dad burst out laughing, followed by Ryan and Luke, and after a few beats the twins and I are cracking up as well, my head thrown back as Nathan's shoulders shake with his chuckles.

And, God, it feels good. Normal. Freeing in a crazy, cathartic sort of way.

This is what families do, after all. They love and hate. They fight and yell. They joke and laugh all in the same breath. They cry with you, for you, and sometimes even because of you. But they always, always have your back. And they're always there for one another no matter what.

Leaning over Nathan, I offer him a hand and pull him back up to his feet. "Well, that's going to leave a big-ass bruise, I reckon. Pun intended, of course."

"Figured." He glares at me, and I can't help but snicker as he pulls his hand free to rub his sore behind.

Just then Linda hiccups, and we all turn around to look at her. "I'm sorry. Oh, God, I'm so sorry, boys. I didn't mean to go and get all emotional on you. I just can't believe that we're all here. That you're a dad, Sebastian, and that everyone is doing so well." Her voice breaks and she sniffles a little, still trying to hold in her tears. "It seems only yesterday you were all little boys yourselves. Cute, naughty little beasties, running around your father's place. Sebastian leading you into all kinds of mischief. And now Sebastian's a family man, and you're all grown up ... I don't know. It just hit me."

I chuckle. "Aww, Linda, we're all still the same. Definitely naughty."

"And cute," Mason adds.

"And I'm still very much leading these assholes into mischief every other day. We're just not as young any more. That's all." I put an arm around her and kiss her head.

"Hey! Speak for yourself, old man," Luke protests, pretending to punch me in the gut with me flinching, and we all laugh again, the atmosphere in the room light as Linda dries her tears.

I'm about to offer everyone a drink when a familiar surge of energy rushes through me, raising all the tiny little hairs on my body, making me turn just in time to see Alice come in.

Our eyes meet across the room, and I swear her face lights up like fucking Christmas.

"Alice, my dear!" Linda pats my cheek, a big smile on her face before she rushes off to hug Alice.

Guess Alice's face is not the only one that lights up.

Alice hugs Linda and then Dad. "What's got you all laughing like this?"

Luke smiles. "Your husband, what else?"

"Has he been making threats again? We talked about this," she mouths, and I roll my eyes to the heavens.

"It wasn't like that," I mutter, right before I have to rescue her from my savage younger brothers who clearly know nothing about respect. Or boundaries, it seems. "Hey! Hey! Put my wife down, you dogs," I bite off when Nathan lowers Alice to her feet and Mason picks her up.

Ryan chuckles and holds out his hand to Luke. The boys all snicker as I glare at them and wrap my arms around a giggling Alice.

"Possessive bastard," Luke states, before holding out a twenty, which Ryan then takes. "I thought you'd last longer than that."

"Oh, God," Alice mutters, turning crimson red. Shit, they're placing bets on how quickly I'll go ape.

"Come." I pull Alice by the hand, determined to ignore the assholes. For now, at least. "Let's go sit at the table. I'm sure the food won't be long now." Yeah, let them have their fun. I have a feeling that pretty soon I won't be the only possessive bastard around here.

"Blimey, it smells wonderful in here. No wonder I'm starving," Dad says as soon as we walk into the dining room and begin taking our usual seats.

We all agree, and Luke and I begin serving everyone their drinks. The table looks lovely, with small pink flower arrangements and various food trays along its centre.

Then the bread and cheeses start going around, as well as the prosciutto and smoked salmon canapés, and our conversation flows naturally, more so than ever now that these Sunday lunches at our place are quickly becoming a thing.

"Is this one of your recipes, Alice?" Linda asks after the main dish is finally served and we all start to dig in.

"Actually, it's Penelope's." Alice smiles sweetly before wiping her mouth. "And a special one at that, since it's a very old family recipe, dating all the way back to her great-grandmother's time. It's already been passed down through three generations of women—going on four—and if we all like it today, Penelope promised to also give it to me."

"Oh, wow. That is special," Linda gushes. "And will you use it in your next book? 'Cause, I promise, I'll be the first one in line to buy it if you do."

Alice shakes her head. "Some things are too special to sell. I think this is one of them."

I rest my arm on the back of her chair, pick up her hand and gently kiss the back of it.

Forty minutes later, dessert is served—a rich tiramisu cake accompanied with real Italian espressos, the perfect ending to our little feast. I place a kiss on Alice's temple and lean back in my chair, scanning the table as everyone I love talks, laughs, and gestures to each other, and for a moment my heart swells.

I feel blessed. Truly blessed to have each and every one of them. To have them back in my life.

And again, it's all thanks to my wonderful wife, without whom this wouldn't have been possible.

Without whom I wouldn't have made it here, happy and surrounded by family, complete and healing.

Because that's what this feels like. Like I'm healing. Like the wound that's been festering in my heart for so long has finally closed, allowing me to move on with my life. Allowing me to see clearly for the first time ever since Mum died.

A deep sense of calm descends over me as I think about her, making me smile.

It's been happening a lot lately. This feeling of joy, of happiness whenever I remember her, instead of the hurt and guilt I usually felt regarding her death.

All that pain and grief is no longer clouding my mind, making me realise just how angry I've been. Towards Mum, God, the universe, even Dad. Blaming them for her death, for my wounds. Blaming myself when in reality there was no one to blame. It wasn't anyone's fault. I was just too young, too inexperienced to understand. To deal with such loss. To deal with the weight of surviving when she did not.

Now I wonder if she's watching over us. If she's proud of me. If she likes the man I've become.

Because I do. I like the man I am now. I like the husband, the father, the brother, the son. I like the best friend.

Most of all, I like the fact that I've managed to find my way back. Because this is it. This is home.

And home is wherever my Alice is.

The End

Prologue Mel and Luke

Arthur

The phone rings twice before a husky female voice answers on the other side. My little sidekick. The brains behind this operation besides mine.

"Mum! Hi! I'm so glad you called. Just give me a second to step away from my desk, all right?"

I smile.

This is what I like about her. The woman is a natural-born actress, not to mention resourceful and cunning as fuck.

"I thought we agreed you wouldn't call me at work," she whispers as the sound of a heavy door opening and closing comes down the line. The fire escape stairs, I'm sure.

"And I thought you said you'd take care of Sebastian and the money," I growl. "Yet Sebastian is fine and so is his wife. Not to mention they keep fucking finding my money."

"I don't know what you want me to say. I did everything I could. It's not my fault Alice forgave him so quickly."

"Well, an anonymous email and siccing a crazy bitch on them was never gonna cut it, was it?" I sneer.

"No. It wasn't. Not when we didn't have the right target to begin with."

"What do you mean?"

She blows out a breath. "I mean that Sebastian was never in charge of the investigation. Luke was."

I rub my eyes. Fuck, we could've saved so much time and money if we'd only known. Still ... "You're sure?"

"Positive."

I smile slowly. Well, I guess it really is true. When a door closes, the Devil finds you a fucking crawl hole. "Darling, you're gonna have to move the money again."

"I'm already working on that. And the bigger chunk is already safe and secure in Switzerland. They'll never find it, trust me."

"I'll believe it when I see it." I light a cigar. "Listen, I want you to put some money in an account for my daughters."

"What? Here in the UK?"

"No. No. Nothing like that. I want you to open an offshore account in their names, deposit a couple of hundred thousand pounds and leave a trail. Make it easy for the Hunters to find, as well as any paperwork you'll need to set it up. Easy, not obvious, though."

"I'll need their signatures."

"You're creative, I'm sure you'll think of something."

She sighs. "And may I ask why I'm putting myself through so much trouble?"

"Because, my dear, Luke has always had a soft spot for my Melanie, and we're going to use his weakness against him."

"But he'll think she was involved in the whole thing. He'll think she was helping you."

"Yes, and he'll want nothing more than to take his revenge on her. He won't be able to resist."

"I still don't get how that's going to help us. Not to mention that Luke will drain the accounts as soon as he finds them."

"Just do it and make sure he finds the evidence. That should give us enough time to hide the rest of the money and disappear. As for Mel and Luke, I know he's only kept his distance all these years because he always thought she was too good for him. If he thinks she's tainted, that she's dirty with all this mess, I'd say all bets are off, wouldn't you?"

She laughs. "Oh, Arthur, your own daughter? Don't you have a heart?"

"No pain, no gain, my dear. And Mel is the best distraction we could've prayed for."

"And your other daughter?"

"The bigger the distraction, the better our chances are of getting away. Surely you can't argue with that."

"No ... no, I can't." She exhales heavily. "OK, I'll start the proceedings right away."

With a long sigh of satisfaction, I grin and disconnect the call.

Luke is young and smart. But I have one advantage over him. Melanie.

And yes, I'm confident I'm going to win.

Dear Reader

Thank you so much for taking the time to read Seized ... Body and Mind. This is my first attempt at writing a contemporary romance, and I thoroughly loved the experience.

I hope you enjoyed reading it just as much as I have enjoyed writing it for you.

If you have a moment, please leave a review on Amazon. Honest reviews from the readers help the authors, and your fellow readers find books they will love. Thank you for supporting me and my work.

Don't forget to sign up for my Newsletter to receive up to date information on new releases, sales, sneak peeks, giveaways and other exclusive content.

Link: on my Instagram account and Facebook page.

Instagram: @alexmellowauthor
Facebook: @alexmellowauthor

Writing romance because bad boys and ruthless billionaires don't always make an appearance in real life.

Acknowledgments

To my readers. I thank you from the bottom of my heart. I feel truly blessed and honoured to have you reading my work.

Thank you to my editor RJ Locksley. Kind, respectful and immensely talented, you helped me make this book better and for that you'll always have a special place in my heart.

Thank you to Murphy Rae. You brought my vision to life with your magic and cover design super powers. I'm obsessed. You are a queen.

Thank you to Brittny Wroblewski. You are so gifted and lovely, and I'm so glad Murphy brought us together. I adore my logos and all my social media graphics and could not be happier with the end result.

Thank you to my husband. You always support me no matter what, cheering me on and believing in me. Without your help and love none of this would be possible.

Thank you to my son. You make everything worthwhile. I love you to the moon and back.

Thank you to my crazy family and friends. You are always there for me, pushing me and making me want to do better.

I love you all!

To my husband and son ...

The only bright lights I'll ever need in my life.
Everything I do is for you.

About the Author

Alex Mellow

BOOKS

Alex Mellow lives with the two loves of her life, her darling husband and son, in London.

Her time is divided between her passion for writing and, of course, her beloved little family.

At home, when she's not writing or running after a very active toddler you can find her reading, watching a good movie or trying to do some exercise. Lol. At least she tries.

Printed in Great Britain
by Amazon

40769393R00233